Praise for the novels of #1 *New York Times* bestselling author Debbie Macomber

"Debbie Macomber brings the people of Promise, Texas, to life as she blends drama, romance and adventure."

—*RT Book Reviews* on *Caroline's Child*

"Macomber is a skilled storyteller."

—*Publishers Weekly*

"Debbie Macomber tells women's stories in a way no one else does."

—*BookPage*

"With first-class author Debbie Macomber, it's quite simple—she gives readers an exceptional, unforgettable story every time, and her books are always, always keepers!"

—*ReadertoReader.com*

"Whether [Debbie Macomber] is writing lighthearted romps or more serious relationship books, her novels are always engaging stories that accurately capture the foibles of real-life men and women with warmth and humor."

—*Milwaukee Journal Sentinel*

"No one writes better women's contemporary fiction."

—*RT Book Reviews*

DEBBIE MACOMBER

Texas Nights

mira

▶ mira

ISBN-13: 978-0-7783-6987-5

Recycling programs
for this product may
not exist in your area.

Texas Nights

Also available from Debbie Macomber and MIRA Books

Blossom Street

The Shop on Blossom Street
A Good Yarn
Susannah's Garden
Back on Blossom Street
Twenty Wishes
Summer on Blossom Street
Hannah's List
The Twenty-First Wish
  (in *The Knitting Diaries*)
A Turn in the Road

Cedar Cove

16 Lighthouse Road
204 Rosewood Lane
311 Pelican Court
44 Cranberry Point
50 Harbor Street
6 Rainier Drive
74 Seaside Avenue
8 Sandpiper Way
92 Pacific Boulevard
1022 Evergreen Place
Christmas in Cedar Cove
  (*5-B Poppy Lane* and
  A Cedar Cove Christmas)
1105 Yakima Street
1225 Christmas Tree Lane

The Dakota Series

Dakota Born
Dakota Home
Always Dakota
Buffalo Valley

The Manning Family

The Manning Sisters
  (*The Cowboy's Lady* and
  The Sheriff Takes a Wife)

The Manning Brides
  (*Marriage of Inconvenience* and
  Stand-In Wife)
The Manning Grooms
  (*Bride on the Loose* and
  Same Time, Next Year)

Christmas Books

A Gift to Last
On a Snowy Night
Home for the Holidays
Glad Tidings
Christmas Wishes
Small Town Christmas
When Christmas Comes
  (now retitled *Trading
  Christmas*)
There's Something About Christmas
Christmas Letters
The Perfect Christmas
Choir of Angels
  (*Shirley, Goodness and Mercy,
  Those Christmas Angels* and
  Where Angels Go)
Call Me Mrs. Miracle

Heart of Texas

Texas Skies
  (*Lonesome Cowboy* and
  Texas Two-Step)
Texas Nights
  (*Caroline's Child* and
  Dr. Texas)
Texas Home
  (*Nell's Cowboy* and
  Lone Star Baby)
Promise, Texas
Return to Promise

Midnight Sons

Alaska Skies
  (*Brides for Brothers* and
  The Marriage Risk)
Alaska Nights
  (*Daddy's Little Helper* and
  Because of the Baby)
Alaska Home
  (*Falling for Him,*
  Ending in Marriage and
  Midnight Sons and Daughters)

This Matter of Marriage
Montana
Thursdays at Eight
Between Friends
Changing Habits
Married in Seattle
  (*First Comes Marriage* and
  Wanted: Perfect Partner)
Right Next Door
  (*Father's Day* and
  The Courtship of Carol Sommars)
Wyoming Brides
  (*Denim and Diamonds* and
  The Wyoming Kid)
Fairy Tale Weddings
  (*Cindy and the Prince* and
  Some Kind of Wonderful)
The Man You'll Marry
  (*The First Man You Meet* and
  The Man You'll Marry)
Orchard Valley Grooms
  (*Valerie* and *Stephanie*)
Orchard Valley Brides
  (*Norah* and *Lone Star Lovin'*)
The Sooner the Better
An Engagement in Seattle
  (*Groom Wanted* and
  Bride Wanted)
Out of the Rain
  (*Marriage Wanted* and
  Laughter in the Rain)
Learning to Love
  (*Sugar and Spice* and *Love by Degree*)

You…Again
  (*Baby Blessed* and
  Yesterday Once More)
The Unexpected Husband
  (*Jury of His Peers* and
  Any Sunday)
Three Brides, No Groom
Love in Plain Sight
  (*Love 'n' Marriage* and
  Almost an Angel)
I Left My Heart
  (*A Friend or Two* and
  No Competition)
Marriage Between Friends
  (*White Lace and Promises* and
  Friends—And Then Some)
A Man's Heart
  (*The Way to a Man's Heart* and
  Hasty Wedding)
North to Alaska
  (*That Wintry Feeling* and
  Borrowed Dreams)
On a Clear Day
  (*Starlight* and
  Promise Me Forever)
To Love and Protect
  (*Shadow Chasing* and
  For All My Tomorrows)
Home in Seattle
  (*The Playboy and the Widow*
  and *Fallen Angel*)
Together Again
  (*The Trouble with Caasi* and
  Reflections of Yesterday)
The Reluctant Groom
  (*All Things Considered* and
  Almost Paradise)
A Real Prince
  (*The Bachelor Prince* and
  Yesterday's Hero)
Private Paradise
  (in *That Summer Place*)

Debbie Macomber's
  Cedar Cove Cookbook
Debbie Macomber's
  Christmas Cookbook

CONTENTS

CAROLINE'S CHILD   9

DR. TEXAS   211

THE PEOPLE OF PROMISE, TEXAS

Nell Bishop: Thirtysomething widow with a son, Jeremy, and a daughter, Emma; her husband died in a tractor accident.

Ruth Bishop: Nell's mother-in-law; lives with Nell and her two children.

Dovie Boyd: Runs an antiques shop and has dated Sheriff Frank Hennessey for ten years.

Caroline Daniels: Postmistress of Promise.

Maggie Daniels: Caroline's five-year-old daughter.

Dr. Jane Dickinson: The new doctor in Promise.

Ellie Frasier: Owner of Frasier's Feed Store.

Frank Hennessey: Local sheriff.

Max Jordan: Owner of Jordan's Town and Country.

Wade McMillen: Preacher of Promise Christian Church.

Edwina and Lily Moorhouse: Sisters; retired schoolteachers.

Cal and Glen Patterson: Local ranchers; brothers who ranch together.

Phil and Mary Patterson: Parents of Cal and Glen; operate a local B and B.

Louise Powell: Town gossip.

Wiley Rogers: Sixty-year-old ranch foreman at the Weston ranch.

Laredo Smith: Wrangler hired by Savannah Weston.

Barbara and Melvin Weston: Mother and father to Savannah, Grady and Richard; the Westons died six years ago.

Richard Weston: Youngest of the Weston siblings.

Savannah Weston: Grady and Richard's sister; cultivates old roses.

Grady Weston: Rancher; oldest of the Weston siblings.

CAROLINE'S CHILD

One

Clutching the mail in one hand, Grady Weston paced the narrow corridor inside the post office. He glanced distractedly at the row of mailboxes, gathering his courage before he approached Caroline Daniels, the postmistress.

His tongue felt as if it'd wrapped itself around his front teeth, and he was beginning to doubt he'd be able to utter a single sensible word. It shouldn't be so damned difficult to let a woman know he found her attractive!

"Grady?" Caroline's voice reached out to him.

He spun around, not seeing her. Great. Not only was he dreaming about her, now he was hearing her voice.

"Open your box," she instructed.

He fumbled for the key and twisted open the small rectangular door, then peered in. Sure enough, Caroline was there. Not all of her, just her brown eyes, her pert little nose and lovely mouth.

If he'd possessed his brother's gift for flattery, Grady would have said something clever. Made some flowery remark. Unfortunately all he managed was a gruff unfriendly sounding "Hello."

"Hi."

Caroline had beautiful eyes, dark and rich like freshly brewed coffee, which was about as poetic as Grady got. Large and limpid, they reminded him of a calf's, but he figured that might not be something a woman wanted to hear, even if *he* considered it a compliment. This was the problem, Grady decided. He didn't know how to talk to a woman. In fact, it'd been more than six years since he'd gone out on an actual date.

"Can I help you with anything?" she asked.

He wanted to invite her to lunch, and although that seemed a simple enough request, he couldn't make himself ask her. Probably because their relationship so far hadn't been too promising. Calling it a "relationship" wasn't really accurate, since they'd barely exchanged a civil word and had never so much as held hands. Mostly they snapped at each other, disagreed and argued—if they were speaking at all. True, they'd danced once; it'd been nice, but only when he could stop worrying about stepping on her toes.

Who was he kidding? Holding Caroline in his arms had been more than nice, it had been *wonderful*. In the month since, he hadn't been able to stop thinking about that one dance. Every night when he climbed into bed and closed his eyes, Caroline was there to greet him. He could still feel her softness against him, could almost smell the faint scent of her cologne. The dance had been ladies' choice, and that was enough to let him believe—hope—she might actually hold some regard for him, too. Despite their disagreements, *he'd* been the one she'd chosen to ask.

"You had lunch yet?" Grady asked, his voice

brusque. He didn't mean to sound angry or unfriendly. The timbre of his voice and his abrupt way of speaking had caused him plenty of problems with Maggie, Caroline's five-year-old daughter. He'd been trying to get in the kid's good graces for months now, with only limited success. But he'd tried. He hoped Caroline and Maggie gave him credit for that.

Caroline's mouth broke into a wide grin. "Lunch? Not yet, and I'm starved."

Grady's spirits lifted considerably. "Well, then, I was thinking, seeing as I haven't eaten myself..." The words stumbled all over themselves in his eagerness to get them out. "You want to join me?"

"Sure, but let me get this straight. Is this an invitation, as in a date?"

"No." His response was instinctive, given without thought. He'd been denying his feelings for her so long that his answer had come automatically. He feared, too, that she might misread his intentions. He was attracted to Caroline and he wanted to know her better, but beyond that—he wasn't sure. Hell, what he knew about love and marriage wouldn't fill a one-inch column of the *Promise Gazette.*

Some of the happiness faded from her smile. "Understood. Give me a few minutes and I'll meet you out front." She moved out of his range of vision.

Grady closed the box, but left his hand on the key. How could anyone with the skills to run a thriving cattle ranch in the Texas Hill Country be such a fool when it came to women?

He rapped on the post-office box hard enough to hurt his knuckles. "Caroline!" Then he realized he had to open the box. He did that, then stared through it and shouted for her a second time. "Caroline!"

Her face appeared, eyes snapping with impatience. "What's the rush?" she demanded. "I said it'd take me a few minutes."

The edges of the postbox cut into his forehead and chin and knocked his Stetson askew. "This *is* a date, all right?"

She stared back at him from the other side, and either she was overwhelmed by his offer to buy her lunch or surprised into speechlessness.

"All right?" he repeated. "This is a date."

She continued to look at him. "I shouldn't have asked," she finally said.

"I'm glad you did." And he was. He could think of no better way to set things straight. He hadn't invited her to lunch because he needed someone to pass the time with; if that was what he'd wanted, he could have asked his sister, Savannah, or her husband or Cal Patterson—or any number of people. No, he'd asked Caroline because he wanted to be with *her.* For once he longed to talk to her without interference or advice from his matchmaking sister. It didn't help to have Maggie there hiding her face in her mother's lap every time he walked into the room, either. This afternoon it'd be just the two of them. Caroline and him.

Grady respectfully removed his hat when she joined him in the lobby.

"This is a pleasant surprise," Caroline said.

"I was in town, anyway." He didn't mention that he'd rearranged his entire day for this opportunity. It was hard enough admitting that to himself, let alone Caroline.

"Where would you like to eat?" he asked. The town had three good restaurants: the café in the bowling alley; the Chili Pepper, a Texas barbecue place; and a Mexican restaurant run by the Chavez family.

"How about Mexican Lindo?" Caroline suggested.

It was the one he would have chosen himself. "Great."

Since the restaurant was on Fourth Avenue, only two blocks from the post office, they walked there, chatting as they went. Or rather, Caroline chatted and he responded with grunts and murmurs.

Grady had long ago realized he lacked the ability to make small talk. Unlike his younger brother, Richard, who could charm his way into—or out of—anything. Grady tried not to feel inadequate, but he was distinctly relieved when they got to the restaurant.

In a few minutes they were seated at a table, served water and a bowl of tortilla chips along with a dish of extra-hot salsa. He reached for a chip, scooped up as much salsa as it would hold and popped it in his mouth. He ate another and then another before he noticed that Caroline hadn't touched a single chip.

He raised his eyes to hers and stopped chewing, his mouth full.

Caroline apparently read the question in his eyes. "I don't eat corn chips," she explained. "I fill up on them and then I don't have room for anything else."

He swallowed and nodded. "Oh."

A moment of silence passed, and Grady wondered if her comment was a subtle hint that she was watching her weight. From what he understood, weight was a major preoccupation with women. Maybe she was waiting for him to tell her she shouldn't worry about it; maybe he was supposed to say she looked great. She did. She was slender and well proportioned, and she wore her dark brown hair straight and loose, falling to her shoulders. In his opinion she looked about as perfect as a woman could get. Someday he'd tell her that, but not just yet. Besides, he didn't want her to think he was only interested in her body, although it intrigued him plenty. He admired a great deal about her, especially the way she was raising Maggie on her own. She understood the meaning of the words *responsibility* and *sacrifice*, just like he did.

She was staring at him as if she expected a comment, and Grady realized he needed to say something. "You could be fat and I'd still have asked you to lunch."

Her smooth brow crumpled in a puzzled frown.

"I meant that as a compliment," he sputtered and decided then and there it was better to keep his trap shut. Thankfully the waitress came to take their order. Grady decided on chicken enchiladas; Caroline echoed his choice.

"This is really very nice," she said and reached for the tall glass of iced tea.

"I wanted us to have some time alone," he told her.

"Any particular reason?"

Grady rested his spine against the back of his chair and boldly met her look. "I like you, Caroline." He didn't know any way to be other than direct. This had gotten him into difficulties over the years. Earlier that spring he'd taken a dislike to Laredo Smith and hadn't been shy about letting his sister and everyone else know his feelings. But he'd been wrong in his assessment of the man's character. Smith's truck had broken down and Savannah had brought him home to the ranch. Over Grady's objections she'd hired him herself, and before long they'd fallen in love. It came as a shock to watch his sane sensible sister give her heart to a perfect stranger. Still, Grady wasn't proud of the way he'd behaved. By the time Laredo decided it'd be better for everyone concerned if he moved on, Grady had wanted him to stay. He'd gone so far as to offer the man a partnership in the ranch in an effort to change his mind. Not that it'd done any good. To Grady's eternal gratitude, Laredo had experienced a change of heart and returned a couple of months later. Love had driven him away, but it had also brought him back.

Savannah and Laredo had married in short order and were now involved in designing plans for their own home, plus raising quarter horses. Savannah, with her husband's active support, continued to grow the antique roses that were making her a name across the state.

In the weeks since becoming his brother-in-law, Laredo Smith had proved himself a damn good friend and Grady's right-hand man.

"I like you, too," Caroline said, but she lowered her gaze as she spoke, breaking eye contact. This seemed to be something of an admission for them both.

"You do?" Grady felt light-headed with joy. It was all he could do not to leap in the air and click his heels.

"We've known each other a lot of years."

"I've known you most of my life," he agreed, but as he said the words, he realized he didn't *really* know Caroline. Not the way he wanted, not the way he hoped he would one day. It wasn't just that he had no idea who'd fathered Maggie; apparently no one else in town did, either. He wondered what had attracted her to this man, why she hadn't married him. Or why he'd left her to deal with the pregnancy and birth alone. It all remained a mystery. Another thing Grady didn't understand about Caroline was the changes in her since her daughter's birth. In time Grady believed she'd trust him enough to answer his questions, and he prayed he'd say and do the right thing when she did.

Their lunches arrived and they ate, stopping to chat now and then. The conversation didn't pall, but again he had to credit Caroline with the skill to keep it going. Half an hour later, as he escorted her back to the post office, Grady was walking on air.

"I'll give you a call tomorrow," he said, watching her for some sign of encouragement. "If you want," he added, needing her reassurance.

"Sure."

Her response was neither encouraging nor discouraging.

"I'd like to talk to Maggie again, if she'll let me."

"You might try this afternoon, since she's spending the day with Savannah."

This was news to Grady, but he'd been busy that morning and had left the house early. He hadn't spoken to Savannah other than a few words over breakfast, and even if he'd known Maggie was staying with his sister, he wouldn't have had time to chat with the girl that morning.

"I'll make a point of saying hello," he said. His heart lifted when it suddenly struck him that he'd be seeing Caroline again later in the day, when she came to pick up Maggie.

They parted. Whistling, Grady sauntered across the asphalt parking lot toward his truck. He felt damn good. The afternoon had gone better than he'd hoped.

He was about to open the cab door when Max Jordan stopped him.

"Grady, have you got a moment?" The older man, owner of the local Western-wear store, quickened his pace.

"Howdy, Max." Grady grinned from ear to ear and didn't let the somber expression on Max's face get him down. "What can I do for you?"

Max shuffled his feet a couple of times, looking uncomfortable. "You know I hate to mention this a second time, but Richard still hasn't paid me for the clothes he bought three months ago."

The happy excitement Grady had experienced only moments earlier died a quick death. "It was my understanding Richard mailed you a check."

"He told me the same thing, but it's been more than two weeks now and nothing's come. I don't feel I should have to wait any longer."

"I don't think you should, either. I'll speak to him myself," Grady promised.

"I hate to drag you into this," Max muttered, and it was clear from his shaky voice how much the subject distressed him.

"Don't worry about it, Max. I understand."

The older man nodded and turned away. Grady climbed into his truck and clenched the steering wheel with both hands as the anger flooded through him. Leave it to his brother to lie and cheat and steal!

What infuriated Grady was that he had no one to blame but himself. He'd allowed Richard to continue living on the Yellow Rose. Allowed him to tarnish the family name. Allowed himself to believe, to hope, that the years away had changed his brother.

All his illusions had been shattered. They were destroyed like so much else Richard had touched. He'd done his damnedest to ruin Grady, and he'd come close. But Richard had succeeded in ruining his own life—his potential to be a different person, a worthwhile human being.

Charming and personable, a born leader, Richard could have accomplished great things. Instead, he'd used his charisma and personality to swindle others, never understanding that the person he'd cheated most had been himself.

Six years earlier Richard had forged Grady's signature and absconded with the cash their parents had left—cash that would have paid the inheritance taxes on the ranch and covered the burial expenses. Grady and Savannah had found themselves penniless following the tragedy that had claimed their parents' lives. It'd taken six long, backbreaking, frustration-filled years to crawl out of debt. Grady had sacrificed those years to hold on to the ranch while Richard had squandered the money. When it had run out, he'd returned home with his tail between his legs, looking for a place to stay until he received a severance check from his last job—or so he'd said.

Deep down Grady had wanted to believe in Richard. His sister had begged him to let their younger brother stay. But she didn't need to beg very hard or very long for him to relent. Unfortunately it had become apparent that a liar and a cheat didn't change overnight—or in six years. Grady's brother was the same now as the day he'd stolen from his family.

Despite the air conditioner, the heat inside the truck cab sucked away Grady's energy. It should have come as no surprise to discover that Richard had lied to him again. This time would be the last, Grady vowed.

Oh, yes, this episode was the proverbial last straw.

His days in Promise were numbered, Richard Weston thought as he sat on his bed in the bunkhouse. It wouldn't be long before Grady learned the truth. The whole uncomfortable truth. Actually he was surprised he'd managed to hold out this long; he credited that to his ability to lie effectively. But then, small-town folks were embarrassingly easy to dupe. They readily accepted his lies because they wanted to believe him. The years had finely honed his powers of persuasion, but he hadn't needed to work very hard convincing the business owners in Promise to trust him. Being born and raised in this very town had certainly helped. He nearly laughed out loud at how smoothly everything had gone.

Actually Richard did feel kind of bad about leaving a huge debt behind. Max Jordan was decent enough, even if he was an old fool. Billy from Billy D's was okay, too. One day—maybe—when he had money to spare, he'd consider paying everyone back. Grady and Savannah, too. That would shock his uptight brother.

It might all have worked if Richard could've persuaded Ellie Frasier to marry him. He experienced a twinge of regret. He must be losing his knack with women. Nothing could have shocked him more than Ellie's informing him she'd chosen Glen Patterson, instead.

Damn shame. Glen was a real hick, not all that different from Grady. Why Ellie would marry Glen when she could have had *him* was something he'd never understand. Women were fickle creatures, but until recently he'd been able to sway them to his way of thinking.

Not Ellie. How he would've loved to get his hands on her inheritance. That money would have gone a long way toward solving his problems. Well, it didn't do any good to cry over might-have-beens. He was a survivor and he'd prove it—not for the first time. Nothing kept Richard Weston down for long.

Calculating quickly, Richard figured he had only a few days before everything went all to hell. He was ready. Grady seemed to think he idled away his days, but Richard had been working hard, preparing what he'd need. He'd been planning for this day almost from the moment he'd gotten back to Promise. Grady needn't worry; before long Richard would be out of his brother's hair.

Sure he had regrets. He'd thought about returning to Promise lots of times over the years, but he'd never suspected it would be for the reasons that had driven him here now.

When he'd first arrived on the ranch, he'd felt a faint stirring of emotion. It'd been a little less than six years since he'd set foot on the old homestead. Those feelings, however, hadn't lasted long and were completely dead now, especially since Grady had tossed him out of the house and forced him to sleep in the bunkhouse.

Richard couldn't grasp what it was that had kept his father and now his brother tied to a herd of four-footed headaches. He hated cattle, hated the way they smelled and bawled, the way they constantly needed care. Hated everything about them. This kind of life was never meant for him. Sadly no one appreciated that he was different. Better, if he did say so himself. Not even his mother had fully recognized it. Unfortunately neither did Savannah. Now that she'd married Laredo, she was even less inclined to side with him.

Sad to say, his time on the Yellow Rose was drawing to a close.

"Richard?"

Maggie Daniels peeked into the bunkhouse. The kid had become something of a pest lately, but he'd always been popular with children. They weren't all that different from women, most of them, eager for his attention.

"Howdy, cupcake," he said, forcing enthusiasm into his voice. "Whatcha doin'?"

"Nothing. You want to play cards?"

"I can't now. How about later?" He leaned against the wall, clasping his hands behind his head.

"You said that last time." Her lower lip shot out.

Yup, kids were just like women; they pouted when they didn't get their way.

"Where's Savannah?" Richard asked, hoping to divert the kid's attention.

"In her garden."

"Didn't I hear her say something about baking cookies this afternoon?" He hadn't heard any such thing, but it'd get rid of the kid.

"She did?" Excitement tinged Maggie's voice.

"She told me so herself. Chocolate chip, my favorite. Why don't you ask her, and when you're finished you can bring me a sample. How does that sound?"

Maggie's eyes lit up and Richard laughed. He loved the fact that she preferred him over Grady. His big lug of a brother didn't know a damn thing about kids. It was comical watching him try to make friends with Maggie. She wouldn't have anything to do with him, and for once in his life Richard outshone his big brother.

"Come on, I'll go with you," he said, changing his mind. "We'll go talk to Savannah about those cookies."

"She's busy in her rose garden."

"But not too busy for us." Richard felt certain that was true. Savannah had a soft spot in her heart for the child and could refuse Maggie nothing. If he'd asked her on his own, chances were he wouldn't get to first base, but with Maggie holding his hand, Savannah was sure to capitulate.

For some reason Richard wanted one of those cookies. And he wanted it now.

He wasn't sure why—maybe just to pull Savannah's strings a bit. But Richard prided himself on getting what he wanted. Whenever he wanted it.

"You're full of surprises, Grady Weston," Caroline muttered to herself as she drove down the highway toward the Yellow Rose. The afternoon had dragged even though she'd been busy. Despite the heavy flow of traffic in and out of the post office, Caroline had frequently glanced at her watch, counting down the hours and then the minutes until closing time. And until she saw Grady again…

His invitation to lunch had caught her by surprise. She'd all but given up hope that he'd ever figure it out. In the past six months she'd done everything short of sending him a fax to let him know she was interested. When it came to romance, Grady Weston was as blind as they come. Not that she was any better; it'd taken her years to work up enough courage to give love a second chance.

She'd dated occasionally but never found that combination of mutual attraction and respect with anyone except Grady. Unfortunately she wasn't sure he recognized his own feelings, let alone hers. Twice now she'd decided to forget about him, and both times he'd given her reasons to believe it might work for them. Like showing up this afternoon and taking her to lunch.

She sped up, hoping their lunch date really *was* a beginning. She wanted a relationship with Grady, a romance—maybe even marriage eventually. Oh, my, but she did like him. He was honest, loyal, hardworking. She admired the way he'd struggled to hold on to the ranch despite grief and crippling sacrifices. Year after year she'd watched him do whatever it took to keep the Yellow Rose, to keep what was important to him and Savannah.

Caroline and Savannah had always been close, but never more so than now. Caroline's mother had died the year before, and it was Savannah who'd stood by her side and cried with her. Having buried her own mother, Savannah understood the grief that suffocated Caroline those first few months. It was also during that time that Maggie had grown so attached to Savannah, who'd become like a second mother to her. It pleased Caroline that her daughter loved Savannah as much as she did herself.

However, the five-year-old felt no such tenderness for Grady. Caroline sighed as her thoughts drifted to their rocky relationship. Grady's loud voice had made the child skittish from the first, and then one afternoon when Maggie was feeling ill, she'd phoned Savannah. Grady had answered the phone with a brusque demand, and from that moment forward Maggie would have nothing to do with him.

It was a problem, and one that continued to bother Caroline. If a romantic relationship developed between her and Grady the way she wanted, the way she dreamed, then Maggie and Grady would need to make their peace. True, Grady regretted the incident and had tried to undo the damage, but the child was unrelenting in her dislike of him.

As she reached the long gravel driveway leading to the Yellow Rose, Caroline decreased her speed to make the turn. A few moments later the large two-story ranch house came into view. Rocket, Grady's old dog, lumbered stiffly down the porch steps to greet her, tail wagging.

Laredo was working in the corral while Savannah stood at the fence watching him put their prize stallion through his paces. Maggie was with Savannah, her feet braced against the bottom rail and her arms resting on top. When she heard the car, she leaped down and dashed toward her mother.

Maggie hurled herself into her arms as soon as Caroline stepped out of the car. "Me and Savannah baked cookies!" Her young voice rang with glee. "And Richard said he never tasted better. He ate five cookies before he could stop himself." She slapped both hands over her mouth as though she'd blurted out a secret.

"How many did you eat?" Caroline wanted to know. It would be just like Richard to let the child spoil her dinner with cookies.

"Too many," Savannah answered for her, giving Caroline an apologetic half smile.

"We'll have a late dinner," Caroline said, dismissing her friend's worries. "I had a big lunch." She was about to tell Savannah about her lunch date when Grady burst out of the barn.

"Have you seen Richard? Has he shown up yet? He's got to be around here somewhere." Grady's face was distorted with rage.

Maggie edged closer to Caroline and wrapped her arm around her mother's waist.

"Grady," Savannah said in that low calming way of hers.

If Grady noticed Caroline, he gave no indication.

"Did I hear someone call for me?" Richard said, strolling out of the house as though he hadn't a care in the world. He was a handsome man, lean and muscular, probably the most attractive man Caroline had ever known. But in Richard's case the good looks were superficial. She'd watched as he skillfully manipulated and used others to his own advantage. Even Grady and Savannah. She was amazed that Grady had allowed him to continue living on the ranch—yet at the same time, she understood. Like Savannah, Grady wanted to believe that Richard had changed.

Grady whirled around at the sound of Richard's voice. "We need to talk." His voice boomed and Maggie hid her face against Caroline's stomach.

"Max Jordan said he hasn't been paid," Grady shouted.

A shocked look stole over Richard. "You're joking! He didn't get the check? I put it in the mail two weeks ago."

"He never got it because you didn't mail it."

"What do you mean?" Richard demanded.

The two men faced off, Grady's anger spilling over

in every word and Richard looking stunned and hard done by.

"Grady, please," Savannah said, hurrying toward her older brother and gently placing a hand on his arm. "Now isn't the time to be discussing this. Leave it until later."

"She's right," Richard said. "In case you hadn't noticed, we have company."

It was obvious that Grady had been so consumed by his anger, he'd barely realized they weren't alone. "Caroline," he murmured, and his face revealed both regret and delight. He seemed uncertain about what to say next. "Hello."

"How's my cupcake?" Richard asked, smiling at Maggie.

The little girl loosened her grip on Caroline's waist, turning to Richard as he spoke. He threw his arms open and she raced eagerly toward him.

"That's my girl," Richard said, catching Maggie and sweeping her high into the air. He whirled her around, the pair of them laughing as if it'd been days since they'd seen each other.

Savannah sidled closer to Caroline. "Grady's been looking for Richard all afternoon," she said in a quiet voice, "and he's been conveniently missing until now."

Caroline understood what her friend was saying. Richard had played his cards perfectly, appearing at the precise moment it'd be impossible for Grady to get a straight answer from him. Then he'd used Maggie's childish adoration to make Grady look even more foolish.

"Maggie," Caroline called.

Richard set the child back on her feet. Together the two of them joined Caroline and Savannah.

"I do believe Maggie has stolen my heart," he said, his eyes bright with laughter.

"Does that mean you'll marry me?" Maggie asked, grinning up at him.

"Sure thing."

"Really?"

"He won't marry you," Caroline said, reaching for her daughter's hand.

"Don't be so certain," Richard countered. He crouched down beside Maggie, but he was looking at Caroline.

"Hi, Maggie," Grady said, choosing that moment to try again. The anger had faded from his face, but he still held himself rigid.

Caroline gave him credit for making the effort to win Maggie over.

Her daughter wasn't easily swayed, however. She buried her face in Richard's shoulder.

"There's no need to be afraid of Grady," Richard whispered to Maggie—a stage whisper that carried easily. Then he smiled in a way that suggested Grady was wasting his time. In other words, Grady didn't have a snowball's chance in hell of convincing Maggie he wasn't an ogre. Richard's meaning couldn't have been clearer.

"I don't like Grady," Maggie announced, pursing her lips.

"Maggie!" Caroline admonished her.

"She's right, you know," Richard said, teeth flashing in a wide grin. "Grady just doesn't get along with kids, not like I do."

Caroline clamped her mouth shut rather than reveal her thoughts. She didn't trust Richard, *couldn't* trust him, not after the way he'd used his family. Used anyone who'd let him.

"I'm thinking Maggie needs someone like me in her life," Richard said. "Which means there's only one solution."

"What's that?" Caroline knew she was a fool to ask.

"You could always marry me," he said and leaned over far enough to touch his lips to Caroline's cheek. "Put me out of my misery, Caroline Daniels, and marry me."

"Oh, Mommy, let's do it!" Maggie shouted, clapping her hands. "Let's marry Richard."

Two

Grady was pleased that his sister had convinced Caroline and Maggie to stay for dinner. Now all he had to do was behave. It never seemed to fail—whenever he had a chance to make some headway with Maggie, he'd do something stupid. He wanted to blame Richard, but as usual he'd done it to himself.

His brother brought out the very worst in him. As Grady washed up for dinner, he hoped this evening would give him an opportunity to redeem himself in both Caroline and Maggie's eyes.

The table was already set and the food dished up in heaping portions. A platter of sliced roast beef rested in the middle, along with a huge bowl of mashed potatoes, a pitcher of gravy, fresh corn on the cob and a crisp green salad. There was also a basket filled with Savannah's mouthwatering buttermilk biscuits. His sister was one fine cook. He'd miss her when she moved into her own house with Laredo. But it was time, well past time, that she had a home and a life of her own. He knew from his talks with Laredo that they'd already started to think about adding to the family.

"Dinner looks wonderful," he said. Grady made an effort these days to let Savannah know how much he appreciated her. Over the years he'd taken her contributions for granted, discounting her efforts with her roses and her fledgling mail-order business—a business that now brought a significant income. He'd even made fun of her goats, which he considered pets rather than livestock. Now that she was married and about to establish her own home, Grady recognized just how much he was going to miss her.

Savannah flushed with pleasure at his praise.

The compliment had apparently earned him points with Caroline, too; she cast him an approving smile. Grady held in a sigh. He needed all the points he could get when it came to Caroline and Maggie. If everything went well, this evening might help him recapture lost ground with the child.

Everyone began to arrive for dinner. With the scent of the meal wafting through the house, it wasn't long before all the chairs were occupied—except for one. Richard's. It was just like his spoiled younger brother to keep everyone waiting.

"Where's Richard?" Maggie asked, glancing up at her mother.

Grady was asking himself the same question.

"He's coming, isn't he?" Maggie whined.

Even from where he stood Grady could sense the little girl's disappointment.

"I don't know, sweetheart," Caroline answered.

"There's no need to let our meal get cold," Grady said. If Richard chose to go without dinner, that was fine by him. If anything, he was grateful not to have his brother monopolizing the conversation, distracting both Caroline and Maggie. Grady pulled out his chair and sat down. Laredo, Savannah and Caroline did so, as well. The only one who remained standing was Maggie.

"What about Richard?" she asked in a small stubborn voice.

"I guess he isn't hungry," Caroline said and pulled out the chair next to her own for Maggie.

"He promised he'd sit next to me at dinner."

"It isn't a good idea to believe in the things Richard promises," Grady said as much for Caroline's ears as for her daughter's. He hated to disappoint the five-year-old, but it was God's own truth. Richard was about as stable as beef prices. His loyalties constantly shifted toward whatever was most advantageous to him, with little concern for anyone else.

His playful marriage proposal to Caroline worried Grady. She'd laughed it off, but Grady found no humor in it. Apparently his brother knew Grady was interested in Caroline and thus considered her fair game. It would be typical of Richard to do what he could to thwart any romance between Caroline and Grady by making a play for her himself. Grady knew that made him sound paranoid, but he thought his fears were justified. Experience had been an excellent teacher.

He reached for the meat and forked a thick slice of roast beef onto his plate, then passed the platter to Caroline.

Maggie folded her arms and stared defiantly at Grady. "I'm not eating until Richard's here."

"Maggie, please," Caroline cajoled. She glanced at Grady, her eyes apologetic.

"Grady yelled at Richard."

Once again Grady was the culprit. "I shouldn't have

yelled, should I?" He was careful to speak in a low quiet voice. "I do that sometimes without thinking, but I wasn't angry at you."

"You were mad at Richard."

No use lying about it. "Yes, I was."

"And now he won't come to dinner."

"I think Richard has other reasons for not showing up," Caroline explained as she placed a scoop of mashed potatoes on her daughter's plate. "Do you want one of Savannah's yummy buttermilk biscuits?"

Maggie hesitated for a long moment before she shook her head. "I won't eat without Richard."

"Did I hear someone call my name?" Richard asked cheerfully as he stepped into the kitchen. "Sorry I'm late," he said, not sounding the least apologetic. He pulled out his chair, sat down beside Maggie and reached for the meat platter all in a single graceful movement.

Caroline's child shot Grady a triumphant look as if to say she'd known all along that Richard hadn't lied to her.

Grady's appetite vanished. For every step he advanced in his effort to make friends with Maggie, he seemed to retreat two. Once more Richard had made him look like a fool in front of the little girl. And once more he'd allowed it to happen.

"Is it true you want to marry my mom?" Maggie asked Richard with such hopefulness that the question silenced all other conversation.

"Of course it's true." Richard chuckled, then winked at Caroline.

"I think you should," Maggie said, hanging on Richard's every word.

Grady didn't speak again during the entire meal. Not

that anyone noticed. Adored by Maggie, Richard was in his element, and he became the center of attention, joking and teasing, complimenting Savannah, even exchanging a brief joke with Laredo.

Caroline was quiet for a time, but soon, Grady noted, Richard had won her over just as he had everyone else. Despite his disappointment, Grady marveled at his brother's talent. Richard had always savored attention, whereas Grady avoided the limelight. It had never bothered him before, but now he felt a growing resentment, certain Caroline was about to be caught by the force of Richard's spell. Other than Ellie Fraiser, Grady had never known any woman to resist his brother's charms. Ellie was the exception, and only because she was already in love with Glen Patterson, although neither of them had recognized the strength of their feelings for each other—until Richard interfered. Indirectly, and definitely without intending it, Richard had brought about something good. Still, if it hadn't been for Glen in Ellie's life, Grady wondered what would have happened. That, at least, was one worry he'd escaped.

As soon as he could, Grady excused himself from the table and headed toward the barn. He would have liked to linger over dinner, perhaps enjoy a cup of coffee with Caroline on the porch, but he could see that was a lost cause.

Not until he'd stalked across the yard did he recognize the symptoms. Damn it all, he was *jealous*. The only woman he'd ever cared about, and Richard was going to steal her away. The problem was, Grady had no idea how to keep him from Caroline.

To his surprise Laredo followed him outside. Like Grady, his brother-in-law was a man of few words.

"Don't let him get to you," Laredo said, leading the way into the barn.

"I'm not," Grady told him, which wasn't entirely a lie. He knew the kind of man Richard was; he knew the insecurity of Richard's charm. He didn't like the fact that his brother was working on Caroline, but he wasn't willing to make a fool of himself, either. Other men had made that mistake before him. Glen Patterson, for one. The poor guy had come off looking like an idiot at the Cattlemen's Association Dance. Richard and Glen had nearly come to blows over Ellie, with half the town looking on. They might have, too, if Sheriff Hennessey hadn't stepped in when he did.

"Good." Laredo slapped him on the back and the two went their separate ways.

Grady didn't stay in the barn long. He gave himself ample time to control his resentment, then decided that, while he wasn't going to accept the role of fool, he didn't intend to just give up, either. He'd tried to make sure Caroline understood that their lunch today was more than a meal between friends. Hell—despite what she'd said—he didn't know if she even considered him a friend.

Grady found her sitting on the porch with Savannah sipping hot tea. Maggie sat on the steps cradling her doll. He strolled toward the women, without a clue what to say once he joined them. He supposed he'd better learn a few conversational rules, he thought grimly, if that meant he'd have a chance with Caroline.

The two women stopped talking as he approached, which led him to surmise that he'd been the topic of conversation. He felt as awkward as a schoolboy and, not sure what else to do, touched the rim of his hat.

Savannah, bless her heart, winked conspiratorially at him and stood. "Maggie," she said, holding out her hand to the little girl, "I found one of my old dolls this afternoon. Would you like to play with her?"

Maggie leaped to her feet. "Could I?"

"You bet."

As Savannah and Maggie disappeared into the house, Grady lowered himself onto the rocker his sister had vacated. He felt as tongue-tied and unsure as he had that afternoon. Taking a deep breath, he forced himself to remember that he'd been talking to Caroline all her life. It shouldn't be any different now.

"Beautiful night, isn't it?" he commented, thinking the weather was a safe subject with which to start.

"Those look like storm clouds to the east."

Grady hadn't noticed. He gazed up at the sky, feeling abashed, until Caroline leaned back in her rocker and laughed. He grinned, loving the sound of her amusement. It was difficult not to stare. All these years, and he hadn't seen how damn beautiful she was. While he could speculate why it'd taken him this long, he didn't want to waste another minute. It was all he could do to keep his tongue from lolling out the side of his mouth whenever he caught sight of her. He longed to find the words to tell her how attractive she was, how much he liked and respected her. It wasn't the first time he'd wished he could issue compliments with Richard's finesse.

"Come on, Grady, loosen up."

"I'm loose," he growled and noted how relaxed she was, rocking back and forth as if they often sat side by side in the evening. His parents had done that. Every night. They'd shared the events of their day, talked over plans for the future, exchanged feelings and opinions.

The memory of his mother and father filled his mind. Six years, and the pain of their absence was as strong now as it had been in the beginning. Some nights Grady would sit on the porch, the old dog beside him, and silently discuss business matters with his father, seeking his advice. Not that he actually expected his father to provide answers, of course; Grady was no believer in ghosts or paranormal influences. But those one-sided discussions had helped see Grady through the rough years. It was during those times, burdened with worries, that he'd been forced to search deep inside himself for the answers. And on rare occasions, he'd experienced moments when he'd felt his father's presence more intensely than his absence.

"You've gotten quiet all of a sudden," Caroline said.

"I want to talk to you about Richard." His words were as much a surprise to him as to Caroline.

"Oh?" Her eyebrows rose.

"I realize you must find his attention flattering, but like I said earlier it isn't wise to believe anything Richard says." The lazy sway of her rocking stopped. "I know you probably don't want to hear this," he added. It wasn't pleasant for him, either. Regardless of anything between them, though, Grady's one concern was that Richard not hurt Caroline.

"I appreciate what you're doing, but I'm a big girl."

"I didn't mean to suggest you weren't. It's just that, well, Richard has a way with women."

"And you assume he's going to sweep me off my feet, is that it?" The teasing warmth in her voice was gone, replaced by something less friendly.

"You think I want to say these things?" he asked, inhaling sharply. "It isn't really you he's interested in, anyway."

"I beg your pardon?"

Grady wished he'd never introduced the subject. Clearly Caroline wasn't going to appreciate his insight, but once he'd started he couldn't stop. "Richard knows how I feel about you and—" He snapped his mouth closed before he embarrassed himself further. "I'm only telling you this because I don't want you to get hurt again." He didn't know what madness possessed him to add the *again*. He realized the moment he did that Caroline had taken his advice the wrong way.

Grady had never asked her about Maggie's father, didn't intend to do so now. Heaven knew she was touchy enough about the subject. The only other time he'd said something, months earlier, she'd been ready to bite his head off.

"This discussion is over," she said, jumping to her feet.

"Caroline, I didn't mean— Oh, hell, be angry if you want." With an abrupt movement, he got out of the chair, leaving it to rock wildly. Once again he'd botched their conversation. "It appears you don't need any advice from me."

"No, Grady, I don't."

It damaged his pride that she'd so casually disregard his warning. "Fine, then, for all I care, you can marry Richard." Not giving her a chance to respond, he stalked away, absolutely certain that any hope of a relationship was forever ruined.

His fears were confirmed less than an hour later when he left the barn and saw her again. She was in her car with the driver's window rolled down. Richard was leaning against the side of the vehicle, and the sound of their laughter rang in the twilight.

The unexpected twist of disappointment and pain caught Grady off guard. Well, that certainly answered that.

Caroline must have noticed him because Richard suddenly looked over his shoulder. Grady didn't stick around. It was too hard to pretend he didn't care when he damn well did. His stride was full of purpose as he crossed the yard and stormed into the house, sequestering himself in the office.

His emotions had covered the full range in a single day. He'd taken Caroline to lunch and afterward felt... ecstatic; there was no other word for it. Before dinner he'd been like a kid, thrilled to see her again so soon. Now, just a few hours later, he'd been thrown into despair, convinced beyond doubt that he'd lost whatever chance he might have had with her.

It was enough to drive a man to drink. He sat in the worn leather desk chair and pulled open the bottom file drawer. His father had kept a bottle of bourbon there for times when nothing else would do, and Grady had followed the same practice. The bottle was gone—which had happened before. Grady suspected Richard, with good reason, but at the moment he didn't really care. He wasn't much of a drinking man. A cold beer now and then suited him just fine, but he'd never enjoyed the hard stuff.

The knock on the office door surprised him. "Who is it?" he barked, not in the mood for company.

"Richard." His brother didn't wait for an invitation but opened the door and sauntered in. He immediately made himself at home, claiming the only other chair in the room. He leaned back, locked his fingers behind his head and grinned like a silly schoolboy.

"So what's up with you and Caroline?" he asked.

Grady scowled. The last person he wanted to discuss with his brother was Caroline. "Nothing."

His denial only served to fuel Richard's amusement. "Come on, Grady, I've got eyes in my head. It's obvious you've got the hots for her. Not that I blame you, man. She's one nice-looking woman."

Grady didn't like Richard's tone of voice, but prolonging this conversation by arguing with him would serve no useful purpose. "Listen, Richard, I've got better things to do than sit around discussing Caroline Daniels with you."

"I don't imagine it would take much to talk her into the sack, either. She's already been to bed with at least one man—what's a few more? Right?"

Grady ground his teeth in an effort to control his irritation. "I don't think it's a good idea for us to discuss Caroline." He stood and walked over to the door and pointedly opened it.

"I wouldn't mind getting into her bed myself one of these days," Richard went on.

Despite everything he'd promised himself, Grady saw red. He flew across the room and dragged his brother out of the chair, grabbing him by the front of his shirt.

Richard held up both hands. "Hey, hey, don't get so riled! I was only teasing."

Grady's fingers ached with the strength of his grip. It took a moment to clear his head enough to release his brother.

"You don't want to talk about Caroline, fine," Richard said, backing toward the door. "But you can't blame a guy for asking, can you?"

Driving home, Caroline realized she not only distrusted Richard Weston, but thoroughly disliked him. Before she'd left the Yellow Rose, he'd gone out of his way to let her know that Grady had asked Nell Bishop, a local widow, to the Cattlemen's Dance earlier in the summer. What was particularly meaningful about the information was that Caroline knew how hard Savannah had tried to convince Grady to invite *her.* He almost had. She remembered he'd come into the post office a few days before the dance, but within minutes they'd ended up trading insults. That was unfortunate. He *had* mentioned the dance, though, leaving her to wonder.

Their verbal exchanges were legendary. Only in the past couple of weeks had they grown comfortable enough with each other to manage a civil conversation.

Now this.

Caroline didn't believe Richard. She strongly suspected that almost everything out of his mouth was a lie. If the story about Nell *was* true, she would've heard about it. To the best of her knowledge Nell hadn't even attended the dance. Not that it was unusual for her to avoid social functions—it was widely known that Nell continued to grieve for Jake, the only man she'd ever loved. He'd been her high-school sweetheart, and their affection for each other had been evident throughout the years. Caroline had often wondered if Nell would remarry.

"Ask her." Caroline spoke the words aloud without realizing it.

"Ask who, Mommy?" Maggie looked at her mother.

"A friend." She left it at that.

"About what?"

"Nothing." She smiled at her daughter and changed the subject.

As it turned out she had the opportunity to chat with Nell sooner than she'd expected. The following afternoon on her way home from work Caroline stopped at the local Winn-Dixie for a few groceries.

She collected what she needed and pushed her cart up to the checkout stand—behind Nell.

"Howdy, friend," Nell said cheerfully. "Haven't seen you in a while."

"Nell!" Caroline didn't disguise her pleasure. "How are you?"

"Great. I've been working hard on getting the word out that I'm turning Twin Canyons into a dude ranch. The brochures were mailed to travel agents last week."

Caroline admired her ingenuity. "That's terrific."

The grocery clerk slid Nell's purchases over the scanner, coming up with the total. She paid in cash, then glanced around. "Jeremy!" she called. "Emma." She reached for the plastic bags, giving a good-natured shrug. "I warned those two not to wander off. I know exactly where to find them, too—the book section. They're both crazy about books, especially The Baby-sitters Club books and that new series of kids' Westerns by T. R. Grant. I can't buy them fast enough."

Caroline recognized both series. T. R. Grant was the current rage; even Maggie had wanted Caroline to read her his books. Maggie was still a bit young for them, but it wouldn't be long before she devoured Grant's books and The Baby-sitters Club by herself.

"Have you got a moment?" Caroline asked, opening her purse to pay for her own groceries.

"Sure." Nell waited while Caroline finished her transaction. "What can I do for you?"

As they walked toward the book display at the far end of the Winn-Dixie, Caroline mulled over the best way to approach the subject of Nell and Grady. She wasn't sure why she'd allowed Richard to upset her, especially when she believed it'd all been a lie. Not that she'd blame Grady for being attracted to Nell. In fact, at one time she'd believed they might eventually marry. They seemed right together somehow; both were ranchers and both had struggled against what seemed impossible odds.

In the back of her mind Caroline had always suspected that when the time was right, they'd discover each other. Grady and Jake had been good friends, and Grady had been a pallbearer at Jake's funeral. Grady and Nell were close in age and would make a handsome couple. Grady was an inch or two over six feet, with a broad muscular physique not unlike Jake's. There weren't many men who'd suit Nell physically, since she was nearly six feet herself.

"I hope you don't think I'm being nosy, but I heard a rumor…" Caroline blurted before she lost her nerve. This was even more embarrassing than she'd feared.

"About what?" Nell frowned.

Caroline drew a breath and held it until her lungs ached. "About you and Grady Weston."

Nell frowned again. "Me and Grady?"

Caroline nodded.

"Grady's a friend," Nell said. "I've always liked him

and if I were ever to consider remarrying, I'd certainly think about Grady."

Caroline broke eye contact. This wasn't what she'd wanted to hear.

"He's a good man and he'd make an excellent husband and father," Nell continued, then asked a probing question of her own. "Is there any reason you're asking?"

"Not really."

"He asked me to the dance last month," Nell added, as if she'd suddenly remembered.

So it was true. Caroline's spirits sank.

"In fact, I received two invitations to the dance within a few hours." This was said with a note of amusement.

"Two? Grady and who else?"

Nell's mouth widened in a smile. "You aren't going to believe this, but both Grady Weston and Glen Patterson asked me to the dance."

"Glen?" That was a kicker, considering he was now engaged to Ellie Frasier. Those two were so deeply in love it was difficult to imagine that little more than a month ago Glen had invited Nell and not Ellie to the biggest dance of the year. In the end he'd gone by himself and then he'd practically come to blows with Richard over Ellie. Richard—always the spoiler.

"I don't know what was in the air that day," Nell murmured. "Grady and Glen calling me up like that."

"Did you go to the dance?"

"Briefly," Nell said, "but Emma had an upset stomach that day. I made an appearance, said hello to some friends I don't see often and left shortly after the music started."

"Grady was there," Caroline said, fondly recalling their one dance. Ladies' choice, and she'd been the one to approach him. Those few short minutes in Grady's arms had been wonderful. Afterward she'd hoped he'd ask her to dance himself, but he'd wandered back to where he'd been sitting with Cal Patterson and hadn't spoken to her again. Caroline had felt bitterly disappointed.

"...any reason?" Nell asked.

Caroline caught only the last part of the question. "Reason?" she repeated.

"That you're asking about me and Grady?"

"Not really," she said, then figured she owed her friend the truth. "He asked me to lunch the other day."

"And you went?"

Caroline nodded.

"And you had a good time?"

"A great time," Caroline admitted.

Nell shifted the weight of the groceries in her hands. "Listen, Caroline, if you're worried about there being anything romantic between me and Grady, don't give it another thought. Grady's one of the most honorable men I know, but—" her voice dipped with emotion "—I'm still in love with Jake."

"Oh, Nell." Caroline hugged her friend.

"Oh, damn it all," Nell said, blinking furiously. "I've got to scoot. I'll see you soon, okay?"

"Sure." It would be good to sit down and talk with her friend. Both their lives were so busy it was difficult to find the time.

"Jeremy. Emma." Nell called her children again, and the two came running.

Caroline waved them off and headed toward the

parking lot, deep in thought. So, what Richard had told her was true. This was what made him dangerous. He tossed in a truth now and then just to keep everyone guessing. But for once, she wished he'd been lying.

Grady had been pensive ever since the night Caroline stayed for dinner, Savannah observed. He sat at the kitchen table, supposedly writing out an order for Richard to pick up at the feed store later that afternoon. But for the past five minutes, all he'd done was stare blankly into space.

Savannah had to bite her tongue. Laredo had repeatedly warned her against any further matchmaking efforts between her brother and Caroline, but he might as well have asked her to stop breathing. Grady was miserable and Caroline hadn't been any happier. If it was within her power to bring them together—these two people who were so obviously meant for each other—what possible harm could it do?

Considering that thought, Savannah poured her brother a fresh cup of coffee.

Grady glanced up and thanked her with an off-center smile.

"Something on your mind?" she asked. If he voluntarily brought up the subject, all the better.

"Nothing important," he murmured and reached for the steaming mug. He raised it tentatively to his lips, then glanced at her as if tempted to seek her advice.

Savannah held her breath, hoping Grady would ask her about Caroline. He didn't.

"The church dinner's this weekend," she said, speaking quickly.

Grady responded with what sounded like a grunt,

the translation of which she already knew. He wasn't interested.

Savannah glared at him. If she wrung his neck, she wondered, would he have any idea why? "Caroline's bringing her applesauce cake," she added casually. "Her mother's recipe."

At the mention of her friend's name, Grady raised his head. "Caroline's going to the church dinner?"

"Of course." At last, a reaction. Her brother might be one of the most intelligent men she knew, but when it came to women he was the class dunce. "I'm bringing my chicken teriyaki salad," she added, as if this was significant.

"Is Laredo going?"

"Yes, and Ellie and Glen and just about everyone else in town."

"Oh."

Savannah figured she was due a large heavenly reward for her patience. *Oh.* Was that all he could say? Poor Caroline.

"It isn't a date thing, is it?"

Savannah didn't know how to answer. If she let him assume everyone was bringing a date, it might scare him off. On the other hand, if she said nothing, someone else might ask Caroline.

"This shouldn't be such a difficult question," Grady said, glaring at her.

"Yes and no. Some people will come with dates and some won't."

He mulled that over. "Does Caroline have a date?"

Savannah had to restrain herself from hugging Grady's neck and crying out for joy. He wasn't as dense as she'd thought. "Not that I know of." This, too, was said casually, as though she hadn't the least bit of interest in Caroline's social life.

"Oh."

Grady was back to testing her patience again. She waited an entire minute before she ventured another question.

"Are you thinking of inviting her and Maggie?"

"Me?" Grady's eyes widened as if this were a new thought.

"Yes, you," she returned pointedly.

"I'm…thinking about it," he finally said.

Her face broke out in a smile and she clapped her hands. "That's wonderful."

"What's wonderful?" Richard asked, wandering into the kitchen. He reached for a banana, peeled it and leaned expectantly against the kitchen counter.

Grady and Savannah exchanged looks. "The church dinner," she answered for them both.

"Yeah, I heard about that," he said with his mouth full. "Either of you going?"

"I think so." Again Savannah took the initiative.

"Then I'll give some thought to attending, too."

Both Grady and Savannah remained silent.

"I should probably have a date, though, don't you think?" He pondered his own question. "Caroline. I'll ask Caroline," he said triumphantly. "She'll jump at the chance to go with me."

Three

"You're a damn fool, that's what you are," Grady muttered as he barreled down the highway toward Promise, driving twenty miles over the speed limit.

The reason for this hasty trip had to do with Caroline Daniels. By dinnertime he'd recognized that either he made his move now and invited her to the church dinner or let Richard beat him to the punch. Of course, he could have just phoned and been done with it, but that didn't seem right, not when anyone on the ranch could pick up a telephone receiver and listen in on the conversation. By anyone, he meant Richard. Besides, Grady preferred to talk to Caroline in person; it seemed more…meaningful.

He'd never been good at this courtship thing, but damn it all, he wasn't going to let his brother cheat him out of taking Caroline and Maggie to that church dinner. Richard wasn't interested in Caroline—Grady was sure of it—any more than he'd fallen head over heels in love with Ellie Frasier. His brother was far more concerned with cheating him out of the pleasure of Caroline's company. Except that he had no intention of standing idly by and letting it happen.

Once he'd made his decision, Grady knew he should act on it. Naturally there was always the risk that he'd arrive at Caroline's with his heart dangling from his sleeve only to learn that Richard had already asked her out for Saturday night.

Even knowing he might be too late didn't stop him. He wanted to attend the dinner with Caroline and Maggie more than he'd wanted anything in a long while. It surprised him how much.

The drive into town, during which he thought about the approach he'd take with Caroline, seemed to take no time at all. His goal was to ask her to be his date before Richard did, and at the same time keep his pride intact if she refused. No small task, considering past experience.

He parked in front of Caroline's small house and leaped out of the truck cab. Eager to get this settled, he took the steps up to her front door two at a time and leaned on the buzzer.

Caroline opened the door, her face registering surprise.

"Grady, hello." She recovered quickly and held the screen door wide.

"Would you like to sit outside for a spell?" he asked, instead gesturing toward the porch swing. Since he was nervous about this entire thing, staying outside in the semidarkness felt more inviting than her well-lit living room.

"Sure."

She glanced over her shoulder, and Grady noticed Maggie playing by herself in the background. She had her dolls sitting around a small table and was chatting amicably as she stood in front of her play kitchen cooking up a storm. He grinned at the sight.

Caroline sat down, but Grady found it impossible to keep still.

"Did Savannah phone?" he asked. It would be just like his sister to give Caroline a heads-up. He hadn't announced where he was going when he left the ranch, but Savannah knew. After all, she was the one who'd steered him in this direction in that less-than-subtle way of hers. Grady tolerated Savannah's matchmaking only because he wasn't opposed to her efforts to promote a romance between him and Caroline. Frankly he could use the help. He wasn't keen, however, on letting her know that.

"Savannah phone me?" Caroline repeated. "No, she hasn't."

Grady released a sigh, and some of the tension eased from between his shoulder blades. "What about Richard?"

"What about him?"

"Have you spoken to him recently—say, in the last four or five hours?"

"No," she answered curtly. "Is there a reason for all these questions?"

Grady could see that Caroline was growing impatient but he needed the answers to both questions before he could proceed. "Of course there's a reason," he snapped, annoyed with his lack of finesse when it came to romance. "I don't want to end up looking ridiculous, thanks to Richard."

"What's Richard got to do with anything?" Caroline demanded.

"If he's been here first, just say so and I'll be on my

way." The thought of Richard and Caroline together did funny things to his stomach. He'd never been a jealous man; it was an unfamiliar—and unpleasant—sensation. But he wasn't about to let Richard walk all over him.

"It seems to me, Grady, that you don't need Richard in order to look ridiculous. You do a damn good job all by yourself!"

Her words took him by surprise. He exhaled, counting to ten, in an effort to calm his racing heart, then leaned against the porch railing and faced her. "All I want to know is if Richard already asked you to the church dinner."

Her eyes briefly widened when she understood the reason for his unexpected visit. Caroline smiled slowly and sweetly. It was a smile he'd seen all too rarely from her. He found it difficult to look away.

"Why do you want to know?" she asked.

"I told you," he blurted out. "If Richard's already asked you, then I'll save my breath."

"What if I said he hasn't asked me? Does that mean you will?"

His pride was a fierce thing and had gotten him into trouble with her in the past. He tucked his hands in his back pockets, shrugging as if it was of little concern. "I might."

Caroline set the swing in motion and relaxed enough to cross her legs. She was wearing shorts, and the movement granted him the opportunity to admire those legs.

"Let me put it like this," Caroline said after a moment. "If Richard *had* asked me, and I'm not saying he has, I'd turn him down."

"You would?" This gave Grady second thoughts. If she'd turn down his brother, there was nothing to say she wouldn't do the same with him. "What about me?" he asked before considering the question.

"But you haven't asked me," she reminded him.

If she was leading him on a merry chase, he swore he'd never forgive her. "Will you…would you and Maggie be my date for the church dinner Saturday night?"

The joy that lit her eyes was all the answer Grady needed. His heart felt as if it might fly straight out of his chest.

"We'd love to go with you," Caroline answered without hesitation.

"That'd be great. Great!" He started to leave, but caught the toe of his boot on a toy Maggie had left on the porch and damn near fell on his face. Not that it would have mattered. He was too happy to let a minor humiliation detract from his pleasure.

He was halfway to his truck when Caroline stopped him. "Do you want me to meet you at the church?" she called out.

"No." What kind of date did she think this was, anyway? "I'll pick you both up." Just so there was no room for misunderstanding, he added, "This is a date, Caroline."

"Any particular time?"

Details. Leave it to a woman to be concerned about something like that. "When do you want me?"

"Six-forty-five sounds about right."

"Then that's when I'll be here."

She walked to the porch steps and wrapped her arm around the white column. "I'll look forward to seeing you Saturday."

It would have been the most natural thing in the world to jump up and shout, he was that happy. Happy enough to feel almost drunk with it. Damn it all, he hadn't even kissed Caroline yet. If he got giddy from a little thing like this, he could only begin to imagine what it would be like the first time they made love.

Reverend Wade McMillen liked nothing better than social gatherings at the church, and this one was special, celebrating the one hundred and twentieth anniversary of the date Promise Christian Church had been established. He'd been ministering to this small but growing flock for five years now. It was his first assignment, and friends in the ministry had told him there was something special about a minister's first church. This had certainly proved to be the case with Wade. The parishioners who crowded the church hall were as much his family as the people he'd left behind.

Raised in Houston, Wade had been around cattle ranchers and oil men from the time he was old enough to pull on a pair of cowboy boots. No one was more surprised when he was called to the ministry than Wade himself. His experience in Promise had shown him that he loved his work more than any other occupation he might have chosen.

Long tables at the far end of the hall were heaped with a variety of some of the best home cooking in Texas. Main courses, salads, desserts. Once the food had been readied, Wade led the assembled families in grace, then stayed out of the way while the women's group got the buffet lines going. His role in all this was to make sure dinner went smoothly and everyone had what he or she needed.

"In my opinion," Louise Powell said, pulling Wade aside, "Savannah Smith's teriyaki salad with *chicken* should be considered a main course and not a salad. It's misleading for those of us who're watching our weight to be tempted with salads that under normal circumstances would be considered a main course."

Louise and her friend Tammy Lee Kollenborn had been a trial to Wade from the start, but he wasn't alone in his struggles with these two women. Heaven help him if he inadvertently crossed either of them.

"I'm afraid I'm the one to blame for that," Wade explained, attempting to sound apologetic. "Savannah put it on the table with the main courses, and I suggested that since it was technically a salad, it belonged there."

"I see," Louise said and tightly pinched her lips together, letting him know she disapproved.

"I'll make sure I don't make that mistake again," he said. "Perhaps next year you'd volunteer to help the women's group set up the hall. I'm sure they'd appreciate your advice on such important matters as what should and shouldn't be considered a salad."

"I'll do that," she said with a tinge of self-righteousness. She patted his hand and excused herself to return to her husband.

The buffet line had dwindled down to only a few stragglers, and rather than become embroiled in any more culinary controversies, Wade reached for a plate and a set of silverware, then stepped to the end of the line.

He scanned the group, looking for an empty seat. The circular tables seated eight, perfect for accommodating four couples. The Royal Heirs, the seniors' social group, occupied four of those tables. No space there.

Ellie Frasier and Glen Patterson sat in a corner of the large bustling hall with their friends. There were a few empty spaces, but their table would fill up soon. He enjoyed Ellie and Glen and was counseling them before their wedding. They'd been in for three sessions now, and he had a strong feeling they were well suited. Their marriage would be a good one, built on a foundation of friendship.

Savannah and Laredo Smith were sitting next to Ellie and Glen. Now, there were two he'd never suspected would be right for each other. Savannah was a gentle soul, a special woman who'd touched his heart. Laredo had drifted into town; somehow he and Savannah had been drawn together. Love had changed them both, Savannah especially. Looking at them now, just a short time after their wedding, it was difficult to remember that they'd been together only months rather than years.

Frank Hennessey, the town sheriff, got in line behind Wade. "This is a great spread, isn't it, Rev?"

"As I've said more than once," Wade reminded the other man, "Promise Christian has some of the best cooks in the state of Texas."

"Amen to that." Frank handed Dovie Boyd a plate before reaching for one himself. Both close to retirement age, the two had been seeing each other for as long as Wade had served the community, but apparently didn't have plans to marry. Wade had never questioned them about their relationship. That was their business, not his. He was fond of Frank and Dovie. He found their company delightful and was happy to let Dovie spoil him with a home-cooked meal every now and then. The woman was a wonder with apple pie.

One of Nell Bishop's children raced across the room, and Wade's spirits lifted. He'd sit with Nell, he decided. The widow might feel like odd man out, being there without a date, and since he was alone himself, well, it would work nicely. Nell was a safe dinner companion; everyone knew she wasn't interested in remarriage. If Wade chose to dine with one of the single ladies, some women in the congregation, Louise Powell and Tammy Lee Kollenborn in particular, were sure to read it as a sign of incipient romance.

So Nell was the perfect choice. No pressures there. Not only that, he had a great deal of respect and affection for her family. He'd enjoy spending the evening with them.

But Nell was sitting with her mother-in-law and their table was full.

Wade had to admit he felt lonely. Everyone present seemed to be part of a couple, and those who were single had found partners. Even Grady Weston had a date, and frankly, Wade was pleased with his choice. He'd long admired Caroline Daniels; she and Grady seemed right together, a thought that had occurred to him more than once since Savannah's wedding.

Not until Wade was at the end of the dessert table did he spot the ideal location. He smiled, amused that the vacant seat was at the very table he'd considered moments earlier. The empty spot was next to Cal Patterson. Wade got along just fine with the rancher, although the man had a reputation for being prickly. Cal sat with his brother Glen, but Glen wasn't paying him any heed. The younger Patterson's concentration was held by Ellie, and rightly so.

"Mind if I join you?" Wade asked Cal.

"Mind?" Cal muttered, sliding his chair over to give Wade ample room. "I'd be grateful."

"This is a great way to celebrate the church's birthday, isn't it?" Wade asked, digging into his food with gusto. He never ate better than at church dinners.

"Growing up, I can remember looking forward to the third Saturday in July," Cal said. "My mom made her special baked beans every year. Still does. Apparently the recipe's been handed down from one generation to the next for at least a hundred years. If I remember right, it originally came from back East."

Wade took a forkful of the baked beans and nodded approvingly. "Mmm." He chewed slowly, savoring every morsel. "There's a lot to be said for tradition, especially when it tastes this good."

"She only bakes 'em once a year and it's always for the church." Having cleaned his own plate, Cal pushed back his chair and folded his arms. Wade's gaze followed Cal's. Grady and Caroline stood in the dessert line with Savannah and Laredo. The four were engaged in conversation and appeared to be enjoying themselves.

"Grady and Caroline make a handsome couple, don't they?" Wade asked, testing the waters with the older Patterson brother. This couldn't be easy on him, especially after Cal's own unfortunate experience a few years earlier. His wedding had been canceled just two days before the ceremony. Cal had taken the brunt of the embarrassment when his fiancée abruptly left town.

Wade and Cal had shared some serious discussions afterward and bonded as friends. But Cal hadn't mentioned Jennifer's name, not in all the time since. The subject of marriage appeared to be taboo, as well. More than once Wade had been tempted to remind Cal not to judge all women by Jennifer's actions. It might be a cliché, but time really was a great healer. When Cal was ready, Wade believed he'd date again.

"It's about time Grady opened his eyes," Cal said, grinning.

"About Caroline?"

"Yeah. Those two have been circling each other for a year, maybe more. If one of 'em didn't make a move soon, I was going to rope 'em together myself."

Wade chuckled, enjoying the image.

"Seems that every time Grady gets close to making a move, something happens and he takes off like a jackrabbit."

Little Maggie Daniels raced past at that moment, and Wade caught her about the waist to keep her from colliding with Nell Bishop's son. "Whoa there," he said, laughing. "What's the big hurry?"

Maggie covered her mouth and giggled. "Petey was chasing me."

"Be careful, understand?"

Maggie bobbed her head, and Wade pointed to the corsage on her wrist. "Who gave you flowers?"

"Grady," Maggie answered with such pride her entire face lit up. Her eyes fell to the pink and white carnations on her wrist. "He yells sometimes."

"Does it bother you?"

Maggie had to think about that a moment before she shrugged. "He bought Mommy flowers, too. She was surprised and so was I, and when Mommy asked him why, he said it was 'cause we're special."

"You are very special." Wade smiled.

Maggie's return smile revealed two missing front teeth. "Mommy likes him," she said, and Wade had the feeling that she'd decided perhaps Grady wasn't such a bad guy, after all.

Petey Bush approached. "Wanna hold hands?" the six-year-old boy asked.

Maggie looked to Wade for permission. "I think it'll be all right," he advised.

She nodded solemnly and the two children strolled off hand in hand.

"It's a sorry day when five- and six-year-olds have an easier time getting a date than we do, don't you think?" Cal asked him.

A sorry day indeed, Wade mused.

Caroline had a wonderful time at the dinner. A *perfectly* wonderful time, she reflected as they walked out to Grady's truck. Everything about the evening had been like a dream. Not once had she exchanged a cross word with Grady. Not once had they disagreed. Not once had he yelled at Maggie. There just might be hope for them.

Maggie, worn-out from the evening's activities, fell asleep between them in the truck. She slumped against Caroline, her head in her mother's lap. When Grady pulled up in front of the house, she was still asleep. It seemed a shame to disturb her.

Grady must have thought the same thing, because he turned off the engine and made no move to get out of the truck. The only light available was from a quarter moon set crookedly in the dark Texas sky.

Night settled about them. Neither one of them spoke. For her own part, Caroline wanted the evening to last as long as possible. If it never ended, that was fine with her.

"I had a lovely time," she finally whispered.

"Me, too."

She assumed he'd open the truck door then and was pleased when he didn't.

"It was sweet of you to bring Maggie and me flowers."

"It was the only way I could tell you how much—" He halted midsentence.

"How much...?" she prodded.

"I like you both," he finished.

"Do you, Grady?" she asked, her voice low.

"Very much." He brought his hand to the side of her face, and Caroline closed her eyes, delighting in the feel of his callused palm against her cheek. Smiling to herself at how far they'd come, she leaned into his hand.

"Do you think it'd wake Maggie if I kissed you?" he asked, whispering.

Caroline didn't know, but she was prepared to risk it. "I'm game if you are."

Still Grady hesitated. "This is the first time Maggie's been willing to have anything to do with me. I don't want to ruin that."

"If you don't kiss me *now,* Grady, I swear I'll never forgive you!"

He laughed softly and without further delay took her face between his hands. Once again Caroline shut her eyes, just for a moment, treasuring these rare moments of intimacy.

Slowly Grady bent toward her and she angled her head to accommodate his movement. His mouth was so close to hers. So close she could feel his breath against her skin. So close she could sense his longing—and admit her own. Yet he hesitated, as did she.

Caroline realized—and she suspected that Grady did, too—that everything between them would be forever changed if they proceeded with this kiss. It was more than an ordinary kiss. It was a meeting of two hearts, an admission of vulnerability and openness.

Caroline wasn't sure who moved first, but chose to think of what followed as a mutual decision. An inexorable drawing together.

The kiss was gentle, almost tentative. His hand drifted to the back of her neck, urging her forward.

Grady kissed her again, and this time his mouth was more demanding, more insistent. Within only a few seconds, Caroline felt as though she'd experienced every possible emotion. When he released her, his breath was ragged.

"I'm sorry, I—"

Rather than let him ruin everything with an apology, she kissed the corner of his mouth.

Maggie stirred and they both froze. Caroline prayed her daughter wouldn't awake, wouldn't unconsciously end these precious moments with Grady.

"Is she asleep?" he asked, speaking so quietly she had to strain to hear. His voice was more breath than sound.

"Yes…"

They waited breathlessly. When it seemed he wasn't going to kiss her again, Caroline took the initiative and leaned toward him. The strength of their attraction stunned her. It was as though they couldn't get close enough. Their mouths twisted and strained in a passionate desperate kiss, but that lasted only a moment.

Then sanity returned. Reluctantly they eased away from each other. Grady rested his shoulders against the seat cushion, tilted back his head and sighed deeply.

Caroline swallowed. "I'd better get Maggie inside," she whispered.

"Right." When he opened his door, the light blinded Caroline and she was grateful when he immediately closed it, making the least noise possible.

Coming around to her side, he opened the door, helped her out and then reached for Maggie, carrying her toward the house. Caroline had expected to carry Maggie herself. She'd always done so; she was accustomed to it. Grady's action brought to life a complexity of feelings—gratitude, relief, even a slight sense of loss.

"You get the door," Grady said.

Caroline unlocked the door. With only a night-light to guide them, she led him to Maggie's bedroom at the rear of the house. She folded back the covers on the bed and Grady carefully set the little girl down. Caroline removed her daughter's shoes and put them aside.

Grady smoothed the hair from Maggie's brow, touched his fingertips to his lips and pressed his hand to the little girl's brow. The gesture was so loving, so *fatherly,* that Caroline had to turn away.

Grady followed her into the darkened hallway. She continued to the front door. She didn't want him to leave but dared not ask him to stay.

"Thank you again," she whispered. "For everything." The front door remained open and light spilled in from the porch.

Grady didn't move.

Slowly she raised her eyes to his. The invitation was there, and it was simply beyond her to refuse him. He held his arms open. Less than four steps separated them, but she literally ran into his embrace. He caught her about the waist, and she wrapped her arms around his neck. They kissed again with an urgency that left her weak, an urgency that drained her of all thoughts save one—the unexpected wonder and joy she'd discovered in his arms.

Until that night, Caroline hadn't realized how lonely she'd been, how long the nights could be. In Grady's arms she felt whole and needed and beautiful.

When the kiss ended, she buried her face in his neck.

"I could hold you forever," he whispered.

"I could let you." She felt his smile.

"Don't tempt me more than I already am," he warned.

It was heaven knowing he found her attractive. He held her close while she struggled to regain her composure. Caroline was grateful for those few quiet moments before he slowly released her.

He placed his hands lightly on her shoulders. "I want to see you again."

"Yes." It didn't matter when or where.

"Soon."

She was almost giddy with the wonder of what was happening. "Please."

He smiled and, as though he couldn't help himself, he kissed her again.

Their kissing only seemed to get better and better. "Why did it take you so long?" she asked when she'd recovered enough to speak.

"Because I'm a pigheaded fool."

"I am, too." No need denying it. She was as much at fault as Grady.

"No more."

"No more," she echoed.

"Tomorrow," he suggested. "I can't wait any longer than that to see you again."

"Okay. When? Where?"

"Can you come out to the ranch?"

"Yes, of course. I'll come after church."

"Wonderful," he whispered and kissed the tip of her nose. "Perfect."

She slipped her arms around his middle. "Oh, Grady, is this really happening or am I dreaming?"

"Nothing gets more real than the way you make me feel."

She smiled. Never would she have believed that Grady Weston was a romantic.

"About Maggie…"

He stiffened, and she stopped him by pressing her index finger against his lips. "Don't worry about her. Everything will work out."

"I don't mean to frighten her."

"I know."

"Did she like the flowers?"

Caroline kissed the underside of his jaw. "Very much."

"Did you?"

"More than I can say." She trailed kisses toward his ear and reveled in the way his body shuddered against hers when she tugged on his earlobe with her teeth.

"Caroline," he breathed. "You're making this impossible."

"Do I really tempt you?"

"Yes." His voice was low but harsh. "You don't have a clue."

Actually she did. "Kiss me one more time and then you can leave."

He hesitated, then gently captured her face between his hands and angled his mouth toward hers. The kiss, while one of need, was also one of elation, of shared joy. All this time they'd wasted, all the time they'd let pride and fear and doubt stand between them.

Caroline needed him and he needed her. Savannah, a woman with real insight into people, had tried to tell her that. And Caroline knew she'd tried to convince Grady, too. She was aware of Savannah's matchmaking efforts because her friend had told her; she was also aware that Savannah had been frustrated by one setback after another.

Caroline supposed she was as responsible for those setbacks as Grady. She'd always been attracted to him, but felt confused, unprepared. She'd been hurt terribly once and with that pain had come fear. For years she'd been afraid to love again. To trust again.

Deep within her, she recognized that Grady would never abandon her. Not Grady. He was as solid as a rock.

His final kiss was deep and long.

It took a moment for Maggie's voice to break through the fog of her desire.

"Mommy! Mommy!"

Grady groaned and reluctantly let Caroline go.

She turned to find Maggie standing in the dim light, rubbing the sleep from her eyes. "What is it, sweetheart?"

Maggie ignored the question and, instead, glared at Grady. "What are you doing to my mommy?" she demanded.

Four

Sunday morning was the one day of the week Jane Dickinson—*Dr.* Jane Dickinson, she reminded herself—could sleep in. Yet it was barely six and she was wide awake. Tossing aside the sheet, she threw on her robe and wandered barefoot into the kitchen.

"Texas," she muttered. Who would've believed when she signed up for this that she'd end up in the great state of Texas? The hill country was about as far as anyone could get from the bustling activity of Los Angeles.

Jane had *tried* to make a go of life in small-town America, but she was completely and utterly miserable. In three months she hadn't managed to make a single friend. Sure, there were lots of acquaintances, but no real friends. Never in her life had she missed her friends and family more, and all because of money. She'd entered into this agreement with the federal government in order to reduce her debts—three years in Promise, Texas, and some of her medical-school loans would be forgiven.

Maybe she should just admit she'd made a mistake, pack her bags and hightail it out of this godforsaken town. But even as the thought entered her mind, Jane realized that wasn't what she wanted. What she wanted was to find some way to connect with these people, to become part of this tight-knit community.

The residents of Promise seemed willing enough to acknowledge that she was a competent physician specializing in family practice. But they came to see her only when they absolutely had to—for prescription renewals, a bad cough or sprain that couldn't be treated at home. Jane's one major fault was that she wasn't Dr. Cummings. The man had retired in his seventies after serving the community for nearly fifty years. The people of Promise knew and trusted him. She, on the other hand, was considered an outsider and, worse, some kind of Valley Girl or frivolous surfer type.

Despite her up-to-the-moment expertise, she had yet to gain the community's confidence. Everything she'd done to prove herself to the people of Promise had been a miserable failure.

Rejection wasn't something Jane was accustomed to dealing with. It left her feeling frustrated and helpless. In medical school, whenever she felt overwhelmed and emotionally confused, she'd gone jogging. It had always helped clear her thoughts, helped her gain perspective. But she hadn't hit the streets even once since she'd come here. With a new sense of resolve, she began to search for her running shoes, reminding herself that *she* was the one who'd agreed to work in a small community. She was determined to stick it out, even if it killed her.

Dressed in bright yellow nylon running shorts and a matching tank top, she started out at an easy nine-minute-mile pace. She jogged from her living quarters next to the health clinic down the tree-lined streets of

Promise. The community itself wasn't so bad. Actually it was a pretty little town with traditional values and interesting people. Ranchers mostly. Down-to-earth folk, hardworking, family-oriented. That was what made her situation so difficult to understand. The people were friendly and welcoming, it seemed, to everyone but her.

Jane turned the corner onto Maple Street. At the post office she took another turn and headed up Main. A couple of cars were parked in front of the bowling alley, which kept the longest hours in town; it was open twenty-four hours on Saturdays and Sundays. It wasn't the bowling that lured folks at all hours, but the café, which served good solid meals and great coffee at 1970s prices.

Jane's feet pounded the pavement and sweat rolled down the sides of her face. She'd barely gone a mile and already her body was suggesting that she hadn't been exercising enough. She knew she'd ache later but didn't care; she was already feeling more optimistic.

She rounded the corner off Main and onto Baxter, running past the antique store owned and operated by Dovie Boyd. Dovie lived in a brick home just around the corner. Despite the early hour, she was standing in the middle of her huge vegetable garden with her watering can in hand.

Jane had often admired the older woman's lush garden. The pole beans were six feet high, the tomatoes bursting with ripeness and the zucchini abundant. Jane marveled at how one woman could possibly coax this much produce from a few plants.

"Morning," Jane called.

Dovie smiled and raised her hand in response.

Jane continued down the street, full steam ahead.

She'd gone perhaps twenty yards when she realized it'd happened to her again. She'd never been a quitter in her life and she wasn't going to start now. She did an abrupt about-face and headed back.

Dovie looked surprised to see her.

Jane stopped and, breathing heavily, leaned forward and braced her hands on her knees. "Hello again," she said when she'd caught her breath.

Without a pause Dovie continued watering. "Lovely morning, isn't it?"

"Beautiful," Jane agreed. Slowly she straightened and watched Dovie expertly weave her way through the garden, pausing now and again to finger a plant or pull a weed.

"Do you have a minute, Mrs. Boyd?" she asked, gathering her nerve. She rested her hands against the white picket fence.

Widening her eyes, Dovie turned. "What can I do for you, Dr. Dickinson?"

"First, I'd like it if you called me Jane."

"Then Jane it is."

The older woman's tone was friendly, but Jane sensed the same reserve in her she'd felt in others.

"What am I doing wrong?" She hadn't intended to blurt out the question like that, but couldn't help herself.

"Wrong?" Dovie set the watering can aside.

"What's wrong with *me?*" she amended.

"I don't think anything's wrong with you." The other woman was clearly puzzled by the question. "What makes you assume such a thing?"

Attitudes were so difficult to describe. How could she explain how she felt without sounding snobbish or self-pitying? But she had to try.

"Why am I standing on this side of the fence while you're on that side?" Jane asked as she paced the cement walkway. "Why do I have to be the one to greet others first? People don't like me, and I want to know why."

Dovie lifted one finger to her lips and frowned, apparently deep in thought. "You did greet me first, didn't you?"

"Yes, but it isn't only you. It's everyone." Jane paused, struggling with her composure. "I want to know why."

"My goodness, I'm not sure. I never realized." Dovie walked toward the short white gate and unlatched it, swinging it open. "Come inside, dear, and we'll sit down and reason this out."

Now that Jane had made her point, it would have been rude and unfair to refuse, but to her embarrassment she discovered she was close to tears.

"Sit down and make yourself comfortable," Dovie said and gestured toward the white wrought-iron patio set. "I'll get a pot of tea brewing. I don't know about you, but I tend to think more clearly if I have something hot to drink."

"I... Thank you," Jane said, feeling humble and grateful at once. The few moments Dovie was in the kitchen gave her time to collect herself.

Soon Dovie reappeared carrying a tray with a pot of steaming tea and two delicate china cups, as well as a plate of scones. She set it down on the table and poured the tea, handing Jane the first cup.

Jane felt a bit conspicuous in her tank top, sipping tea from a Spode cup, but she was too thankful for Dovie's kindness to worry about it.

"All right now," Dovie said when she'd finished pouring. "Let's talk." She sat down and leaned back in her chair, pursing her lips. "Tell me some other things that have bothered you about Promise."

Jane wasn't sure where to start. "I have this...this sense that people don't like me."

"Nonsense," Dovie countered. "We don't know you well enough to like or dislike you."

"You're right. No one knows me," Jane murmured. "I need a friend," she said with a shrug, offering the one solution that had come to her.

"We all need friends, but perhaps you need to make more of an effort to give people a chance to know you."

"But I *have* tried to meet people," she said in her own defense.

Dovie frowned. "Give me an example."

Jane had a list of those. An inventory of failures cataloged from the day she'd first arrived. "The party for Richard Weston," she said. It was the first social event she'd attended in the area. Richard had been warm and friendly, stopping her on the street and issuing a personal invitation. Jane had been excited about it, had even told her family she was attending the party. But when she got there, she'd ended up standing around by herself. The evening had been uncomfortable from the start.

As the new doctor in town Jane appeared to be a topic of speculation and curiosity. The short newspaper article published about her earlier in the week had added to the attention she'd garnered. People stared at her, a few had greeted her, asked her a question or two, then drifted away. Richard had been the star of his own party, and the one time he'd noticed her, she was sure he'd forgotten who she was. For a while she'd wandered around, feeling awkward and out of place. Mostly she'd felt like a party crasher and left soon after she'd arrived.

"You *were* there, weren't you?" Dovie murmured with a thoughtful look.

"Yes." Not that it'd done Jane any good.

"You came in a suit and high heels, as I recall," Dovie added.

"I realized as soon as I arrived the suit was a mistake," Jane said. At the time she'd felt it was important to maintain a professional image. She was new in town and attempting to make a good impression.

"And then jeans and a cotton top to the Grange dance."

"I didn't realize it was a more formal affair." She hadn't lasted long there, either. "I wasn't sure what to wear," Jane confessed. She'd come overdressed for one event and underdressed for the other. "But," she said hopelessly, "I had no way of knowing."

Dovie nodded, silently encouraging her to continue.

"I showed up for the Willie Nelson Fourth of July picnic, too, but no one bothered to tell me Willie Nelson wouldn't be there." That had been a major disappointment, as well.

Dovie giggled and shook her head. "The town council's invited him nine years running, and he's politely declined every year, but we've never let a little thing like that stand in our way. This is Willie Nelson country!"

"Someone might have said something." Jane didn't take kindly to being the only one not in on the joke.

"That's something you can only learn by living here. Next year, you'll know."

If I'm here that long, Jane thought.

"Another thing," she said. "What's all this about a ghost town?" Jane asked next.

Dovie's expressive eyes narrowed. "Who told you there was a ghost town?"

Jane wondered at the swift change in her newfound friend. "I overheard two children talking. One of them mentioned it."

"Don't pay any attention to those rumors, understand?"

"Is there one?"

"That's neither here nor there," Dovie said, but not unkindly. "We have other more important matters to discuss."

"Such as?"

Dovie's head came back. "You." Her face was set, her voice firm. "You're right, you do need a friend."

"Are you volunteering to take me under your wing?" Jane asked and hoped Dovie understood how very grateful she'd be.

"I'm too old." Dovie's response was fast. "I'm thinking of someone more your age." She tapped her index finger against her chin. "You and Ellie Frasier would get along like gangbusters. Unfortunately Ellie's busy getting ready for her wedding just now, so you'll need to be patient."

"Oh." Jane's voice was small.

"Until then, you and I have our work cut out for us."

Jane frowned, not sure she understood. "What work?"

Dovie's expression told Jane she'd overlooked the obvious. "We need to find out what's wrong with everyone in this town. I've decided there's nothing wrong with *you,* Dr. Jane. It's everyone else, and I'm determined to find out what."

"All the comforts of home," Richard Weston said out loud. He stood in the middle of the dirt road that ran through the ghost town. "Bitter End, Texas," he continued, "population one." He laughed then, the sound echoing down the long dusty street littered with sagebrush and rock.

Hitching his thumbs in the waistband of his jeans, he sauntered down the dirt road as if he owned it, and for all intents and purposes, he did.

For the time being Bitter End was his home. He was proud of the good job he'd done carving out a comfortable place for himself. He figured he'd be stuck here for a while. How long wasn't clear yet. A man on the run didn't have a lot of alternatives.

Everything was about to catch up with him. His brother already knew he hadn't paid that old coot Max Jordan, and he wasn't going to be able to hide all the other charges he'd made, either. Although Grady's business account had sure come in handy. But he'd stretched his luck to the max in Promise.

Time to move on. Hide again, only no one would ever think to look for him here. He was as safe as a babe cuddled in his mother's loving arms. Richard had a sixth sense about when to walk away. He'd come to trust his instincts; they were what had kept him out of prison this long.

Richard kicked the toe of his snakeskin boot into the hard dry ground. He'd arrived in Promise penniless, miserable and afraid to glance over his shoulder for fear the law—or worse—was hot on his tail. He'd decided to head back to Promise on the spur of the moment, when he awoke one morning and found himself outside El Paso without money or transportation. Hitchhiking, he made his way to the central part of the state.

Luck had blessed him all his life. He hadn't been back long before he discovered Savannah had visited Bitter End. As soon as his older sister mentioned the ghost town, he'd known what to do.

Little by little Richard had managed to squirrel away supplies, making the trek so often he no longer lost his way. Each day he managed to take something from the ranch or buy supplies on ranch credit. In the beginning it was little things, items not easily missed. Seldom-used equipment no one would notice was gone. Gradually he'd worked in the larger pricier necessities. He'd been clever about it, too.

Still congratulating himself, Richard walked up the old wooden steps to the boardwalk. He sat down in the rocking chair he'd discovered in one of the buildings and surveyed the town. His domain.

He'd been born under a lucky star, Richard told himself, and its shine hadn't faded. He marveled anew at the crafty way he'd charged much of what he needed. Grady didn't have a clue, either. Richard would charge something nonsensical like tractor parts to Grady's account, knowing no one would think to question that. Later, making sure it wasn't the same salesclerk, he'd return the part and use the credit to purchase what he really needed. In the weeks since his return he'd accumulated all the comforts of home, and the best part was that it had been at his brother's expense.

"Oh, yes, I'm going to be real comfortable now," he said, grinning broadly. Tucking his hands behind his head, he leaned back. "Thanks, Grady," he said with a snicker.

Slowly his smile faded. None of this hiding out would be necessary if the situation with Ellie Frasier had worked out differently. It would have been easy to let that sweet young thing soothe away his worries, but his hopes had died a humiliating death, thanks to Glen Patterson.

Why any woman would choose some cowboy over him was beyond Richard. Clearly Ellie had no taste. In the beginning he'd been drawn to the inheritance her daddy had left her, figuring he'd talk her into marrying him, get his hands on the money and then skip town.

As time progressed and he came to know Ellie, he'd actually found himself thinking about sticking around and making a go of life in Promise. Money in the right places would put an end to his current troubles. For a while he'd toyed with the idea of getting involved in local politics. Promise could use a mayor like him, not some hick but a man with an eye to the future. Then maybe for once he'd be able to stay out of trouble, make a new life for himself. Start over. But unfortunately it hadn't panned out.

Standing, Richard glanced at his watch. He hadn't moved here yet, so he had to be conscious of the time. Although his sister and brother hadn't said much, they were aware of his absences, and he didn't want to arouse their suspicions.

Richard headed to where he'd parked the pickup. After several failed attempts, he'd found a new way into the town, one that didn't necessitate a long walk.

The wind whistled behind him, a low plaintive cry that sent shivers down his spine.

"Oh, no, you don't," he said. Naturally there'd been talk about ghosts in Bitter End. The one time he'd brought Ellie with him, she'd been squirming out of her skin in her eagerness to leave. She claimed it was a feeling she had, a sense of oppression. His sister had said she, too, could feel something weird in the old town.

Yeah, right.

Not Richard, at least not until that very moment. The wind increased in velocity, whistling as he walked away, his back to the main street.

"I don't hear anything, I don't feel anything," he said aloud, more in an effort to hear the words than to convince himself.

The sensation, or whatever the hell it was, didn't dissipate until he was safe inside his brother's dilapidated truck. With the doors locked Richard relaxed, suspecting he'd viewed one too many episodes of *Tales from the Crypt*.

As he drove off, another thought entered his mind. Caroline Daniels.

He had no real interest in her himself, but he could have her and he knew it. His brother was sweet on Caroline; that was easy to guess, just from the way Grady looked at her. It might be rotten of him, Richard thought with a grin, but he sure did love to play the spoilsport.

His brother had as much charisma as an overripe tomato, yet Grady was the one sitting pretty on a prosperous ranch, living high, while Richard had to worry about where his next meal was coming from. Some things in life just weren't fair, and if he wanted to even them out a little, he could see no harm in it. Besides, he subscribed to the idea that, regardless of the star he was born under, a man made his own luck. Or, at least, enhanced it.

"You don't know how good you've got it, big brother," Richard said. It shouldn't be hard to lure Caroline away from Grady—and it didn't hurt any that her kid was crazy about him. Kids had always liked him, and Richard had encouraged them. For some reason a lot of people put stock in their kids' opinions and preferences. As far as he was concerned, it didn't matter a damn what some kid thought, although he didn't mind using a child to manipulate the parent.

Maggie was a great example. She preferred him over Grady, which made him the leading man when it came to winning her mother's affections. He found Caroline kind of irritating, though; he didn't care for the way she looked at him.

What he enjoyed most of all was playing himself off against his brother. He loved it when he could frustrate Grady, but his older brother made it much too easy; he took all the fun out of it. Well, not *all* the fun. Poor old Grady—would he never learn? Richard smirked. When he was around, Grady didn't stand a chance with the ladies.

Grady felt like a kid waiting for prom night—a kid who had a date with the prom queen. The chance to see Caroline again was worth cutting short his sleep. It meant getting up earlier than usual to deal with morning chores. But he'd managed, surprising Wade as much as he did Savannah and Laredo when he slipped into the pew two minutes before services were due to start.

He hadn't come to hear the sermon, but he figured God would forgive that. He'd come for Caroline. She sang with the choir, and the possibility of seeing her again so soon after the church dinner was irresistible.

Grady still walked on air after last night's kisses. Even Maggie's interruption hadn't ruined the evening. He'd been at a loss for words when she'd stumbled upon Caroline and him with their arms locked around each other. Rather than try to explain, he'd left the matter in Caroline's capable hands and departed soon afterward.

The last thing she'd said before he walked out the door was that she'd stop by the ranch Sunday afternoon.

Mere hours away.

The service was upbeat, and Wade's message caused him to nod his head in agreement a number of times. The minister used humor and lots of anecdotes, which made for an interesting sermon. Before he realized it, the hour was over and the congregation dismissed with a benediction.

Pastor Wade McMillen stood in the doorway as people left. "Good to see you, Grady," he said, giving Grady's hand a hearty shake. "But somehow I don't think it was my sermon that interested you."

Grady grumbled some noncommittal reply. Damned little escaped Wade's attention. As if to prove him right, Wade caught Jeremy Bishop by the shoulder, stopping him on his way out the door.

"That must have been an interesting book you were reading in church," he said with an encouraging smile.

Jeremy squirmed uncomfortably before he reached inside his shirt. With obvious reluctance he withdrew a slim paperback novel.

"T. R. Grant?" Wade said and cocked one eyebrow at the title.

Jeremy's eyes grew round. "You've never heard of T. R. Grant?"

"Can't say I have," Wade admitted.

"He's great!"

Wade chuckled. "I'm sure he is. Maybe I should read him, too."

"I've read everything he's ever written. I can lend you one of his books if you want."

"I'll take you up on that offer." Wade ruffled the boy's hair and returned his attention to Grady. "I see that things are developing nicely between you and Caroline Daniels."

Grady tensed. He had no desire to discuss his private life.

As if he knew that, too, Wade slapped him lightly on the back. "It took you long enough," he said with a laugh. Before Grady could respond, Wade had begun talking to someone else.

Grady met Caroline on the front lawn. He saw her speak to Wade, then glance at him, smiling shyly. The yard was crowded with people visiting and chatting, but everyone appeared to fade from sight as Caroline approached.

"Hello again," he said, which was probably the stupidest thing he'd ever uttered. Not that he cared.

"Hello." Her voice had a deep breathless quality.

"Were you able to reassure Maggie?" He'd felt bad about leaving her to make the explanations, but feared any effort on his part wouldn't have come out right.

"She understands."

"But does she approve?"

Caroline's eyes avoided his, which was answer

enough in itself. "It isn't up to Maggie to approve or disapprove of whom I kiss."

He exhaled slowly and would have said more except that he couldn't stop looking at Caroline. She was so damn pretty, any coherent thought didn't stand a chance of lasting more than a second or two. It was her eyes, he concluded, a deep rich shade of chocolate. No, he decided after a moment, it was her soft brown hair. He remembered the silky feel of it bunched in his hands when he'd kissed her. He remembered a whole lot more than the feel of her hair...

"So you're coming to see Savannah this afternoon?" he asked, trying to redirect his thoughts. If he continued in this vein much longer, he'd end up kissing her right then and there just to prove how real last night had been.

"No."

Grady's disappointment was sharp. "You're not? But I thought—"

"I'm coming to see you."

His heart, which had gone sluggish with discouragement, sped up, and he could feel his pulse hammering in his neck.

"Hi, Grady," Maggie said, joining her mother. She clung to her mother's arm and looked up at him with a slight frown.

"Hi, Maggie. I hear you're coming out to the ranch this afternoon."

The child continued to stare at him, and although she made no comment, Grady saw the way she moved protectively close to her mother.

"Did Savannah tell you about the new colt we have?" She nodded.

"He's only a few days old, but he's already handsome. I bet you'd like to see him."

Again she nodded.

Grady glanced at Caroline. "Do you think Maggie's old enough to visit the colt?"

"I can, can't I, Mommy?" Maggie twisted around and gazed up at her mother with imploring eyes.

"I think it should be all right, as long as you stay with Grady."

"I will, I will," she promised.

"That new colt needs a name," Grady added. "Maybe you could help us decide what to call him."

Her eyes got huge. "Could I really?"

"If you can think of a decent name for such a handsome boy. We'll let you take a gander at him first, pet him a few times and then give you the opportunity to think up a name."

"That's kind of you, Grady," Caroline said.

They walked toward the parking lot, in no particular hurry. "What time will you be by, do you think?" he asked, restraining himself from saying she should come right that minute.

"Maggie needs something to eat and a nap first."

"She can have Sunday dinner with us—you both could—and then Maggie could nap. Savannah'll be more than happy to watch her." After she finished wringing his neck for inviting company without consulting her first. "While Maggie's resting, perhaps you and I could…" For the life of him, he couldn't think of a single respectable thing for the two of them to do.

"Go riding," Caroline inserted. "I'll borrow some jeans from Savannah."

She could have suggested mud wrestling and he would've agreed.

"Well…I suppose we can alter our plans just a little," Caroline said, smiling softly.

It took a moment for the words to sink into his consciousness. "You could? Great."

"Are we going to Savannah's?" Maggie asked, tugging at the sleeve of her mother's dress. "Are we leaving now?"

"It looks that way," Caroline answered.

Maggie clapped her hands, celebrating the good news.

"I'll see you there, then," she said to Grady, opening the passenger door for Maggie. Her daughter leaped inside, eager to be on their way.

Grady opened the driver's side for Caroline. "Drive carefully."

She got in and assured him she would.

Grady stepped away from the car when she started the engine; he watched her back out of the parking space and turn out of the driveway before he realized that he'd attracted a number of curious stares. In particular, he noticed Edwina and Lily Moorhouse studying him.

The two sisters were retired teachers, as prim and proper as the spinster schoolmarms of nineteenth-century Promise. They smiled approvingly in his direction before they leaned toward one another, heads close enough to touch, talking up a storm. He'd been in their classes as a boy and could well recall the speed with which those two could chatter. Two hundred words a minute, he guessed, with gusts up to four fifty.

Their tongues were wagging now, but frankly, Grady didn't care. He was about to spend the afternoon with the woman who'd dominated his thoughts for months. The woman who dominated his dreams.

Grady arrived back at the Yellow Rose less than five minutes behind Caroline. He found her in the kitchen with Savannah, preparing Sunday dinner. She paused when he entered, then glanced around her.

"Did you see Maggie?"

"Maggie?" He shook his head.

"She wasn't on the porch?"

"Not that I noticed." He stuck his head out the door and couldn't see her.

"I told her not to leave the porch." Caroline sighed with impatience. She set aside the tomato she was slicing and reached for a towel.

"She came to me for a carrot not more than a minute ago," Savannah said.

"She probably went into the barn to see the new colt." Grady blamed himself for that.

"She knows better," Caroline murmured. "It's not safe there."

"Don't worry, she's only been gone a minute," Savannah said reassuringly.

"I'll get her," Grady offered, eager to prove to Maggie that he could be as charming and wonderful as Richard.

"Are you sure you don't mind?" Caroline asked.

"Not in the least." Grady headed toward the barn, whistling as he went. The interior was dark after the bright sunlight, and he squinted until his eyes adjusted to the change in lighting.

"Maggie," he called out.

No answer.

"Maggie," he called again.

A soft almost mewing sound followed. Grady whirled around. The noise came from Widowmaker's stall. When he looked inside, Grady's heart froze. Maggie was huddled against the wall, her face white with terror.

Just then, the ill-tempered stallion thrashed out with his hooves, narrowly missing the child.

Five

Grady knew that he had to make his move fast or Maggie could be seriously hurt. Widowmaker snorted and began to paw the floor. Unwilling to give the stallion an opportunity to get any closer to the child, Grady threw open the stall door, grabbed Maggie and literally swung her out of harm's way.

Maggie let out a scream. With his heart pounding, Grady firmly held the squirming child against him, trying to comfort her and at the same time calm his own fears. Unfortunately he failed on both counts.

The barn door flew open and Savannah and Caroline rushed breathlessly inside.

"Mommy! Mommy!"

Grady released Maggie, who raced toward her mother, nearly stumbling in her eagerness to escape his clutches. Caroline held her arms open and the child sobbed hysterically as she fell into her mother's embrace.

"What happened?" Savannah asked.

"Somehow Maggie got into Widowmaker's stall,"

Grady explained. His knees shook so badly he sank onto a bale of hay.

"Dear God," Savannah whispered and lowered herself onto the bale beside him. "Is she hurt?"

Grady didn't think so.

Caroline's eyes were filled with questions, but it was impossible to talk over the sound of Maggie's crying.

"What about you?" Savannah asked. "You didn't get kicked, did you?"

"I'm fine." Which wasn't entirely true. Grady figured just seeing Maggie in that stall cost him five years of his life. God only knew what would have happened if he hadn't gotten there when he had. The thought wasn't one he wished to entertain.

Gathering the child in her arms, Caroline made her way out of the barn. Savannah and Grady followed. His sister returned to the house, but Grady lingered outside, not knowing how to help although he wanted to do *something*. He waited for a clue from Caroline, who sat on one of the porch steps as she cradled her daughter. Maggie continued to sob almost uncontrollably, hiding her face in her mother's shoulder. Caroline stopped whispering to the child and started to sing in a low soothing voice gently swaying back and forth.

Grady pulled out the rocking chair and Caroline's eyes revealed her gratitude as she sat down in it. When the song was finished, she talked softly to Maggie, reassuring the little girl once more that everything was fine and there was nothing to be afraid of.

Grady paced the area in front of the porch, waiting, wondering what he should do next. If anything. Gradually Maggie quieted. Then she straightened and glanced around.

"Hello, princess," he said, remembering that was what his father had called Savannah. It seemed to suit Maggie. "Are you okay?"

Maggie took one look at him and burst into tears. Within seconds she'd buried her face in her mother's shoulder again.

"What'd I say?" he asked, unable to understand what he'd done now. He'd hoped the child would view him as her hero since he'd saved her from certain harm. Apparently that wasn't the case.

"She's embarrassed," Caroline explained.

"Embarrassed?" he shouted, forgetting how his booming voice terrified the little girl. Maggie burrowed deeper into her mother's embrace.

Savannah opened the screen door and stepped onto the porch. "Dinner's ready if anyone's interested," she announced.

Grady wasn't. His appetite was gone. Conflicting emotions churned in him—he felt angry and relieved, frustrated and pleased, confused and happy. He wanted to hug Maggie and thank God she was safe, and at the same time chastise her for giving him the fright of his life.

"I think it might be best if I took Maggie home," Caroline said.

"No." Grady's protest was instantaneous. "I mean, you need to do what you think is best but…" He didn't know what he wanted other than to spend time with her, but now it seemed that wasn't going to happen.

"I'll see if I can settle her down," Caroline offered. She held Maggie in her arms and continued to rock, humming softly.

Grady sat on the top step and marveled at her gentle manner with the child. The way she calmed Maggie helped quiet his own heart. No one seemed to realize it, but he'd suffered quite a jolt himself. Rocket sat next to him, his head nestled on Grady's lap. The old dog had belonged to his father, and in the years since his parents' deaths, Grady had spent many a late night sitting quietly with Rocket. Talking a bit, mostly just thinking. The dog had often comforted him.

When he was sure he wouldn't disturb the child's slumber, Grady dragged the vacant rocker next to Caroline.

"Thank you," she whispered. Reaching out, she squeezed his hand. "I hate to think what could have happened if you hadn't arrived when you did. Maggie knows better. I'll have a talk with her later, but I don't think you need to worry about anything like this again. I don't believe I've ever seen her so frightened."

"I was terrified myself." He wasn't ashamed to admit it.

Caroline closed her eyes as though to shake the image of her daughter in the stallion's stall from her mind.

It was difficult for Grady not to stare at her.

"Go and have your dinner," she said a moment later. "I'm only going to stay a few more minutes."

"I'm not hungry," he said, wishing he could convince her to stay.

"I'm sorry, Grady, for everything."

He gestured with one hand, dismissing her apology.

"I was looking forward to riding with you this afternoon," she said.

He'd forgotten the ostensible reason for her visit. He

shrugged as if it was no big thing. "We'll do it some other time."

She brushed the hair away from Maggie's sweet face. "I'd better go."

The screen door opened and Savannah poked her head out. "Do you want to put Maggie down on my bed?" she asked. "I'll watch her so you two can…" She didn't finish the statement, but Grady knew his sister. She'd been about to say, "so you two can have some time alone together."

Caroline shook her head. "Maggie's had a terrible fright and she's embarrassed because she knows she did wrong. I need to talk to her and it'd be best if I did that at home."

"I'll walk you to your car," Grady offered. He stuffed his hands in his back pockets as he stood up.

"I'm so sorry, Savannah," Caroline whispered.

"I'll see you again soon, won't I?"

"Of course."

Savannah and Grady walked down the porch steps with Caroline holding the sleeping Maggie. "Laredo and I are driving into Fredericksburg to talk to our builder next Wednesday. If everything goes according to plan, we'll be in our own home by October."

The house would be empty without Savannah, but Grady refused to think about it. At least her new home wouldn't be far from the ranch house, no more than a five-minute walk.

"The house plans are ready?"

Savannah looked inordinately proud. "Laredo and I finished going over everything Friday afternoon and gave our approval to the builder. You can't imagine how much time and effort went into that."

They reached the car and Grady opened the passenger door so Caroline could set Maggie down. The child didn't so much as stir when Caroline placed the seat belt around her.

"Seeing as Laredo and I will be gone most of Wednesday, perhaps that would be a good day for you two to get together." Savannah made the suggestion casually, as though she often arranged her brother's schedule.

"Ah…" Grady was a little embarrassed by her obviousness.

"I can come over after work," Caroline said, smiling at him. "But I don't know if the sitter can keep Maggie."

"Bring her with you," Savannah said. "That'll give the three of you time together. It's important for Maggie to feel comfortable around Grady."

He was warming to the idea. "Perhaps we could all go riding," he said. "I've got a nice gentle horse I'll put you and Maggie on." He thought it would be fun to show them the herd and stop at a few special spots along the way. He was proud of the Yellow Rose.

"That would be wonderful!" Caroline sounded enthusiastic; her voice and movements seemed animated, even excited.

"Then it's a date," Grady said.

"I'll see you soon." Savannah turned to leave, hurrying back to the house.

Grady and Caroline stood in the yard, and Maggie slept on contentedly as a cool breeze passed through the open door.

"I'd better get going," Caroline said.

Grady noticed the reluctance in her words, felt it himself.

"I'm glad we had a little time together, anyway."

"Me, too."

There was a moment's silence, then Caroline did something completely out of character, something that stunned him. Without warning, she stepped forward and kissed him.

Caught by surprise, Grady was slow to react. A second later he clasped her in his arms, so deeply involved in the kiss that he didn't care *who* saw them. Even Richard.

Neither one of them was able to breathe properly when the kiss ended. Their balance seemed to be affected, too. Grady gripped her elbows and she held on to his waist.

Their eyes met and she smiled the softest, sweetest, sexiest smile he'd ever seen.

"What was that for?" he asked, his voice thick with passion.

"For saving Maggie."

"Oh." He cleared his throat. "I once saved a wounded falcon."

She kissed his cheek.

"It was hurt real bad."

Her lips inched closer to his.

"Richard broke his arm when he was eight and I carried him home. Will you reward me with a kiss for that, as well?"

"Grady!" she protested with a laugh. "Enough."

He loved the sound of her laughter. Because he wanted to hold her one last time, he scooped her into his arms and swung her around. Throwing back her head, she continued to laugh with such sheer joy it infected his very soul. They hugged for a long time afterward, content simply to be in each other's arms.

This was heaven, Grady told himself. Heaven in its purest form.

Glen was at Frasier Feed early Tuesday evening just as he'd promised. Ellie'd had a long grueling day; not only was the store exceptionally busy, their wedding was less than a month away and there was an endless list of things that needed to be done.

"I'm glad you're on time," she said, smiling at him, loving him. She marveled again at how they'd both been so incredibly blind to their feelings. *Obtuse* was the word for the pair of them.

"Hey, when was I ever late?" Glen teased.

Ellie rolled her eyes and hung the Closed sign in the shop window. She started toward the office where she kept her purse, but hadn't gone far when Glen caught her hand and stopped her.

"Not so soon. Aren't you going to let me know how pleased you are to see me?"

"I see you every day," she reminded him.

"We aren't even married and already you're treating me like an old hat." He wore a woebegone look.

Laughing, Ellie locked her arms around his neck and gave him a kiss he wouldn't soon forget. Neither would she.

"Oh, baby," he whispered, his eyes closed. "How much longer until the wedding?"

"Less than a month." Her head buzzed with everything they still needed to do, to decide and plan. "Sometimes I wish we could just run away and get married."

"That idea appeals to me more and more," he murmured.

Ellie was tempted herself, but reason soon took over. "Your mother and mine would never forgive us."

"In that case, let's live in sin and give them something to really be upset about."

Despite herself, Ellie giggled. "You always make me laugh."

"I'm glad to know you find me a source of entertainment."

"Always," she joked, kissing him again, lightly this time.

He released her with a reluctance that warmed her heart. Ellie retrieved her purse from the office and tucked in her to-do list.

"When are we scheduled to meet with the Realtor?" Glen asked.

"Not until seven." Where they would live had been a major decision. If she moved out to the ranch with Glen and Cal, she'd be commuting to Promise each day. If Glen moved into town, then he'd be the one commuting. In the end they'd decided to buy a house in town. Glen would continue working with his brother for a number of years, but hoped someday to start his own spread. When the time came, they'd buy a ranch closer to town, but that was years in the future.

Glen checked his watch. "Do we have time for a quick bite to eat?"

"If you want."

He growled. "I'm starving."

"All right, cowboy, let's stop at the Chili Pepper for a quick sandwich."

Only a few months ago Ellie's life had been empty

enough to swallow her whole. Her father had died, and then her mother had unexpectedly sold the family home and moved to Chicago. For the first time in her life Ellie had been utterly alone. That was when she realized how much she'd come to rely on her best friend—and eventually know how much she loved him.

They walked to the restaurant and managed to get a booth. Both were familiar enough with the menu not to need one. Ellie ordered the barbecue sandwich and a side of potato salad, and Glen chose a slab of the baby back ribs. He also asked for a pitcher of ice-cold beer.

"Dovie took me to lunch this afternoon," Ellie said when the beer arrived.

"Anything going on with her these days?"

"She wanted to know how the wedding plans were coming along, and..." Ellie hesitated.

"And?" he prodded, pouring them each a beer.

"Have you met Dr. Dickinson yet?"

"Doc Cummings's replacement? Not officially. Why?"

"Dovie asked if I'd, you know, take her under my wing."

"The doctor?" Glen set his mug down on the table.

"Apparently she's not adjusting to life in Promise."

Glen relaxed against the red vinyl upholstery. "How do you mean?"

"She doesn't fit in, and Dovie seems to think what she really needs is a friend, someone to introduce her to people, show her the ropes."

"Do you have time for this?" Glen asked, zeroing in on Ellie's own concern.

"Not just now."

"Don't think you're going to have a lot of spare time

once we're married, either," he said with a twinkle in his eyes. "I plan on keeping you occupied myself."

"Oh, really?" Although she enjoyed bantering with him, Ellie could feel the heat rise in her cheeks.

"What that doctor really needs is something or someone to occupy her time."

"I suppose you're going to suggest a man," Ellie said.

"You got something against men?"

"Just a minute." Ellie put down her mug too quickly, then used her napkin to wipe up the spilled beer. "You just might be on to something here."

Glen frowned. "What do you mean?"

"Why don't we introduce the new doc to Cal?" An idea was beginning to take shape in her mind and fast gaining momentum.

"My brother?" Glen sounded incredulous.

"Yes, your brother!" She snorted. "Do you know any other Cal?"

Glen stared at her as if seeing her for the first time. "You're not serious, are you?"

"Yes, I am. They're perfect for each other."

Glen slapped the side of his head, pretending there was something wrong with his hearing. "Let me get this straight. The woman I love, the very one who couldn't see the forest for the trees, is about to take on the role of matchmaker."

"It only makes sense."

"You haven't even *met* the woman."

"I most certainly have," Ellie protested.

"When?"

"The Cattlemen's Association Dance," she informed him primly, neglecting to mention that it had been a ten-second conversation and they'd done nothing more than exchange first names.

"Okay, Ms. Romance Expert, explain to me why you think my brother should meet this Mary."

"Her name is Jane."

"Jane," he corrected. "What's so special about her?"

"I don't know," Ellie was forced to admit. "But I do know one thing…"

"What's that?"

"Cal needs someone."

Their meal arrived and Glen reached for a blackened rib and dipped it in the pungent smoky barbecue sauce that was Adam Braunfels's speciality. "Does Cal know his life is lacking?" he asked.

"Not yet."

"Are you going to tell him, or are you volunteering me for the job?"

Glen appeared to find her idea highly entertaining, but she ignored his unwarranted amusement. "Neither of us will need to tell him," she said.

Glen made a show of wiping the sweat from his brow. "Boy, am I relieved."

"Cal will discover this all on his own."

"Listen, honey, I hate to burst your bubble, but Cal's a confirmed bachelor. I don't even remember the last time he went out on a date. He's sworn off women for good."

"You sure about that?"

"Well, it's been more than two years now, and he still isn't over Jennifer."

"Then it's about time he *got* over her." She sounded more confident than she felt, but she wasn't going to let a little thing like male pride stand in her way. Cal needed someone in his life, but he was too stubborn to realize it. Like most of the male sex he simply needed a little help. She'd aim him in the right direction and leave matters to progress as they would.

Eventually Cal *would* see the light; he'd figure it out on his own. As soon as she and Glen were married, Cal would be in that ranch house all by himself. It wouldn't take him long to discover how large and lonely a house could be with just one person living there.

"You look thoughtful," Glen said.

"It's going to be up to us." She nodded firmly.

"Us?" He raised both hands. "Not me! Forget it. If you want to play matchmaker with my big brother, you go right ahead, but don't include me."

A little respect for the validity of her idea—bringing two lonely people together—would have gone a long way, but Glen was having none of it.

"Good luck, sweetheart," he said, reaching for a French fry. "I have to admire your spirit."

"I don't believe in luck," she told him with the confidence of one who knows. "I believe we shape our own destinies." *And occasionally someone else's.*

Late Wednesday afternoon Caroline drove into the yard of the Yellow Rose Ranch. She'd been looking forward to this all week.

As she parked, the screen door opened off the back porch and Grady stepped outside.

Caroline climbed out of the car, and Maggie slipped her small hand into Caroline's as he approached.

"Will Grady yell at me?" Maggie whispered.

"Of course not," Caroline assured her.

Grady smiled at them and it was difficult for Caroline to look away. His face was alight with such pleasure she had to catch her breath. They'd known each other for years, she and Grady; they had a history, most of it unpleasant. Both were opinionated, strong willed. But she'd always admired Grady, always thought him honorable and decent. She'd carefully guarded her heart for a lot of years, and he was the first man, the only man, to get close enough to make her dream again.

"Hi," she said, feeling self-conscious.

"Hello." His gaze left her and traveled to Maggie. He bent down on one knee to be eye to eye with Caroline's daughter. "How are you, princess?"

"Fine." Maggie kicked at the dirt with the toe of her shoe and lowered her head to stare at the ground. "I'm sorry I went into the big horse's stall."

"You were looking for the colt, weren't you?"

Maggie nodded and kept her head lowered. When she spoke, even Caroline had trouble understanding her. "I won't do it again."

"Good for you," Grady said. "It's a wise woman who learns from her mistakes."

"And man," Caroline added.

Grady threw back his head and laughed loudly. At the sound Maggie leaped two feet off the ground and flew into her mother's arms, her own small arms tight around Caroline's neck.

"What'd you say to her this time?" Richard asked as he sauntered out of the bunkhouse.

"Richard!" Maggie twisted around, her face wreathed in smiles.

"How's my cupcake?" Richard asked, holding out his arms to the youngster.

Maggie squirmed free of Caroline's embrace and hurried toward the other man. Richard cheerfully caught her, lifted her high above his head and swung her around. Maggie shouted with glee.

"What are you doing here?" Grady asked, frowning.

The smile on Richard's face faded. "This is my home."

"Not anymore. Nothing here belongs to you."

The message was clear. Grady was telling his younger brother to keep away from Caroline and Maggie.

Richard laughed as if to say the mere suggestion was ludicrous. "How can you bar me from something that was never yours?" he asked. He switched his attention to Maggie.

"Maggie, I think—" Caroline started, but was interrupted.

"I like Richard!" her daughter cried. "Not Grady, *Richard*."

Richard tossed a triumphant gaze at Grady.

"Richard shows me magic tricks and dances with me."

"Grady saved your life," Caroline reminded Maggie. After looking forward to this time with Grady all week, she wasn't about to let Richard ruin it.

Maggie's head drooped against Richard's chin and her arms circled his neck. "I still like Richard best."

"Of course you do," Richard cooed. "All the women in this town do."

"Except Ellie Frasier," Grady said in low tones.

The air between the two men crackled. Richard raised his eyebrows. "Well, well, so my brother knows how to score a point."

"Caroline and Maggie came here to visit me."

"If that's the way you want it," Richard said and

slowly set Maggie down. "I didn't realize they were your exclusive property. It's a shame because Caroline and I might have renewed an old acquaintance. We used to be good friends, remember?"

"We were never friends, Richard," she said, intensely disliking him.

"So that's the lay of the land, is it?" Richard said, with a half smile that implied her words had wounded him. As though his heart was capable of entertaining anything other than selfish pursuits, she thought in disgust.

He walked away then, and despite everything, Caroline experienced a twinge of sadness. She regretted the waste of his skills, his potential. She'd known him all her life, but she didn't really *know* him. She didn't think anyone was capable of fully understanding Richard.

Grady reached for her hand. "I'm sorry, Caroline."

"It's fine. Don't worry about it."

Maggie didn't share her opinion, but Caroline wasn't concerned.

"Would you like some lemonade?" Grady asked her daughter. "I made it specially for you." He sounded downright pleased with himself.

"That sounds yummy, doesn't it?" Caroline said.

Maggie didn't answer.

"We'll take a glass," Caroline responded for both of them.

Grady led the way to the kitchen and got out three glasses. "It dawned on me the other day that I'm going to be living the bachelor life in a few months. I never spent much time working in the kitchen, not with Mom around and then Savannah doing all the cooking." A sadness came over him at the mention of his mother.

Grady wasn't one to openly display his emotions, but Caroline knew that the death of his parents had forever marked him. He never talked about the accident—they'd drowned in a flash flood—or the horrible weeks that followed with the discovery of Richard's theft and disappearance.

"I suspect Wiley and I'll starve to death before the end of the first month," he said, making a lighthearted shift of subject. Wiley had been foreman on the Yellow Rose for as long as Caroline could remember.

"I don't think Savannah will let that happen."

"Can I play with Savannah's dolls?" Maggie asked, tugging at her mother's arm.

"Don't you want to go riding?" Grady asked, sounding disappointed.

Maggie shook her head; Caroline supposed she'd been scared off by the incident on Sunday. It might be a while before she was interested in horses again. In any event, dolls had always been her first choice.

"You be careful with Savannah's things, you hear?" Caroline warned.

"I will," Maggie promised and skipped off, her lemonade untouched.

"She enjoys playing with dolls, doesn't she?" Grady said.

"More than anything."

Grady carried their lemonade into the living room and set both glasses down on the coffee table.

"I imagine you're wondering why we're sitting in here rather than outside," he said.

As a matter of fact she was.

"It's too damned difficult to find a way to hold you if you're sitting in that rocking chair," he confessed.

"Damn it, woman, I haven't thought about anything but kissing you again from the moment you left last Sunday."

It was heaven to hear him say it, and hell to confess it herself. "Oh, Grady, me, too!"

Neither made a pretense of drinking the lemonade. The minute they were on the sofa, they were in each other's arms. Their first kiss was urgent, like a thirsty traveler drinking in cool water, not taking time to savor the taste or feel of it. Their second kiss was more serene.

Caroline wanted this, needed this, and Grady hadn't disappointed her. His own display of eagerness warmed her heart. A delightful excitement filled her, allowing her to hope, to dream.

"Is this really happening to us?" she asked. She shifted around and rested her back against his chest. He spread light kisses down the side of her neck.

"If it's not, don't wake me."

"When did this come about?" She closed her eyes and moaned softly when his teeth nipped her ear, sending shivers up her spine. "Grady," she groaned, half in protest, half in encouragement.

"Kiss me," he pleaded.

He didn't need to ask twice. She twisted around and offered him her mouth. The havoc his touch created within her was much too powerful to resist.

Caroline was too involved in their exchange to hear the door open.

Grady abruptly broke off the kiss. Stunned by the sudden change in him, she didn't notice Savannah for several seconds.

"Oops." Her best friend sounded infinitely cheerful. "I think we came back a little too soon, Laredo."

Six

"This is incredible!" Caroline cried, galloping after Grady. The wind blew in her face as her pinto followed Grady's horse across the wide open range. She hadn't gone horseback riding in ages, and it felt wonderful, exhilarating. Caroline couldn't remember a time she'd experienced such a sense of freedom. Not in years and years. This lighthearted feeling could only be attributed to one thing—the fact that she was falling in love with Grady.

"Come on, slowpoke," Grady shouted over his shoulder, leading her farther from the ranch house. He hadn't said where they were headed, but he seemed to have a destination in mind.

"Where are you taking me?" she called, but either he didn't hear or chose to ignore the question.

Bless Savannah's matchmaking heart. When she'd returned early, she insisted they go riding, saying she'd look after Maggie. Grady and Caroline had both made token protests, but it didn't take long for Savannah to convince them to sneak away.

The day was lovely, not excessively hot for an August

afternoon. Surprisingly it was several degrees cooler than it had been earlier in the week. The grass was lush and green because of the early-summer rains, and the air smelled fresh.

During the past few days Caroline had been giving a lot of thought to her relationship with Grady. Both were mature adults. He'd recently turned thirty-six and she was almost twenty-eight. She knew what she wanted in life, and he seemed to have set his own course, too. She liked him and deeply respected him. Recently, very recently, she'd admitted she was fast falling in love with him. Already she was beginning to believe they could make a decent life together.

Grady crested a hill and stopped to wait for her. His eyes were bright, alive with happiness, and Caroline wondered if the joy she read in them was a reflection of her own.

"Are you ready for a break yet?" he asked.

"I'll rest when you do," she told him, not wanting to hold him up.

"In other words you're willing to follow me to the ends of the earth."

She laughed rather than confess the truth of it. "Something like that."

"Seriously, Caroline, my backside is far more accustomed to a saddle than yours. I don't want to overtax that part of your anatomy."

"I didn't know you were so concerned about the care and comfort of my butt," she teased.

Grady threw back his head and laughed boisterously.

She urged the pinto into an easy trot, and Grady caught up with her in short order. They rode in companionable silence for several minutes. Gradually he led her toward some willow trees growing along the edge of a winding creek. The scene was postcard picturesque.

"There's a nice shady spot here." Grady pointed to a huge weeping willow whose branches dipped lazily into the water.

They paused there. Grady dismounted first, then helped her down. Caroline had been around horses most of her life and certainly didn't need any assistance. But she didn't stop him; she knew he wanted to hold her, and she wanted it, too. She could find no reason to deny either of them what they desired.

He held her a moment longer than necessary and she pretended not to notice. Bracing her hands against his shoulders, she slowly eased her body toward the ground. Even then he didn't release his firm grasp on her waist.

His eyes were intense, focused only on her. Time seemed to stop. Everything around her had an unreal dreamlike quality. Sound filtered lazily into her mind— the whisper of a breeze through the delicate branches of the willow, the creek's cheerful gurgle, the bird song of early evening.

"I used to come here when I was a boy," Grady said. He still held her, but more loosely now. "I used to think it was a magic place."

"Magic?"

"Bandits hid in the tree, waiting to ambush me, but I was too smart for them." Laugh lines crinkled at his eyes as he spoke.

"When I was a little girl, I used to hide in an oak tree in our backyard. I was sure no one could see me."

He removed his glove and brushed a strand of hair from her temple, his callused fingers gentle against her face. "Once I'd rid the place of the bandits, I'd sit and think...and pretend."

"I'd dream," she told him, realizing as she did that this was the first time she'd ever told anyone about the oak tree.

"Any particular dream?" he asked.

"Oh, what most girls dream," she said. "Girls who've read *Cinderella* and *Rapunzel* and *Snow White*—I adored those stories. I'd dream about being a princess in disguise. A handsome prince would fight insurmountable odds to come to me and declare his love."

He grinned. "At your service."

"Oh, Grady, are you my prince?" She felt foolish when she'd said the words, but he looked at her so seriously, all joking gone.

"There's nothing I'd like more," he said in a quiet voice.

The air between them seemed electric, charged with tension, and Caroline was convinced she'd die if he didn't kiss her soon. Judging by the glitter in his eyes, Grady must have felt the same way. He muttered something unintelligible, then unhurriedly lowered his mouth to hers.

He tightened his arms around her waist, almost lifting her from the ground. Caroline ran her fingers through his hair. His Stetson tumbled from his head, but he didn't seem to notice. The kiss went on and on.

Abruptly he broke it off and shook his head. "I shouldn't have done that. I'm sorry. I'm moving too fast. It's just that—"

"No, that's not it."

His hands were in her hair, too, and he held her

against him. With her ear pressed to his heart, she could hear its desperate pounding.

"I can't seem to keep my hands off you," he whispered.

"You don't hear me complaining, do you?"

"No, but…" His chest expanded with a deep sigh. "Oh, hell, Caroline, I haven't made any secret of the way I feel about you."

"It's how I feel, too," she confessed.

Holding her hand firmly in his, he guided her toward the creek, stopping long enough to retrieve a spare blanket from his saddlebag. He pulled back the dangling willow branches and bowed, gesturing her in. "Welcome to my castle."

"Castle?" she repeated. "I thought it was a bandits' hideout."

"Not anymore," he murmured. "I'm your handsome prince, remember?"

All Caroline could do was smile. And if her smile was a little tremulous…she couldn't help it.

He spread the blanket on the ground, and once she was seated, he returned to his saddlebag. To her surprise, he produced a bottle of cool white wine, two stemmed plastic glasses and a piece of cheddar cheese.

"You shock me, Grady," Caroline told him as he opened the bottle with his Swiss Army knife.

"I do?" He glanced up, a look of amusement on his face as he cut the cheese and handed her a slice.

"This is so *romantic*."

"If you think this is something, just wait."

Caroline raised her head. "You mean there's more?" She savoured a bite of the sharp cheddar.

"Much more." He leaped to his feet and returned to

the horses. Again opening a saddlebag, he drew out a small gold-foil box.

"Chocolates?" Caroline squealed with delight.

"I figured these were the kind of thing a man gives a woman when he comes courting." He didn't look at her; instead, he busied himself carefully pouring the wine.

Caroline loved the way he used the old-fashioned term. "*Are* you courting me, Grady?" She'd meant to sound demure, but her question had an urgency about it. "Are you being serious?" She had to know.

"This is about as serious as a man gets," he said and handed her a plastic cup of wine. "Shall we make a toast?" he asked, holding up his glass.

She nodded and touched her glass to his.

"To the future," he said, then amended, "our future."

Caroline sipped the wine. The chardonnay was delicate, smooth, refreshing. One sip and her heart started to pound, the force of it growing with every beat. It took her a moment to realize what was happening.

She was in love, really in love. It both terrified and excited her. And with that realization came another. She needed to tell Grady about Maggie's father. He had a right to know the truth, although the thought of telling him brought a dull ache to the pit of her stomach.

"You're quiet all of a sudden," Grady said.

"I was just thinking." She shrugged off his concern.

"That could be dangerous to your mental health," he teased. He leaned forward, his lips moist with wine, and gently kissed her. His mouth lingered in a series of short nibbling kisses far more potent than the wine.

"I can't make myself stop kissing you," he said, leaning his forehead against hers.

"I can't stop wanting you to kiss me," she told him.

She moved her hands along his neck, loving the feel of his skin. "I...I want to talk to you about Maggie." She closed her eyes, fighting back the tension that gripped her. The sooner she got this over with, the better.

"I'm trying, Caroline, I honestly am."

"I know...but what I want to say doesn't have anything to do with how she feels about you."

Grady went very still.

The heavy pounding of her heart echoed in her ears, drowning out her thoughts. She couldn't look at him while she spoke of that pain-filled time. Before she could stop herself, she was on her feet.

"It's about Maggie's father." She clenched her hands until the knuckles were white. Her stomach tightened. The only one who knew the full truth had been her mother. Caroline was well aware that other family members and certainly her friends had speculated for years about who'd fathered Maggie, but she'd never told them. Never told anyone. Never felt the need until now.

"Caroline, you're very pale. Is this really so difficult for you?"

She bowed her head and exhaled slowly. "It's much harder than I'd thought it would be."

He stood up and moved behind her, placing his hands on her shoulders. "Then forget it. My knowing isn't necessary, not if it upsets you like this."

"But it *is* necessary." He had no idea how much.

"Then you can tell me some other time," he insisted. He bent to kiss the side of her neck. His mouth lingered and her head fell forward. "I want our afternoon to be special. I don't want anything to interfere with that."

"But you have a right to know." She paused and swallowed. What he didn't seem to understand was that telling him wouldn't get any easier. In fact, the longer she waited...

His hands gently stroked the length of her arms. "Let's not spoil our afternoon with memories best forgotten. There'll be plenty of time for you to tell me everything—but not today."

"Aren't you curious? Don't you want to know?"

He released a long sigh. "Yeah, I am," he said after a moment. "Perhaps I'm a little afraid, too. I don't want anything to ruin what we have."

"Oh, Grady." He made it so easy to delay telling him the truth. Easy to thrust it into the future with excuses she was far too willing to accept and he was just as eager to suggest.

"I'm your prince, remember?"

"I remember," she replied dutifully.

"Good." He kissed her then, his mouth touching hers in a quick caress. "Now let's get back to our wine."

He waited until she'd settled herself on the blanket before he handed her the glass he'd refilled. Positioning himself behind her, he eased her against him. Caroline closed her eyes as he gently fingered the fine strands of her hair.

"I told you this is a magic place."

"Mmm."

"Reality will find us soon enough, so let's enjoy the magic while we can."

Caroline had to admit she was willing to do just that.

Maggie put Savannah's dolls back on the bedroom-window seat and looked out again, hoping to see her mommy. She'd gone horseback riding with Grady and they'd been away a long time. Longer than she wanted them to be. She was ready to go home now.

Bored, she put on her backpack and wandered into the kitchen where Savannah was kneading bread dough.

"When's Mommy coming back?" she asked.

"I don't know, sweetheart, but I imagine they'll be here soon."

"Where's Richard?" Maggie asked next.

"I don't know."

"Can I watch television?"

"Of course, but get Laredo to turn it on for you, okay?"

"I can do it," Maggie insisted. She turned on the television at home and it wasn't hard.

"Grady got a new satellite dish and it has three remote controls."

There was his name again. Not only did Grady shout, but he made it so she couldn't prove to Savannah how smart she was.

"Laredo's in the barn, but he'll be finished any minute."

Maggie glanced wistfully toward the barn, but she wouldn't go in there alone, not anymore. The last time, she'd gotten into trouble, and Grady had yelled at her again and grabbed her. He'd been scared, too; she could tell when he pulled her away from the horse and held her.

"I'd do it for you, sweetheart, but I've got my hands buried in bread dough," Savannah explained.

"That's all right." Not wanting to wait inside, Maggie walked onto the porch. She sat on the top step, and Rocket ambled over to lie down beside her. She rubbed his ears for a few minutes because Savannah had told her he liked that. Then she rested her chin on her folded hands, looking out over the ranch yard, hoping she'd find something to do. Something that wouldn't get her in trouble.

She caught a flash of color and saw Richard coming out of the bunkhouse. Her spirits lifted immediately. Leaping off the steps, she raced to his side. "Richard!"

He jerked around, then smiled when he saw her. Maggie liked Richard's smile, but what she enjoyed most were his magic tricks. Once he pulled a coin out of her ear. Another time he had her draw a card out of the middle of a deck and then told her what card it was. He was right.

"Howdy, kiddo," Richard said.

"Wanna play?" she asked, skipping after him.

"Not now."

"Nobody wants to play with me," she said, hoping he'd feel sorry for her and offer a game or a few tricks.

"Sorry, kiddo, I've got things to do."

Maggie's face fell. Everyone was too busy for her. "Can I help?" she asked, thinking if he finished early, he might take time to play.

"No," he said sharply. He sounded almost like Grady when he was mad, and Maggie gasped.

Richard squatted down. "Maybe we can play, after all. How about a game of hide-and-seek?" he suggested. "You go hide and I'll come and find you."

This was great, better than she'd expected. "Okay." Maggie glanced around, looking for a place to hide, somewhere Richard wouldn't find her.

"Are you closing your eyes?" she asked.

"You bet I am, kid."

Maggie didn't like the way he said it, but she was so

pleased to have someone willing to play with her that she didn't care.

"Don't peek," she warned and raced around the corner.

"I wouldn't dream of it," he called after her.

He said that in a way she didn't like, either. Almost as if he was mad but without raising his voice. Maggie tore across the yard, her pack slapping against her back, and hid in Savannah's garden. She liked the smell of the roses. She crouched down under the table on the patio...but Richard didn't come and he didn't come. She got tired of waiting.

He was probably looking in places near the barn, she decided. Sneaking out of the rose garden, she crept on tiptoe closer to where she'd last seen him. Circling around to the other side of the barn, she saw Grady's truck that Richard sometimes drove. He didn't usually keep his truck there. The truck bed was covered with a sort of blanket but bigger.

Richard would never think of looking for her there. The tailgate was down, and by standing on a box she was able to climb inside. The floor hurt her knees and it was dark and warm inside, almost like a cave under the heavy cloth. There was lots of other stuff, too. She found a rolled-up sleeping bag and leaned against it.

"Richard!" she called, thinking he might need help finding her.

Nothing.

It was getting so hot under the blanket that she took off the backpack. Soon her eyes grew heavy with sleep. She decided to put her head down on the sleeping bag, but just for a few minutes until Richard found her.

Just until then.

* * *

This was so easy it was embarrassing, Richard Weston told himself. The pickup, formerly owned by Grady—as he liked to think of it—sped down the road toward Bitter End. No one would think of looking for him there. No one would even guess.

Luckily his brother's head was in the clouds these days. Grady Weston in love—if it wasn't so damn funny, it'd be sad. Grady had fallen in love—for the first time, Richard was sure—at the age of thirty-six—and it wasn't a pretty sight. For a couple of weeks now he'd been walking around the house with his tongue hanging out of his mouth and his eyes glazed over. It was a wonder he hadn't tripped down the stairs and broken his damn neck.

Actually Richard wouldn't have minded doing the dirty deed with Miss Caroline himself. He'd bet that woman was some hot number in the sack. Still, he felt grateful to her for keeping Grady distracted. His blockhead of a brother didn't have a clue what he, Richard, was up to. Before Grady figured it out, he'd be long gone. Yup, it was that easy.

Richard laughed aloud. "Idiots." He hated to say this about his own flesh and blood, but both Grady and Savannah were dolts. It was kind of sad that they'd be gullible enough to let him drive off with several months' worth of supplies. He'd even managed to acquire a small gasoline-powered generator—one he'd put onto his brother's business account, naturally. Of course Grady wouldn't know anything about it for a couple of weeks.

Richard almost wished he could be a fly on the wall when the bills started coming in. Grady would have a conniption. Richard felt a mild twinge of guilt about that, but hell, he didn't have any choice. Not really. He had to eat, and while the portable television might seem an extravagance, it wasn't. How would he know what was going on in the world without watching the evening news? It wasn't like he was going to get cable in the old ghost town, either. All he had were rabbit ears. He'd be lucky to receive one station, possibly two, but that was probably just as well. Otherwise he'd be tempted to laze around and waste his whole supply of gasoline on running the TV.

By the time he reached the turnoff to the dirt road that wound up the far side of the valley, he was lost in his thoughts.

He knew himself well enough to realize he'd find it difficult to stay cooped up in Bitter End, with no companionship and few diversions. There were sure to be times when he'd welcome an excuse to venture into Promise, or any one of the other small towns that dotted the Texas Hill Country.

He couldn't do that, however. Grady was bound to report the truck as stolen, and sure as shootin', Richard would have a lawman on his tail five minutes after he hit the highway. But a stolen vehicle was only a small part of Richard's worries—just one more complication in his already complicated life.

Hell, all the lawmen in three states would give their eyeteeth to get their hands on him. So the last thing he needed was to be pulled in for driving a stolen truck.

A shiver raced down his spine. He didn't want to think about that.

The road grew bumpy and he slowed. For a moment

he thought he heard a sound, a cry of some kind, but he strained his ears and didn't hear it again.

Imagination was a funny thing, he mused. Could be dangerous, too. On a recent visit to Bitter End, he'd had the impression that someone was watching him. Someone or something. A vague feeling, mildly uncomfortable.

He blamed Ellie Frasier for that. She'd given him the willies the time he'd brought her to Bitter End. The minute they'd left the truck, she'd started making noises about this "feeling." He hadn't felt a damn thing, while she'd been practically crawling out of her skin. Naturally that was for the best, since he certainly didn't want her coming back and bringing her friends along.

Ellie hadn't been able to get out fast enough. Whatever the feeling was, it had never bothered Richard—until that last visit. He'd probably just heard too much about this so-called sensation. He didn't understand it, but he was counting it as a plus. The town's reputation for eeriness meant that people would stay away. He'd have to control his own imagination, not let ghost stories and strange noises spook him.

As he neared Bitter End, he reduced the truck's speed. He'd found a spot in the ghost town where he could hide the pickup, so if anyone did happen to stumble in, they wouldn't see it.

He stopped in front of the wooden stable, which leaned heavily to one side. He'd say one thing for the folks who'd originally built this place. They'd been great craftsmen. Most of the buildings still stood, despite their age.

He drove the truck into the decrepit stable and

jumped down from the cab. He was about to close the door when he caught a movement under the canvas tarp.

He froze. Sure enough, he saw it move again. Believing in the element of surprise, he moved quietly to the back of the truck and firmly gripped the edge of the blanket. With no warning, he jerked it away from the bed.

Maggie Daniels screamed and cowered in a corner. It took them both a moment to recover, but she was faster.

"Richard!"

"What the hell are you doing here?" he demanded.

The smile on her face disappeared. "We were playing hide-and-seek, remember? I fell asleep..."

Richard swore.

Maggie's eyes grew round. "If my mommy was here, she'd wash your mouth out with soap."

As far as he could see, Richard had few choices. He could dump the kid on the highway—but would she shut up about where she'd been? He could keep her in Bitter End. Or he could do away with her entirely. Kidnap and murder charges wouldn't look good on his rap sheet. But he might not have any other options.

Damn it, what was he going to do now?

Grady had never been one to idle away time, nor had he been known to sit under a willow tree and soak in the beauty of a summer evening. Not for the past six years, at any rate. It'd taken him that long to get the ranch into the black. He'd earned a decent profit last year and would again this year, God willing. He finally felt good about his life and he didn't want his happiness compromised now with talk of Maggie's father. He tried to convince himself it didn't matter—but it did.

Caroline had wanted to tell him, and curious though he was, he'd persuaded her to wait. Grady recognized that his behavior was uncharacteristic; generally he faced problems head-on. But he knew why he didn't want to hear what she had to say. Admitting it didn't come easy, not by a long shot. Intuitively he feared that once she told him about Maggie's father, nothing would be the same between them. Sitting with her in the shade of the willow tree, holding her close, loving her—these moments were far too special to invade with difficult truths. So he'd delayed the inevitable, hurled it into the future until he felt more ready to deal with it.

Caroline lay down on the blanket beside him, her head resting against his thigh. Lazily he brushed the hair from her face. She was so damned beautiful he could barely manage not to stare at her. Barely manage not to kiss her again. They'd done plenty of that this afternoon. She'd tasted of wine and chocolate, and Grady thought he'd never sampled a more intoxicating combination. Sweet and potent at the same time.

He'd as good as told her he was interested in marrying her. A man didn't go courting otherwise. It was time for him to settle down. Glen was about to make the leap into marriage, and with Savannah married and she and Laredo building their own home, he'd soon be alone. But it wasn't just the events in other people's lives that had convinced him.

It was Caroline and Maggie. Whenever he was with them, he didn't want their time together to end. His life felt empty when they weren't around.

He tried to tell Caroline that, but he couldn't manage the words. He discovered it was damned hard to admit how much he needed someone else. He'd never felt this way before, and it frightened him.

"I could almost go to sleep," Caroline murmured. Her eyes remained closed and he ran his index finger down the side of her jaw. Her skin was soft and smooth. Lovely. *She* was lovely.

Her lips eased into a smile. "You're right."

"Well, I don't know what I'm right about, but I like the sound of those words."

"Every man does," she teased.

"Flatter my ego and tell me why I'm right."

"This place," she whispered. "I don't think I've ever felt so…content. So relaxed."

"Me, neither." Today was the first time he'd spent more than ten minutes here in years, and already they'd been gone at least two hours.

"I wonder…" she began wistfully.

"What?" He bent forward to graze his lips across her brow.

"If you have any other magic tricks up your sleeve."

"That's Richard's specialty, not mine."

Caroline frowned. "You provided a magical afternoon for me," she said. "Wine and chocolates and this beautiful place."

"The kissing wasn't half-bad, either."

Her eyes fluttered open and she gazed up at him with such longing he couldn't possibly have resisted her.

Caroline wrapped herself in his embrace the moment he reached for her. Grady was shocked by the intensity of his own craving. It felt as though he'd waited his entire life for this afternoon and this woman.

His tongue danced with hers and he worked his fingers into her hair, loving the feel of it, clean and silky smooth. Fifty years of this, and he swore he'd never tire of her taste.

"I suppose we'd better think about getting back," he said reluctantly, feeling cheated that their magical time had come to an end.

"How long have we been gone?" Caroline asked. Not waiting for a response, she glanced at her watch. She gasped and jumped to her feet. "Oh, my goodness, we've been away for over two hours!"

"I know."

"But Maggie…"

"She's with Savannah."

"I had no idea we'd been gone this long." She started cleaning up the area, her movements fast and jerky.

"Caroline, you don't have anything to worry about."

She turned slowly to face him, obviously comforted. "Thank you, Grady. I do know that. I'm just not used to…any of *this*." She made a gesture that took in their surroundings, the remains of their picnic and Grady himself.

He helped her mount—because he wanted to, not because she needed any assistance. They rode back to the ranch, joking and laughing, teasing each other the way lovers do.

As the house came into view, his eyes were drawn to its silhouette against the darkening sky. Solid, secure, welcoming. His home had always seemed a natural part of the landscape to him. It belonged there. And for the first time in years, he felt that his life was what he wanted it to be.

It wasn't until they neared the corral that Grady noticed something was amiss. He saw Laredo, and the minute the other man caught sight of Grady and Caroline, he ran into the house, calling for Savannah. She rushed out onto the back porch.

His sister's face was red, her eyes puffy as though she'd been weeping. That wasn't like her.

"What is it?" he asked as he dismounted.

"Oh, Caroline, I'm so sorry." Savannah's voice trembled and she covered her mouth.

Confused, Caroline looked to Grady. "What's wrong?"

Grady walked around his gelding and helped Caroline down from her horse. Her hands trembled as she held his arms.

"Where's Maggie?" she asked, her voice oddly calm.

"That's the problem," Laredo said, moving to stand next to his wife. He slid his arm around Savannah's shoulders.

"You don't know where Maggie is?" Caroline asked, and again Grady heard that strange calm in her voice.

"I... She went outside, and the last time I checked she was sitting on the porch," Savannah cried. "I've looked everywhere, called for her until my voice was hoarse. I don't know where she could have gone."

"Apparently she'd come out to look for me," Laredo said.

"Did you see her?" Grady demanded.

"No." Laredo shook his head.

"Oh, Caroline," Savannah wept, "I'm so sorry! I should never have let her leave the house."

Caroline's fingers dug into Grady's arm. Her eyes were wide and filled with terror when she looked at him, seeking reassurance.

Grady's heart felt like a lead weight in his chest. "We'll find her," he promised.

Seven

The calls lawmen dreaded most were domestic violence and missing children. Frank Hennessey was no exception. The report of a missing child made his blood run cold. He preferred dealing with a drunken belligerent husband any day of the week if it meant he didn't have to see the face of a parent whose child couldn't be found. Frank had never married, never had children, but he'd been a firsthand witness to the agony parents endure when their child disappears. All his years of law enforcement had convinced him there was no deeper pain than the loss of a child.

The call that Maggie Daniels had gone missing came minutes before Frank was due to go off duty. Grady Weston phoned it in. There'd only been one other time Frank had heard Grady sound the way he did this evening, and that was the day his parents had drowned in a flash flood.

"Are you sure she hasn't fallen asleep somewhere in the house?" Frank felt obliged to ask.

"We're sure, Frank." Grady's impatience crackled over the telephone line.

"Was she upset about anything?"

"No, she was excited about visiting the ranch," Caroline answered, apparently from one of the extensions.

"Maggie didn't run away, if that's what you're thinking," Grady told him angrily.

In fact, Frank's questions had been leading to that assumption. It was the most common scenario, even with kids this young. He sighed heavily. He hadn't been around children much, but he'd taken a real liking to Caroline's fatherless child. She was a sweetheart, and the thought of anything happening to her made his insides twist.

"Are you coming out to take a report or not?" Grady demanded.

"I'm on my way." Frank replaced the receiver. Grady sounded as worried and frustrated as he would if he were the child's father. In situations such as this the families were often impatient and angry, lashing out at authority because of their own helplessness. Frank had seen it before. Some of the cases he'd worked on came with happy endings. The lost child was found safe and promptly returned to the parents.

The other cases, two in his career, would forever haunt him. *Missing.* He'd come to think of it as the ugliest word in the English language. The first child had turned up dead; the second was never seen again.

Although the highway was deserted, Frank ran the lights on his patrol car as he sped toward the Yellow Rose Ranch. The entire forty minutes it took him to drive from town, he kept hoping against hope that by the time he arrived, Maggie would've been found. He wasn't a superstitious man, nor did he believe in intuition, but his gut told him that wouldn't be the case.

He was right.

No sooner had he pulled into the yard than the door opened and Grady hurried onto the porch. Caroline was with him, looking paler than he'd ever seen her. Grady's eyes were dark with anxiety.

"Thank you for coming," Caroline said, her voice determined. She was a strong woman and Frank deeply admired her grit.

Grady held the door open for him. "Savannah's got coffee brewing," he said, leading the way into the kitchen.

Frank looked around at the small group assembled there. Laredo had his arm around Savannah, who seemed on the verge of collapse. Her eyes were red and swollen, testifying to the tears she'd already shed.

"It's my fault," she said.

"No one's laying blame," Grady told her, his eyes softening. He brought the coffeepot over to the table where a number of mugs had been set, and he filled each one.

"But I was supposed to be watching her," Savannah explained as Frank doctored his coffee with milk.

"It doesn't matter who was watching her," Caroline said, her voice shaking slightly. "What matters is that we don't know where Maggie is now."

"We'll find her," Wiley Rogers, the foreman, insisted. "Don't you worry about that. Not a one of us will rest until Maggie's found."

Frank had heard words like that before, and he'd watched as families invested every penny of their life's savings in the effort. He'd watched them invest the very heart and soul of their existence in tracing a missing child, sometimes to the point that the entire family was destroyed. He'd assumed when he moved to Promise fifteen years ago that he'd never have to deal with this sort of agony again, but he'd been wrong. It was staring him in the face this very minute.

"Savannah, since you were the last person to see Maggie, why don't we start with you." He withdrew a small notebook from his shirt pocket. "You *were* the last one to see her, right?"

Savannah nodded and Laredo moved closer to his wife's side as if to protect her. Frank pitied her, understood the grief and guilt she must feel. He glanced away and surveyed everyone else in the room.

It was then that he noticed one family member was missing. "Where's Richard?" he asked, interrupting Savannah.

"In town, I suspect," Grady said.

"Driving what?"

"My pickup's missing, so I guess he has that."

Frank walked over to the telephone. "I want him here."

"Of course," Savannah said.

"You don't think he'd take Maggie with him, do you?" Caroline asked, looking to Grady and Savannah for the answer. "I mean, we assumed he left earlier, before Maggie turned up missing, but…" She let the rest fade.

"It isn't a good idea to assume anything." Frank walked over to the wall phone and lifted the receiver. He barked out a few orders, then instructed his deputy to drive through town and find Richard Weston. If Richard wasn't there, Al was to find out the last time anyone saw him and report back to Frank as soon as possible.

While he waited for Al to return the call, Frank finished the interview with Savannah and Laredo. An hour passed before the phone rang. Caroline leaped from her chair and her eyes grew wide and hopeful when Grady reached for the receiver. Without a word he handed the telephone to Frank.

Richard Weston was nowhere to be found. Neither was Grady's truck. No one had seen him, not that day or the day before. Al reported that he wasn't the only one looking for Richard, either, but Frank decided these people had enough trouble on their hands. He didn't intend to add to it.

"You don't honestly think Richard took the child, do you?" Savannah asked after he'd relayed the details of Al's findings.

"At this point I won't discount any coincidence. Maggie's missing and so is Richard."

"But I'm sure he left long before Maggie disappeared," Savannah said.

"I'm not." This came from Laredo. "I saw the truck. And I saw it while Maggie was in the house with you."

Unable to sleep, Caroline sat on the dark porch, her arms wrapped protectively around her middle. Frank had left several hours earlier. There was nothing more he could do; he'd already alerted law-enforcement officers across Texas and in the adjoining states to keep their eyes open for Maggie. Savannah had given the sheriff Maggie's school photograph and he'd taken it into town with him. Soon Maggie's likeness would be seen in every law office in the Southwest. The search was on for Richard, too, with an all-points bulletin issued for his arrest. Caroline knew that had something to do with information the sheriff had received, information about a crime Richard had committed back East. She didn't know what it was, and right now she didn't care. Finding Maggie was the only thing that mattered.

With nothing further to be done at the moment, everyone had turned in for the night. Frank had offered to follow her home, but Caroline refused to leave. If Maggie—she paused and rephrased the thought—*when* Maggie came back, Caroline wanted to be right here at the ranch waiting for her.

Although everyone had gone to bed, she knew no one would sleep well. She accepted one of Savannah's nightgowns and made the pretense of going to bed, too, but the room felt suffocating. Within minutes she'd dressed again and made her way through the house and outside. She sat on the porch steps and stared into the bleak darkness.

It wasn't long before Grady joined her. Wordlessly, with barely a sound, he sat down on the step next to her and clasped her hand. Her fingers tightened around his.

"I'm so afraid." It was the first time she'd verbalized her fears.

"I am, too."

She pressed her head against his shoulder and he placed his arm around her, drawing her close.

"Do you think she's with Richard?" Caroline couldn't shake the thought. They'd both disappeared around the same time, but that made no sense. Richard might be a lot of things, but a child-snatcher wasn't one of them. Caroline could think of no plausible reason for him to take Maggie.

"I can't imagine that even Richard would do anything like this," Grady said, his voice little more than a whisper.

Caroline reminded herself that Frank believed there might be a connection between Maggie's disappearance and Richard's. She just couldn't understand what it might be.

"You should try to sleep," Grady urged.

"I can't." Every time she closed her eyes her imagination tormented her. She couldn't bear the thought of her daughter hurt and crying out for her. But that was what filled her mind and heart and made sleep impossible.

"I can't, either."

"Oh, Grady," she whispered, her voice breaking. "Where can she be?"

He waited a moment before he answered, and she knew he was experiencing the same frustration she was. "I wish I knew."

As the night wore on, it became more and more difficult for Caroline to hope. When she couldn't stand the silence any longer, she buried her face in her hands and cried, "I want my daughter!"

She tried to be strong, but she didn't think she could hold back the tears. Hysteria was edging in on her. She could feel it pushing her closer to the brink.

All at once she was completely wrapped in Grady's arms. She clung to him, shaking almost uncontrollably as she muffled her sobs against his chest. His hold on her was firm, solid, and she needed him as she'd rarely needed anyone in her life. She wept until there were no tears left.

"This might be the worst possible time to tell you this," Grady whispered, his mouth close to her ear. "I love you, Caroline."

"Oh, Grady," she sobbed.

"I know it's new, and it might take some getting used

to, but let my love be your strength for now. Lean on me if you can. Let me help you bear this. I'll do everything in my power to get Maggie back."

She was holding him, clutching his shoulders, like a lifeline. "I love you, too," she whimpered, but didn't know if he'd heard her.

"We'll get through this," he promised. "We'll find Maggie."

He sounded confident and sure, and she clung to the promise of his words.

"It's going to be all right, understand?"

She nodded, desperately wanting to believe him.

Oh, God, she prayed, *please bring my little girl home.*

But God seemed far away just then.

Maggie's eyes were sore from crying, but she didn't want Richard to hear her because he'd already gotten mad and yelled at her. She huddled in the corner of the old stone building that used to be a store. It was getting dark, but there was still some light coming in through the open door. Richard had told her not to leave the room and then he'd disappeared. Maggie didn't like Richard anymore, even if he *could* do magic tricks.

He was mean and he said bad words and he threw things, too. After he found her hiding in the back of Grady's pickup, he started acting like Billy Parsons when he had a temper tantrum at his brother's birthday party. The only thing Richard didn't do was throw himself down on the ground and start kicking.

Her stomach growled, but Maggie had already looked around for something to eat and hadn't found anything. She wished she'd gone horseback riding with her mommy and Grady. She was afraid of horses after last Sunday—but not nearly as afraid as she was now.

"Richard," Maggie said, risking his wrath by walking out of the store. "I want to go home now, okay?"

"Yeah, well, you can't have everything you want." He was sitting outside and he had a big bottle in his hand. Every now and then, he'd take a drink. Her mother had told Maggie it wasn't good manners to drink out of a bottle, but she didn't tell Richard that because he'd only yell at her again.

"Can we go back to the ranch?" she asked.

"No." He growled the word at her and laughed when she leaped back, frightened by the harsh sound of his voice. "I've got an idea," he said, leaning toward her. "Why don't you go fall in an empty well and save me a lot of trouble?"

Maggie hurried back into the old store and sat down on the lone chair. When it grew dark, she ventured over to the stable where he'd parked the truck. There was enough moonlight to find her way, but she walked very carefully, afraid of holes in the road and snakes...and Richard. Climbing into the bed of the pickup, she curled up with the sleeping bag she'd found earlier. She was cold and hungry and more afraid than she'd ever been in her whole life.

Every once in a while she could hear Richard singing. He played his guitar and sang, but his voice didn't sound right. It was like he'd mashed all the words together. She used to think he had a good voice; she didn't think so anymore.

Soon she fell asleep and didn't awake until light peeked through a crack in the stable door. She was so hungry her stomach hurt.

She clambered out of the truck and walked back to the main street. The early morning was very still.

Richard was asleep in the rocker. His guitar lay on the wooden sidewalk, and he'd slouched down in the chair with his feet stretched out. His arms dangled over the edges of the rocker until his fingertips touched the ground close to the empty bottle. His head lolled to one side.

"Richard," she whispered. "I'm hungry."

He opened his eyes and blinked a couple of times.

"I'm hungry," she repeated, louder this time.

"Get out of here, kid."

"I want my mommy," she said, and her lower lip wobbled. "I don't like it here. I want to go home."

Richard slowly sat up and rubbed his face. "Get lost, will ya?"

Maggie didn't mean to, but she started to cry. She'd always thought Richard was her friend, and now she knew he wasn't.

"Stop it!" he shouted and scowled at her.

Sobbing, Maggie ran away from him.

"Maggie," he called after her, but she didn't stop, running between two of the buildings.

"Damn it."

Maggie pretended not to hear him and, thinking he might try to follow her, she crept down the side of a building, then slipped inside another store.

The town was old. Really, really old. Older than any place she'd ever been. It smelled old. None of the buildings had paint, either. It sure seemed like no one had lived here for a long time. Some of the places had stuff inside. The store had a table and chair and shelves. But there were only a few cans sitting around—they looked kind of strange, like they might burst. Plus a cash register. She'd tried to get it to work, but it wouldn't open for her.

Maggie wasn't sure what kind of shop this had been, but it had a big cupboard. Maybe she could hide from Richard there. She opened the door and saw that it had shelves. On one of the shelves was a doll. A really old one, with a cotton dress and apron and bonnet. The doll's face had been stitched on. It wasn't like any doll she'd ever seen. The only one she owned with cloth arms and legs was Raggedy Ann, but her clothes were bright and pretty. This doll's clothes were all faded.

"Are you scared, too?" she asked the doll.

The stitched red mouth seemed to quaver a bit.

Suddenly she heard Richard's footsteps outside.

"Maggie, damn it! You could get hurt racing around this old town."

Maggie didn't care what Richard said—she didn't like him. She crouched down inside the cupboard and shut the door, leaving it open just a crack so she could see out.

"Are you hungry?" he called. She watched him stop in the doorway, staring into the building. Maggie's heart pounded hard and she bit her lower lip, afraid he might see her.

"Come on, kid," he growled.

Maggie clutched the old doll to her chest and closed her eyes. She wanted Richard to go away.

"I'm going to cook breakfast now," he said, moving away. He continued down the sidewalk with heavy footsteps. "When you're ready, you can come and eat, too."

Maggie waited a long time and didn't move until she

smelled bacon frying. Her stomach growled again. It'd been hours and hours since she'd eaten.

Her grip on the doll loosened and she looked into its face again. It was a sad face, Maggie realized, as if the doll was about to cry. Maggie felt like crying, too. She missed her mommy.

Slipping her backpack off her shoulders, Maggie opened it and carefully tucked the sad doll inside.

"I cooked you some bacon and eggs," Richard called.

This time Maggie couldn't resist. She pushed open the cupboard door and slowly walked out of the old building.

"There you are," Richard said, holding out a plate to her.

Maggie didn't trust Richard anymore and moved cautiously toward him. If he said something mean, she was prepared to run.

"I'm sorry I yelled at you," Richard told her.

"What about the bad words?"

"I'm sorry about those, too."

"Will you take me home now?" she asked, standing in the middle of the dirt street.

Richard stood by the post where people used to hitch their horses. He didn't look like he was sorry, even if he said he was.

Maggie's stomach was empty and making funny noises.

"You really want to go home now?" Richard asked. He sounded surprised that she'd want to leave. He made it seem like she was supposed to be having fun.

"I want to see my mommy."

"Okay, okay, but we need to talk about it first." He

set the plate of food aside and sat down on the steps leading to the raised sidewalk.

"Why?"

He scratched his head. "Do you remember Grady getting mad at Savannah about coming to the ghost town?" he asked.

Maggie nodded. Grady had been real upset with Savannah when he found out she'd been to the town. Savannah had come to look for special roses, and Grady had stomped around the house for days. Even Laredo wasn't happy when Savannah wanted to come back and look for more roses.

"Now, this is very important," Richard said, his voice low and serious. "You mustn't let anyone know where you've been, understand?"

Her chin came up a little. "Why not?"

"You love your mommy, don't you?"

Maggie nodded.

"If anyone finds out you've been here..." He stopped and glanced in both directions as if he was afraid someone might be listening. "If anyone finds out, then something really bad will happen to your mother."

Maggie's eyes grew big.

"Do you know what ghosts are?" Richard asked.

"Melissa Washington dressed up in a sheet and said she was a ghost last Halloween," Maggie told him.

"There are good ghosts and bad ghosts."

"Which kind live here?" Maggie whispered.

"Bad ones," he whispered back. His voice was spooky. She wondered if he was trying to scare her on purpose.

"Bad ones?" she repeated faintly.

"Very bad ones, and if you tell anyone, even your

best friend, then the bad ghosts will find out and hurt your mother."

"How…how will they hurt Mommy?"

"You don't want to know, kid." He squeezed his eyes shut and made an ugly face, as if just telling her about it would upset him.

Maggie blinked, not sure she should believe him.

"Remember when Wiley cut his hand and Savannah had to wrap it up for him?"

"Yes…"

"That's what bad ghosts will do to your mommy, only it wouldn't just be her hand."

Maggie forgot all about the smell of bacon. Wiley's hand had bled and bled. Blood had gotten everywhere, and she could remember being surprised that one hand had so much blood in it. Just looking at it had made her feel sick to her stomach.

"You wouldn't want anything bad like that to happen to your mommy, would you?"

Maggie shook her head.

"I didn't think so."

"Can I go home now?"

He studied her for a long time. "You won't tell anyone?"

"No."

"Cross your heart?"

"Cross my heart." She made a big X over her heart.

"I'd hate to see your mommy hurt, wouldn't you?"

Maggie nodded.

"Then maybe it'd be all right if I took you home."

Maggie sighed with relief. She was tired and hungry, and all she wanted was to see her mother again.

Richard helped her into the cab of Grady's truck. He

made her curl up on the seat and keep her head down so she couldn't see as they drove away. Every time she closed her eyes she thought about a bad ghost and what might happen to her mother if she told anyone where she'd been. She still wasn't sure if Richard was lying, but she couldn't take any chances. She remembered how angry Grady had been with Savannah. When she asked her mother about it, Caroline had explained that Savannah had gone to a dangerous place. Now Maggie understood why Grady was so upset. That town was really creepy, and the more she thought about it, the more she believed there were bad things in those buildings.

The ride was bumpy and she was tossed about, but Richard wouldn't let her sit up and look out the window until they were on the real road.

"Remember, kid, you never saw me. Got that?"

"I never saw you," she repeated solemnly.

"Your mother's life depends on you keeping your trap shut. You wouldn't want your mother dead, would you?"

"No."

"Good. Just remember that the first time you're tempted to tell someone where you were."

"I'll remember. I won't tell." Maggie didn't want her mommy to die. Not like her grandmother. Or Savannah's parents. Or Emma Bishop's daddy.

Richard didn't drive her all the way back to the Yellow Rose. He stopped at the top of the driveway, leaned across her and opened the truck door.

"Remember what I said," he told her again. His eyes were mean.

"I'll remember," she promised, and before he could change his mind, she climbed out of the truck. She stumbled as she jumped down and fell, scraping her elbows. She began to cry, hardly noticing that Richard had driven off, tires squealing.

With her backpack hitting her shoulder blades, Maggie raced toward the ranch house. The driveway was long and her legs felt like they were on fire before the house finally came into view.

Grady stood on the porch with a cup of coffee, but the moment he saw her, he gave a loud shout and flung the cup away. Then he leaped off the porch without using any of the steps and ran toward her.

Almost immediately afterward, her mother threw open the screen door and placed both hands over her mouth. Then she started running, too. Maggie had never been so happy to see her mother. She was even glad to see Grady. He waited for Caroline and let her go to Maggie first. Maggie liked that.

Her mother caught her in her arms and held her tight, then started to cry. She was worried about the bad ghosts, Maggie reasoned. She didn't need to be afraid, because Maggie wouldn't tell. Not anyone. Not ever.

Grady wrapped his arms around them both. He closed his eyes the way people did in church when they prayed. When he opened them again, he smiled at her. Maggie liked the way he smiled. It was a nice smile, not mean.

"Boy, we're glad to see you," he said.

Savannah wiped the tears from her face as she strolled along the pathway in her rose garden. But this morning she didn't appreciate the beauty of the roses. Nor did she find the solace she normally did here. If she lived to be a hundred years old, she didn't want to go through another day like the past one.

Although Caroline had repeatedly told her it wasn't her fault that Maggie had turned up missing, Savannah blamed herself. She'd been preoccupied with baking bread, her head full of the romance developing between her brother and her best friend. What she *should* have been doing was keeping careful watch over her best friend's child.

"I thought I'd find you here." Laredo walked up from behind her.

She didn't want him to know she'd been crying, but wasn't sure she could hide it.

"Sweetheart, why are you still upset? Maggie's home safe and sound."

"I know."

"Then what's bothering you?"

Her chest tightened, and she waited until the ache eased before she answered. "My brother."

Laredo clasped her shoulders. "Richard?"

She nodded. "He was involved in Maggie's disappearance. I know it."

"I have to admit it's mighty suspicious."

"Maggie won't say a word. Everyone's tried to get her to say where she was, but she refuses. Even Frank Hennessey can't get her to budge."

"It doesn't matter. She's home now."

"But it *does* matter," Savannah said passionately. "Laredo, tell me, where did Grady and I go wrong?"

"Sweetheart, your brother's an adult who makes his own decisions. You didn't do anything wrong. You're his sister, not his mother, and even if you were, I'd say the same thing. Richard is his own person, responsible for himself."

"In my head I agree with everything you're saying, but that doesn't take away the pain."

Laredo guided her to the patio set and made her sit down in one of the white wrought-iron chairs.

"I was the one who convinced Grady to let him stay."

"Yes, but that's because Richard's your brother."

"If I'd listened to Grady that first night, none of this would have happened."

"Oh, my love, that's the risk of having a gentle heart. Someone's bound to take advantage of it. I'm sorry it had to be your own brother."

"He's hurt so many people." That was what troubled Savannah most. It wasn't just she and Grady who'd been hurt, but others. Who knew how many? Wherever he'd spent the past six years, she had no doubt he'd left victims behind. People like the shopkeepers in Promise. He'd defrauded them, humiliated them, and ultimately *she* was the one to blame. Savannah didn't know if she could forgive herself. "I should've let Grady kick him out that first day," she muttered fiercely.

"You don't think he's coming back?"

She shook her head. "All his things are gone."

"Everything?"

She nodded and swallowed tightly. "Including Grady's truck."

Laredo swore under his breath. "Did Grady talk to Sheriff Hennessey?" he asked.

Savannah looked down at her clenched hands. "Yes," she said, her voice small. "That was when he learned…"

"Learned what?"

She sighed. "There's more, Laredo. Richard's charged

thousands of dollars' worth of goods in Promise. He owes money to everyone in town. There was never any check. He didn't intend to pay for any of the things he charged and now he's gone." She squeezed her eyes shut in an effort to keep the tears at bay. "You should have seen the look on Grady's face when Frank told him. It was the same look he had six years ago—when he found out what Richard did then. After Mom and Dad died..."

Savannah hadn't thought herself capable of such intense anger. She looked her husband in the eye and said, "I think I hate my own brother."

Eight

Richard had been gone a week. To Grady, his brother's disappearance was both a blessing and a curse. Only now was Grady getting a complete picture of the damage Richard's extended visit had wrought. Every day since his brother had vanished, a fistful of new bills arrived, charges Richard had made using the family's accounts.

The bills were stacked on Grady's desk, and whenever he looked at them, his anger mounted. He'd made a list of money owed and checked it three or four times before he could grasp the full extent of what Richard had done.

While a majority of businesses in town accepted credit cards, ranchers tended to avoid them. Grady carried only one, and it was tucked in the back of his wallet for emergencies. All his purchases were paid for with cash or put on account, then paid in full at the end of each month.

In the weeks since his return, Richard had taken it upon himself to run into town to pick up supplies, and Grady had let him. Sending his worthless brother on errands had seemed innocent enough, and it freed up Laredo, Wiley and him for the more serious ranching chores. What Grady didn't know was that every time Richard had driven into town, he'd charged clothing, expensive liquor, all kinds of things, on the family accounts. It added up to nearly eight thousand dollars, not including the money still owed on some of his earlier purchases. Richard had masterfully hidden what he'd done, robbing Peter to pay Paul, returning goods and buying other things with the credits. He'd managed to disguise his actions using a number of clever cons. Merchants had trusted him. Trusted the Weston name.

Now Richard was gone, and just like six years earlier, Grady was stuck with the mess he'd left behind.

Unable to tolerate looking at the stack of past due notices, Grady grabbed his hat and abandoned his office. The day was hot, although it was only nine in the morning, and he was supposed to meet Wiley and the hired hands near Gully Creek.

He was halfway to the barn when he saw Frank Hennessey's patrol car coming down the driveway, kicking up a plume of dust in its wake. Grady paused and waited for the lawman. With any luck Frank would have some word about Richard and the stolen truck. Whereas Grady hadn't filed charges against his brother six years ago, he felt no such compunction now. He wanted Richard found and prosecuted to the full extent of the law.

Richard deserved a jail term, if for nothing more than the agony he'd caused Caroline by kidnapping Maggie. Until the day he died, Grady wouldn't understand what had prompted his brother to steal away with the child.

For her part Maggie seemed to have made a full recovery. Thank God. She clung to Caroline, but that was understandable. She refused to talk about where she'd gone or who she'd been with, but anyone with half a brain knew it'd been Richard. If Grady had anything for which to thank his useless brother, it was that he'd had the common decency to bring Maggie back to her mother.

Frank parked the patrol car in the yard and slowly climbed out of the driver's seat. "Morning, Grady." He touched the brim of his hat.

"Frank." Grady nodded in greeting. "I hope you've come with good news."

"Good and bad, I'm afraid," Frank said. By tacit agreement the two men headed toward the house for coffee. Savannah was busy in her office, updating her rose catalog on the computer, but she'd recently put on a fresh pot.

Grady poured them each a cup but didn't sit down. When it was a question of receiving news about Richard, he preferred to do it standing up.

"What have you learned?" Grady asked, after giving Frank a moment to taste the coffee. He leaned against the kitchen counter and crossed his ankles. Frank remained standing, as well.

"First, your truck's been found."

This was an unexpected and pleasant surprise. Grady had driven the old Ford pickup for ten years now, and he'd grown attached to it. The thought of being forced to buy a new one had rankled, especially in light of the mounting bills.

"Richard abandoned it in Brewster," Frank said, "and stole another."

While he wasn't surprised, Grady would almost

rather lose his truck permanently than have his own brother steal some other rancher's vehicle.

"It was a newer model," Frank said with a soft snicker. "Apparently yours was a bit too old to suit his image."

Grady didn't miss the sheriff's well-placed sarcasm.

"Only this truck had an additional advantage," Frank muttered.

"What's that?"

"The owner kept a rifle mounted in the back window."

Grady took a moment to mull over the information. "You don't think Richard would actually use it, do you?"

The lawman shrugged. "Given the right set of circumstances, I wouldn't put it past him."

Grady had never thought of Richard as violent. He'd proved himself to be a weasel and a lowlife, but the fact that he might be brutal enough to use a weapon against another human being surprised even Grady. "What makes you think that?" Grady asked, afraid of what Frank was going to say. Last night he'd alluded briefly to something Richard had done back East, but at the time they were all too concerned about Maggie to give it much thought. "What do you know about Richard?"

The sheriff had never been one to hedge, and he didn't do so now. "It gives me no pleasure to tell you this, but there's been an arrest warrant issued for him from New York City."

"New York? On what charge?"

"The list is as long as my arm," Frank said with real regret. "Extortion for one. Richard's been involved in a number of scams, most of them bilking immigrants from Central and South America. Apparently he fed them a pack of lies, luring them into the country with promises of housing and jobs. Promises he had no intention of keeping. He set them up in warehouses in horrible conditions, forced them into menial jobs from which he collected most of their pay. It made big news on the East Coast when his activities were uncovered. Somehow he managed to scrape together the bail, then hit the road the minute he was freed."

Grady had been angry at his brother and furious at himself, too, for allowing Richard to worm his way back into their lives with his hard-luck story. Richard had taken advantage of his family; that was bad enough. But to learn he'd made a profession of stealing from others made Grady sick. How was it that his own brother—born of the same two parents, raised in the same household—could have lowered himself to such depths? If he lived to be an old man, Grady would never understand what had turned Richard into the type of person who purposely hurt others.

"I'm sorry to be the one to tell you this, Grady," Frank said again.

"I realize that." His voice sounded strange even to his own ears.

"When and if we find Richard, I won't have any choice but to arrest him."

"I understand." Grady wouldn't expect anything less. It was what his brother deserved.

"I talked to the New York district attorney this morning. The state wants him bad. Apparently there's been quite a bit of press regarding his arrest and the charges brought against him. He's hurt a lot of people, Grady."

"What happened to him? What made Richard the way he is?" The questions were rhetorical; Grady didn't actually expect the sheriff to supply an answer.

Frank shook his head. "Hell if I know. I liked Richard. He was always charming and clever—but somehow that turned into conniving and untrustworthy. Why he's like that, I couldn't say. Over the years I've met other people who were just as rotten, and I don't believe environment or bad circumstances is always the explanation. Your parents were God-fearing folk, and they raised him right. The fault lies within Richard himself."

Although Grady already knew as much, it helped to have a lawman as experienced as Frank confirm it.

"Eventually Richard will be caught," Frank said, as if he felt the necessity to prepare Grady for the inevitable. "And when he is, he'll be headed straight for prison."

It hurt to think of his brother doing jail time, but Grady's sympathies went out to all the people Richard had cheated, himself included.

Grady walked Frank out to his patrol car, then made his way to the barn. He whistled for Rocket and stopped abruptly when the dog didn't come. Rocket's hearing was getting bad, and he'd grown arthritic; these days, he mostly enjoyed lazing about on the front porch. But he still liked to accompany Grady to the barn. Just to reassure himself, Grady decided to check on his dog. Rocket had belonged to his father and was already middle-aged—seven years old—at the time of the accident. In the hard, financially crippling years that followed, the dog had become Grady's constant sidekick and friend. He'd shared his woes, frustrations, joys and sorrows with Rocket, and the old dog always gave him comfort.

A smile came to him when he saw the dog lying on

his usual braided rug. He whistled again. "Come on, boy, we've got work to do."

Rocket remained still.

As Grady approached the front porch, his steps slowed. He wasn't sure when he realized his faithful companion was gone, but by the time he reached the porch steps, his heart was full of dread.

"Rocket," he whispered and hunkered down beside the dog.

One touch confirmed the worst. Rocket had died, apparently in his sleep.

An intense sadness settled over Grady. On a ranch dogs came and went, and he'd learned the downfall of becoming too attached to any one animal. But Rocket was special. Different. Rocket was a loyal intelligent dog—the best dog he'd ever had; Rocket was also the last tangible piece of his father.

His throat ached and he bowed his head for several minutes, not even trying to fight back the tears.

Once he'd composed himself, he sought out his sister. He found her working in her garden. "I need a shovel," he announced without emotion, as if he didn't know where one was kept.

As he knew she would, Savannah guessed immediately that something wasn't right. "What happened?"

He steeled himself and told her. "Rocket's gone. It looks like he died in his sleep."

He watched as the sadness transformed her face. Tears filled her eyes. "Oh, Grady, I'm so sorry. I know how much you loved him."

"He was just a dog," he said with a stoicism he didn't feel.

"Not an ordinary dog," she added gently.

"No, not ordinary," he agreed, the pain of loss tightening his chest. "If you agree, I'd like to bury him in your garden by the rosebush you named after Mom."

She nodded mutely.

They worked side by side, brother and sister. Grady dug the grave, grateful for the physical effort that helped vent his pain. Again and again he was forced to remind himself that Rocket was just a dog, like a dozen or more who'd lived and died through the years. But he couldn't make himself believe it.

When he finished, he placed a rock as a marker. Savannah stood beside him.

"Goodbye, Rocket," she whispered.

"Goodbye, old friend," Grady said.

Savannah sobbed and turned into his arms. Grady held her, battling back emotion himself. An image came to mind, a memory—his father crouched down and Rocket running toward him, leaping into his arms, joyfully licking his face. Their reunion would be a happy one, but Grady knew there'd be a hole in his heart for a long time to come.

"I'm glad we could finally meet for lunch," Ellie Frasier said, sliding into the booth at the bowling alley café.

Jane Dickinson smiled in welcome. She'd been waiting ten minutes, but she tended to be early, a habit her family had instilled in her. This lunch date was something she'd really looked forward to, although it had been difficult to arrange with both their schedules so busy. But Dovie had encouraged Jane to meet Ellie, mentioning her in almost every conversation.

Jane had come to think of Dovie as a mentor and friend. Stopping to talk with her that first morning she'd gone for a jog had been one of the smartest things she'd done since moving to Promise. Unfortunately Dovie was still the only person in town she knew on a first-name basis. Despite her efforts to become part of the community, friendly gestures from the other residents of Promise were few and far between.

"So…Dovie thought it would be a good idea for the two of us to get to know each other," Ellie said, reaching for the menu.

"I realize you're getting married soon," Jane said as a means of starting the conversation. "You must be terribly busy…"

Ellie nodded. "The wedding's only a couple of weeks away." A wistful look stole over her face.

Jane recognized that look—it was the look of a woman in love. Jane envied her happiness. After medical school and then working as an intern, followed by her residency at a huge public-health hospital in Los Angeles, there hadn't been time in her life for anything other than medicine. Now she was trapped in Texas with only one friend and zero prospects for romance.

Ellie did little more than glance at the menu before she set it aside.

Jane had spent several minutes reading over the selections, but had failed to make a choice. "You know what you're going to have?"

"I almost always order the chicken-fried steak."

The thought of all those fat grams was enough to make Jane feel queasy. Even the salads listed on the menu were ones she normally avoided—coleslaw with mayonnaise dressing, for instance. Most of the food was battered and fried. Even the vegetables. Okra coated in cornmeal and cooked in a deep fryer. The same with tomatoes. It was a wonder anyone lived beyond twenty-five in this town. The eating habits here were probably the unhealthiest she'd seen in years. It was time the people of Promise caught up with the latest information on health and diet.

"The chicken-fried steak is great," Ellie coaxed when Jane continued to study the menu.

The waitress arrived with her pad and pen. Ellie gave the woman her order, then chatted briefly while Jane reviewed her choices one last time.

"I'll have a green salad with avocado if you've got it."

The waitress—Denise, according to her name tag—wrote it down on her pad.

"With dressing on the side."

Denise exchanged a scornful glance with Ellie before she called the order in to the kitchen. The woman's reaction was typical of what Jane had encountered the past few weeks.

"What did I do that was so wrong?" Jane asked, leaning forward.

"First off, we Texans pride ourselves on our food."

"The diet around here is appalling," Jane blurted without thinking. "Everything is loaded with fat. Chicken-fried steak, barbecued meat, chili without beans—doesn't anyone appreciate the high fiber content of kidney beans?"

"It's exactly this attitude that's causing your problems, Doc."

"What attitude? All I'm trying to do is set better health standards for the community! It's a wonder you aren't all dead or dying."

"And a wonder you haven't been tarred and feathered," Ellie snapped.

Jane's mouth sagged open. She might have laughed if Ellie hadn't looked so serious.

"You want to know why people are unfriendly?" Ellie asked. "Perhaps you should look at how *you* come across. Rude, superior and know-it-all! The only reason I agreed to talk to you is because of Dovie, who for reasons I don't understand has taken a liking to you."

The woman was spitting mad, and other than pointing out a few basic truths, Jane still didn't know what she'd done that was so offensive.

"As far as everyone in this town is concerned, you can take your salad-eating wine-sipping butt and go back to California. We don't need some surfer chick telling us what's good for us, understand?"

Jane noted that the other customers had gone quiet. Several heads nodded in agreement. "I see," she said, struggling to hold on to her composure. "But unfortunately I've signed a contract and I'm stuck here for three years. So if I'm going to live in this community—"

"Then I suggest you change your high-and-mighty ways."

Swallowing her pride, Jane nodded. "I'm probably going to need a little help."

"You need a lot of help."

Jane decided to let that comment slide. "I'd appreciate a few words of advice."

Ellie didn't answer right away. "You sure you're up to this?"

Jane smiled. As far as she could see, she didn't have any choice. "Be gentle, all right?"

A smile cracked Ellie's lips. "I'll try."

Jane sighed. They'd started off on the wrong foot, but she sensed Ellie could be an important ally, and she badly needed a friend her own age. Dovie was kind, but it would take more than the assistance of one woman to help her fit in.

"Denise." Ellie waved her arm and called for the waitress. "Doc wants to change her order."

"I do?"

"You said you're willing to learn. Now's your chance. Your initiation, if you like. First, I'll teach you how to eat like a Texan. We can both diet tomorrow."

Jane swallowed, then nodded. "What is it I want to order?"

Ellie motioned to the waitress. "The doc here will have the chicken-fried steak, fried okra and an extra scoop of gravy on her mashed potatoes."

"All *right,*" Denise said with smiling approval, writing it on her pad. "Do you want a side salad with that?" she asked.

It would probably be the only healthy part of the entire meal. "Sure." Jane was about to remind her to leave off the dressing, when Ellie added, "Put the dressing right on top of it, too, will you, Denise?"

The waitress grinned from ear to ear. "Not a problem."

Jane decided then and there that either she'd adjust to life in Texas...or die trying.

Maggie gasped and bolted upright in bed, unsure for a moment where she was. Her skin felt clammy, and she was breathing fast. A moment later she realized it had only been a dream. She'd been in the town again, the one with the bad ghosts. Richard was in her dream, too. He was looking at her and his face kept getting wider and longer as if he were staring at her through a wavy mirror.

His voice boomed loud, too, and he kept telling her what would happen to her mother if Maggie told anyone where she'd been. Again and again she promised him she wouldn't tell, and she hadn't. Not anyone. Not even her dolls.

Kicking aside her blankets, Maggie stole out of the bedroom and sneaked down the hallway, guided by the night-light, to her mother's bedroom. She stood and watched her mother sleeping, checking to make sure she was safe and no bad ghosts had gotten her.

"Maggie?" Her mother's eyes fluttered open.

"I had a bad dream," Maggie whispered.

Her mother tossed back the sheet, silently inviting Maggie into bed with her. Maggie was glad; it was a rare treat to sleep with her mommy. She climbed onto the bed and her mother wrapped an arm around her, then gently brushed the hair from her brow.

"Was it a very bad dream?" she asked.

"A scary one," Maggie told her.

"Do you want to tell me about it?"

Maggie shook her head. She didn't want to think about Richard ever again. She remembered that he didn't know she'd taken the doll, and if he found out, he might send the bad ghosts after her. As soon as she could, Maggie had removed the doll from her backpack and hidden it inside a big tin in her closet. No one knew it was there. Not Mommy. Not Richard. Not anyone.

Safe in her mother's arms, Maggie closed her eyes.

"You're not frightened now, are you?"

Maggie shook her head, but it wasn't true. "A little," she confessed.

"Did I tell you Grady's coming over tomorrow after church, and we're going to the park for a picnic?"

Maggie's spirits buoyed. "We are?" Usually they went out to the ranch and visited with Savannah and Laredo, too.

"Does that sound like fun?"

Maggie nodded eagerly. "Will Grady push me on the swing?"

"If you ask him."

Maggie closed her eyes again and sighed deeply. "Grady's not so bad. I'm sorry his dog died." She'd liked Rocket.

She felt her mommy nod. "He's going to miss him."

"I'm going to miss him, too," Maggie said. "Maybe we can make Grady feel better."

"He doesn't frighten you anymore?"

Maggie shook her head. "He does a little when he yells, but if I plug my ears I don't really hear it."

"He doesn't mean to yell, it's just…part of his nature."

Maggie wasn't entirely sure what that meant. But she knew that ever since the morning Grady found her running down the driveway and she saw his face light up with a smile, she'd liked him better. Until then, she'd never seen Grady smile, not a real smile, anyway. He'd hugged her again and again that day, and her mommy, too. Later he'd taken her into the barn and held her hand so she wouldn't be afraid of Widowmaker and let her see the new colt.

Grady had reminded her that she had yet to choose a name for him. She'd chosen "Moonbeam," and Grady said it was a pretty name. Wiley had teased him about it and said it sounded like one of those hippie names from the sixties—whatever that meant—but Grady had insisted Moonbeam was it. She'd chosen well.

"I think Grady's special," Maggie announced suddenly. She no longer felt any doubt. Richard had been fun at first, but he wasn't a real friend.

"I do, too," her mommy said softly.

Caroline had readied the picnic basket and cooler before church, packing everything that didn't need to be refrigerated. It had been Grady's idea to go on a picnic in Pioneer Park and she suspected she knew why. Ever since she'd brought up the subject of Maggie's father, he'd been waiting for her to tell him. She wished now that she'd ignored his advice the day they'd gone horseback riding. The day Maggie disappeared. It would make everything far less complicated now. She pushed the worry to the back of her mind, determined to have a good time. If the subject arose, she'd deal with it then.

The park sat in the very center of town and took up four square blocks. It had a wading pool for toddlers, as well as Promise's one and only swimming pool, complete with diving board. The grass was lush and green and meticulously groomed. A statue of a pioneer family stood proudly in the middle, along with a plaque that described the pioneers' role in Texan history. The paved walkways all led directly toward the statue.

Maggie loved the playground, and Caroline appreciated Grady's willingness to indulge her child. Ever since that terrible night, Grady had given special attention to her daughter.

Caroline didn't know what she would have done without Grady. That night had been a turning point for all of them. For her and Grady, and for Grady and Maggie.

The doorbell rang and Maggie screamed from inside her bedroom, "I'll get it!" Caroline heard her race for the door.

The only person it could be was Grady. He'd followed them home from church, driving the old Ford pickup, which had been returned to him a few days before. Maggie had already changed out of her Sunday-school dress and into shorts. Caroline wore a sleeveless yellow cotton dress, with a wide straw hat and sandals, the same clothes she'd worn to the service. Grady sent her a purely masculine look of approval as Maggie dragged him by the hand into the kitchen.

"It's Grady," Maggie announced unnecessarily. "Can we go now?"

"Soon. I've got to load up the potato salad and fried chicken first."

"Mommy makes the best potato salad in the world," Maggie said. "She lets me peel the hard-boiled eggs and help her stir."

"No wonder it's so good," he said and glanced from Maggie to Caroline.

The look, however brief, made Caroline wonder if he was speculating about who had fathered her child. Then again, she might be imagining it. Every time they were together, she became obsessed with her secret, with the need to tell Grady. She loved this man and she feared what would happen once he learned the truth.

"Go put on your running shoes," Caroline instructed her daughter. Maggie dashed out of the room, eager to comply.

Grady watched Maggie go before turning his attention to her. "I didn't embarrass you in church this morning, did I?"

"No," she answered, wondering what he was talking about.

"I couldn't keep my eyes off you."

"I didn't really notice…" She hated this tension, this constant fear that any look he gave her, any silence, meant he was wondering about Maggie's father. Soon, she promised herself. She'd tell him soon. Perhaps even today.

Grady gripped her about the waist and they kissed, sweetly and unhurriedly. "I didn't hear a word of Wade's sermon," he whispered into her hair, holding her close.

"Me, neither." But not for the reasons he assumed.

"Wade stopped me on the way out the door," Grady said, grinning, "and told me there'd be a test on the sermon next week. Not to worry, though, he was willing to share his notes."

Caroline managed a smile. "I think Wade's the best thing that's happened to Promise Christian in a long time."

"You're the best thing that's happened to me," Grady whispered. "Ever." He reluctantly let her go when Maggie tore into the kitchen.

The five-year-old was breathless with excitement. "I'm ready!" she cried.

Caroline added the potato salad and fried chicken to the cooler, and Grady carried it to his pickup. The three of them piled into the front and drove to the park.

Caroline noticed that Maggie was especially quiet on the short drive. She was concerned the child might be reacting to her tension. But Maggie's spirits lifted the instant they arrived at the park. Grady lugged the picnic supplies to a vacant table, and while Caroline covered it with a plastic-coated tablecloth, Maggie insisted on showing Grady her favorite swing.

"Go on, you two," Caroline said, waving them away. Once again she noticed—or thought she did—the way Grady studied Maggie. Briefly she wondered if he'd guessed.

Determined to ignore her worries, at least for the moment, Caroline spread a blanket on the grass in a shady area. When she'd finished, she slid the cooler beneath the table and out of the sun.

The sound of Maggie's laughter drifted toward her, and Caroline looked up to discover her daughter on the swing set with Grady standing behind her.

"Higher!" Maggie shouted. "Push me higher!"

Grady did, until Caroline held her breath at the heights the swing reached. She pressed her hand to her mouth to keep from calling out a warning, knowing she could trust Grady with her daughter. She gasped once when the swing buckled, but Grady swiftly caught it and brought it back under control.

Eventually he stopped the swing and Maggie returned to earth. Squealing with delight, she still had energy left to run back to their picnic table.

"Did you see, Mommy?" Maggie cried. "Did you see how high Grady pushed me?"

Caroline nodded. "I saw."

"I could touch the sky with my feet. Did you see? Did you see?"

"Yes, baby, I saw."

The afternoon was lovely. After they ate, Maggie curled up on the blanket and quickly fell asleep.

Now, Caroline commanded herself. *Tell him now.* But

she couldn't make herself do it, couldn't bear to see the look in his eyes when he learned the truth. Avoiding his gaze, she brushed the soft curls from her daughter's brow.

"Any effects from her night away from home?" Grady asked. "Has she told you anything of what happened?"

"Not a word, but she woke up last night with a nightmare and wouldn't tell me about it."

"Poor thing."

Caroline gazed down at her slumbering child, loving her with an intensity that went beyond anything she'd ever known, even the strong love she felt for Grady. "She's back, safe and sound, and for that I'm grateful."

"I am, too."

Caroline leaned against Grady, letting him support her weight, his hands resting on her shoulders.

"Savannah reminded me that it's Maggie's birthday next week. I'd like to give her something special, but I need to ask you about it first. She seems quite taken with Moonbeam, so—"

"You're giving her the colt?" Caroline could barely believe her ears. At the same time she realized that the mention of Maggie's birthday created a natural opening to talk about her child's father. To reveal his name.

No! she couldn't tell him, Caroline thought in sudden panic.

"Of course we'll keep Moonbeam at the ranch."

While the offer was tempting, horses weren't cheap to maintain.

"The gift includes room and board." Grady answered her question even before she could ask it.

"That's generous of you."

"She's going to be six, right?"

"Yes."

His gaze softened as he studied the little girl. "You said once that you'd dated Cal."

Caroline felt as though her lungs had frozen. This was as close as Grady had come to asking her outright about Maggie's father.

"I did," she said and looked away. He reached for her hand. "Now that Richard's gone—"

"Do you mind if we don't talk about my brother?" Grady said, interrupting her. "I want to escape him for a few hours if I can."

"Of course, but—"

"I'd much rather concentrate on other things just now, like how good you feel in my arms."

Caroline closed her eyes.

"It doesn't matter, Caroline," he whispered close to her ear.

"What doesn't matter?"

"About Maggie. I already love her."

"I know. It's just that..." Caroline liked to think she would have continued if Maggie hadn't chosen that precise moment to awake.

"Can we go swing again?" she asked Grady.

He grinned. "This time let's bring your mother, too. All right?"

Maggie took Caroline's hand and the three of them headed toward the swing set, the subject she was about to broach shelved once again.

The day ended far sooner than Caroline and Maggie would have wished. Grady dropped them off at seven and went to check in with Frank Hennessey. Caroline assumed it had to do with Richard, but she didn't ask and he didn't volunteer.

The light on her answering machine was flashing, and while she unpacked the picnic basket, she played it back.

"It's Savannah. Give me a call when you get home."

Tucking the phone to her ear, Caroline punched out her friend's number. As she waited for Savannah to answer, she set the leftovers in the refrigerator.

"Hi, it's me, Caroline. You called?" she asked when Savannah picked up the receiver.

"I did." Savannah sounded pleased about something but didn't elaborate. In fact, she appeared to be waiting for Caroline to speak first.

"Um, Savannah, was there a particular reason you called?" Caroline finally ventured.

"Aren't you going to tell me, or is it a big secret?"

"Savannah, *what* are you talking about?"

The line went silent. "He didn't ask you?"

"Ask me what?"

"Oh, dear," Savannah said with an exaggerated sigh. "When he left this morning, Grady was as fidgety as a drop of cold water on a hot skillet."

"Maybe he's got heat rash," Caroline teased. "Now tell me what this is all about."

"Grady," Savannah said as if that much should be obvious. "And then in church, the poor man couldn't keep his eyes off you."

"This isn't making a lot of sense, Savannah Smith."

"And I was so sure, too."

"Sure about what?" Caroline demanded.

"That Grady was going to ask you to marry him."

Nine

Every pew in Promise Christian Church was filled
for the wedding of Ellie Frasier and Glen Patterson.
Glen had asked Cal to be his best man and Grady to
serve as one of the ushers. Grady had agreed before
he learned that he was expected to wear a tuxedo. He
wasn't sure how a man could breathe with a shirt but-
toned up that tight.

The main advantage of being in the wedding party
was that Caroline was one of Ellie's bridesmaids. Grady
had never realized that four women all wearing the
same dresses could look so different. In his—admit-
tedly biased—opinion, Caroline was the most beautiful. Savannah, of course, was a close second.

Since it was the hottest time of the year, Wade Mc-
Millen kept his sermon short. Ellie and Glen exchanged
their vows as both their mothers sat in the front row
quietly weeping. The Moorhouse sisters sobbed loudly,
and Dovie Boyd dabbed at her eyes, as well. Even the
coolly composed Dr. Dickinson, sitting beside Dovie,
sniffled a bit as the *I do*'s were said.

Grady met Frank Hennessey's eye as they exited the

church. Frank had his arm protectively around Dovie, and his expression seemed to say that he had plenty of years on Grady and he still didn't understand what made women weep at weddings.

The reception was held at the Grange Hall and, on this Saturday afternoon, there were as many cars parked out front as the night of the big summer dance. The table closest to the door was stacked high with elegantly wrapped wedding gifts.

Grady ended up spending most of his time in the reception line, but once again he was compensated by having Caroline at his side.

"Ellie looks so beautiful," she said when the last guest had made her way through the line.

Grady's patience when it came to these formal affairs was limited. He felt tired and hungry. "Do you want something to eat?" he asked with a longing glance at the buffet table.

"I've got to help Ellie change out of her wedding dress," she told him.

"You mean we can take off these fancy duds?" He eased his index finger between the starched collar and his neck.

"Not us. Just Ellie and Glen."

"Not fair," he complained.

"Go help yourself to some dinner and I'll be back before you know it." She kissed his cheek, and while it was only a sample of what he wanted, he'd take what he could get.

"Where'd Caroline go?" Cal asked, coming up behind Grady in the buffet line.

"To help Ellie change out of her dress." Grady thought that made him sound like an expert on wedding etiquette, but he wouldn't have had a clue if Caroline hadn't told him.

"Who designed these starched shirts, anyway?" Cal muttered, "The Marquis de Sade?"

"I wouldn't doubt it." Grady reached for a plate. It'd been hours since he'd last eaten. Between that and the afternoon's exertions, he was starved.

"Glen's a married man now," Cal said as if it had only now hit him.

"Does that bother you?" Grady asked, thinking there'd be a big adjustment in Cal's life. Grady had heard Glen was moving into town with Ellie; apparently, they'd put money down on a house.

"Doesn't bother me at all—but it would if he hadn't married Ellie. Those two are good together."

Grady felt the same way. Cal and Glen had been his neighbors all his life. Neighbors and best friends. The three of them were as close as family, and yet Grady had to wonder if he knew Cal as well as he thought he did. Again and again he'd mulled over the news that Cal had once dated Caroline, but he firmly believed Cal would have married her if he'd been the baby's father.

Grady had given up trying to work out who Maggie's father was. He felt certain it had to be someone he knew, perhaps trusted, otherwise she wouldn't hesitate to tell him. Whenever they were together he watched her struggle with herself. The one time she'd been ready to tell him, he'd stopped her. He wanted to kick himself for that now. This secret was tormenting her—and him, too.

Last Sunday on their picnic, he'd tried to reassure her that it didn't matter. He loved Maggie and he loved her. Apparently he'd failed, because she seemed more apprehensive than ever.

"Glen looks at Ellie the way you look at Caroline," Cal said casually.

"It's that noticeable, is it?"

Cal nodded. "You could say that."

They carried their plates to a recently vacated table in the far corner of the hall.

Grady stacked the empty plates to one side and pulled out a chair. Cal sat across from him. "I'm thinking of asking Caroline to marry me," he said, mentioning it in an offhand way. It was the first time he'd said it aloud. He watched Cal's reaction, closely.

"All right!" Cal grinned. "I wondered how long it'd take you. I've always liked Caroline."

"I love her." Grady had no problem admitting it, and if Cal had any leftover emotion for her, he'd rather they cleared the air now.

"Then what's the holdup?"

Grady felt a surge of anger, not at the question but at the answer. He stabbed his fork into a thick slice of ham as he waited for the bitterness to leave him. This was a day of shared joy, and he refused to allow his brother to ruin it.

Cal propped his elbows on the table. "My guess would be that Richard's got something to do with this. I thought he wasn't around anymore."

Without elaborating, Grady told him about the latest fiasco involving Richard. Cal and Frank Hennessey were the only two people with whom Grady would discuss his worthless brother. He supposed Cal had told Glen; that was only natural, and fine with him. Six years earlier, when Richard had disappeared with the inheritance money, Cal had advised Grady to press charges against him. Grady had agonized over it and in the end decided not to. Now he wondered if he'd made the right decision.

Few other people knew of Richard's treachery.

Savannah might have told Caroline, but he couldn't be sure. Of all the women in town, Caroline had been the most sensible about Richard and his attentions. Grady admired her for seeing through his brother and not being taken in by his easy charm. Nearly everyone had been deceived by his flattery and suave ways, but not her.

"Richard's gone," Grady said, answering his friend, "and yet he isn't. He left behind damn near eight thousand dollars in debts."

Cal gave a low whistle.

Grady told him how his brother had charged things on local accounts all around town. Clothes, liquor, food, even camping and ranch supplies, although God only knew what he intended to do with them. Frankly, Grady didn't *want* to know.

"They aren't your debts," Cal was quick to remind him. "The bills have Richard's signature on them."

"But he put them on the family accounts."

Cal sighed in resignation. "You paid them, didn't you?"

"I didn't have any choice." It was the Weston name that stood to be tarnished. Grady knew he wouldn't be able to look his friends and neighbors in the eye when his own brother had bilked them, unless he himself made good on the debts. Which he had. That eight thousand had nearly wiped out his savings, but he'd get by, just as he always had.

Earlier in the week he'd checked out engagement rings in the jeweler's window, and he'd realized he wouldn't be able to buy as big a diamond as he wanted for Caroline; he also realized it was more important to be debt-free.

Cal was about to ask him something else when Frank Hennessey abruptly pulled out a chair and joined them. He cast them a grateful look. "I'm safe for now," he said in a low voice.

"Safe from who?" Grady asked, puzzled. Frank normally didn't run from anything or anyone.

Frank threw back his head with a groan. "Dovie. The woman's got that look in her eye again."

Cal and Grady exchanged glances. "What look?" Cal ventured.

"Marriage. I...I've been telling her for the last ten years that one day I'd marry her. I meant it at the time, but I tell you, boys, the mere thought is enough to make my blood run cold. I can see now I'm not the marrying kind—I'm just not! I've got to get *her* to see that." He hunched forward. "But I don't want to upset her, either."

"I thought—assumed that you and Dovie had, you know, an understanding," Grady whispered.

"We do," Frank said. "But every once in a while she reminds me of that stupid promise and I find an excuse to delay it, and she's satisfied for another few months. Then we attend a wedding or one of her friends has an anniversary, and she brings the subject up again. You'd think after this length of time, she'd figure we've got a pretty good arrangement. You'd think she'd be willing to leave well enough alone." He gave a long-suffering sigh. "I'm crazy about Dovie, but marriage isn't for me."

Grady began to speak, but Frank cut him off. "Weddings are dangerous things, boys. Dovie took one whiff of those orange blossoms, and next thing I knew she had that look."

"Why does she want to get married?" Cal asked, voicing Grady's own thoughts. If she'd been content for ten years without a ring on her finger, she obviously wasn't as keen on marriage as she let on.

"Dovie says a ten-year courtship is long enough. Either I follow through or this is it." Frank shook his head sadly. "I should never have said anything to her about marriage," he muttered, "but I couldn't help myself. I thought I'd lose her if I didn't propose, so I...sort of... did. At the time I actually believed we could make a go of it. Now I know marriage just wouldn't work. Not for me, anyway."

"Give her time to accept reality," Grady suggested.

Frank shook his head in despair. "You don't know Dovie like I do."

"You're sure you don't want to marry her?" The question came from Cal. Cal's mother and Dovie were good friends.

"It isn't that at all," Frank said. "I don't want to get married, period. It has nothing to do with Dovie. She's the best thing that ever happened to me."

"But you told her you would."

"I know," Frank admitted. "The thing is, most of the time she's as happy with our arrangement as I am. We live separate lives. She has her shop and her interests, and I have mine, and we both like it that way. We see each other just about every day and, hell, she knows how I feel about her."

"But you won't marry her, no matter what?"

"I told you, marriage and I aren't compatible." Frank looked at them mournfully. "I like my life just the way it is." The sheriff slowly exhaled. "The two of you understand, don't you, seeing that neither one of you is married, either?"

Cal glanced quickly at Grady, eyebrows raised. "This isn't a good time to be asking Grady that," he said.

"What?" Frank said with a moan. "You aren't thinking about getting married, are you?"

"As a matter of fact, I am."

Frank swore under his breath. "Caroline, isn't it?"

Grady nodded, not hiding his grin.

"She's a fine woman, but damn it all, this is going to send Dovie into wedding overdrive."

"I haven't asked Caroline yet," Grady said.

"Thank God, because once Dovie learns you two got engaged, I won't hear the end of it."

"I can't guarantee Caroline's answer."

"Do you honestly think she'll refuse?" Frank asked in a way that said he knew the answer. "It's fairly obvious how you feel about each other."

"Naturally I'm hoping…"

"Why borrow trouble?" Cal asked. "Of course she'll say yes. Why shouldn't she?"

Ten years, Dovie mused darkly. She'd wasted ten years of her life on that ungrateful lawman. Arms folded, she paced her living room, back and forth, back and forth, trying to walk off her anger.

It wasn't working.

By the time they left Ellie and Glen's wedding reception, Dovie was barely speaking to Frank. He didn't have a lot to say, either—which was just as well. He'd proposed to her shortly after they'd met, and all these years she'd waited. All these years she'd believed in him and hoped and loved him.

Well, she'd better smarten up and accept the truth. Frank never intended to marry her and, really, why should he? He enjoyed all the delights of married life with none of the responsibilities. Twice a week he spent the night, and in the morning she made him breakfast and handed him his clean laundry and sent him on his way with a kiss.

No more.

There'd been only one other man in Dovie's life, and that was her husband. But Marvin had been dead thirteen years now. And for ten of those years she'd pined after a lawman who claimed to love her, but apparently not enough to marry her.

A light knock sounded on her back door. It had to be Frank Hennessey—the only person in the entire world who came to her in the dark of night. And Dovie knew why he'd come. Well, he could forget it. She had a thing or two to say to him.

She marched through the house and threw open the door, startling Frank.

"If you're here for the reason I think you are, then you can turn around and go right back home." She pointed in the direction of his parked car.

He blinked. "Dovie, sweetheart, you don't mean that." He removed his hat and wore the anguished look of a misunderstood and badly maligned male.

"I certainly do mean it, Franklin Hennessey." She would have slammed the door on him, but he'd stuck his foot in.

"We have a good life just the way it is," he said enticingly.

"If I'm so happy about our lives, then why do I feel this ache in my heart? Why can't I sit through a wedding without dissolving in tears? I want you to marry me, Frank."

The pained expression returned. "Oh, Dovie, I can't do that."

"Can't or won't, Frank?"

He didn't answer and she knew why.

"I love you, Dovie." The words were a low purr.

"You *say* you love me, but you won't do anything to prove it," she spit, folding her arms and refusing to look at him.

"I can't tell you how sorry I am. I always thought… I believed one day I'd be able to…to take the plunge. But I realize now that marriage would never work for someone like me."

"Then we're at an impasse. I guess the reality is that you won't marry me. Not now and not ever."

"But it's not because I don't love you!"

"So either I accept you the way you are or—"

"Our arrangement has worked so far, hasn't it, my love?" he asked, his eyes pleading.

"Or I break off this dead-end relationship," she continued, ignoring his words.

Frank went pale. "Oh, Dovie, you wouldn't do that."

Dovie drew a deep breath and the anger vanished. A peace of sorts came over her, a calmness. "I have to, Frank—for my own self-respect, if nothing else."

He stared at her as though he didn't understand.

It hurt to say the words, but either she did this or she'd never be able to face herself in the mirror again. Squaring her shoulders, she smiled sadly and said, "It'd be best if we didn't see each other anymore."

The sheriff's mouth dropped open. "Dovie, please! Be reasonable about this."

"It's over, Frank." She straightened and looked him straight in the eye.

"Okay," he agreed, unmistakable regret in his voice. "If that's the way you want it."

Dovie's hand gripped the door handle. "Goodbye, Frank," she said.

"Good night, Dovie." As though in a daze, he turned and left.

Tears clouded her eyes, but she refused to let them fall. She'd loved Frank for ten years, and it would be a major adjustment to untangle her life from his, but she'd do it and be a stronger woman for it.

A loud knock on the windowpane of her back door made her jump. Dovie answered it to find a bewildered-looking Frank standing on the other side.

"I just want to be sure we understand each other," he said, holding his hat in both hands. "Are you saying you don't want me stopping by on Wednesday and Saturday nights anymore?"

She rolled her eyes. "That's exactly what I'm saying."

"I see." He seemed to ponder her words for a moment. "What about dinners on Sunday?"

"I think we should put an end to that, as well."

"Afternoon tea at your shop?"

"You can find some other woman to spend your afternoon break with," she suggested, even though the thought of him seeing anyone else nearly destroyed her.

"There isn't another woman in the world I'd rather be with than you."

A slow smile eased up the corners of her mouth.

"Then the answer is simple. Marry me the way you promised."

Frank ground his teeth. "I can't, Dovie. I wish to hell I could, but it's impossible. I just can't do it."

"There are certain things I can't do, either, Frank." She softly closed the door.

Caroline knew this dinner was different the minute Grady phoned to invite her. He was formal and polite—as if he was planning something other than a casual evening out.

"He's going to ask you," Savannah insisted. "I'm sure of it." It'd been a week since Ellie and Glen's wedding, and the topic of love and marriage hadn't strayed far from her best friend's mind.

"Have you thought about how you'll respond when he does?"

Caroline had thought of little else for an entire week. Not her response, should he bring up the question of marriage, but *his* response once she told him the truth about Maggie. The conversation lay before her like a stretch of deep treacherous water. They'd need to get through that before she'd be able to consider her reply.

She figured he'd introduce the matter of marriage over dinner. Everything pointed to that. Rumor had it that he'd been seen in the jewelry store earlier in the week. In fact, he'd made a number of trips into town.

He'd stopped by the post office three times, which was highly unusual. If she saw him in town even once a week that was a surprise; three times was almost unheard of.

Maggie was spending the night at Dovie's, so Caroline had the luxury of a free afternoon in which to indulge herself without the constant interruptions of a six-year-old. She soaked in a perfume-scented tub, painted her toenails and curled her hair with a hot iron, all the while praying everything would go smoothly.

This was supposed to be the night of her dreams. But by the time Grady arrived to pick her up, she was a nervous wreck. The hours of anticipating his reaction had left her tense and jittery. Not knowing how he'd feel, what he'd say, was almost more than she could take.

The doorbell rang precisely at six, reminding her that even in small things, Grady Weston was reliable, a man who kept his word. His eyes widened with appreciation when he saw her, and she realized every minute she'd spent in front of the mirror had been worth it.

"I didn't think it was possible for you to look more beautiful than you did at Ellie's wedding," he said with the sincerity of a man not accustomed to giving compliments.

"Thank you." She twirled around to give him a full view of her new dress. "Do you like it?"

"Oh-h-h, yes. Where's Maggie?" he asked, glancing around.

"With Dovie. She's spending the night."

He handed her a bottle of wine as if he'd suddenly remembered it was in his hands.

"Shall I open it now?" she asked.

"Sure. If you want."

He followed her into the kitchen, and as she searched for a corkscrew, she saw him pacing the room, his lips moving.

"Grady?"

His head shot up and he looked startled.

"Did you say something?"

He shook his head in quick denial.

She found the corkscrew and gave it to him. While he wrestled with the cork, Caroline took out two wine-glasses.

"This isn't going to work," he announced and set the bottle down on the countertop, the cork half-out.

"That's the only corkscrew I have," she said.

"I'm not talking about the wine." He pulled out a kitchen chair and with both hands on her shoulders urged her to sit. Then he finished opening the wine, a white zinfandel, and poured them each a glass.

He drank down the first one in three gulps; after that, he immediately refilled his glass.

"If your parents were alive, I'd talk to them...but it's just you and me. So—I'll say what I have to say."

"What you have to say?" she repeated, her eyebrows arched. Despite her own anxiety, she couldn't help enjoying his discomfort. Just a little.

He pointed his finger at her as he struggled with the words. "I have to do this now. If I wait any longer, I'll say or do something stupid, and the entire evening will be ruined." His eyes were warm, openly revealing his love. "And that isn't what I want."

"What *do* you want, Grady?" she asked in a soft voice.

He reached for his wine and took a deep swallow.

"Wine is usually sipped," she murmured.

"I know," he said, "but I need the fortification."

Caroline's heart swelled with emotion. "Oh, Grady, I love you so much."

He stared at her for a long wonder-filled moment. "I love you, too." He smiled then, sweetly. "I practiced this proposal a dozen times on the drive into town, and now

I find myself completely at a loss. I don't know where the hell to start."

"The fact that you love me is a good opening."

"But I have to tell you so much more."

"Love is only the beginning..." This was where she needed to explain the past, but she couldn't. Not now, in the most wonderfully romantic moment of her life. Not when the man she loved with all her heart was about to ask her to share his life.

"I'm free to love you," he said.

"Free?" she repeated, not understanding.

"Richard's gone."

She frowned and felt a sudden chill race down her bare arms. "What does Richard have to do with this?"

"Everything." She could feel the anger coming from him. She swallowed, waiting for him to elaborate.

"Richard has been a thorn in my side for six long years. He's my brother, and for that reason alone, a part of me will always love him. But I refuse to allow him to dictate my life a minute longer than he already has."

"What...what do you mean?"

"I'm finished dealing with the problems my brother created. I refuse to pick up any more of the pieces, or accept any further responsibility for the disasters he's left in his wake. I'm not paying another debt of his. Every minute of the last six years has been spent struggling to regain ground Richard stole from me. I resent every one of those wasted minutes, and I refuse to deal with his mistakes anymore."

Caroline wasn't sure how she could remain upright in her chair, why she didn't pitch to the ground.

The harshness left Grady's eyes as he looked at her. "As I said, I'm no longer tied to Richard or his troubles,

so I can tell you how much I love you. Maggie, too."
The anger dissipated and his features softened with
love. "I'm free to ask you to share my life, Caroline, if
you'll have me."

He hesitated, and when she didn't immediately respond, he said gently, "I'm asking you to marry me."

The choking in her throat made it impossible to respond.

"Is the decision that difficult?" He sounded a little
hurt.

"No…"

"I did it all wrong, didn't I?" he muttered. He thrust
a hand into his coat pocket and produced a velvet ring
case. "Give me another chance to do this the way you
deserve."

"Grady—"

"No, don't say anything. Not yet." Then he opened
the small velvet box. "It took me thirty-six years to find
the woman I want to be with for the rest of my life, and
that woman is you, Caroline Daniels."

She pressed both hands over her mouth, her eyes
filled with tears.

"Would you do me the honor of becoming my wife?"

She tried to speak and found that she couldn't.

"Just nod," he suggested.

"I can't," she finally managed, her voice cracking.

"Can't nod?"

"I can't marry you…" She stood up, then walked to
the sink and stared out the window. This was the most
difficult thing she'd ever done, outside of burying her
mother. Only now she felt as if it was her heart she was
laying to rest. Her heart. And her future.

"You're saying no?" He was clearly shocked.

"I can't because…" She stopped, unable to continue.

"You *can't* marry me?"

"No."

"Is that your final answer?"

She dared not turn around and look at him. "That's my final answer," she said in a monotone.

She heard him retreat, his heavy steps taking him as far as the living room. Without warning, he rushed back into the kitchen.

"Just one damn minute," he shouted. "I don't accept that. You just finished telling me how much you love me!"

She couldn't deny it and so she said nothing.

"If you're going to reject my proposal, then at least have the decency to look me in the eye when you do it."

Slowly, her heart breaking, she turned toward him.

"Tell me to my face that you don't want to marry me," he demanded.

Her chin came up. "I won't marry you."

Grady's jaw was clenched. *"Why not?"* The two words were like knives.

"Because if you married me…" she began, gazing straight ahead. She couldn't go on.

"I'm not good enough for you, is that it?"

"No!" This was said with all the conviction of her soul.

"Then say it," he yelled. "Just say it."

"Because if you married me," she started again, "you'd be left to deal with yet another one of Richard's mistakes."

He frowned darkly. Then he understood, and a look

of horrified disbelief came over him. "Are you saying
that *Richard* is Maggie's father?"

Caroline hung her head and nodded.

Ten

Richard was Maggie's father. Nothing Caroline could have told him would have shocked Grady more. The news went through him like a bolt of lightning. He was speechless with surprise, then numb with disbelief. Richard? His no-good, cheating, irresponsible brother was the father of Caroline's child? It was more than he could take in. More than he could accept.

Once his mind had cleared enough to let him respond, he asked the obvious questions. "When were you lovers? I don't remember the two of you so much as dating."

"We didn't, not in the normal sense." She reached for her wine. "I was in San Antonio in college, my senior year," she said, her voice low. "It was finals week. Knowing how crucial it was for me to do well, my mother didn't tell me what'd happened to your parents until after the exams. I felt horrible, sick to my stomach the moment she told me. I was furious with her for not letting me know. I'd always loved your mother. Your father, too." She inhaled deeply.

"You weren't at the funeral, were you?"

"No—because I didn't hear about it in time."

"Then how does Richard play into this?" He realized he sounded irritated; he couldn't help it. Damn it all, he was furious. Exasperated, too. The numbness was wearing off, and in its stead, a slow-burning anger began to build. Once again his brother had found a way to cheat him. Nothing in his life, *nothing,* was untainted by that bastard and his fiascos.

"San Antonio was his first stop after he took the money," Caroline continued.

Grady's eyes narrowed. "So you know about that? The theft?"

She nodded. "Savannah told me," she said. "Years later."

Grady pulled out a chair and sat down. He didn't think his knees would support him much longer.

"It was one of those flukes," Caroline went on. "I was gassing up at a service station and Richard pulled in. He didn't recognize me at first, but I told him how sorry I was about his parents." She looked away and took another steadying breath. "He seemed broken up about it."

"Broken up enough to walk away with the forty thousand dollars that was our inheritance," Grady mumbled.

"We had coffee together and he told me how he'd found your mother's and father's bodies."

"That's a lie!" Grady cried, knotting his fists in outrage. "Frank Hennessey found them and came and told us." How like Richard to seek all the sympathy!

"I know it's a lie now," she whispered, "but at the time I didn't have any reason not to believe him."

Grady vowed to stay quiet, seeing as every time he spoke, it interrupted the story, and this was one he very much wanted to hear.

"He broke into sobs and…and said he hadn't been able to bear the pain and after the funeral had blindly driven off, not knowing where he was going or how he'd gotten to San Antonio. He said he hadn't eaten or slept in days."

"And you believed him?" Grady shouted.

"He'd suffered a terrible loss." She raised her voice. "So, yes, I believed him."

Grady wiped a hand down his face. "I'm sorry, I didn't mean to yell."

"I…I didn't, either."

Despite the apology, he struggled with his temper. "It's something of a shock to learn that the woman I love has slept with my brother."

She didn't respond, but Grady could see that his words had hit their mark. He didn't want to hurt her, but he felt a sick ache in every part of his being, and lashing out was a natural response. Even when he knew he was being cruel and unfair. He hated himself for it, but couldn't seem to hold back.

To Caroline's credit she didn't retaliate or ask him to leave. He admired her restraint and wished his own response had been more generous, more forgiving. In time, perhaps, he could be, but not now. Definitely not now.

After a silence Caroline picked up her story. "He was an emotional mess and I took him home with me. We weren't in the house five minutes when he fell asleep on the sofa. I phoned my home and my mother confirmed that Richard had disappeared the afternoon of the funeral. I…I didn't tell her he was with me. I should have. I realized that too late, but my sympathies were with Richard. He'd received a terrible shock and—"

"No less terrible than what Savannah and I suffered."

"I know, but he was with me and you were here in Promise." She clenched her hands in her lap. "Don't you think I've gone over this a million times since? Don't you think I have my regrets, too?"

He nodded, hating himself for being angry and unable to keep his emotions under control. Every time he thought about Richard being Maggie's father, a fierce kind of outrage gripped him.

"Do...do you want me to continue?"

"Yes," he replied, mentally preparing himself for what was to follow.

"According to Richard, he was overcome with grief, running from his pain and...and he'd found me."

"It was fate, right?" Grady's sarcasm was heavy.

"Yes..."

"He spent the night?"

"Yes." Her voice grew small. "I made up a bed in the living room for him, but in the middle of the night he came into my bedroom and said he needed someone to hold."

"And you let him?"

"Yes."

"I suppose he felt all better in the morning, then?"

"Grady, it wasn't like that."

Her voice grew strong, then defiant. He stared at her, and for a moment almost hated her. But it wasn't possible; he loved her too much. No one else possessed the power to hurt him like this. Loving Caroline and Maggie had brought him such joy, but it made him vulnerable, too. Vulnerable to pain and to anger. Vulnerable to a lot of emotions that were unfamiliar to him. Uncomfortable emotions.

He wasn't sure he wanted to experience them again, not if it made him feel like this.

All at once sitting became intolerable and he jumped to his feet. "Was it rape?"

She took a long time answering. "No. That's not Richard's way. But I was inexperienced and he…he used my naïveté."

It came to Grady, then, what she was telling him. "He seduced you, didn't he?"

"I was young and a virgin. I thought he was the most handsome man in the world. He was hurting—both his parents had died in a tragic accident—and he'd turned to me for comfort. I didn't mean to let him make love to me, but he was so convincing, and before I realized what was happening, he was in bed with me, kissing me, telling me how much he needed me to take away this terrible pain. I tried to tell him I couldn't do that, but he wouldn't listen and then…he climbed on top of me and—"

"How long did he stay at your place?" Grady asked, thinking how desperately he and Savannah had searched for Richard. His sister had been close to a nervous collapse those first few days following the funeral.

"I woke up alone the next morning." She swallowed and wrapped her arms around her waist as if warding off a sudden chill. "He was gone. Without a word, without a note. Gone."

"When did you realize you were pregnant?"

"Six weeks later. I didn't know what to do. I was in denial and then in shock. It was horrible enough knowing I'd slept with a man who didn't care about me, who'd used me for his own purpose. Later, after a doctor confirmed the pregnancy, I had no way of contacting him to let him know."

"Did you think he'd leap up and offer to marry you?" Grady knew he sounded sarcastic but couldn't restrain himself.

"No…but I thought he should know."

Grady said nothing, not wanting to ask the obvious question, and then he found it impossible to keep silent. "Does he know now? Is that why he took Maggie? Because he learned he had a child?"

"No!" she cried. "He knows nothing. I didn't even put his name on the birth certificate."

"Why'd he bring her back, then?"

"How should I know? But I'm grateful, terribly grateful, that he did."

So was Grady.

"Maggie's *my* child," Caroline said with open defiance. "There's none of her father in her."

Grady wanted to believe that. Now that he knew the truth though, it was obvious Maggie was his brother's child. Biologically, at any rate. Maggie had Richard's eyes and his dark hair.

"When he came back, did he try to pick up where you'd left off?" This was another one of those questions it hurt to ask because he feared the answer. And, he saw, another one of those questions that cut Caroline to the quick.

"No," she whispered. "When Richard first returned, I was terrified he'd figure out Maggie was his daughter and try to take her away from me. Don't you remember how I avoided the ranch after he first got home?" Her voice grew tight with remembered anxiety. "In the beginning I invented one excuse after another not to stop by. Every time I was near him I was afraid he'd say something about that night, and then I realized..." She paused, then covered her mouth with one hand and closed her eyes.

Grady's arms ached to hold her, but he remained where he was, steeling himself against her. "Realized what?"

"That...that he didn't even remember. I was just another face, another body. He'd used me the same way he'd used people his whole life. He might have suspected he'd...he'd been to bed with me, but he couldn't be sure, so he kept quiet."

"You're positive about that?"

"With Richard how can anyone be positive about anything? But it was just that one time and it was so long ago. I'm sure there've been a hundred women since."

They were silent for several moments before Grady spoke again. "Does anyone else know?"

She shook her head.

"Savannah?"

"I think she might have guessed, but we've never discussed the subject, and I've never come right out and told her."

"Then what makes you think Savannah's guessed?"

"I saw her look at Maggie once and then at Richard. Later I saw Richard's baby book in the kitchen and I knew she'd been comparing photographs."

So his sister knew, which left Grady to wonder how many other people in Promise suspected. How many others were laughing at him behind his back?

Grady decided it was time to leave. He'd heard everything he could bear to listen to for one evening.

"Thank you for telling me. I know this wasn't easy—and I appreciate your honesty. You needn't worry—your secret is safe with me."

"It wouldn't work, Grady," she said sadly, her eyes full of tears. "I can see that now. It just wouldn't work with you and me."

Then, weighed down by a sadness that seemed to encompass all the grief and despair he'd ever felt, he walked out the door. He had her answer. He loved her, had asked her to be his wife and she'd rejected him. Now he understood why.

"Mommy," Maggie whispered as Caroline lay on the living-room sofa, "are you sick?"

"I'm fine, honey."

"Then how come you're crying?"

"I'm sad, that's all," she said, discounting her pain for her daughter's sake.

"Why are you sad?" Maggie pressed.

"There's a pain deep inside here," she said, flattening her hands over her heart.

"It's not going to bleed, is it?"

"No." Although a physical wound would be easier to endure.

In two days she hadn't heard from Grady, but then, she hadn't expected to. Twice Savannah had phoned, but Caroline had let her answering machine take the calls. She wasn't up to talking, even to her best friend.

"Are you going to bleed?" Maggie asked her again, her small face stiff with fear.

"No, Maggie. What makes you ask?"

The child didn't answer and Caroline slid over on the couch to give her room to sit down. The little girl curled up with her, and Caroline held her tight. It took a long time for the tension to leave Maggie's body. Eventually she drifted off to sleep and that, in Caroline's eyes, was a blessing.

Such a release didn't come for her, but she longed for it. At least when she was asleep, Grady's face wasn't there to haunt her. Awake, though, she couldn't escape the image of his shocked expression when he'd learned the truth.

The accusation, the blame, the disgust. By the time he left, he could barely tolerate being in the same room with her.

Caroline hugged Maggie, and to her amazement soon found herself drifting off. She must have slept because the next thing she knew, Maggie was shaking her shoulder with one hand and holding the portable telephone with the other.

"It's Savannah," she said.

Caroline could see it would be impossible to delay talking to her friend any longer. She sat up and took the receiver. "Hi," she said, still groggy and slightly confused.

"It's Savannah. Are you all right?"

"I'm fine," she lied.

"If that's the case, why haven't you returned my calls?"

"I'm sorry, but I just didn't feel like talking."

Savannah hesitated, then blurted, "Good grief, what's the matter with you two? You sound as miserable as Grady."

Caroline had nothing to add to that.

"I'm coming over," her friend announced.

"Savannah, no! Please." But the line had already

been disconnected and Caroline realized there was no help for it. Savannah Smith was a woman on a mission, and she wouldn't rest until she'd done whatever she could to straighten things out between these two people she loved. Two people who loved each other, according to Savannah. Well, she was right. Caroline did love Grady and was confident he loved her. Just not enough.

Knowing Grady's sister was coming to visit, Caroline washed her face and applied fresh makeup. The last thing she needed was for Savannah to return to the ranch with tales of Caroline pining away for want of Grady—however true that might be. She changed into a fresh shirt and jeans, then ran a comb through her hair.

Savannah arrived less than an hour later, storming into the house like an avenging angel. Caroline was ready with a fresh pitcher of iced tea, waiting for her in the sunny backyard patio. Maggie played contentedly in her sandbox, building castles with imaginary friends.

"All right," Savannah said, the minute they sat down. "What happened?"

"You mean Grady didn't tell you?"

Savannah gave a soft snicker and rolled her eyes. "All he'd say was that what happened is between you and him."

"He's right."

"I can't stand this, Caroline! He asked you to marry him, I know that much."

"He told you?"

"He didn't have to—I saw the diamond. Which means if he has it and you don't, you must've turned him down. But that doesn't make any sense. You love Grady."

Caroline said nothing.

"You *do* love him, don't you?"

"Yes." But that wasn't the issue.

"Then, Caroline, why would you reject him? I don't understand. I know it isn't any of my business, but it hurts me to see two people so obviously in love this unhappy."

Caroline didn't mean to start crying. The tears embarrassed her and she blinked rapidly, praying Savannah wouldn't notice. But of course she did and wasn't about to pretend otherwise.

Leaning forward, Savannah placed her hand on Caroline's arm. "Oh, Caroline, please tell me. I want to help."

"You can't. No one can."

Savannah wasn't so easily dissuaded. "You helped me when Laredo left, don't you remember? When he went back to Oklahoma, I was in so much pain I didn't know if I'd survive it, and you were there for me. It wasn't so much what you said, although I recall every word. It was your love and friendship that helped me through a horrible time. Let me help you now."

Caroline cupped the cold glass of iced tea with both hands. "He did ask me to marry him, and you're right, I refused."

"But why?"

"He…he said he was free to ask me because he was finished dealing with his brother's mistakes. Finished cleaning up after Richard." She inhaled and didn't exhale for several seconds. "I had to tell him. He has a right to know."

"About Maggie?" Savannah asked gently.

As Caroline suspected, Savannah had guessed that Richard was Maggie's father. She nodded.

"But why did you refuse his proposal?"

"I love Grady, but I don't want him to consider Maggie and me a burden. Just one more responsibility he's dealing with because of his brother. Another screwup in a long list."

"Doesn't Grady understand that Richard used you, too?"

"I'm not sure he does," she breathed. "It was too much of a shock."

Savannah sat back in her chair and tapped her finger against her lips. "Well, this certainly explains a great deal."

"Grady would feel I'd broken a confidence by discussing this with you," she felt obliged to remind her friend.

"You needn't worry about that."

"Why not?"

Savannah grinned. "My brother isn't speaking to me at the moment."

"Oh, Savannah."

"Not to worry. He isn't speaking to anyone."

So Grady wasn't taking this any better than she was. "He growls when one of us even dares to mention your name. Oh, and I heard him on the phone the other day. Apparently he was talking to Frank Hennessey because he said—or rather, shouted—that he wanted his bastard of a brother brought to justice."

"I take it there's no word about Richard?"

"None." Savannah shook her head. "It's as if he's vanished off the face of the earth, and at this point I don't really care. Richard deserves what he gets, as far as I'm concerned. Especially after this latest fiasco."

Caroline frowned, not understanding. "What fiasco?"

Savannah sighed. "He didn't tell you, did he?" She didn't wait for a response. "Grady can be too noble for his own good sometimes. Richard charged eight thousand dollars' worth of goods on the family accounts."

"No." Caroline felt sick to her stomach just knowing their brother was capable of something this underhand and cruel. Richard was well aware how long it had taken Grady to regroup after the family lost its money. Money stolen by Richard. Then, just when Grady was financially able to get back on his feet, up popped Richard again. *Up pops the weasel.*

"He paid off every bill with his own money. Laredo and I wanted to share the expenses with him, but Grady refused. Seeing that we're newly married and building a home now, he wouldn't hear of it. Laredo wouldn't leave it at that—he said we're all partners and the money should come out of the business. But Grady said no. I don't have to tell you how stubborn he can be."

"You see?" Caroline said. "For the last six years all Grady's done is work to clean up Richard's messes. I'd just be one more."

"You don't honestly believe that, do you?"

"Yes, Savannah, I do."

"Then you don't know my brother." Savannah smiled slightly. "Give him time. Grady isn't that easily discouraged. He may need a few days to work things out, but he'll be back."

Caroline *wanted* to believe it, but she was afraid to hope.

"He loves you and Maggie. Mark my words, he isn't going to take no for an answer."

Caroline shook her head helplessly. She'd seen the pain in Grady's eyes, seen the shock and grief. She was just one more problem his brother had left behind, and he wanted out.

Caroline didn't blame him.

Eleven

Grady was in one bad mood. He'd been angry and cantankerous all week, to the point that he could barely stand his own company. Wiley said he'd rather chase strays than put up with Grady's foul temper and had left him to finish the repairs on the fence line by himself.

Grady had been doing the backbreaking work all afternoon, and although he'd managed to replace several rotting posts and make other fixes, his mind was a million miles away. Actually only about forty miles away. And while his hands were busy digging fence holes his thoughts were on Caroline.

"Damn it all to hell," he muttered and threw down the shovel. He'd finally finished for the day. Sweat poured from his brow, and his chest heaved from the physical exertion. "Damn it," he said again. He *should* be happy. The sale of the herd was scheduled and his financial problems would soon be over. Beef prices were up slightly. So why *wasn't* he happy? All he could think about was one headstrong woman who was too damn proud for her own good. What in the hell did she mean when she said a marriage between them wouldn't work? Why the hell not?

He could stand there stewing in the hot September sun or he could do something about it, Grady decided. Only he wasn't sure what. He tossed his tools into the back of the pickup, then drove at breakneck speed toward the house.

Savannah was working in her garden when he pulled into the yard. Her head was covered with a wide-brimmed straw hat, and she wore a sleeveless summer dress and an apron. The minute she spotted him she stepped out of the flower garden, a basket of freshly cut roses dangling from her arm.

"Grady?"

"Woman's a damn fool," he said, heading into the house. He took the porch steps two at a time. It didn't surprise him that his sister followed him inside; he would have been disappointed if she hadn't.

"I assume you're talking about Caroline," she said as she set the roses on the kitchen table.

"Is there anyone more stubborn than Caroline Daniels?" He paced the floor of the large kitchen, unable to stand still.

"Only one person I can think of," she said, smiling slightly. "And that's you."

"Me?" Grady considered himself a reasonable man. "Caroline rejected *me*. Not the other way around."

"Did she now?" Savannah removed a vase from the cupboard above the refrigerator. Grady recognized it as one that had belonged to their mother—crystal, sort of a bowl shape. He'd always liked it. Savannah began deftly arranging the roses.

"I asked Caroline to marry me," Grady said impatiently. He'd never intended to tell anyone what had happened, but the events of that evening burned inside him. It was either tell Savannah or scream it from the rooftop.

"So I understand," she murmured.

Grady had had it with women and their subtle messages. While he might normally have appreciated Savannah's reserved manner, it infuriated him just now.

"What exactly do you understand?" he demanded.

"Two hurting people, if you must know. Two people deeply in love with each other, neither one fully appreciating or—"

"She said no," he cut in. "She wasn't interested in being my wife—said it wouldn't work. Said it twice, as a matter of fact."

"Did she now?"

Grady slapped his hat against the edge of the counter. "If you have something to say, Savannah, just spit it out."

"Well, since you asked…" She gave him a demure smile. "It seems to me—and of course I could be wrong—that Caroline might have said no, but that wasn't exactly what she meant."

"I'm a simple rancher. If she said no and meant something else, then she should've come right out and *said* what she meant. I'm not a mind reader."

"Neither am I," Savannah stated. "But really, how else did you expect her to respond?"

"A yes would have sufficed."

"And what was she supposed to do then? Wait until your wedding day to casually mention that her child is also your niece?"

"No. It doesn't matter who fathered Maggie. I'm offering to be her daddy, to make her my own."

"Exactly!" Savannah rewarded him with a wide grin. "Bingo, big brother! Now collect your prize."

The woman was speaking in ridiculous riddles. "Damn it, Savannah, what do you mean by that?"

"You should be able to figure it out."

He frowned.

Savannah sighed loudly. "I believe what you said was, *It doesn't matter who fathered Maggie.* Now tell me, why is that?"

"Why?"

"Yes, why?" she repeated.

"Because I'm asking to be her father."

The smile was back in full force. "Very good, Grady."

His frown deepened.

"You're almost there, big brother." She added a long-stemmed yellow rose to the vase.

"Almost? I've been there and back a thousand times in my mind. Why do I have to fall in love with the most stubborn woman in the entire state of Texas? What did I ever do to deserve this?"

"I don't know, but if I were you, I'd thank God every day of your life for a woman as wonderful as Caroline."

He stared at her.

"*If* you're lucky enough to convince her to be your wife, that is," Savannah said.

"As far as I'm concerned she has to come to me now." A man's pride could only take so much, and Caroline had run roughshod over it one time too many.

Savannah shook her head. "Wrong."

"Wrong?" Grady didn't see it like that, but he was desperate enough to listen to his sister's crazy reasoning.

"You were doing so well there, too," she said with

another sigh. "Grady, I've never known you to be a man who took no for an answer. It's just not like you to roll over and play dead."

"I'm not playing dead!"

"You're just acting that way?" She made the statement a question, which irritated him even more.

"Either you don't love Caroline as much as I believe, or—"

"I love her and I love Maggie, too. When Maggie was missing, it felt as if a part of me was gone. When I saw she was safe and sound, I damn near broke into tears myself."

Savannah, ever patient, ever kind, beamed him a dazzling smile. "I'm not the one who needs to hear this, you know."

"So you're telling me I should ask Caroline again." Even as he spoke, he was shaking his head. "Not in this lifetime." In his view, it was Caroline's turn to risk her pride. If she wanted to change her mind, she could let him know. He grabbed his hat and walked out the back door.

"Where are you going?" his sister asked.

Until that moment he hadn't been sure, then in a flash he knew. "I'm going to give Caroline a chance to change her mind."

Edwina and Lily Moorhouse had just stepped up to the counter when the door to the post office flew open and Grady Weston stepped inside.

The two elderly women turned to look at him; so did Caroline. He was staring straight at her, and she could tell he was breathing fire.

"Caroline—"

She instantly returned her attention to the Moorhouse sisters. "Can I help you?" she asked ever so sweetly, ignoring Grady. Her heart was pounding like a frightened kitten's, but she refused, *refused,* to allow Grady to intimidate her.

"You can talk to the Moorhouse sisters until Kingdom come, and it isn't going to help. Eventually you're going to have to speak to me, too."

Edwina's eyes rounded as she glanced at her sister. "It's Grady Weston again."

"I have eyes in my head, sister. I can see it's Grady."

"Fit to be tied, from the looks of him."

"Indeed."

Despite the way her heart raced, Caroline found herself smiling.

"I do think he's constipated again, sister."

Lily studied him, tapping her foot. "Prunes, young man, eat prunes. They'll do wonders for your disposition."

Grady scowled at her, but Caroline knew it would take a lot more than that to intimidate the retired schoolteacher.

"Listen here, Grady Weston, I wiped your nose in third grade, so don't you be giving me dirty looks. My, oh my, but you always were a headstrong boy."

It was clear Grady wasn't going to be drawn into a verbal exchange with the two women.

"In some ways," Lily mused, "your stubbornness was a characteristic I admired."

Edwina slapped a ten-dollar bill onto the counter. "We'd like a book of stamps, Caroline."

"Of course." Caroline handed her the stamps with her change.

"Good day."

"Good day," Caroline replied, watching them leave.

"Good day, young man," Edwina said as she passed Grady and winked.

Caroline wasn't sure what to make of the wink. If Grady noticed it, he didn't let on.

He touched the brim of his hat and stepped around the two women in his rush to reach the counter.

"Can I help you?" Caroline asked, lowering her gaze for fear of what he might read in her eyes.

"As a matter of fact you can." Grady's voice echoed in the room.

She waited, figuring he wasn't going to ask for stamps.

"I'm here to talk some sense into you."

"Grady, listen—"

"Hear me out first. The last time we spoke I asked you to marry me and you turned me down."

Caroline doubted he'd ever fully comprehend how difficult it had been to reject him. She'd wanted to say yes more than anything she'd ever wanted in her life. But no self-respecting woman willingly entered a marriage if she believed she'd be a burden to her husband. Even loving him the way she did, she couldn't do that to him. Couldn't do it to herself.

"Be warned," he said, lowering his voice.

"Warned?"

"This time I'm not taking no for an answer."

"Grady, please…" He made this so damned hard.

"Sorry, it's too late for that. I don't want anyone but you."

She looked away rather than meet his gaze.

"For the past six years I've worked day and night

and done without—just so I could make up for what we lost because of Richard. He's stolen six years of my life, Caroline. He's robbed me and Savannah of too much already, and I'll be damned if I'll let him rob me of anything else."

"I...I don't understand."

"If you allow Richard to stand between us now, it'll be one more thing my brother's taken from me. But this time I'm not the only person he's hurting. He's hurting you and Maggie, as well. Is that what you want?"

"No." Her voice sounded weak, unconvincing.

"You appear to have doubts."

"I... There's more than just me to consider," she said.

"Okay, let's talk about Maggie."

Slowly Caroline raised her eyes to his. Her daughter had to come first. Always. "What about Maggie?"

"I love her, too." It was the first time Grady had mentioned his feelings for her child, the first time he'd said this. "I'm looking to be more than your husband, Caroline. I'm looking to be Maggie's daddy."

She bit her lower lip.

"My brother might have fathered this child, but I'll be the one to raise her, to love her, to kiss her skinned knee. I'll put her to bed at night, sit with her when she learns to read, teach her how to ride Moonbeam. Me, not Richard."

It was a long speech for Grady, and every word was heartfelt. Caroline knew that in her bones, sensed it deep inside. They were the words of a man who understood that fatherhood was more than biological. Much more.

"Oh, Grady..."

"Is that all you have to say?"

"I—"

The door opened and Nell Bishop walked in with Jeremy and Emma. "Hello," she said with a cheerful wave as she headed for her post-office box.

"Hello, Mr. Weston."

"Howdy, Jeremy."

"We're going swimming in the pool," Emma announced.

Nell sorted through her mail. "Come on, you two," she said and steered her children toward the door. She paused to look back at Grady and Caroline. "Everything all right?" she asked cautiously.

"Yes," Grady barked.

Caroline nodded.

Nell, who'd been married to a man as stubborn and lovable as the one standing there in front of her, smiled. "Yes, I can see that everything is coming along nicely." Then she and her children left.

"What'd she mean by that?" Grady demanded.

Caroline shrugged. "You'll have to ask her."

"Well?"

The gruff question caught her by surprise. "Well, what?"

"Are you going to change your mind about marrying me or not?"

"I—"

"You're a fool if you turn me down."

"Honestly, Grady—"

"You aren't likely to get a better offer."

This last comment irked her no end. "What makes you so sure?" she snapped. "Look, Grady," she began before he could answer, "let me ask you a question. Do you love me?"

"You know I do."

"You might have said so."

"I did," he insisted.

"When?"

"The first time I proposed."

"Oh." Well, that *was* true. But everything hinged on how *much* he loved her. "I'm afraid we'd be a burden to you."

"How?"

Caroline swallowed. "Every time you look at Maggie—and me—you'll be reminded of Richard. That's what I'm afraid of. We'd be just another problem Richard left for you to fix."

"That's not the way I see it, Caroline. I told you, remember? I won't let Richard take another thing away from me. And you know what? For the first time in his life, my brother has given me something wonderful. He's hurt me, true, but he's also blessed me—in you. In Maggie."

"But—"

"Obviously the question is, do *you* love *me?*" he said. "You seem to be the one having trouble making up your mind."

"I love you so damn much," she confessed.

No sooner had the words left her lips than Grady reached across the counter for her. Their positions, the obstacle between them, made the kiss awkward. It hardly mattered. They'd kissed countless times by now, but no kiss had ever meant this much.

It was a meeting of their hearts.

His mouth was warm and urgent against hers.

"We're getting married," he whispered.

"Yes," she whispered back. She whimpered when he

deepened the kiss, then wrapped her arms around his neck and invited the exploration of his tongue.

The sound of someone entering the post office broke them apart. Caroline looked up guiltily, feeling a little shy.

Dovie Boyd stood in the foyer. She nodded toward them. "Hello, Grady. Caroline."

"Hi, Dovie," Caroline said, grateful Dovie wasn't a gossip. She shuddered to think of the consequences if someone like Louise or Tammy Lee had happened upon them in each other's arms.

"You're the first to hear our good news," Grady said, taking Caroline's hand. He grasped it firmly in his own, then raised it to his lips. "Caroline has agreed to be my wife."

Dovie's eyes grew wide. "Congratulations! I couldn't be happier." She opened her purse and took out a linen handkerchief. "I really...couldn't...be...happier," she said, sniffling and dabbing at her eyes. "You're a wonderful couple and...and I think it's just wonderful, really I do." She turned abruptly and walked out, apparently forgetting what had brought her to the post office in the first place.

Grady, Caroline and Maggie sat on the front-porch swing. "Will I call you daddy?" Maggie asked Grady.

"Of course. If you want to."

She nodded. "Then I'll have a daddy."

"Yes, princess, you'll have a daddy."

"And Mommy will have a husband."

"And Grady'll have a family." He tucked his arm around Caroline's shoulder, loving her so much.

"Us," Maggie said and tossed her arms in the air. "Your family is us."

"What do you think of that?" Caroline asked her daughter.

Maggie considered the question a moment, looked up at Grady and slowly grinned. "You don't do magic tricks," she said, "but I like you better 'cause you love me and Mommy."

"That," Grady said, "is very true. You're both very easy to love."

"I'm glad you think so," Caroline whispered and leaned her head against his shoulder, utterly content.

* * * * *

DR. TEXAS

One

Texas is the only state big enough to hold your dreams. Someone had told Dr. Jane Dickinson that when she signed up for this gig. But whoever it was obviously hadn't lived in Promise.

With medical-school bills the size of the national debt, signing a three-year agreement to practice medicine in the Texas Hill Country in exchange for partial payment had seemed the perfect solution. Whatever romanticizing she'd done when she'd first thought about making the move from urban California to the heart of rural America had faded with the reality of her situation. Texas had bugs practically as big as pit bulls and she'd always been somewhat phobic about insects, whether they were of the crawling or flying variety. More serious, more disturbing, was the fact that she simply didn't fit in with this community. People were never less than polite, but they hadn't accepted her. They came to her as a last resort—if they couldn't cure whatever ailed them on their own—and then complained because she wasn't Doc Cummings. Being fresh out of medical school, female and a good fifty years younger than the beloved practitioner hadn't helped, either.

But although Jane was lonely and often at loose ends, she felt that she'd begun to make strides. Becoming friends with Dovie Boyd had a lot to do with that. The older woman owned an antique shop with the small Victorian Tea Room tucked in one corner, and she'd generously offered Jane not only friendship but advice. Life had taken a decided turn for the better since that first morning Jane had spoken to Dovie.

Her last scheduled patient for the day had left, and so had Jenny Bender, her receptionist. Jane sat at her desk, leaning comfortably back in her chair. The makeup she'd applied that morning had long since dissolved in sweat, and her feet ached. It'd been a busy day, which was a good sign. It meant that more people of Promise were coming to trust her skills.

Ellie Patterson was due to return from her honeymoon this week, too. Her second new friend was a local businesswoman. They'd recently met, thanks to Dovie. Jane liked Ellie's no-nonsense approach to life, her quick wit and down-to-earth attitude. After having lunch together, Jane could tell they had the potential to become good friends. She hoped that was the case, because at this point she needed all the friends she could get.

A distinct noise in the outer office cut into her thoughts, and Jane stood up to investigate.

"Is someone here?" she called, walking out of her office.

Nothing.

"Hello," she tried again, wondering if she was beginning to hear things.

"Dr. Jane?" A child's voice came from the waiting room.

Jane found six-year-old Maggie Daniels standing just inside the clinic door. "Oh, hi, Maggie."

The little girl's pigtails fell forward as she lowered her head. "Hello."

Maggie's mother was Promise's postmistress, and the post office was next door to the health clinic. She'd talked to Caroline Daniels a number of times and had heard just a day or two ago that Caroline and a local cattle rancher, Grady Weston, were now engaged.

"Where's your mother?" Jane asked. It was unusual for Maggie to come to the clinic by herself.

"At work," she answered, still keeping her head lowered. Her arms were wrapped protectively around her stomach.

Jane knelt down in front of her. "Are you feeling all right, Maggie?"

The little girl shook her head.

"Where do you feel sick?"

"My tummy."

Jane brushed the hair from the child's forehead and checked for fever. Maggie's skin was cool to the touch. "Does your mommy know you're here?"

Maggie's head flew up, her eyes wide with alarm. "No! Please don't tell her, okay?"

"But if she doesn't know where you are, she might worry."

"She said I could play while she finished work. Mrs. Murphy had to drop me off early today 'cause she had a dentist appointment."

Jane assumed Mrs. Murphy baby-sat Maggie after school.

"Is something at school bothering you?" Jane guessed, thinking this stomachache might be linked to an incident there. School had been in session a little more than two weeks. That Maggie didn't want her mother to know where she was aroused Jane's suspicions. Perhaps Maggie had gotten into trouble with her teacher and was worried about what would happen when her mother found out. Either that, or she suffered doubts or fears regarding her mother's recent engagement.

"I like school," Maggie said, and her face brightened. "I'm in first grade this year."

"But you're not feeling well?"

The little girl shook her head, sending her pigtails swaying. "My tummy hurts."

"Okay," Jane said. "Maybe we'd better have a look." She held out her hand to Maggie, who slipped her own small one into Jane's.

"You won't tell Mommy?" Maggie pleaded again.

"Not if you don't want me to," Jane said, although she wondered if it was wise to make such a promise. But it was clear the child was deeply upset about something. While Jane didn't have a lot of training in pediatrics, she suspected that if she hadn't reassured Maggie, the child would have bolted.

Playing the situation by ear, Jane led Maggie into the examination room and lifted her easily onto the table.

"Take off your backpack and I'll listen to your tummy," Jane instructed, picking up her stethoscope.

Slowly and with obvious reluctance Maggie did as she was asked, but when Jane went to move the backpack off the table, Maggie grabbed it back and clung to it. Jane realized immediately that whatever bothered the child was in that backpack.

"Is there something important in your bag?" Jane asked casually.

Maggie nodded. She tucked her chin tight against her chest. Finally, hesitantly, Maggie opened the zipper. Twice she paused and glanced up at Jane as if questioning the wisdom of continuing.

Jane allowed the girl to make the decision on her own. Apparently Maggie had decided to trust her, because once she had the bag completely open, she withdrew an old dilapidated-looking doll. It was either a replica of an antique or the genuine thing, although that didn't seem likely. Either way, the doll had seen better days. It was falling apart. The face appeared handstitched, the once red lips faded to a pale pink. The muslin dress had probably been white but was now a washed-out shade of yellow. The dull calico apron had frayed edges. Despite its condition, the doll had a certain appeal. At one time it must have been the muchloved toy of some young girl.

"I want you to keep it," Maggie said in a small tense voice as she held out the doll.

"But I couldn't do that," Jane protested.

"Please..." Big tears welled in Maggie's dark eyes. "I took it..." She clutched her stomach with both arms. "I'm sorry for taking her away from—" She stopped and her lower lip started to wobble, but she quickly pulled her emotions together.

"Can't you take it back to the person it belongs to?" Jane asked.

Maggie shook her head vigorously, the pigtails whipping about her face.

Jane frowned. "So you want me to keep her for you?"

Maggie nodded.

Perhaps that was the best solution. Again Jane followed her instincts, which told her that pressing Maggie to tell her anything more was a mistake. The little girl clearly regretted having taken the doll and wasn't sure how to handle the situation now.

"All right. I'll do that." She could display the old doll in her office in the hope that whoever owned it would come to her and ask. That would save Maggie the embarrassment of having to return it.

"I promise to take good care of your friend," Jane said solemnly. She helped Maggie down from the table. "Come on, let's find a new home for your doll." Perhaps later Jane could make a few discreet inquiries. Dovie might know something or have a suggestion, since she owned an antique shop—although the older woman seemed unusually distracted at the moment. Jane assumed it had something to do with Frank Hennessey, the local sheriff, who'd been Dovie's longtime male friend. Apparently they'd had some kind of argument and were no longer seeing each other.

Maggie slipped her hand into Jane's as they walked into the small office once occupied by Doc Cummings. The most logical place to set the doll was on the bookshelf, which looked out into the hallway. Anyone passing by was sure to see it.

Carefully Jane put the toy on the top shelf. "Okay," she said and took a step back. "What do you think?"

The youngster smiled and released a great sigh. "My tummy doesn't hurt anymore."

"That's wonderful." A miracle cure, Jane mused; she must be a better doctor than she'd imagined. "If you want to come and visit your friend, you're welcome to do that anytime," Jane told her.

Maggie shook her head, then whirled around. "Mommy's calling," she said. Racing down the hallway, she grabbed her backpack from the examination table and flew toward the waiting room. She paused abruptly and looked back. "Thank you, Dr. Jane."

"You're welcome," Jane said with a smile.

Then Maggie disappeared out the door.

If only dealing with her other patients was this easy.

Dovie Boyd was miserable. She wandered between the lush rows of her garden, picking ripe tomatoes from her heavily laden plants. Her only consolation was that Frank Hennessey probably felt even worse than she did. For ten years they'd been friends. More than friends. During those years they'd talked frequently of marriage—with Dovie generally bringing up the subject. Frank had been a bachelor all his life; Dovie understood that marriage would be a big change for him and had been patient. No, she thought now, she'd been stupid. Although she loved Frank, she'd never been completely comfortable with their arrangement. He knew that, which must be why he'd made promises he didn't intend to keep. When she pressured him about it after Ellie Frasier and Glen Patterson's wedding, he owned up to the fact that he simply couldn't marry her. He loved her, he claimed, but he wasn't the marrying kind. He just couldn't do it.

The truth had been painful, but she'd lived long enough to recognize something else. Either she accepted Frank and their relationship the way it was or she broke it off.

She broke it off. Not that it was an easy decision. She missed him. Missed their afternoon chats over coffee, missed their romantic dinners and sitting on the porch gazing at the stars, sipping a nice glass of East Texas wine. She missed cuddling up with him at night, too. For the better part of nine years Frank had spent two nights a week with her.

Her twenty-five-year marriage to Marvin had been a good one, although to her regret they'd remained childless. She'd loved her husband and grieved deeply for him when he died.

That was thirteen years ago. She'd still been young enough then to want a man in her life—was young enough still! Frank had courted her for two years before they'd become lovers. She would never have believed she'd allow a man into her bed without the benefit of a wedding band. But she had, trusting with all her heart that Frank would one day marry her. In retrospect she wondered how she could have let the arrangement continue this long.

In other years Dovie would pick two or three large green tomatoes for Frank; this year she left them to ripen on the vine. There wouldn't be any fried green tomatoes for Frank Hennessey. The thought saddened her, reminding her that there was a gap in her life, that she'd lost an important person. But this break, no matter how painful, was necessary, she told herself.

Just then Frank's patrol car rounded the corner and Dovie's heart accelerated. Although tempted, she looked away, pretending not to notice.

"Hello, Dovie," he called softly.

She glanced in his direction. He'd come to a stop and rolled down the car window.

"How are you?" he asked in that sweet seductive

way he had. He'd always used that tone when he wanted Dovie to know how much he loved her.

Slowly she turned to look at him. "Very well. Thank you for asking," she said, then continued down the row, picking tomatoes. No sooner had the words left her lips when she heard his car door slam. It demanded an effort of will not to get up and move toward him. She fought a desperate urge to stare at him, to indulge her heart and her eyes. Frank was a fine-looking man even now as he neared retirement age. He'd maintained a trim physique and most people wouldn't guess he was sixty.

"Seems your garden has a lot of tomatoes this year," he commented. He remained on the sidewalk, following her from the opposite side of the picket fence.

"Seems that way," she said after a moment, wondering at the wisdom of allowing this conversation. All it did was remind her how unhappy she was without Frank, how much she missed him. From the glances he sent her, she knew he missed her, too. She also knew he was trying to wear down her resolve.

"How've you been?" Frank pressed when she didn't elaborate on the abundance of her garden.

"Wonderful." She prayed God would forgive her the lie.

"I'm afraid I can't say the same. I miss you, Dovie. Nothing seems right without you."

Nothing seemed right for her, either, but she wasn't about to admit it. What made this breakup so difficult was that she loved Frank. Despite that, she couldn't go on with their arrangement. It wasn't the life she wanted. She craved what most women of her generation did— and maybe most women, period. Commitment, emotional security, an open acknowledgment of love.

"I miss you, sweetheart," he said again in a soft sad voice.

"Then marry me, Frank."

His eyes narrowed. "We've been through this a hundred times. Dovie, you know how I feel about you. I'd give my life for you. You're the best thing that's ever happened to me. If I were to marry anyone, it'd be you, but I *can't,* Dovie, I just can't."

It hurt to hear the words, but she was glad he'd said them because this forced her to remember that nothing would ever change between them.

"I love you, Dovie! I'm doing my damnedest to understand why everything's different and all because I told you the truth. None of this would've happened if I hadn't admitted I couldn't go through with marriage."

"We've already said everything that needs to be said," she told him, shifting the weight of the basket from one arm to the other.

"Let me help you with that," Frank offered. "That's much too heavy for you."

He was halfway to the gate before she stopped him. "I can manage on my own."

He gripped two pickets so tightly that his knuckles whitened. His blue eyes implored her. "Dovie, please."

Already she could feel herself weakening, and she forced herself to be strong. It'd been less than two weeks. Sooner or later Frank would understand. This wasn't a game, or an ultimatum or an attempt to manipulate him. They just saw things differently; it was as simple as that. He'd made his decision and she'd made hers. He would simply have to accept that she wasn't giving in or changing her mind.

"I need to go inside. Good seeing you again, Frank.

I hope you have a pleasant evening." Then she headed toward the house and didn't look back.

After setting the tomatoes by the sink, Dovie reached for her phone and punched in her best friend's number.

Mary Patterson operated the local bed-and-breakfast with her husband, Phil, and the couple had been friends of Dovie's for years. Although Dovie was well aware that others knew of her arrangement with Frank, the only person she'd actually confided in was Mary.

"Frank was just here," Dovie announced when Mary answered the phone. Her hand clenched the receiver and she closed her eyes, distressed by the brief confrontation. It had left her feeling weak and light-headed.

"What did he say?" Mary asked.

"That he misses me and wishes things could go back the way they were before."

"You refused to listen, right?"

"Right," Dovie answered.

"Good!" Mary said with conviction. "That's exactly what you *should* do."

Her support was something Dovie badly needed just then. "He said he's miserable."

"As well he ought to be!"

"I am, too, but I suppose I'm more determined than I am miserable."

"Oh, Dovie." Mary's voice was full of sympathy. "I know how hard this is on you. But Frank's strung you along all these years, promising to marry you, and then he decides he can't go through with it. You should sue him for breach of promise."

"I wouldn't do that."

"I know."

"It's just that I feel so alone," Dovie confessed. "In some ways this is as difficult as when Marvin died."

"This *is* a death," Mary said compassionately. "The death of a relationship."

Her friend was right, Dovie realized sadly. She'd been able to bury her husband, lay him and their lives together to rest. She'd taken the time she needed to heal, the time she'd needed to grieve, and then when the worst of the pain was over, she'd opened her antique shop. Starting the business had helped her get through the first lonely year. What she needed now, Dovie decided, was a diversion, something that would see her through the long difficult weeks ahead.

"I'm thinking of traveling," Dovie announced, although the thought had only just come to her.

"Traveling?" Mary echoed. "Where?"

"I'm not sure—possibly Europe. I've heard about the wonderful antiques you can get there. I'll make it a buying trip," she said, warming to the idea. Not only would it be her first trip abroad, she'd be able to write it off as a tax deduction.

"When?" Mary asked.

"I…I'm not sure yet, but I'll talk to Gayla Perkins at Adventure Travel in the morning."

"Dovie…" For the first time Mary hesitated. "This sounds drastic."

"I need to do *something* different," Dovie said. "Otherwise I'm afraid I'll give in to Frank."

"Will you travel alone?" Mary asked.

Dovie hadn't gotten that far in her planning. "It looks like I'll have to."

"Take a cruise, then," Mary advised.

"A cruise?" Dovie hadn't thought of that. "I don't know..."

"You might meet someone." Mary's voice rose with enthusiasm. "They have short ones, three and four days. I understand the prices are reasonable and there's plenty of single men."

Dovie didn't want any other man in her life.

"A cruise would be perfect for you," Mary went on. "I read not long ago about certain cruises that specialize in matching up singles. That'd be ideal."

"Oh, Mary, I don't know..."

"What's not to know? You want to travel, and if that's the case, then do it in style."

"A cruise," Dovie said slowly, letting the idea grow more familiar.

"Not just an ordinary cruise," Mary corrected, "but a short one especially for singles. Can you imagine how Frank's going to feel when he hears about that?"

Dovie figured she had no business caring about Frank's feelings one way or the other, but she did. A dozen times a day she had to remind herself that Frank Hennessey was no longer part of her life. They were no longer a couple. She had her own life to live, and the time had come for her to explore other possibilities. Yes, a singles' cruise could be just the thing.

"I'll do it," Dovie said. "First thing tomorrow. I'll call Adventure Travel."

"You won't be sorry," her friend assured her.

Dovie had a strong feeling Mary was right.

The alarm woke Cal Patterson at the usual hour. He rolled out of bed and stretched his arms high above his head, yawning loudly. On his way into the bathroom, he caught his reflection in the mirror and stopped to stare at himself. Hmm. Not much to look at. He wondered at this sudden need to examine his features. Probably had to do with Glen and Ellie getting married, he decided.

He'd grown pensive since the wedding. He'd found himself entertaining a number of intriguing notions after Ellie and his brother had left on their honeymoon. Like the fact that he missed Glen. Really missed him.

Glen. Married.

Even after the wedding, it still didn't seem possible. They were brothers and partners in the Lonesome Coyote Ranch. Both had been born here, and as far as Cal was concerned he'd die here, too. The ranch was his life, his blood, his soul.

Glen was like him, a rancher at heart. Their ancestors had settled in Texas a century and a half before, and the family had been ranching one spread or another ever since. When the time was right, Cal suspected Glen would buy his own ranch, one closer to town since Ellie would need to travel in every day.

Cal had finished dressing when he heard a door close downstairs.

"Don't tell me you're still sleeping?" a voice called up. "What the hell kind of ranch are you running here?"

Glen? His brother was supposed to be on his honeymoon! Cal started down the stairs. "What are you doing here?" Cal shouted.

"I go away for a few days and this whole place goes to hell in a handbasket."

Cal reached the bottom of the stairs, and the two brothers stared at each other. It'd barely been ten days since the wedding and yet it felt as if they'd been apart for ten years. They hugged with the fierce love of brothers who were also close friends.

"How was the Gulf?" Cal asked, breaking away and moving toward the kitchen to make a pot of coffee.

"Terrific," Glen said, "although Ellie and I didn't get outside much."

Cal hadn't expected that they would, seeing as this was their honeymoon. "I didn't think you were due back for a couple of days yet."

"We weren't, but you know Ellie. She was worried about the feed store."

"And you were worried about the ranch."

Glen rubbed the side of his jaw. "Not...worried, exactly."

The two laughed and Cal grabbed a couple of mugs. "So, is married life everything you hoped for?"

"More," Glen said wistfully. "I knew I loved Ellie," he continued, his voice thoughtful, "but I didn't realize exactly how much until this past week. I feel like I'm the luckiest man alive. Hey, Cal? You might want to think about making the leap one day yourself."

Cal let the comment slide and poured them each a cup of coffee. He handed one to his brother. "Ellie is special," he said.

Glen sugared his coffee, and they talked business for the next forty minutes, then headed to the barn for the start of their day.

By the afternoon it was difficult for Cal to remember that Glen had ever been away. They'd worked together for so many years they didn't require words to communicate. As soon as they'd finished delousing the calves, Glen made a beeline for the barn and his favorite gelding, Moonshine. He groomed the big bay, then washed up. "I'll see you in the morning," he said on his way out of the barn.

Cal grinned to himself at his brother's eagerness to hurry home to his bride. "Sure thing," he said, waving him off. Although Glen had spent most of his free time with Ellie before they got married, she'd often driven out to the ranch. Cal had enjoyed watching their exchanges, and he'd especially relished being the beneficiary of Ellie's delicious homemade dinners. She'd taken a few cooking lessons from Dovie, mostly in preparing basic meals, the kind Cal liked. Well, she could practice on him as often as she wanted. He wasn't much of a cook himself, but managed to fry up a decent steak every so often.

"Damn, I almost forgot," Glen said halfway out the barn door. "Ellie wanted me to ask if you had plans Friday night."

"Plans?"

"For dinner," Glen answered as if that should be obvious.

"I don't have anything special going," he said. Already his mind was full of the meals she'd served in the weeks leading up to the wedding. Memories of her roast chicken and garlic mashed potatoes made his mouth water. "If she's thinking of inviting me over, you tell her I accept."

Glen looked surprised. "You sure about this?"

"Why shouldn't I be?"

"Well…" Glen's mouth widened in a grin and he slowly shook his head. "No reason. I'll tell Ellie to count on you for Friday night."

"You do that."

Cal walked his brother out. He stood there for a moment, watching the dust plume as Glen's truck barreled out of the yard and down the long driveway. Not for the first time in the past ten days Cal wondered what his own life would be like now if he'd married Jennifer Healy.

Two years earlier Cal had been engaged. But less than forty-eight hours before the wedding Jennifer had changed her mind and abruptly left town. She'd given him no explanation.

But Cal knew why she'd done it. She'd wanted him to be something he never could.

He'd loved her, or had convinced himself he did. But she'd had other plans for him, plans she didn't divulge until the wedding arrangements were made. Jennifer seemed to believe that once they were husband and wife, she'd be able to convince him to sell his half of the ranch to Glen. Her scheme included moving him to San Antonio or Houston. Even now, two years later, Cal couldn't imagine himself living in big-city America. It shocked him that a woman he loved, the woman he'd intended to marry, didn't understand that a city the size of Houston would slowly kill him. He was a country boy, through and through.

When he'd adamantly refused to give in to her demands, Jennifer had walked out, leaving him to deal with the embarrassment of canceling the wedding at the last minute. And yet—perhaps it was ego, he didn't know—he had the distinct feeling that if he'd asked, she might have stayed.

But he hadn't asked, hadn't believed the relationship was worth saving. Her preference for leaving the ranch, leaving Promise, would have always been an issue between them. She would have held his decision against him and they'd have argued about it again and again. So he'd let her go. He realized in that moment that he'd given his heart to a woman who would have abused his love.

After Jennifer left, his attitude toward women had undergone a swift change. He found them untrustworthy and deceptive. Glen and others had tried to convince him that not all women were like Jennifer. Deep down Cal believed that, but he wasn't willing to give anyone that kind of power over him a second time. He'd learned his lesson well.

His new sister-in-law was an exception. He'd always been fond of Ellie and was understandably proud that he was the one to figure out how Glen and Ellie felt about each other long before either of them had a clue. Actually, considering how anti-romance he'd become, that was little short of amazing.

Ellie was a sweetheart and Glen was a lucky man. His sister-in-law was an idealist, though. She firmly believed in the power of love. While that might prove true for others, it hadn't for him.

Cal never intended to marry. He was thirty-six and set in his ways. His life was full and he didn't have room in it for a relationship; he'd made damn sure of that. Whenever he was tempted to let his guard down and fraternize with the enemy, something would happen to remind him that women weren't to be trusted.

Given time, he thought cynically, ninety-nine percent of the female population would turn on a man. He'd seen it happen. Well, maybe not in Promise—not often, anyway. He could actually think of a few success stories. Glen, of course. His parents. Savannah Weston and Laredo Smith. And now his best friend,

Grady Weston, was engaged to Caroline Daniels; he supposed their marriage stood a chance if anyone's did. But he was still convinced he was right. Anyway, Texas men weren't prone to "sharing their pain." You wouldn't find a cowboy crying his eyes out on some talk show about a woman who'd done him wrong. In Texas men sat around and drowned their sorrows in beer. If they mentioned their troubles, it was in words no television channel could air. And ten to one, if a man had problems, there was a woman involved.

Cal headed back to the house. He'd grab something easy for dinner and then tackle some paperwork. Come Friday, Ellie would be cooking up something memorable.

He paused in his tracks as he recalled that sly smile of Glen's when he'd asked about Ellie's cooking.

Then it hit him like the proverbial bolt of lightning. Ellie had invited him all right, but no one had said anything about her doing any cooking. His brand-new sister-in-law intended to set him up with one of her girlfriends. She was fixing to play matchmaker.

It'd be a cold day in hell before Cal would sit still for that.

Two

Jane was astounded—and delighted. Only two days home from her honeymoon, and Ellie Frasier Patterson had already dropped in to visit her. Jane was between patient appointments, so she and Ellie spent a few minutes catching up on news. Then Ellie announced that Jane would be joining her and Glen for dinner that Friday night.

"But—"

"You don't have an option here," Ellie said with a grin. "You need a Texas education and you're going to get it."

Jane took half a second to think it over. "I'll be there." She'd asked for help. Why turn it down when it was offered?

"Be at the Chili Pepper at seven Friday night," Ellie instructed on her way out the door.

Jane made a note in her weekly planner, then sat back in her chair with a triumphant smile. Finally, after spending six months in this town, she was making progress. This would be her first night out with people her own age, and she looked forward to it.

On Friday night she arrived at the restaurant precisely at seven. The place was packed. She glanced around and then saw Ellie wave her arm to get her attention. Ellie, her husband, Glen, and a man Jane recognized as Glen's brother were sitting in a booth in a far corner. Jane waved back and wove her way between the tables toward them.

"Hello," she said, raising her voice to be heard above the country-and-western tunes blaring from the jukebox.

"You remember Glen," Ellie said indicating the man sitting next to her. "And my brother-in-law, Cal."

"It's good to see you both again," Jane said, smiling brightly.

The rancher stood—reluctantly, Jane thought—to allow her to slide into the booth next to the wall, opposite Ellie. It concerned her a little that Ellie hadn't said anything about this being a double date; Jane wondered if Ellie's brother-in-law had been kept equally in the dark. Probably, or he wouldn't be here. She'd seen him around before, and although she hadn't known his name until now, she thought Cal Patterson was one of the rudest unfriendliest men she'd ever *not* met.

He was good-looking, or could be if he bothered to smile. Tall and lean, he had that rough-and-tumble cowboy appeal.

One glance from Cal gave her the answer she'd suspected. He, too, had been duped, but judging by his fierce scowl, he thought she was in cahoots with Ellie.

Jane's high hopes for the evening died a sudden and painful death.

"I'm so glad you could make it," Ellie said and

handed Jane a menu. Cal sat next to her as stiff as new rope and about as welcoming.

The waitress brought over a pitcher of beer and four mugs. Willie Nelson's plaintive voice rolled from the jukebox just then, and Jane's mouth gaped in astonishment as the entire restaurant began to sing along with him. She would've joined them had she known the words.

"If you're going to live in Texas you gotta love Willie Nelson," Ellie informed her when the tune was finished.

"Not just Willie, either," Glen added, "but country music in general."

"I like Garth Brooks," Jane told them, although she was familiar with only a couple of his songs. "And Johnny Cash."

"That's a good start," Glen said, giving her a friendly smile. He lifted a mug to his lips, having waited for the froth to settle, and Jane reached for her own. She wasn't much of a beer drinker, preferring white wine, but when in Rome...

Cal sampled his beer, too. "If you're serious about living in Texas, then you'll need at least one button on your car radio set to a country-and-western station."

Jane was surprised by his remark. "I am serious," she told him. Other than an awkward greeting, this was the first time he'd spoken directly to her.

"She wasn't born here," Ellie said, smiling, "but she came as soon as she could."

Everyone laughed.

The waitress returned for their order—barbecued ribs, baked beans and coleslaw all around—and soon afterward brought a second pitcher of beer. Jane had yet to finish her first glass, but both men were ready for another.

"What else do I need to do?" Jane asked. "If I want to become a Texan, I mean."

"Clothes are important," Ellie said, "but I can help you with that later."

Jane smoothed her skirt. She'd already learned that lesson the hard way. She'd worn a business suit to a party soon after her arrival and had been sadly over-dressed for the occasion. Most everyone else had been in jeans and tank tops. A couple of months later, she'd attended a dance and had dressed casually only to discover it was a formal affair. She'd felt like a fool and stayed no more than a few minutes, feeling completely out of place.

"That's where I've seen you," Cal said. "You were at the party Richard Weston threw for himself, weren't you?"

Jane nodded. She'd only been in town a few days when she'd met a handsome congenial rancher who'd invited her to a party. She hadn't known a soul in Promise, and his was the first friendly face she'd seen. Richard had stopped her on the street and insisted that anyone as beautiful as she was had to come to his party. She'd arrived terribly overdressed and hung around feeling unwelcomed and uncomfortable for more than an hour.

"Whatever happened to Richard?" Jane asked. "I saw him around town a few times, but not recently."

The other three went strangely silent and then exchanged looks as if they weren't sure how much to tell her.

Jane stared at them. "Did I ask something I shouldn't have?" Without knowing it, she'd apparently entered forbidden territory. She couldn't prevent a small sigh from escaping. It'd been this way from the beginning—like being in an alien culture, with no one to guide her or tell her the rules. Or explain the native customs, she thought wryly.

"It's just that Richard Weston is...a sad case."

"Sad?" she echoed dutifully.

"He's all foam and no beer," Glen said. "He's hurt a lot of good people and, worse yet, the ones he's abused most have been his own family."

"Richard arrived back in town after being away six years," Cal muttered. "He made a nuisance of himself and caused a lot of trouble for Grady and Savannah before he disappeared."

"I...I didn't know," Jane said. She'd talked to Richard briefly a couple of times. Their first meeting, when he'd invited her to the party, had been pleasant enough, but the subsequent encounter had left her with the distinct impression that the man was frivolous and irresponsible; apparently her assessment hadn't been far off. She frowned, thinking through the relationships. Okay, Richard was the younger brother of Grady and Savannah, and Savannah was married to...Austin? No, Laredo Smith. Grady had recently become engaged to Caroline Daniels. Even after several months, Jane had a hard time keeping track of all the connections.

"Yeah. Richard disappeared not long ago," Ellie said.

"With Grady's truck," Cal added. "That's Richard for you." He shook his head as though the mere mention of the other man's name disgusted him.

"He stole his own brother's truck?"

"And a lot more." This from Cal, too.

"I don't think we need to worry about him coming

back, though," Glen said, sounding sure of himself. "He's gone for good, and all I can say is good riddance."

The others nodded in agreement. A moment of silence followed.

"Do you know about the Bubbas?" Ellie asked, abruptly changing the subject. "Have you met any?"

"Just a couple of the youngsters I've examined who have that nickname."

"There's much more to being a Bubba than a name," Glen told her, grinning once more. "You don't have to be *called* Bubba to be one. There's your basic Bubba, and then there are your different variations, according to what state you live in."

Jane was quickly getting lost. "Perhaps it'd be best if you defined what a Bubba is. A Texas Bubba," she qualified, not wanting to be confused by any other Southern Bubba-types.

"Well," Glen drawled, "that's not as easy as it sounds."

"Sure it is," Cal said. "He drives a beat-up truck with a rifle or fishing pole in the gun rack."

"And carries a fifty-pound sack of dog food in the bed of his truck," Ellie said, "which he probably bought from me."

"He's got a case or two of empty beer and soda cans rolling around on the floor on the passenger side of the cab."

"Is he one of those guys who wears a monster belt buckle?" Jane asked eagerly.

Glen and Cal glanced at each other. "All Texans wear giant belt buckles," Glen informed her kindly.

"Yes, I know, but Bubba buckles are smaller and their bellies are bigger."

"You got it!" Ellie and Glen chorused.

Ellie took a swallow of her beer. "So, Jane, you need a bumper sticker. It's not just a Bubba thing. Everyone in Texas has at least one. Three or four are better."

"Okay." This didn't sound difficult. "What should it say?"

"Touch my truck and you die," Cal suggested.

"I don't drive a truck," Jane said with a smile. "I could buy one, though, if I need to."

He grinned, too, and Jane was surprised by the way it transformed his features. Gratified, too. It made him as attractive as she'd guessed it would. "Buying a truck won't be necessary," he told her.

"Insured by Smith and Wesson," Glen said next.

Jane rolled her eyes. "I don't *think* so."

"Don't mess with Texas," Cal continued.

"I'd better start taking notes," Jane said in a mock-serious voice, reaching for her purse. This was fun, especially now that Cal seemed to have loosened up some. Was it the beer—or the company?

"She needs a hat," Ellie announced just as their dinner was served.

"A hat?"

"A lady Stetson," Glen tossed in and picked up a dripping barbecued rib with both hands.

"A hat doesn't mean a damn thing if she doesn't ride," Cal said as he offered the platter of ribs to Jane.

She helped herself to one, then carefully wiped her fingers on the rather inadequate paper napkin.

"Ride? As in horse?" She looked from Glen to Cal and then to Ellie.

"You're right, Cal," Ellie said, frowning thoughtfully. She nodded in Jane's direction. "You're gonna have to learn to ride."

Jane bit into the pungent smoky-tasting rib, enjoying it more than she would ever have believed. "You're sure about this?" she asked. "I have to ride?"

"Positive."

"Okay," Jane said with some reluctance. "Do you know of anyone who gives lessons?"

"Lessons?" Glen asked, and the three burst into spontaneous laughter.

Jane didn't know what she'd said that was so funny.

"Everyone around here grows up with horses," Ellie explained apologetically. "Most of us were sitting in a saddle before we could walk."

"Then what does someone like me do?"

The question appeared to give them pause. "I don't know," Glen replied at last. "Laredo Smith's raising quarter horses. He might agree to give you lessons."

"I doubt he has the time," Cal inserted. "Laredo and Savannah are building a house, and Laredo's trying to do as much of the work as he can himself. Last I saw they had a good start on it."

"Well, we need to come up with someone who can teach you to ride," Ellie said. She looked sharply at Cal, but Jane noticed that Ellie's brother-in-law was ignoring her. She had a feeling Ellie hoped Cal would jump in and volunteer. Cal didn't, and Jane suspected he wanted nothing more to do with her. It was a pity because she would've liked to know him better.

Cal hadn't been keen on this evening from the moment he'd realized Ellie wasn't cooking dinner at her own house—and even more so when he figured out she was matching him up with the town doctor. He would've put an end to her less-than-clever method of throwing Dr. Texas in his face if he hadn't worried about annoying his new sister-in-law. He'd known Ellie for years, but the relationship was different now, and he had to respect that. When the evening was over, he'd make sure Ellie understood he didn't appreciate her matchmaking attempts.

When Jane had first shown up at the restaurant, he'd been prepared to remain closemouthed and unfriendly. The last thing he'd wanted was to give the impression that he was interested in dating some city slicker. Far from it. But soon the beer had loosened his inhibitions and he'd begun to enjoy the lighthearted conversation. He considered Jane's eagerness to adapt to Texas downright charming. When she'd offered to buy a truck to go along with his suggestion for a bumper sticker, he found himself almost taken with her. Damn it, he liked her attitude. Despite appearances, she knew how to have a good time, and as for turning Texan, she was obviously willing to try.

The bill arrived for their dinner and Glen reached for it. "We'll split it," Cal said.

"How much do I owe?" Jane asked, bending down for her purse.

Cal placed his hand on her arm. "It's taken care of."

Ellie beamed him a smile dazzling enough to blind him. He wasn't sure what had made him offer to pay for Jane's dinner. This wasn't a date, wasn't even *close* to one. But hell, he figured he owed the woman that much after the unfriendly way he'd started off the evening.

"What do you want to do now?" Glen asked his wife.

"How about bingo?" Ellie suggested, looking at the others.

"Bingo?" Jane repeated.

"Sure. There's a game every Friday night in the room above the bowling alley," Ellie said. "You'll love it. Just consider it part of your Texas education."

"I...don't think I've ever played," Jane confessed. "But if you think I should..."

"Don't you worry," Cal said, impressed once more with her willingness to fit in. "It's not difficult to learn."

Since the bowling alley was only a couple of blocks away, they decided to walk. Cal wasn't sure why he tagged along. His intent had been to beg off after dinner and join his friends at Billy D's, the local watering hole. Of course Glen wouldn't be around, and probably not Grady, either. Jimmy Morris and Lyle Whitehouse would be shooting the breeze as usual—not that Cal was a big fan of Lyle's. The guy was far too ready to take offense and want to settle things with his fists. Anyway, Cal realized that, when it came right down to it, he was enjoying himself with his brother and Ellie. Doc Texas wasn't bad, either, although he was determined to make sure she realized this wasn't a real date.

The upstairs room of the bowling alley was set up with tables and chairs for the twice-weekly bingo sessions. A concession stand in the back of the room sold cold drinks, popcorn and hot dogs. Lloyd Bonney, a retired rancher who'd moved into town a couple of years ago, called out the numbers from his position at the front.

They purchased three bingo cards each and were heading for a table near the electronic bingo board when Cal saw his parents. He groaned inwardly. It would be just like his mother to read far more into their little four-some than was warranted. Mary Patterson refused to accept that her oldest son wasn't interested in marriage. She kept insisting she wanted grandchildren and it was his duty to provide them. Cal was convinced Ellie and his brother would be more than happy to handle that task; he only wished she'd stop harassing *him* about it.

"You want to sit by Mom and Dad?" Glen asked after they'd waved to their parents. Cal growled his reply and his brother laughed. "That's what I thought."

They located some space at one of the long tables, and the two women ended up sitting between the brothers, which was fine, Cal supposed—although to the casual observer it might look as if Jane was *with* him. He wasn't much of a talker and felt grateful that Ellie and Jane carried on a nonstop conversation. Cal shook his head, amused at the way women could chatter. He never did understand how they could have so much to say to each other.

Lloyd flipped a switch and the electronic board lit up. The air machine bounced the lightweight balls bearing the bingo letters and corresponding numbers.

Because Jane was new to this, Cal watched her cards for her during the first game, checking to be sure she caught the number on each of them.

"*B*-fifteen," Lloyd called.

Cal checked his own card and closed off the appropriate box. The other two didn't have fifteen in the *B* row. Once again he glanced over at Jane's row of cards and saw that she'd missed one. He pointed it out to her.

"Oh, thanks," she said and smiled her appreciation.

A smile. Just a smile, and yet it warmed his heart. He was startled by his reaction. It was so…unexpected.

Damn it, something must be wrong with him to take a smile, a simple expression of thanks, and make more of it than was warranted. Obviously he'd had one too many beers.

The evening wore on, and while Cal didn't have any luck, Glen bingoed once for a twenty-five-dollar purse. The last game was the grand finale, Blackout Bingo, where every number on the card had to be closed in order to win the two-hundred-dollar grand prize.

As he had all evening, Cal glanced over at Jane's cards after he'd checked his own numbers. Other than that one time, she hadn't missed any. Lloyd had called out forty-five numbers or so when he noticed that one of Jane's cards was nearly filled. She had four blank spaces compared to his best one, which showed at least ten. The next two numbers Lloyd called were both on Jane's card.

He could feel her excitement growing. Five numbers later she had only one open space. She needed *O*-sixty-four. Jane closed her eyes, propped her elbows on the table and crossed the fingers on both hands.

Two numbers later Lloyd called, "*O*-sixty-four."

Together Cal and Jane screamed, "BINGO!"

Cal hadn't meant to yell, but he was damn near as excited as Jane. She leaped to her feet and hugged Ellie and then Cal, as though this two hundred dollars was two hundred thousand.

"Congratulations," Cal said. He couldn't help being delighted. Jane's excitement was contagious.

"Two hundred dollars," she breathed, as if this was more than she'd seen in her entire life. Lloyd personally counted out the money, placing the bills in her hand.

Clutching them in her fist, Jane wildly hugged Ellie again.

Ellie laughed. "I told you that you'd like this game."

"I *love* this game." Jane pressed the money to her heart. "I'm gonna buy me a real Texas outfit. You want to come along and make sure I get what I need?"

"You're on," Ellie replied as Jane tucked the money into her purse.

Afterward Cal and Glen stopped and greeted their parents.

"Mom, Dad, this is my friend Jane Dickinson," Ellie said, saving Cal the embarrassment of introducing her and then explaining that technically she wasn't his date. He was grateful that Ellie had taken the initiative; otherwise his parents might get the wrong idea. His mother didn't need any encouragement to match him up.

"Good to see you dating again," his father said, blindsiding him.

He'd expected his mother to comment on Jane's being with him, but not his father. "This isn't a date," Cal felt obliged to correct him, and not entirely for his dad's sake, either. It saved Jane the need to correct his father's assumption.

"Congratulations on your win, Jane," Mary said. It was easy to read what his mother was thinking—from the look in her eyes, she was already envisioning grandchildren.

After exchanging pleasantries and saying goodbye to his parents, they walked back to the Chili Pepper where they'd left their vehicles. Glen opened the truck door for Ellie and helped her in.

"I had a wonderful time," Jane said, her blue eyes

bright with pleasure. "My best since moving here. Thanks so much for including me."

"How're you getting home?" Glen asked when he apparently realized she hadn't come in a car.

"I walked. It's only a few blocks."

"Would you like a ride?" he asked. Cal probably would have offered but was pleased that his brother had done it first. If Glen hadn't, he'd be obliged, and he didn't want her to think he was seeking out her company.

"I appreciate the offer, but I feel like walking. Thank you, though."

Glen climbed into his truck and backed out of the parking space as Ellie waved farewell.

Cal opened his pickup door, prepared to leave himself. "Sure you don't want a ride?" he said, trying not to sound reluctant.

"Positive. Good night, and thanks for dinner. That was really sweet of you."

Cal stood waiting by the open door until Jane had crossed the main intersection. Only then did he climb into his truck and start the engine. Checking the rearview mirror for traffic, he caught sight of Jane ambling down the street. He sighed, silently cursing himself. He didn't feel right leaving her to walk home on her own. She might not be his date or even his friend, but damn it all, he felt responsible for her safety. Especially when she was walking around with her bingo winnings in her purse. Promise didn't have a crime problem, but it didn't hurt to be cautious.

Cal cut the engine and climbed out of his truck, then raced after her.

She glanced up at him in surprise when he reached

her. "I'll walk you home," he said gruffly, matching his steps to hers.

She blinked as if she wasn't sure what to say. "Thank you."

He shoved his fingers into the small pockets at the top of his jeans. They walked in silence, neither of them making an effort to talk. Two blocks off Main Street, Cal was glad he'd decided to escort her home. The streetlight on Fourth Avenue had burned out, and the sidewalk was darker than a bowl of black bean soup.

"Perhaps you'd better give me your arm," Cal suggested halfway down the block.

She did, and he tucked her hand in the crook of his elbow. Oddly, he *enjoyed* doing this small thing for her.

"That's something you and Ellie and Glen forgot to mention," Jane said suddenly.

"What's that?"

"The men in Texas are real gentlemen."

"My momma didn't raise no Bubbas," Cal said, joking, and they both laughed. It felt good to laugh, and Cal had done more of that in the past few hours than he had in months.

"Listen," he said impulsively as they neared the small house behind the health clinic, "are you serious about learning to ride?"

"Very much so."

"All right, then I'll teach you."

"You will?"

Cal wasn't sure what had prompted the offer, but since he'd blurted it out, he couldn't very well back down now.

The light from her porch illuminated her face. She looked like the original California girl with her short sun-bleached hair and eyes as blue as the Pacific. Already Cal was calling himself a damned fool and he hadn't even given Jane her first lesson. Maybe someone should offer to give *him* a lesson—on how to keep his stupid mouth shut.

Savannah Smith had made the appointment to see Dr. Jane Dickinson Tuesday morning. She hadn't been feeling well the past few weeks and thought it was time for a general checkup. Besides, she had her suspicions.

In the past half year her life had undergone a number of drastic changes. First and foremost, she'd met Laredo; they'd fallen in love and were now married. About the time Laredo had come into her life, her brother Richard had reappeared after a six-year absence. Thanks to her influence, Grady had allowed Richard to stay at the ranch, which was more than charitable of him, seeing as their brother had stolen from them—and that Grady's inclination had been to turn him away. Apparently she'd still had some lessons to learn regarding Richard. Painful ones.

Savannah had desperately wanted to believe he'd changed, but then, so had Grady. Against his better judgment, her brother had given Richard opportunity after opportunity to prove himself. In the end, when he disappeared with Grady's truck, it was exactly what she'd learned to expect. Only this time he didn't steal only from them; he'd also charged thousands of dollars' worth of goods and services in town. It was a matter of pride and principle to Grady that those bills be paid.

The merchants in Promise had accepted the charges because of the Westons' good name, and Grady wouldn't let Richard disgrace it or ruin a hundred years of excellent credit. The money had come out of the profits from selling off the herd; it was money that could have been spent in other ways, money that would have benefited the Weston ranch, the Yellow Rose.

Savannah's bout of ill health had started shortly after Richard's sudden departure. She'd done her best to hide it from her husband, but Laredo knew something was wrong because he'd been the one to suggest she make the appointment. Sitting in the examination room now, Savannah silently prayed that the diagnosis was what she suspected.

The door to the examination room opened and Dr. Dickinson walked in. It was a bit unsettling to have a doctor younger than she was. Particulary after all those years of seeing old Doc Cummings.

"Hello," Dr. Dickinson said, smiling. She held out her hand and Savannah shook it. This must be a big-city thing, she thought, because generally women in rural Texas didn't shake hands.

"I'm pleased to meet you," Savannah answered. This was their first actual meeting, although they'd seen each other at various events.

The physician sat down on the chair across from her. "You haven't been feeling well?"

Savannah nodded. "My stomach's been queasy, usually in the morning and often late in the afternoon, too."

"Any other symptoms?"

"I'm so tired lately. The other night it was all I could do to stay up past eight, which is ridiculous."

The doctor made a notation on her chart. "Anything else?"

"Well…yes. My period's two weeks late."

This information was written on the chart, as well. "I understand you were recently married."

Savannah nodded. "In June."

"Are you using any form of birth control?"

Savannah found such talk excruciatingly embarrassing. "Uh, usually," she answered, blushing hotly.

"I'd like to do a urine test," the doctor said.

"Okay. So do you think I might be pregnant?"

Dr. Dickinson's answering smile was warm. "You're showing all the symptoms."

Savannah let out a deep breath as that confirmation settled over her. Pregnant. So soon? She'd known it was the likely reason for her nausea and tiredness—not to mention the missed period. But...pregnant? Somehow, it didn't seem possible, and yet she supposed it was inevitable considering their haphazard methods of birth control.

After a brief physical examination Savannah provided a urine sample. Waiting for the test results seemed to take forever when in reality it was only minutes. Savannah's emotions ran the entire spectrum. She felt mostly an overwhelming sense of joy—a joy so deep and profound it was difficult not to leap up and shout with it. Simultaneously she was aware that the timing could hardly be worse. She and Laredo had spent much of the summer drawing up plans for their own home. Every penny they'd managed to pull together had gone into the project. Now wasn't exactly the ideal time to announce she was going to have a baby.

The door opened and the doctor returned. "Congratulations, Savannah. You're going to be a mother."

Savannah's hands flew to her mouth and tears welled in her eyes.

"How do you feel about this pregnancy?" the physician asked.

"I...it's a surprise. I mean, it is and it isn't. I realize it shouldn't be, but..." She realized she was babbling. "I'm happy. Very happy."

"I'd like to set up a series of appointments for you, plus I'd like to start you on a regimen of vitamins."

"All right."

"Good," Dr. Dickinson said. "So I'll see you in a month." Then she gently patted Savannah's back and left to attend to the next patient.

Savannah's head continued to buzz as she drove back to the ranch. To her amazement Laredo was waiting for her when she pulled into the yard. He hurried over to the truck and opened the door the second she'd parked.

"What did the doctor have to say?" he asked before she had time to climb out. His eyes revealed his anxiety.

"Oh, Laredo, you aren't going to believe this. We're pregnant!"

"Pregnant?"

"Oh, please tell me you're glad. Because I am. I swear I could explode!"

They walked into the kitchen and Laredo pulled out a chair and sat down. "Pregnant," he said again, as if he couldn't quite believe it.

Savannah nodded, studying this man she loved beyond all reason. As she knew it would, a slow easy smile spread across his face. "Pregnant," he said more loudly this time. "My wife's going to have a baby! Just wait until my mother hears about this."

Savannah smiled. Their love was the most profound wonder of her life. And as she'd now discovered, it was only the beginning.

Her husband leaped to his feet and caught her in his arms. "We're going to have a baby!"

"I know the timing's bad…"

"The timing's perfect. You're perfect. Life's perfect." He threw back his head and laughed, and then he kissed her.

"Hey, you two," Grady said when he stepped into the kitchen. "What's going on?"

Three

For the first time since Jane had come to Texas, she felt a sense of belonging. Friends made all the difference. Her evening out with Ellie, Glen and Cal had cheered her immensely, and within a few days she'd followed all their instructions. She had a Texas bumper sticker, a Willie Nelson cassette in her car, and she routinely listened to the Brewster country-and-western station. A shopping spree with her bingo winnings plus a chunk of her savings had netted her an outfit Annie Oakley would've been proud to wear. Not only that, her first riding lesson was scheduled for Friday afternoon. If she got any more Texan, she wouldn't recognize herself!

Thursday-afternoon traffic in the clinic was slow; she hadn't seen a patient in more than two hours. Attaching her beeper to her waistband, she headed toward Dovie's antique shop, taking the rag doll Maggie Daniels had brought her. Every time she entered the office the old-fashioned doll smiled at her with its faded pink lips, looking somehow forlorn, as though it—she— wanted to pour out her sawdust heart. If anyone could help Jane locate the doll's rightful owner, it was Dovie.

Her friend seemed to be experiencing a lull in business, too. Dovie's face broke into a welcoming smile when Jane walked into the shop.

"Jane, how are you?" Dovie asked, rushing over to hug her. She had to skirt wooden tables and dressers and chairs, all draped and dangling with jewelry and scarves. Jane was impressed by the quantity and quality of Dovie's wares.

"I'm terrific," she answered.

Her arm around Jane's waist, Dovie led her to the Victorian Tea Room and poured them each a cup of fragrant lemon tea. When she'd finished, she asked about Friday night's dinner.

Jane talked nonstop for ten minutes, relating the highlights of the evening. She mentioned winning at bingo and that Cal had walked her home and volunteered to teach her to ride.

"Cal?" Dovie sounded shocked. "Cal Patterson?"

"I know. I was surprised myself. At first I could tell he wasn't thrilled to be paired up with me. He seemed to think I'd finagled this matchmaking myself, but after a while, he was fine." She grinned. "You could say he underwent an attitude adjustment." She considered Cal a gentleman in an age when chivalry was all but dead. He'd gone out of his way to escort her home, out of regard for her safety. That certainly hadn't been required, but Jane appreciated it. In the days since, she'd thought quite a lot about him.

Dovie's eyes twinkled with delight. "You're exactly what that young man needs."

"I met his parents, too."

"Mary and Phil are two of my dearest friends," Dovie told her.

Jane sipped her tea, then lifted the bag with the doll onto her lap. "Actually I have a reason for stopping by other than to let you know how everything went last Friday." She opened the bag and carefully withdrew the fragile toy.

Dovie's eyes widened when she saw it. "Where in heaven's name did you find that?"

Jane hesitated. "I'm not at liberty to say."

Dovie's brows rose a fraction of an inch.

"I will tell you that someone brought it to me—feeling a lot of guilt. Apparently this person took the doll and shouldn't have, and for reasons I can't understand is unable to return it. I was hoping you might know who the rightful owner is."

Dovie turned the antique in her hands and thoroughly examined how it was constructed. "I'd swear it's authentic."

"You mean this *is* a real antique?" Jane asked, wondering where and how six-year-old Maggie could have come by it.

"She's real and probably worth quite a lot of money."

"You're joking." The doll was ready to fall apart.

"I'm not." Dovie gave the toy back to Jane with some hesitation. "Are you sure you can't tell me the name of the person who gave you the doll?"

Jane shook her head. "I wish I could, but I'd be breaking a confidence."

Dovie accepted her answer. "Do you have any idea where this unnamed person got the doll?"

"Didn't say." In retrospect, Jane realized there were any number of questions she should have asked Maggie. But the child had been in quite a state, sick with regret and worry. At the time it'd seemed more important to reassure the little girl than to worry about the doll's owner.

"There's only one place I can imagine finding anything like this," Dovie said, her look thoughtful. A frown slowly formed, furrowing her brow.

"Where's that?" Jane asked.

"It doesn't seem possible...but there's been talk about it lately and I have to wonder. The doll might have come from... Bitter End."

It was Jane's turn to lift her eyebrows. She'd never heard of the town and was fairly certain she would have remembered one with such an unusual name. "Bitter End?"

"That's the name the settlers chose more than a hundred and thirty years ago, after the Civil War. If I remember my history correctly, the journey across Indian territory and through the war-ravaged South was harrowing. Not a family came through the trip unscathed. Parents lost children and children lost parents from Indian attacks and disease. By the time they reached the Texas Hill Country, their faith had nearly been destroyed."

"Times were so difficult back then," Jane said, remembering that the now-common childhood diseases were often the source of death.

"Those pioneers faced hardship after hardship," Dovie continued. "Overcome with bitterness, the town's founding fathers decided to name their community Bitter End."

"I've never heard of it."

"Few have," Dovie said. "It's a ghost town now."

"Really? You've been there?" Jane asked, her curiosity keen. She'd never dreamed something like that existed in this vicinity.

"Have I been to Bitter End?" Dovie's laugh was abrupt. "I'm sorry to say I haven't. I'd like to and perhaps one day I will. The only reason I even know about it is because of something my father said years ago."

"I'd like to go there," Jane said. She'd always been a history buff, and visiting a ghost town would be a wonderful adventure.

"Jane, I hate to disillusion you," Dovie said kindly, "but I don't even know if the old town is still standing."

"Could you give me directions?"

"If I knew where it was, possibly, but there are no paved roads. It's somewhere up in the hills. You need to remember this is a real ghost town."

"But what happened? Why did everyone leave?" Jane's mind filled with questions.

Dovie looked as though she regretted bringing up the subject. "I don't have a clue. No one does. At one time I believe the town was quite prosperous—a fast-growing community. My father said he'd even heard that the railroad was scheduled to lay track there, but all of that changed overnight."

"Overnight?" The details were becoming more and more intriguing. "Something drastic must have happened."

"A natural catastrophe, perhaps," Dovie suggested. "No one knows."

"That doesn't make sense," Jane said, thinking out loud. "Tornado, fire, flood—anything like that would have destroyed the whole town. There'd be nothing left. Anyway, why wouldn't they rebuild if that happened?"

"I don't know," Dovie murmured. "My father mentioned it twice in the years I was growing up. As I recall, he said everyone packed up and moved—no one knows why. They abandoned almost everything."

"Then there's a possibility the entire town's intact."

"Yes…I suppose there is," Dovie said.

"Do you know people who've actually been there?"

She took her time answering. "A few."

"Who?"

Dovie was about to speak when the bell above the front door rang, and Sheriff Frank Hennessey walked into the store.

It seemed to Jane that Dovie went pale. "Jane," she whispered, getting to her feet, "don't leave me."

Jane nodded.

"Hello, Sheriff," Dovie said. Her tone lacked its usual warmth.

"Dovie."

The sheriff glanced in Jane's direction, and his look made it clear he wished she wasn't there. In any other circumstances Jane would have made her excuses and left, but Dovie had plainly asked her to stay. However uncomfortable she was, Jane felt obliged to honor her friend's request.

"What can I do for you, Sheriff?" Dovie asked.

Frank Hennessey glanced at Jane again. "Dovie, in the name of heaven, this has got to end," he said in a low urgent voice. "We're both miserable."

"We've already been through this a thousand times. Nothing's going to change."

The sheriff's mouth thinned. "I love you," he whispered.

"So you say." Dovie began to move about the shop,

rearranging things here and there. Frank Hennessey trailed behind her, looking lost and utterly wretched.

When his pleading didn't work, the sheriff tried a different tactic. "What's this I heard about you traveling?" he demanded as though he had every right to know.

"It's time I saw something of the world."

"A *singles'* cruise, Dovie?" His disapproval was evident.

Dovie sighed expressively. "Who told you?"

"Does it matter?"

"As a matter of fact it does because I want to be sure that whoever it was has nothing more to report."

"You didn't want me to know?" The sheriff's tone had gone from irritated to hurt.

"What I choose to do with my life from here on out, Frank Hennessey, is *my* concern, and only mine."

He stiffened. "You don't mean that."

"Yes, Frank, I do." Dovie had completed one full circle of the shop. She stopped in front of the table where she and Jane had been drinking tea. "You remember Dr. Dickinson, don't you?"

The sheriff gave Jane little more than a perfunctory nod.

"Good to see you again, Sheriff Hennessey," Jane said, but she doubted he'd even heard.

His gaze remained on Dovie. "This has gone on long enough," he said, and he no longer seemed to care whether or not Jane was privy to their conversation. "I'm crazy about you. It's been damn near three weeks, and we're no closer to settling this than we were then. I need you, Dovie! It isn't like you to be unreasonable. I don't know who put this craziness in your head, but it's got to end, for both our sakes. Can't we resolve this?"

"Resolve this?" Dovie repeated as if she found the statement amusing. "What you mean is, can't I give in to you. It's not going to happen, Frank. You've made your decision and I've made mine, and that's all there is to it."

"Damn it, Dovie, would you listen to reason?"

"There's nothing more to discuss," Dovie said, not quite disguising the sadness in her tone. "I think it'd be best if you left."

Frank stared at Dovie in disbelief. Then, in an act of pure frustration, he slapped his hat against his thigh and stormed out of the shop, leaving the display windows shaking.

Dovie sank into the chair and Jane noticed that her hands were shaking. "I'm sorry to subject you to that, Jane," she said, her voice as shaky as her hands.

"Are you all right?" Jane asked, truly concerned.

"No," Dovie admitted, "but I will be in time."

"Are you really going away?"

"Yes. I've booked a three-day cruise, but not a singles' one. Mary Patterson suggested that, but I'm not interested in getting involved again—at least not this soon."

"You love Frank, don't you?" Jane probed gently.

"Yes, fool that I am. I do. But he's stubborn, and unfortunately so am I." She didn't elaborate, but Jane had a pretty clear picture of the problem. Dovie wanted a ring on her finger, and Sheriff Hennessey wasn't about to relinquish his freedom. From the looks of it, they were at an impasse.

"You'll enjoy the cruise," Jane said, wanting to encourage her friend in the same kindly way Dovie had encouraged her. "And it'll do you a world of good to get away for a while."

"I'm sure you're right." Dovie made an unsuccessful attempt at a smile. "I talked Mary and Phil Patterson into coming along with me, and by golly, we're going to have the time of our lives."

She said this, Jane noted, as though the person she most needed to convince was herself.

It came as a surprise to Cal to realize he was actually looking forward to seeing Jane Dickinson again. By Friday afternoon he was ready to teach that California gal everything she cared to know about the joys of riding.

From his brother Cal learned that Ellie and Jane had been shopping and Jane had purchased an entire Western outfit, complete with hat and cowboy boots.

They'd talked briefly by phone earlier in the week, and Cal had suggested Jane come to the ranch at five o'clock, since the days were growing shorter now.

Accustomed to women being late, Cal didn't actually expect her to show up on time. He was pleasantly surprised when her car turned into the yard at five minutes to five.

She parked, then opened the car door and gingerly stepped out. Her clothes were so new they practically squeaked.

"This really is very kind of you," she said, smiling.

Cal walked all the way around her, amazed by the transformation a few clothes could make. She looked great. Terrific. If he didn't know better, he'd have assumed she'd been born and raised in the great state of Texas. At least, until she opened her mouth, and then all doubt was removed. She didn't sound anything like a Texan—but he didn't feel he should hold that against her.

"What do you think?" she asked, holding her arms out at her sides.

"Your Wranglers seem a little stiff, but other than that, not bad. Not bad indeed!"

"Did you check out my bumper sticker?" she asked.

He hadn't, so he turned to look—and roared with laughter. Sure enough, she'd gotten a sticker. It read: *Texas Crude*.

"Not only that, I'm listening to Reba, Clint, John Berry and Alabama."

Cal loved it. "Wonderful."

She laughed and he discovered that he liked the sound of it. Soon he was chuckling himself, and for no damn reason that he could think of. Hmm. Something like this could ruin his reputation as a curmudgeon.

"You ready?" he asked.

"Ready as I'll ever be," she said, then exhaled a deep sigh.

Cal led the way. He'd already chosen Atta Girl for her and brought the horse out of the paddock. Atta Girl was a gentle chestnut mare who'd delivered six foals over the past ten years. Cal trusted her to treat the green-horn with patience.

"This is Atta Girl," he said, rubbing his hand down the mare's neck.

Jane stood directly in front of the animal. "Pleased to meet you," she said with the same seriousness she might have used to address the bank manager.

"She isn't going to shake your hand," Cal said, struggling not to smile.

Jane gave him a glance that said she didn't find him

all that funny, but he noticed she had a hard time containing her amusement, too. It'd been a long time since anyone had affected him this way.

"I thought we'd start with you learning how to saddle her," he said. Once she was familiar with the basics, he'd let her mount.

Jane nibbled her lower lip. "Before I put a saddle on her back, I thought maybe Atta Girl and I should talk this over."

He assumed she was joking, but it soon became obvious she wasn't. Apparently she intended to have some polite conversation with Atta Girl first.

"I thought you might like to get a good look at me," Jane said, just as if she were talking to a person. "It must be frustrating to carry someone around without being able to see who it is."

Cal tried not to roll his eyes, but didn't succeed. At this rate it'd take a month of Sundays to get her on Atta Girl's back.

"She can't really see you, anyway," Cal felt honor bound to tell Jane.

"Do you mean to say you gave me a blind horse?"

He shook his head. "Horses are notorious for having bad eyesight. You notice how far apart her eyes are? How they're on either side of her face?"

Jane looked at one side of Atta Girl's face and then the other.

"Because of that, horses have what you might call a broad view of things, and although they can tell when there's something approaching, what they generally see are shadowy figures."

"Oh," Jane said and tentatively touched the mare's soft muzzle. "In that case, Atta Girl, you need carrots. Lots and lots of carrots. I'll bring you some on my next visit."

"While we're at it," Cal said, "it's probably not a good idea to approach a horse from the rear. It's an ugly way to die."

"How reassuring," Jane muttered.

"Not to worry, you're safe with Atta Girl."

"At least her name isn't something like Killer."

"That was her sire's name," Cal teased.

Jane placed her hands on her hips. "Are you trying to scare me?"

"Would I do something like that?" he inquired, the picture of innocence. While he had her attention, he told her a number of other facts she should know. Riding information, as well as bits and pieces of horse lore. She listened with complete concentration. Not until she'd grown accustomed to riding would she really experience the thrill of it. Nothing in life could compare with galloping through a field of wildflowers on a warm spring day with the wind in your face.

"What kind of relationship do you have with your horse?" she asked. "Do you think of him the way Roy Rogers thought of Trigger?"

"Probably not." He hoped he wasn't shattering any illusions. "Thunder's a loyal partner, but he's not my best friend. The tricks he knows aren't going to end up on any television show, but he cuts cattle better than any pony I've ever ridden." Cal paused, wondering whether to add the next part. "Also, I'm not having him stuffed when he eventually goes."

Jane looked startled, but recovered quickly. She asked a number of intelligent questions, which he answered to the best of his ability.

"You ready to saddle her up?" he asked.

Jane drew a deep breath and nodded.

Having been around horses his entire life, Cal had no fear of them. Respect, yes, but not fear. Jane was intimidated; following his example, though, she refused to show it. Nor would she allow her intimidation to stop her from getting on with the lesson.

Cal brought out the brushes, a blanket, the saddle and tack. He taught her by demonstrating and then letting her do it herself. Atta Girl was everything he'd expected. To his amusement Jane stopped what she was doing several times, walked around to the horse's head and spoke to her. Anyone might have thought they were actually communicating.

"You're sure this isn't too much trouble for you?" she asked Atta Girl next.

"Jane," Cal muttered, thinking she was quite possibly the most sensitive person he'd ever met. Also the most ridiculous, but he found himself more entertained than annoyed.

By the time she had the saddle on, it was close to seven and twilight was beginning.

"We'll save the actual ride for another lesson," he said. "But it'd be a shame if you didn't at least mount her after all this."

Jane's expression was skeptical. "You think I should? Tonight?"

He nodded, then watched as she walked around to discuss the prospect with Atta Girl. "Does she have any objection?" Cal asked as a joke.

"She doesn't seem to," Jane said, apparently taking him seriously.

"I'll help you adjust the stirrups," he said. It was a

skill that demanded experience and time. "You're doing great."

"I'll bet that's what they said to Custer before the Battle of Little Big Horn," she complained, then put her foot in the left stirrup and heaved herself up.

Apparently the cinch wasn't as tight as it should have been, because before he could warn her, the saddle slid sideways, sending her directly under Atta Girl's stomach. Jane let out a cry of alarm while Atta Girl pranced about in an effort to maintain her balance. Cal held his breath, fearing the mare would inadvertently step on Jane. To his amazement he watched her roll out from under the horse and leap to her feet. Indiana Jones had nothing on Dr. Texas!

"Are you okay?" Cal asked. Everything had happened so fast he'd barely had time to react. He took hold of Atta Girl's reins and quickly reassured the frightened mare by speaking gently to her.

"That does it," Jane said breathlessly, her hand over her heart.

"You're quitting?" Cal asked, not that he blamed her. She'd had quite a scare.

"No, I'm joining Weight Watchers. I damn near downed that poor horse."

Cal stared at her, then started to chuckle. The laughter came from deep inside him, and nothing could have held it back. Nothing. It was as though two years of fun and laughter had been confined inside him, waiting for precisely this moment. A few hours with Jane Dickinson, and all the pent-up enjoyment of life came spilling out of him in waves of unrestrained delight.

"Well, I'm glad you find this so funny," she said.

Tears ran down his cheeks and he wiped them aside

with the back of his hand. "Damn, but I can't remember when I laughed so hard." Jane crossed her arms, and not wanting his reaction to offend her, he gave her a brief hug. "You're a good sport, Jane."

She muttered something unintelligible.

"And listen, there's no need for you to lose weight—you're perfect just the way you are. The saddle slipped because the cinch wasn't tight enough. It had nothing to do with your size."

She seemed none the worse for wear and within seconds she was smiling, too. "You're willing to give me another lesson?"

"You bet, Dr. Texas."

Her smile broadened.

In fact, Cal could hardly wait. This was the most fun he'd had in years. Even Jennifer, the woman he'd loved enough to marry, had never provoked this much reaction in him—apart from the anger and humiliation he felt when she'd dumped him.

"Next week?" Jane asked.

Cal nodded, but waiting an entire week for her second lesson was too long. He wanted to see her again soon.

"Can you make it Tuesday, Dr. Texas?"

She laughed. "You bet, cowboy—and at least my jeans are broken in now."

Jane returned to her house, threw off her clothes and soaked in a hot tub. She couldn't very well claim she was saddle sore, seeing that she hadn't so much as managed to sit on a horse. But she'd taxed rarely used muscles in her effort to avoid being trampled by Atta Girl.

All Cal had done was laugh, and while he might have

been amused, she'd been frightened out of her wits. But all's well that ends well, she decided, not sure if it was the desire to learn to ride or her attraction to Cal that had prompted her to agree to a second lesson.

She liked him. A lot.

Climbing out of the tub, she dressed in a light robe, made some popcorn for dinner and settled down in front of the television with a rented video. The tape had just started when the phone rang.

It was so rare for her phone to ring that she stared at it for a moment. Any emergency calls came through her beeper. At last she picked it up.

"Hello?"

"Janey, it's Mom. How are you, sweetheart?"

"I'm feeling wonderful." She reached for the remote control and stopped the movie. Since her arrival in Promise she'd tried to hide her unhappiness from her parents. Now she was eager to share the good news of making friends and becoming part of the community.

"You sound terrific."

"Listen, honey," her father said, speaking from the extension, "your letter arrived this afternoon. What's all this about a ghost town?"

Excited after her discussion with Dovie, Jane had written home, elaborating on the story, adding bits of speculation and her decision to learn everything she could. From what Dovie had said, the frontier town was real; information had been passed down from one generation to the next. But still, a person could grow up believing in some historical "fact" and later learn it had been a legend with little or no basis in reality.

"Do you honestly believe there's such a place as Bitter End?" her mother asked.

"I don't know, but I'd like to find out."

"How do you intend to do that?" her father wanted to know. "You didn't tell us in your letter."

"I don't know…" Dovie had told her there weren't any roads leading to the ghost town, and a quick survey of an area map revealed a thousand spots where the old town might be.

"I'm as fascinated by all this as you are," her mother said. "I've always loved history, too."

"What interests me is the mystery involved," Jane murmured.

"You mean why everyone left the town?" her father asked.

"Yes. If I understood Dovie correctly, the town was thriving. Then overnight everyone just packed up and moved away. Actually they came here, to Promise."

"And nobody knows why they abandoned one town and founded another," her mother said.

"That's right. No one seems to know. Dovie's never been there herself, but from what she told me there's a good possibility the entire town is still standing."

"But it's over a hundred years old."

"Over 130. As far as I've been able to find out from reading state history, the original settlers were probably a mixed bag of immigrants, outlaws and Southern sympathizers who'd lost everything in the Civil War. That was pretty typical of the people who came to Texas at that time. Most of them had packed up what was left of their worldly belongings and traveled here, hoping to put the war behind them."

"I'm fascinated," her mother said again. "I'll do some research and see if I can find any books that mention Bitter End."

"Thanks, Mom, that'd be great."

"It sounds from your letter," her father said, "as if you're enjoying Texas. This last letter was a lot less… reserved than before."

Jane chuckled. "Well, I've got a complete cowgirl outfit now, and one of the local ranchers calls me Dr. Texas."

It was her father's turn to chuckle. "Don't let him give you any ideas. You're Dr. California, understand?"

She did. She was following in her grandfather's and her uncle Ken's footsteps. As soon as her student loans were paid off, she'd be joining her uncle's medical practice in Los Angeles. One day she'd inherit the practice. Uncle Ken claimed she was his favorite niece. While a couple of her cousins had shown an interest in medicine, she was the only one who'd taken it seriously. The schooling had been difficult, her internship and residency demanding. She'd given up every aspect of a social life and been left to deal with a huge debt.

Her parents had helped her out financially, but medical school was expensive. Her uncle had offered to help, too. Still, when the opportunity arose to wipe out most of her debt by working in Texas, she'd leaped at the idea. Three years was nothing. The time would pass before she knew it, or so she'd believed.

Her first six months in Promise had proved otherwise.

Until recently.

Until she met Cal Patterson.

Four

Late Monday night Frank sat in his patrol car outside Dovie Boyd's home, mulling over what he should do next. He was miserable, and he knew she was, too. He'd loved Dovie for a lot of years, but this was the first time he'd encountered her stubbornness. It was enough to drive a man to drink.

Louise Powell, dressed to the hilt in her Texas trash, complete with star-shaped sunglasses and a silvery hat with a rhinestone band, had approached him at the bowling alley café. She'd let it drop that Dovie had booked a singles' Caribbean cruise. Now if that didn't beat all. Louise had gotten the information from Gayla Perkins at the travel agency and had taken great delight in rubbing his nose in it.

It was downright embarrassing. Here was the town gossip, flapping her tongue all over the county, telling everyone who cared to hear that Dovie was seeking greener pastures.

His fingers tightened around the steering wheel as he reviewed his options. He'd tried, heaven knew he'd tried, but damn it all, he loved Dovie and he didn't want to lose her, especially to another man.

He checked his wristwatch and knew she hadn't gone to bed yet. He sighed deeply, remembering the times they'd cuddled up together on her big feather bed, watching television. She'd made the everyday routines of life special, adding her own little touches here and there. She sun-dried the bedsheets, then stored them with woven lavender wands so that when he crawled in beside her he felt their cool crispness and breathed in the light perfumed scent of summer.

Dinner, too, was something special. Dovie set her table with a linen cloth and napkins, using china and real crystal. She could serve home-baked macaroni and cheese with the panache of the finest restaurant.

Damn, but he missed her.

Swallowing his pride, Frank stepped out of the car and approached the house. He had to try one last time. If he couldn't get her to listen to reason tonight, then he'd have no choice but to accept her decision.

As was his habit, he parked the car around the corner, out of sight from the street, and approached through the backyard. He missed their nights together more than he would've thought possible. He knew Dovie, and she was lusty and vital, a real woman with a woman's needs. It was a source of consolation to realize she must miss their nights together, too.

He knocked lightly on the back door and waited, hat in hand.

The porch light went on and he saw her pull aside the lace curtain and peek out. It was several long seconds before she unlocked the door and opened it.

"Hello, Dovie." He kept his gaze lowered. Coming to her like this wasn't easy.

"Frank."

He didn't speak, but merely raised his eyes to hers. He loved her, as much as he was capable of loving any woman. Surely she knew that! But he wasn't the marrying kind. He couldn't help it; he needed his freedom in order to breathe. Marriage, even to Dovie whom he adored, would feel like a noose around his neck.

Everything had been perfect. They'd each had their own lives and a life together, too. He had his house and she had hers. Two nights a week he joined her for mutual pleasure. He was willing to do whatever it took, short of marriage, to return to that arrangement.

"It's not true," she said, breaking the silence, "about the singles' cruise. I don't know who told you that, but I'm not looking for another man."

A weight seemed to lift from his shoulders. So she wasn't seeking out someone else. Although he was grateful, all he could manage was a nod.

"I've just decided to do some traveling," she told him.

"Why?" That was another thing he'd always loved about Dovie—she enjoyed the simple pleasures in life. She shunned luxuries, content with a walk in the moonlight when he would gladly have taken her out for an evening at a fancy restaurant.

"I've lived my entire life in Promise," she explained. "If I don't travel now, I never will. I understand the Caribbean is lovely and I've always dreamed of visiting the islands there. At one time I thought I'd see it with—"

"I'll take you." If all she wanted was a trip, a vacation away, he'd book their passage in the morning. No questions asked. Anywhere in the world she wanted to go.

"As your wife, Frank?"

The bubble of hope he'd felt burst with her words. "Oh, Dovie, you know I can't do that."

"Yes, I do know. That's why I'll be traveling without you."

The frustration was almost intolerable. "Don't you miss me?" he cried. He ached with the need to hold her.

She looked away but not before he saw the sheen of tears in her eyes.

"I miss you so much," she whispered.

"Oh, Dovie." He reached for her hand and kissed her palm. "Can't we work this out like two adults? I love you and you love me. It's all we need, all we've ever needed."

Her skin was silky smooth and touching it fired all his love, all his passion. "Let me spend the night." His eyes pleaded with her.

Her long hesitation gave him hope.

"No," she finally whispered.

"Dovie, you don't mean that!"

"I do mean it." She eased her hand from his grasp.

Frank couldn't believe this was happening. He'd come so close to convincing her—and he wasn't about to give up without a fight.

"I'm a man with strong needs," he said, hoping that would influence her.

"I love you, but I'm not sleeping with you again, Frank, not unless we're married."

"Dovie." He groaned her name. Damn it, the time had come to play hardball, acquaint her with a few facts. "There are other women in Promise who'd welcome my attention." He was a handsome cuss and he knew it, but there wasn't a woman in the world he wanted more than Dovie Boyd.

"Yes, I'm sure any number of them would," Dovie said.

Frank saw the hurt in her eyes and was furious with himself for suggesting he'd consider seeing anyone else. But he'd tried everything possible to get her to listen to reason.

"Perhaps another woman *would* be the best answer," Dovie murmured. She stepped back from the threshold.

He opened his mouth to tell her he'd been only bluffing, but he wasn't given the opportunity. Dovie's door was closed firmly in his face. He stared at it in stunned silence.

Hell and damnation, the woman drove him crazy! It'd serve her right if he did go out with someone else. Maybe then she'd realize what she was giving up; maybe then she'd come to her senses. Yup, that was what he'd do, Frank decided. She was taking a fancy cruise and plenty of eligible men were bound to come sniffing around. Well, he was entitled to some compensations, too.

Eventually, he hoped she'd accept that, even though he loved her with all his heart, he wasn't about to let her or any other woman maneuver him into marriage. In a few months he'd be sixty-one years old. He'd managed to avoid marriage so far. Why would he change now? Marriage was a trap, especially for a man like him— despite those sentimental beliefs of Dovie's.

But as soon as she learned he was seeing another woman, she'd be back. What had begun as a bluff now sounded like a good strategy. Dovie needed some competition; that way she'd realize how good they'd had it. One thing about Dovie, she was a fast learner.

Frank felt another faint stirring of hope. Before long, he told himself, Dovie would be begging him to come back.

Early Tuesday afternoon Ellie stepped outside the feed store and inserted a few coins in the pop machine. The morning had been hectic and she was grateful for this respite, however brief. She opened the can of soda and saw Jane Dickinson walking across the street.

"Jane," she called, raising her hand in greeting. "Come on over."

Jane returned the wave, glanced both ways, then crossed the street.

Ellie's father had recognized early in his career the importance of customer relations. He'd strived to make the feed store a friendly place in which to conduct business. He'd wanted to give ranchers and anyone else who dropped off an order a cozy place to sit and chat. The large shaded porch had been furnished with chairs and a pop machine for that purpose.

She and Glen had spent many an afternoon in this very spot. They'd been friends long before they'd fallen in love—a love it took them far too long to recognize or acknowledge. Even now, a month after their wedding, it astonished her that they could have been so blind to their feelings.

"Hi," Ellie greeted Jane. "I heard about the riding lesson," she said carefully.

Jane smiled and claimed an empty seat beside Ellie. "It went okay—I think. Cal's teaching me with Atta

Girl, and other than damn near toppling the mare, I did fine."

Glen had told Ellie the story of the saddle slipping during Jane's first lesson. He reported that Cal had laughed so hard in his telling of the story he was almost incomprehensible. It'd taken Glen a while to understand what had happened.

"Actually I'm amazed you're willing to go back for a second lesson, seeing the way Cal behaved," Ellie said, wanting to kick her brother-in-law for his lack of manners.

At the mention of his name, Jane's face brightened. "He was great," she said. "Patient and gentle."

Ellie wondered if she was having a hearing problem. It wasn't possible that they were referring to the same person. *"Cal?"*

Jane eyed her. "Yes, Cal. He's the one who's teaching me."

"I've never heard him referred to as patient and gentle, at least not since Jennifer— " Ellie stopped abruptly.

"Who's Jennifer?" Jane asked.

Ellie sighed inwardly. She'd already mentioned Cal's former fiancée so she might as well continue. "She and Cal were…friendly at one time."

"Friendly?"

"An item."

"How much of an item?"

Ellie could see there was no help for it. "They were engaged."

Jane didn't respond right away. "I see."

Ellie wouldn't have said another word if Jane hadn't pressed. Would have preferred it that way. Apparently Cal was quite taken with the new doctor, and she didn't want to be responsible for upsetting this hopeful turn of events.

"Do you mind telling me what happened?"

That was difficult. If this had concerned anyone other than Cal, Ellie would have suggested Jane simply ask him. But for the past two years Cal had closed himself off from most people as a result of the broken engagement. And he'd rejected the possibility of any other relationship with a woman. Ellie didn't want to scare Jane off; if anything she wanted to encourage a romance between these two lonely people.

Glen had been shocked when he learned that Cal had offered to teach Jane to ride. Even Ellie had been surprised. And delighted. Naturally she'd *hoped* he'd volunteer, but she'd believed it'd take some champion finagling on her part. The last thing she'd expected was for Cal to volunteer on his own.

Ellie hesitated, wondering how much she should say. "There isn't really that much to tell."

"I don't mean to pry," Jane said.

"Well…you should probably know," Ellie said. "Cal never did tell us exactly what went wrong. He loved Jennifer. Anyone looking at the two of them could see the way he felt about her."

Jennifer, though, wasn't the type Ellie would have chosen for her brother-in-law, but then, Cal hadn't sought her opinion. Glen hadn't been impressed by Jennifer, either, but like Ellie, had kept his views to himself. Ellie had met Jennifer, who'd worked at a local branch of a large bank, in the course of business. She'd quickly decided Jennifer Healy was selfish and manipulative, an opinion shared by a number of other people Ellie knew.

"I gather they disagreed about something, and two

days before the wedding," Ellie continued, "Jennifer called the whole thing off. She gave him back the ring and left town."

"Moved?"

"To Houston. Glen heard sometime later that she was living with a salesman."

"She walked out two days before the wedding," Jane repeated slowly.

"A big family wedding," Ellie elaborated. "Cal was stuck with phoning all the guests and telling them the wedding was off. He had to return gifts, cancel all the arrangements… Humiliating, huh? Naturally, everyone speculated about what had gone wrong. But Cal didn't want to answer questions, so he retreated. Didn't come into town for months."

"It must have been a painful time for him."

Ellie nodded. "He wasn't the same afterward."

Jane's eyes asked the obvious question although she didn't voice it.

Ellie answered it, anyway. "He likes you, Jane. You know something? In two years you're the first woman he's done more than speak a few gruff words to."

"Me?" Jane flattened her palm against her chest.

"Yes. I know I'm right. He likes you."

Jane laughed and shook her head. "I don't think so."

"He's teaching you to ride, isn't he?"

"Yes, but I suspect that's because he felt sorry for me."

Ellie dismissed the excuse with a shake of her head. "You don't know Cal the way I do. Since Jennifer walked out on him, his attitude toward women has been less than charitable. Trust me, he's interested in you."

* * *

With Ellie's words ringing in her ears, Jane headed out to Lonesome Coyote Ranch for her second riding lesson. It'd been four days since her last one and she was looking forward to learning more. About horseback riding, yes, but also about Cal Patterson.

Ellie had said it'd been two years since Cal's broken engagement. Two years since he'd participated in anything social. What her friend didn't know was that it'd been even longer for Jane. She was twenty-eight years old and couldn't remember her last real date. There'd been a few get-togethers with other medical students, but even these had been severely curtailed during her internship and residency. When it came to dating, high-school girls had more experience and finesse than she did.

Cal was already in the yard when she arrived. "Howdy," he greeted her.

"Hi." She walked away from her parked car. As she'd jokingly said on Friday, her jeans were less stiff this time. The boots, however, still felt awkward, but eventually she'd get used to wearing them, or so Max Jordan had assured her.

Cal's smile was warm. "I wasn't sure you'd show."

"Why not?"

He chuckled. "Ellie tells me it was exceptionally rude to laugh at your, uh, accident. She says I should apologize."

Jane shrugged off his apology, such as it was. "I'm willing to put the incident behind us if you are."

"I am." He led the way toward the barn. "Atta Girl's been waiting for you. She'd like a second chance, too."

The first part of the lesson went well, as they reviewed what she'd learned the last time. She saddled Atta Girl herself, making sure to check the cinch, then mounted the mare with a boost from Cal and a minimum of fuss.

"How does it feel?" he asked, taking the reins and leading Atta Girl into the corral.

"I didn't realize I'd be this high off the ground." She gripped the saddle horn with both hands. Once they arrived at the fenced area, Cal gave her the reins, and Jane held on for dear life.

Cal had her ease Atta Girl forward in a slow walk. Not bad, she decided. In fact, it was kind of exciting.

"This is great!" she called out. Some of her excitement must have communicated itself to Atta Girl, because the mare increased her speed.

"Ride the horse, not the saddle," he reminded her.

"I know," she shouted back. His advice, however, did little good. Try as she might, Jane felt her rear bouncing hard on the unyielding saddle. She'd bounce up and slam down against the leather with a force powerful enough to jar her molars. Fearing she was about to lose her hat, she held on to it with one hand.

"Are you sure I'm doing this right?" she shouted to Cal, certain she wouldn't be able to maintain her balance another minute. The ground looked a long way down.

Cal mounted his own horse and rode next to her, circling the corral. She envied the grace with which he rode; it was as if man and beast moved as one, just the way those cowboy books said. Jane attempted to work her body in unison with Atta Girl's movements, but couldn't find the appropriate rhythm, despite her efforts.

"How…am…I…doing?" Each word vibrated as she rebounded against the saddle.

"You're a natural," Cal assured her. He slowed the gelding's pace and Atta Girl followed suit. Jane's rear end was grateful, not to mention the rest of her. She would never have guessed that her *teeth* would hurt after a riding lesson.

"Will I ever feel as comfortable in a saddle as you?" she asked, envying his skill and grace. She marveled that he hadn't so much as worked up a sweat.

"Give it time," he said.

Together, side by side, they circled the corral, keeping to a walk. By the time Cal guided her to the gate and helped her dismount, she'd begun to feel like a real rider.

Except for the fact that her legs almost went out from under her when her boots touched the ground. She waited for the numbness to fade, adjusted her jeans and took her first steps. Once she was assured that her teeth were intact and her head wasn't in danger of falling off, she was able to talk.

"I hurt less after a forty-mile bicycle ride," she said, rubbing her derriere with both hands.

"You're still a tenderfoot."

"It isn't my feet that are tender," she countered.

Cal threw back his head and laughed, although she didn't think she'd been that funny. "I don't know anyone who makes me laugh the way you do," he said.

"I just speak the truth," she muttered, and he laughed again.

He helped her remove the saddle and rub down Atta Girl, then invited her to the house.

For a bachelor's place, the house was meticulous. The kitchen countertops were spotless. Either he didn't cook or he cleaned up after himself. Judging by the guys she'd known in medical school, he was a rare man if it was the latter.

"Thirsty?" he asked, opening the refrigerator. "Want a drink?"

"Please."

He took out a couple of cans of soda and handed her one. They sat at the kitchen table, Jane wincing as her rear end made contact with the hard wooden seat.

"You doing anything Friday night?" Cal asked casually, then took a deep swallow of soda.

"Nothing important," she said, thinking he was asking about her next riding lesson. "What time would you like me to be here?"

"Here?" He frowned. "I was inviting you to dinner."

At first Jane was too stunned to answer. Cal Patterson was asking her out on a date. A real date. It'd been so long since she'd been asked that she didn't even recognize it when she was. "I'd be—" she flashed him a smile "—delighted. I'll look forward to seeing you Friday night."

When he walked her to her car a few minutes later, he told her that her riding was progressing nicely.

She grinned. "That's because I've got a great teacher."

Cal opened her car door. "I'll pick you up at seven," he said. "That okay?"

"Seven," she agreed and hoped he didn't hear the nervousness in her voice. She had a *date,* a real date. With Cal Patterson.

Maybe Texas wasn't so bad, after all.

Friday night Cal shifted the hangers from one side of his closet to the other, looking for a decent shirt. He didn't know what in hell had prompted him to invite Jane to dinner.

Then again, he *did* know. He liked her. Fool that he was, he'd allowed her to get under his skin. He blamed Ellie for this. Blamed and thanked, depending on how he felt at any given moment.

He could add Grady Weston's name to the list of troublemakers. First, his brother decides to marry Ellie. Then not a month passes before Cal's best friend from childhood announces *he's* engaged, too. Grady was going to marry Caroline Daniels, the postmistress. Cal shook his head. The men in Promise were deserting bachelorhood in droves.

Cal had no intention of joining their ranks. Asking Jane to dinner might be misconstrued as romantic interest in the town's new doctor, but that wasn't the case. He liked her, enjoyed her company, but considered her safe. She was a California girl, born and raised. A city girl. In three years' time, she'd be heading back where she belonged, where she fit in. What appealed to him was the way she could make him laugh. And hell, stuck as she was in small-town Texas, he felt sorry for her.

That was it, Cal decided as he jerked a clean shirt off the hanger and put it on. He knew she was all alone down here; he was just being nice to an out-of-state girl, inviting her to share a meal and a few laughs. After that he wouldn't see her again, he vowed. Except for their riding lessons, of course.

He hadn't actually expected her to show up for the second lesson, not after the way he'd reacted to her fall off the saddle. A smile touched the corners of his mouth as he remembered her Butch Cassidy roll beneath Atta

Girl's belly. My, oh, my, could that woman move. Which led to thoughts he immediately censored…

He fastened the shirt snaps and eased into a clean pair of Wranglers. He wasn't going to a lot of trouble for this dinner, no sir. Nor had he mentioned it to his brother. Glen would make more of it than was there, and he'd for sure tell his wife. Cal did *not* want Ellie to know about this.

A Johnny Cash tune drifted into his mind and he whistled along—until he realized what he was doing and abruptly stopped. He hadn't whistled in years. What the hell was happening here?

The forty-minute drive into town was accomplished in no time at all, or so it seemed. He'd take Jane to dinner as promised, then the minute they were finished he'd escort her home, head to Billy D's and meet up with his friends. On Friday night Billy's was always packed.

Another thing he'd do, Cal determined as he walked the short distance from the curb to Jane's front door, was have a little heart-to-heart with the doc. He had to explain that while this evening was a pleasant diversion, this was not a relationship with a future. It wasn't a relationship, period.

As gently as he could he'd tell her that he wasn't interested in her romantically. There wasn't any point in it, seeing that she'd be returning to California and he was staying here. Being the kind of guy he was, honest and straightforward, he didn't want to mislead her into believing something could develop out of this. It was just a dinner. One dinner.

He rang her doorbell and waited. He might even say something right away. Get it over with quickly.

The door opened and Cal's jaw dropped. Wow. Jane

was beautiful. She wore a two-tone blue denim ankle-length skirt with a matching blouse. The buttons were big silver-dollar coins. With her sparkling blue eyes and short blond hair, she looked sophisticated. Western *and* sophisticated. Sort of L.A. meets San Antonio. It was all he could do not to slobber.

"I'll be ready in a moment," she said, holding open the screen door.

Cal removed his hat when he walked into the small house. He remained standing while she reached for her purse and clipped the beeper onto her black leather belt.

"I'm on call," she said, explaining the beeper.

"You clean up real good," he said once he found his voice.

She smiled. "You don't look so bad yourself."

"Any place special you'd like to eat?" he asked.

"You choose."

Not that there was much choice. The Chili Pepper was the best restaurant in town, but they'd eaten there the week before. The café in the bowling alley served damn good chow, but it wasn't the type of place to take Dr. Texas, especially with her dressed to the nines. That left the Mexican Lindo, which he suggested.

"I'm game," she said.

The restaurant was less than five blocks away and the weather was accommodating, so they walked. They were led to a corner booth and Cal felt grateful for that, since it afforded them a measure of privacy. They'd barely sat down when the waiter delivered a bowl of corn chips and fresh salsa. Jane glanced at the menu and quickly made her decision.

"Cheese enchiladas," she told him before he could ask.

Cal selected chili verde, one of his favorites.

He asked for a beer, and because she was on call, Jane ordered an iced tea. They were just beginning to relax when Jane's beeper went off.

She removed it from her belt and read the code. "There's an emergency," she said. "If you'll wait a couple of minutes, I'll phone the service."

"Sure." This was what he wanted, Cal tried to tell himself. She was offering him a perfect out, and he should be thankful. He hadn't stopped to think about the questions their being together were sure to raise. Lots of questions, especially from his family and friends.

Jane was gone only a couple of moments. "It's Jeremy Bishop," she said, hurrying back. "Nell thinks he's broken his arm. She's driving him to the clinic now."

"Is it bad?"

"I won't know until I see him. I'm sorry, Cal, but I have to go."

"I understand," he assured her.

Her eyes showed her regret before she turned and walked quickly out the door. As soon as she was gone, he realized she'd be alone at the clinic. Nell was an emotionally strong woman, but Jeremy was her son and she might need someone to talk to while Jane dealt with the boy's injury.

Cal signaled the waiter. "Can you bring me the bill?"

The young man was clearly flustered. "But you haven't eaten yet. If there's a problem…"

"There's no problem," Cal said. "Dr. Dickinson had an emergency and I've decided to leave myself."

The waiter nodded gravely. "Your order just came up. Would you like a takeout box?"

"Sure," Cal said. He hadn't thought of that.

When the waiter finished transferring the dinners

to cardboard containers, Cal paid for them and made his way to the clinic.

He arrived at the same time as Nell, Jeremy and Nell's other child, Emma. Nell looked pale and distraught. She'd wrapped Jeremy's arm in a pillow; he was obviously in pain and his face was streaked with tears.

"Hello, Jeremy," Jane said, taking charge immediately.

Cal wasn't sure she realized he was there until she turned. "Oh! Hi, Cal."

"I thought I'd keep Nell company in the waiting room," he said.

"Good idea." She thanked him with a smile. Cal put their dinners on the reception desk and guided Nell to a chair, while Jane slid an arm around Jeremy's shoulders and steered him toward the examination room.

"I want to be with my son," Nell insisted.

"I'll come for you in a few minutes," Jane promised, "but first I need an X-ray to see what we're dealing with here."

Nell accepted the decision and sank into her chair. She stared straight ahead, her features sharp with fear. "I found him by the tractor," she whispered.

Cal wasn't sure she was talking to him, but he understood the significance of what she was saying. Nell had been the one to find her husband trapped beneath a tractor. The vehicle had turned over on him and crushed him, and she'd been powerless to do anything but hold his hand while he died.

"Jeremy climbed up on it even though I've warned him repeatedly to stay away."

"Seems to me he's learned his lesson," Cal said. "I

don't think you'll have any problem keeping him away from now on."

Nell smiled, and Cal wondered if he should stick around or head over to Billy D's. To his surprise he discovered he had no real desire to join his friends. He'd much rather stay right where he was and help Nell— and Dr. Texas.

Five

"In a month you'll be husband and wife," Reverend Wade McMillen said, leaning back in his leather chair in the study.

It didn't seem possible, but the wedding date had sneaked up on her. Caroline had discovered that putting together a wedding, even a small one involving just family and a few close friends, had demanded every spare moment she had.

"A month," Caroline repeated, glancing at Grady. They'd been attending counseling sessions with Wade for the past few weeks. Even now, Caroline had a difficult time taking it all in. She'd loved Grady for years, but had hidden her feelings behind a prickly attitude. It used to be they couldn't stay in the same room without sparks flying and tempers flaring. They ignited fireworks now, too, but for other reasons.

"It doesn't seem possible," Grady said, his gaze holding Caroline's.

"You're as ready now as you'll ever be," Wade said, grinning at them. "I've counseled a lot of couples in my time. I often get a feel for the relationship before the vows are spoken. And I'm confident the two of you are going to have a strong secure marriage."

Grady reached for Caroline's hand and squeezed her fingers. "I feel that way, too."

Caroline nodded, her love for Grady clear to see.

"No problems with Maggie?" Wade asked.

"None," Caroline assured him. There'd been a time when the child had been terrified of Grady's booming voice, but no longer. Her six-year-old was enthralled with him. Caroline had no doubt of his love for her daughter. The day Maggie had disappeared, kidnapped by Richard Weston, Grady had proved how deeply he cared for the child. And for her.

"She isn't showing any bad effects from the time she was missing, then?" Wade went on.

"Not that we can tell," Caroline replied. "She seems to be sleeping better these days. She hasn't woken up with nightmares recently, either." Caroline frowned, shaking her head. "No matter how hard I tried, though, I couldn't get her to tell me about her dreams—or what happened when she was gone. Then overnight, the bad dreams stopped. She's her normal cheerful self again."

"She talks about me becoming her daddy and seems genuinely excited about it," Grady added.

Wade looked at him. "You were worried you were somehow the cause of Maggie's nightmares?"

"Yeah, but now she's more accepting of me and more affectionate than ever."

Caroline nodded; she was pleased that Grady had started the adoption process. "I'm convinced that whatever was troubling her is somehow connected to the time Richard had her."

"Richard," Wade repeated, his brow furrowed. "Has anyone heard anything from him or about him lately?"

"Not a word," Grady said. "I know the sheriff's pretty frustrated. It's like Richard's disappeared off the face of the earth."

A chill raced down Caroline's spine every time she thought about Grady's brother. He'd hurt a lot of people, but what infuriated her more than anything was how he'd used and abused his own family. He'd run off with the ranch assets the day the Westons laid their parents to rest, creating untold hardship for Grady and his sister, Savannah. Six years later he'd returned, down on his luck. Grady and Savannah had taken him back in, tried to help him, and once more Richard had proved he couldn't be trusted. After charging thousands of dollars' worth of goods, Richard had disappeared again.

Grady, being honorable and decent, had paid those bills himself rather than have the local businesses absorb the losses. While it meant they wouldn't be starting their marriage with any substantial savings, Caroline loved Grady for being the kind of man he was.

"Shall we schedule the wedding rehearsal?" Wade asked.

Brimming with excitement, Caroline and Grady nodded; soon after, their session was over.

Grady tucked his arm around her waist as they left the church and headed toward the parking lot.

"Have I told you today how much I love you?" Grady asked. He kissed her as he opened the passenger door.

"It's something I'm not going to tire of hearing," Caroline said. Grady's love was a blessing she hadn't expected to receive. She was coming to this marriage with a child and a lot of emotional baggage. Much of that was thanks to Richard, who'd fathered Maggie during a brief and ultimately meaningless liaison. So meaningless he didn't even remember it. Caroline had been terrified that this would make her and Maggie a burden for Grady, another mess of Richard's he had to clean up. She'd been convinced it would be better to let Grady walk out of her life—but he'd refused to let that happen. He loved her and Maggie. When she told him about Maggie's father, his initial reaction had been shock—because she'd kept the truth from him. But he'd recovered quickly and said that the man who raised and loved Maggie would be her *real* father, and that would be him. In the weeks since their engagement Grady had proved his devotion to her and to Maggie over and over again.

"Do we need to pick up Maggie right away?" Grady asked now.

Dovie Boyd had volunteered to baby-sit the little girl during the counseling sessions with Wade. "What do you have in mind?" she asked, leaning her head against his shoulder.

Grady started the truck's engine. "I was thinking we could stop at the bowling alley for a pizza." He glanced at her. "You game?"

"I'm game for anything with you," she assured him. "But I'll need to phone Dovie to make sure Maggie's okay first."

"No problem." He backed out of their parking space and they drove to the bowling alley.

After a quick phone call, Caroline joined Grady in a booth at the café. He got out so she could slip in beside him. Not so long ago, he'd have preferred to sit in the cold rather than share her company, Caroline mused. Now they could hardly bear to be separated by even a table.

"Everything all right with Maggie?" he asked.

"She's fine. Dovie said she's already asleep."

"Hey, first grade is a big step for a kid."

Especially when Maggie had only recently outgrown naps. She fell asleep before her eight o'clock bedtime most evenings.

"Dovie doesn't mind keeping her a bit longer?"

"Not at all," Caroline told him. She didn't mention that she was worried about her friend. Although Dovie hadn't said much about her breakup with Sheriff Hennessey, it had obviously been hard for her; a smile didn't come as easily and she seemed listless, depressed. From what Caroline had seen of the sheriff, he wasn't handling the situation any better.

Caroline wished she could help in some way, but experience had taught her that Frank and Dovie had to work this out themselves. She wasn't optimistic, though. Their relationship had been a long-standing one, and if they were going to reconcile, she suspected it would have happened by now.

"I talked to Glen yesterday and he told me something about Cal," Grady said after they'd ordered the mushroom-and-pepperoni pizza. "You'll never guess."

"When it comes to Cal, you're right—I won't guess."

"He's got a date."

"A date? Cal?" Caroline was shocked. "Who?"

Grady smiled. "The new doc."

"Jane Dickinson?"

"Right. He's teaching her how to ride."

This *was* news. "What possessed him to do such a thing? Cal, the woman-hater."

Grady shrugged. "Hell if I know. I gotta tell you it came as a shock to me, too." He leaned toward Caroline. "Cal didn't even tell his brother. Glen found out from his mother, who heard about it from Dovie, who heard from the good doctor herself."

"Typical," Caroline said with a laugh. "But still, it sounds promising."

Love would change Cal Patterson, and she was anxious to see it happen. Ever since his broken engagement, he'd shut himself off from any association with the opposite sex. Caroline suspected falling in love would have a powerful positive impact on him.

Caroline liked Cal and knew that his friendship was important to Grady. She was pleased that Grady had asked him to serve as best man at their wedding. In every way that counted, Cal was more of a brother to Grady than his own.

"I saw Cal's truck this evening," Grady said.

"Parked outside the health clinic," Caroline guessed.

He nodded. "I have a feeling about this."

"A good feeling, I hope."

"A very good feeling," he said, grinning.

The clock said almost ten before Jane had finished setting Jeremy Bishop's arm and securing it in a cast. After giving Nell instructions for the pain medication, Jane and Cal walked the family outside.

"You were a good patient, Jeremy," Jane told the boy. He'd been in a lot of pain, but despite that, he'd willingly cooperated with everything she'd needed him to do.

"He's got a lot of his father in him," Nell said, looking proudly at her son. She stood outside her car, drawn and tired from the ordeal. "Thank you both," she said.

"I was pretty shaken when we first arrived. I'm afraid if I'd gone into the examination room, I'd have done something stupid—like faint."

Jane had thought the same thing. "You're his mother. It's to be expected."

"You were great with him," Nell told her. "I can't thank you enough."

"That's what I'm here for." It was helping people like Nell and her family that made Jane's job a pleasure. They hadn't really met before tonight, but she'd heard about Nell from Ruth Bishop, a heart patient. Nell was a widow and Ruth's daughter-in-law.

"Go home, get plenty of rest, and if the pain doesn't decrease, give me a call."

"I will," Nell promised, climbing into the car. "Thanks again."

Jane and Cal stood by the door of the clinic until Nell had pulled out of sight.

"You hungry?" Cal asked, his hand on Jane's shoulder.

"Starving," she confessed.

"Me, too."

They warmed the takeout in the microwave and sat side by side on the examination table, holding the cardboard containers on their laps.

"This tastes like heaven," Jane told him between bites. The enchilada sauce and melting cheese dripped from her plastic fork.

"That's because we're hungry."

"I'm sorry our dinner date was ruined." She did feel bad about that. Cal had been thoughtful and patient—bringing them their meal, comforting Nell, sitting here for hours—and she wanted him to know how much she appreciated it.

"I'm not," he surprised her by saying. Her reaction must have shown in her eyes because he added, "It was good to see you in action. You're a damned good doctor."

His praise flustered her and she looked away. "Thank you."

"You were great with the kid," he said and hopped down from the table to toss the container in the garbage.

"I appreciated your help. Nell was frazzled and anxious." She crossed the room to discard her leftovers; when she turned around, she inadvertently bumped into Cal.

His arm shot out to balance her, although she wasn't in danger of falling. The move had been instinctive, but the moment he touched her, she froze. Cal did, too. It was a little thing, of no importance, but it caught her off guard. The shaken look on Cal's face told her he was equally affected.

Then before her instincts could warn her, it happened. Cal bent his head and kissed her. It was almost as though that, too, was an accident. The kiss was hard, quick, their mouths moist and warm. Then it was over.

Jane stared at him, unblinking. Cal stared back. They studied each other for a startled moment. He seemed about to apologize when he suddenly grinned, instead. It was one of the sexiest smiles she'd ever seen. Then he kissed her again.

As kisses went, this one was innocent. Simple. Yet Jane trembled with the aftershock. She'd been too long without a man, she decided. That was why this rancher had such a powerful effect on her senses.

Desperate to steer her mind away from what had just happened, she said, "I…I spoke with Dovie Boyd recently. She happened to mention a ghost town."

Cal frowned, but Jane wasn't sure his displeasure was the result of their kiss or her comment. Possibly both.

"Bitter End," Jane added. "Have you ever heard of it?"

He nodded and shoved his hands into his pockets.

He wasn't forthcoming with any more information. "Then there really *is* a ghost town in the area?" she prodded.

Cal shrugged.

Jane made herself busy about the room, putting away her supplies. "Have you been there?"

He didn't answer until she turned to face him, and even then his eyes avoided hers. "Once, as a kid."

Her excitement grew. "Will you take me there? I'd love to see what it's like now."

"Jane, I can't."

His refusal bewildered her. "Why not?"

"I don't even know if I could find it."

"But we could do that together. I'll be taking more riding lessons, and we've got to move me out of the corral at some point. This would give me a goal, some incentive."

"I don't think so."

"Why not?" Jane could tell he wasn't pleased with her persistence.

"It's dangerous there."

"All I want to do is see it," she said, unwilling to give up without an argument. "One time, that's all I'm asking."

"It's not a good idea."

It was his attitude that got to her—as if she were a child who had to settle for *because I said so* as an excuse. How could he kiss her one moment and insult her the next?

"Is there a reason for this?" she asked, her voice growing cool.

"A very good one."

She waited for him to explain himself, and when he didn't, she said it for him. "It's because I'm an outsider, isn't it? Because I wasn't born and raised here. It's all right for me to give three years of my life to this community, but I'll never be fully accepted." The strength of her feelings shocked Jane. It hurt that he'd categorically deny her the one thing she'd asked.

His features softened. "Jane, that's not it."

"Then what *is* it?"

"First, I don't know where Bitter End is. I really don't. Second, I've got better things to do with my time than wander around the countryside looking for some old town best forgotten."

This was quite a speech for Cal. "But you've already been there once."

"Years ago," he said, "when I was a kid."

"You should be able to find it again."

"Jane, *no*."

The evening had started out with great promise; now this. What Cal Patterson didn't understand was that she was an old hand at getting what she wanted. She'd been forced to acquire the skills, to refine the tactics. Medical school had taught her that. She'd learned how to deal with older physicians who felt women had no place in medicine. She'd come face-to-face with the old-boy network more than once. People assumed this sort of outdated thinking wasn't prevalent any longer, but they were wrong. She'd seen it and dealt with it on a daily basis, and learned there was more than one way to achieve what she wanted.

"I'm sorry to hear you won't help me find the ghost town," she said softly.

"It's no place for a greenhorn."

"I see." Her tone was noncommittal.

He narrowed his eyes. "Why do I have the feeling I'm butting my head against a brick wall?"

So he knew. "I'll find Bitter End with or without you," she said matter-of-factly.

Cal's eyes closed for an instant. "And if I decide not to continue with the riding lessons, you'll have someone else teach you, too?"

"Yes." She wasn't going to lie about her intentions. That was exactly what she'd do if necessary—only she hoped it wouldn't be. "I'd much rather continue with you, though." She took a deep breath. "Cal, I'm not trying to be manipulative here. But I want to see this town. I'll admit I've become kind of obsessed with it. And I'll do whatever it takes to get there."

It was several moments before he responded. "It's not safe in Bitter End."

"So you said."

"The town's...evil."

"Evil? You mean there are *ghosts?*"

"Not that type of evil." He paced the room as though it was impossible for him to stand still any longer. "Grady Weston, Glen and I found Bitter End a number of years ago. I must have been about fifteen at the time, high on adventure. Fearless, like all kids that age. Cocky, some might say."

"I wouldn't have thought that was so long ago," she joked.

He didn't crack a smile. "We searched for weeks, the three of us. It was summer and we went out looking every day we could. We studied maps, even checked out an old journal that had belonged to Grady's father and had a few cryptic hints."

"But you found the town," Jane said, her voice rising with excitement.

"Yes, eventually we located it."

"Did you explore? What was it like? I'd love to see it! Oh, Cal, please reconsider."

His sigh was deep and troubled. "You can't imagine how thrilled we were when we stumbled across it. We'd been searching all that time, and then one afternoon there it was. Surprisingly most of the buildings were intact."

"That's incredible!" Just wait until her mother heard this. She'd want to know every detail.

"But it wasn't what we expected," Cal told her, his eyes somber.

"How do you mean?"

"There's something wrong in that town. Like I said, something evil. We all felt it the moment we rode down the street. The horses felt it, too. The entire time we were there, they were skittish."

"Something evil?" This made no sense to Jane. "What exactly was the feeling like?"

"I've thought about it a lot in the last few months, ever since Grady told me Savannah's been out there."

"Savannah Smith?" Jane wondered if Cal realized he'd handed her a way of locating the town.

"She went there looking for old roses. According to what Grady said, she felt it, too. That same feeling."

"Well, what *was* it?"

Cal shook his head. "It's impossible to describe. I've never experienced anything like it before or since."

"Try," she pleaded.

"Like there's a rope tightening around my chest," he said, struggling to find the words. "A feeling of sadness. Loss. As though more than a century wasn't enough time to wipe out the grief or the agony of whatever happened."

"I'd still like to see it for myself," she told him.

"I figured you would." His tone was resigned.

"Does this mean you'll take me?" She clasped her hands, prayerlike. She didn't want another riding teacher. She liked the one she had. And she wanted Cal to be her guide to Bitter End; if there was danger in the town, she'd rather he was with her.

"All right," he finally agreed. "We'll go look for it."

Overjoyed, Jane threw her arms around his neck and hugged him. The next instant Cal wrapped his arms around her waist and pulled her against him. Without warning, his mouth crashed down on hers. The kiss was urgent. Exciting. Cal didn't give Jane an opportunity to break it off, not that she would have, but gradually, as though he realized what he'd done, he mellowed the kiss. He wove his fingers into her hair, then slowly, cautiously, they began to relax against each other. Jane moved her lips, opening to him—and the excitement built again.

Cal groaned. He twisted his mouth against hers,

seeking more, and Jane was all too willing to comply. She wasn't sure a man had ever kissed her quite like this. With such need, such intensity.

When he broke away, they were both gasping. "I...I think I need to sit down," Jane said, reaching for the nearest chair and lowering herself into it.

"Me, too," Cal said.

Involuntarily she raised her hands to her lips. The kiss had been fierce. Wonderful.

"I didn't mean for that to happen," he said next. But instead of sitting, he stalked about the room.

"I know."

"I think you should realize I've already decided it would be...ill-advised for us to get involved."

He sounded so absurdly formal. Had she been in full possession of her wits, she would have challenged him, demanded to know his reasons. But his kisses had left her senseless. Her own pride played a role in her reaction, too. She just looked at him, unwilling, unable, to respond.

"I don't mean to insult you," he added.

"You didn't," she was quick to assure him, then hesitated, more confused than offended. "Are you saying you want to put a halt to the riding lessons?"

"Not at all. When will you be ready again?"

From the intense look in his eyes, Jane had the feeling he was inquiring about a lot more than horseback riding. "Tomorrow?" She raised her eyes to his. She wasn't shy or cowardly or afraid of risks. Medicine wasn't a career for a woman who was weak at heart. If she had been, Jane wouldn't have lasted a month in medical school.

"I'll see you at three," he said on his way out the door.

"I'll be there," she called after him. It'd take more than stubborn pride to upset her. She had a strong feeling that Cal Patterson had met his match—and an even stronger feeling that she'd met hers.

Richard was bored but he was smart enough to realize that the moment he left Bitter End, he'd risk being caught and hauled to jail.

By now, despite switching license plates, the truck he'd "borrowed" would be listed in a police computer as stolen.

Relieving his boredom by leaving the ghost town was a risk he couldn't afford to take, although it was damned tempting.

Leaning his chair against the side of the old hotel, he strummed a few chords on his guitar. Only, it wasn't nearly as much fun to play without an audience.

He reached for the half-empty whiskey bottle and indulged in a healthy swig. The liquor wasn't going to last, he could see that. He'd drunk twice as much as he'd estimated. His limited supply would need to see him through the next few months. A bottle wasn't much company on the long lonely nights, but it was all he had. Hell, a man took what he could get.

He strummed a few more chords on the guitar and sang halfheartedly. If his life had taken a different turn, he might have entered show business, made a name for himself. He would've enjoyed that.

He returned the bottle to his lips, shuddering at the potency of the drink. Enough liquor would help him forget. Or help him remember. Problem was, he couldn't decide which he wanted anymore.

He tipped back his head and shouted with everything

in him, "Is anyone home?" He waited for a response and was both relieved and disheartened when none came.

Even a ghost might be some company.

According to the days he'd marked off on the calendar, this was Friday night. If he'd still been in Promise, instead of hiding up in this godforsaken ghost town, he'd probably be at Billy D's, drinking with the boys. Shooting the breeze, playing pool or maybe a game of darts.

He'd be singing, too, along with the jukebox. A little David Allan Coe, the ex-con turned singer. His music could get raunchy and off-color, but Richard didn't mind. It was just the thing for a Friday night at the saloon.

But this Friday—and how many others to follow?— Richard would be alone.

What he missed even more was female companionship. He could have had a cozy love nest here had he been thinking clearly. But everything had come down on him and there hadn't been time to find a woman to bring with him—or maybe two.

The loneliness wouldn't be half so bad with a couple of sweet young things to keep him occupied. Yeah, he could've convinced them this was an adventure. And he could've let them fight over him, which was guaranteed to be entertaining. Not too hard on his ego, either. Women didn't walk away when *he* was around. All except Ellie Frasier, now Ellie Patterson. Richard frowned. He didn't know what he'd done wrong. Her choosing Glen Patterson over him hurt his pride.

"She's a fool," he said aloud.

One day Ellie would regret her choice, Richard was

sure of it. She could have married him, instead of that hick Patterson. Everything had gone downhill after that.

The creditors had started closing in and it'd become impossible to hide the charges he'd made on Grady's accounts. As soon as Grady learned the truth, he would have kicked him out. But Richard hadn't given his brother the chance; moving with speed, he'd left Promise before any of it came to light.

He'd carefully worked out every detail of his plan, stocking up on stolen food and supplies for weeks beforehand. It wasn't an easy task, but he'd been at his deceptive best. He was proud of the way he'd pulled it off, too, keeping his activities hidden from the family.

Grady and Savannah were pathetic, really.

As far as Richard was concerned, his brother and sister deserved everything they got. Anyone that trusting needed to be taught a lesson. Richard had burned them twice, and it hadn't been difficult. He wondered if they'd ever learn; he suspected they wouldn't. They weren't the type, neither one of them. He experienced a twinge of guilt but refused to waste time on a useless emotion. Grady and Savannah were nothing short of gullible. He looked at it this way—he'd done them a favor. Taught them a life lesson. He couldn't help it if they were slow learners.

A shooting star blazed across the autumn sky and Richard raised his bottle in salute. He wished he had a woman on his arm, but okay, that wasn't possible. His little home away from home was a damn sight better than a jail cell, and that was where he was headed if the law ever got hold of him.

Life was much too complicated, Richard mused. What had started out as a simple transaction back in

New York had gone sour. The bad taste of it lingered in his mouth, but there was no use fretting about it now.

In addition to his many talents, Richard Weston was a survivor. He might be down but he wasn't out, and once his current troubles came to an end, he'd be back on his feet.

If Ellie had married him, he would've used her inheritance to pay off some rather dangerous debts—and to grease the right palms. But she was with Glen. Stupid woman. She didn't know a good thing when she saw it.

He tipped back the bottle, took another drink and immediately felt worse. He was lonely and restless. All the self-talk in the world wasn't going to change that. While he might be safe, he wasn't happy.

Six

Jane removed the blood-pressure cuff from Ruth Bishop's upper arm and noted the reading on her chart. Ruth's diastolic and systolic numbers were well within the normal range, which was good. The medication was doing its job.

"Overall, how are you feeling?" Jane asked as she reached for her prescription pad to write a renewal.

"Good," Ruth said after a short hesitation.

Jane looked up. "Is there anything else you'd like me to check? You're here now and I'd hate to have you think of something later." Jane held office hours on Saturday morning because it seemed a convenient time for a lot of people. If Ruth decided, once she got home, that she *did* have some other concern, Jane wouldn't be available again until Monday. Not only that, Ruth would have to make the long drive a second time.

Jane waited quietly for a minute or so.

Ruth finally spoke. "Actually it's my daughter-in-law," she said.

Jane sat down and made herself comfortable. It'd taken her a while to realize that, when it came to confidences, people shared at their own pace and in their own way. Not just the people in Promise, Texas, but people everywhere.

"Nell was in last night with Jeremy," Jane said, wanting Ruth to know she was familiar with her daughter-in-law.

"I know. Jeremy said that for a lady doctor you weren't half-bad."

Jane unsuccessfully hid a smile.

"He meant that as a compliment," Ruth said, her cheeks growing pink.

"Don't worry, Ruth, I hear that all the time."

"It's difficult for some folks to get used to the idea of a female doctor."

Ruth wasn't telling Jane something she didn't already know.

"I'm living with Nell," Ruth explained, "helping her out when I can. Encouraging her. It was a blow to both of us when Jake died... I never expected my son would join his father before me." Her eyes teared up, and Jane leaned forward to hand her a tissue. Ruth thanked her in a choked voice and dabbed her eyes.

"So...what about Nell?" Jane asked gently, giving the older woman time to compose herself.

"Early this morning I found her in the living room weeping. That's not like her. She's not a woman who shows her pain. When we buried Jake, it was Nell who remained strong, who comforted the family, who held us all together. I don't know what we would've done without her."

From her psychology classes, Jane remembered that in a family crisis there was usually one member who remained emotionally steady for others to lean on for support. She'd seen the truth of this time and again. Sometimes family members traded roles, almost taking turns, at comforting and helping one another through a crisis.

"Nell shed her share of tears, I know that," Ruth said, "but she did it privately. She loved my son, grieves for him still."

"I'm sure that's true," Jane said. She hardly knew Nell, but the widow was unmistakably a strong independent woman, someone she'd like to call a friend.

"Jeremy's broken arm shook her more than I realized. I wasn't home at the time. The Moorhouse sisters, Betty Knoll and I play bridge on Friday nights. Edwina and Lily bring out their cordial—same recipe Dovie uses—and we let down our hair and relax."

Jane could picture the four older women and suspected they were crackerjack bridge players.

"Nell told me Jeremy had climbed on the tractor. That he fell off and broke his arm." Ruth grew quiet for a moment. "You may not know this, but Jake died in a tractor accident. It must have been terribly upsetting for Nell finding Jeremy by the tractor. Especially since she's the one who found Jake. He was still alive and in shock, but was gone before help could reach him."

"I'm so sorry," Jane murmured. She could only imagine the horror of finding your husband trapped beneath a tractor. Nell had been pale and shaken when she arrived with Jeremy, Jane remembered; she must have been reliving that unbearable time. Thank heaven Cal had been at the clinic and was able to distract Nell while she dealt with the injured boy.

"It's been almost three years since Jake's been gone. It doesn't seem like it could be that long, but it is."

"It's a big adjustment, losing a son," Jane said softly.

"And losing a husband. Last night I found Nell sitting in her rocker by the fireplace," Ruth said, continuing with her story. "It was three in the morning, and when I asked her what woke her up, Nell told me she hadn't been to bed yet."

"Had she been up with Jeremy?" The question was prompted by Jane's concern that perhaps the pain medication hadn't worked adequately. After the shock of a broken bone, Jeremy needed his rest. His mother did, too.

"No. Nell was…remembering." Ruth fell silent for a moment. "I…I worry about my daughter-in-law," she admitted. "It's time she moved on with her life. Met someone else."

Jane said nothing, preferring to let the other woman speak.

"I don't think it's a good idea for her to spend the rest of her life grieving for Jake," Ruth said, her own voice trembling with emotion. "I know…knew my son and he wouldn't have wanted that."

"Have you told her this?" Jane asked.

"Oh, yes, a number of times. She brushes it off. Last summer, for the Cattlemen's Association Dance, she received two invitations. I was ecstatic, thinking it was past time the men in this town paid her some attention."

Jane was thinking Nell had done better than she had herself. No one had asked her, but then, she'd been new to the community and hadn't met a lot of people yet. By that she meant Cal. He would've been her first choice had she known him.

"Nell turned down both offers," Ruth said, pinching her lips in disapproval. "No amount of coaxing could get her to change her mind, either." She exhaled noisily and Jane recognized Ruth's impatience with her daughter-in-law. "As it turned out, Emma had an upset tummy that night, so Nell made a quick appearance at the dance but came home within the hour. I was babysitting and I told her to stay as long as she wanted—have a good time, I said, but she'd have none of it."

It sounded to Jane as though Emma's upset stomach had been a convenient excuse for Nell to hurry home.

"How can I encourage her?" Ruth asked.

This was at the heart of her worries, Jane realized. "You can't," she said.

"But it's been almost three years," Ruth said again.

"Nell has to be the one to recognize when it's time. No one else can do that for her."

"I know, but I'd like her to get out more. Socialize. Spend time with her friends, but she hardly even does that. Nell works too hard and laughs too little."

"It's not something you can force," Jane said. "Nell will know when she's ready."

"I hope it's soon," Ruth murmured. "My son was a wonderful man, but she's too fine a woman to pine for him the rest of her life. Much too fine."

Jane was sure that was true.

Storm clouds darkened the afternoon. Glancing toward the sky, Cal hurried outside. Electrical storms weren't uncommon in the Texas Hill Country, and he wanted his livestock in the shelter of the barn.

The dogs helped him and he'd gotten Atta Girl and a chestnut mare named Cheyenne safely into the barn when he saw Jane's car pull into the yard. Damn, with the approach of the storm, he'd forgotten about the lesson. Despite that, she hadn't been far from his thoughts all day. Not since the moment he'd first kissed her.

He didn't know what had driven him to do anything so foolish, especially after insisting there was no future in this relationship. Impulse, he supposed—an impulse he planned to avoid from now on.

Frightened by the thunder, Moonshine, Glen's favorite gelding, pranced about the yard, making him difficult to catch. He wouldn't have given Glen nearly as much trouble, but there was nothing Cal could do about that now.

The wind howled and the first fat drops of rain fell haphazardly from the sky. "Can I help?" Jane had to shout to be heard.

"Go in the house before you get soaked," Cal ordered. The rain was falling steadily now, and Cal knew it would only grow more intense.

"I can do something!"

He should've known she'd insist on helping him. Dr. Texas wasn't the type who took orders willingly. Cal groaned; he certainly knew how to pick 'em. He couldn't be attracted to a docile eager-to-please female. Oh, no, that would be too easy. Instead, he had to go and complicate his life with a woman whose personality was as strong and obstinate as his own.

Against his wishes, Jane ran to the corral and stood on the opposite side, waving her hands high above her head. To Cal's amazement Moonshine had a change of heart. Either that, or the quarter horse was so unsettled by the sight of a California girl flapping her arms around, he figured the barn was the safest place for him. In an abrupt turnaround, the gelding trotted obediently into the barn, one of the dogs barking at his heels.

Cal followed him inside and out of the rain. He waited for Jane to join him before closing the door. The rain fell in earnest, a real downpour, pounding the ground with such force the drops ricocheted three inches upward.

Cal led Moonshine into his stall. "I didn't think you'd come, what with the storm and all," he told Jane.

"I wasn't sure I should."

It went against his pride to let her know how pleased he was she had.

"Do you want me to drive home?" she asked, sounding oddly uncertain and a bit defensive.

It was the way he'd feel had circumstances been reversed. "You're here now. The weather's a write-off but we'll make the best of it." Which shouldn't be too hard. Dr. Texas looked damn good in her hip-hugging jeans and boots.

He removed his jacket and handed it to her. "Let's make a run for the house." Opening the barn door, he looked out and cringed. The rain was still coming down in torrents and it was almost impossible to see across the yard. They'd be drenched to the skin by the time they reached the house.

Holding the jacket above her head for protection, Jane moved beside him to view the downpour. "My goodness, does it rain like this often?"

"Often enough," he muttered.

"I've never seen anything like it."

Seeing she'd been born and raised in Southern California, Cal could believe that. He'd read about small towns near Death Valley where the children had never seen rain at all.

"You ready?" he asked.

"Any time," she said, with a game smile.

Lightning flashed. Not willing to wait any longer, Cal offered Jane his hand. She clasped it tightly and held the jacket over her head with her free hand. They sprinted toward the house, sliding a bit on the muddy ground. He kept his pace deliberately even, fearing she might slip.

Breathing hard, they burst into the house together. Jane released Cal's hand immediately. The water dripped from him as if he'd just stepped out of the shower, and his clothes were plastered to his skin.

"You're drenched," Jane said and gave him back his jacket. Despite the protection it had provided, her hair and face glistened with rainwater.

"So are you," he said, and for the life of him, he couldn't pull his gaze away from hers.

"Not like you." She moistened her lips with her tongue and that was Cal's downfall. He'd already promised himself there wouldn't be a repeat of the kiss they'd shared last night, but nothing could have stopped him from sampling her lips once more. He leaned forward and pressed his mouth to hers.

He wasn't sure what he expected, but not her sigh of welcome. Nor had he anticipated her stepping farther into his embrace. His breathing grew heavy and so did hers. The kiss deepened and she slipped her arms around his neck and moved even closer. The feel of her soft body against his was enough to make him weak at the knees.

He lifted his head. "I'm getting you all wet."

"I know."

"You shouldn't have come," he whispered, although his head and his heart waged battle.

"Do you want me to leave?"

"No." His response was instantaneous. Direct. Reluctantly he eased her out of his arms. "I'll go change."

"I'll put on a pot of coffee."

He nodded and headed toward the stairway, taking the steps two at a time. Every minute not spent with her felt wasted, and he was a frugal man.

He stripped off his shirt, then flung it aside, drying himself with a towel. He reached for a sweater and pulled it over his head. He'd just donned a clean pair of jeans and had stepped back into his boots when the electric lights flickered and went off.

The house was almost completely dark. Even though it was midafternoon, the heavy black clouds closed out the light.

"Jane," he shouted from the top of the stairs, "are you okay?"

"I'm fine," she called back.

"I'll be right there." Cal draped his wet clothes over the edge of the bathtub and ran a comb through his hair before going downstairs. He got a flashlight from the hallway and found Jane in the kitchen standing next to the stove.

"I guess we'll have to do without the coffee," she said.

"Will wine do?" he asked.

"Great idea." His eyes were adjusting to the darkness and he saw her smile at him.

It would be easy to get lost in one of those smiles. "I'll get a fire going." He took her hand and led her into the living room. He knelt in front of the brick fireplace, arranged the kindling, then placed a couple of logs on top. The match flared briefly and ignited the wood.

Soon a fire burned invitingly, its warmth spreading into the room.

"This is cozy, isn't it?" Jane said, huddling close to the fire.

"I'll be back in a minute with the wine." As it happened, he had a number of bottles left over from the wedding that had never taken place. He'd wanted Glen and Ellie to use the wine at theirs, but Glen had declined, insisting Cal save it for a rainy day. Like right now, Cal thought wryly.

He returned with a corkscrew, two goblets and a bottle of merlot.

He sat on the carpet with Jane, his back supported by the sofa, a glass of wine in his hand. Jane sat next to him, chin resting on her bent knees.

"I'm glad you're here," he said, not looking at her. It was a big admission, seeing as he'd told her—twice— she shouldn't have come.

"I'm glad I'm here, too."

He put his arm around her shoulders and she scooted closer to his side. She turned to him with another one of her potent smiles. It was an invitation to kiss her again, an invitation he wasn't about to ignore.

She wanted his kisses, her smile said. Cal had thought of little else from the moment they sat down in front of the fire. He'd attempted to discipline his response to her, but his resolve weakened by the moment, and he'd all but given up.

He lowered his head and watched as her eyes closed. He could deny himself no longer. The kiss that followed was intense and passionate. He hadn't meant it to be— but he couldn't help it, either. His mouth played on hers until he groaned.

Thunder exploded, and for an instant Cal thought it was the beat of his own heart. Jane had that kind of effect on him. He broke off the kiss and, closing his eyes, leaned his head back against the sofa. Drawing in several deep breaths, he struggled to find his equilibrium.

He couldn't make himself stop wanting her. But it wasn't right; he knew that. This relationship had no future.

At last he straightened and took a sip of his wine. Jane did, too, and he noticed that her hand trembled slightly. His was shaking, too.

He'd rarely been more unnerved. He thought of telling her about Jennifer, then changed his mind, afraid she'd read something more into the information than he intended. And yet he couldn't say what his intentions were.

"Are you cold?" he asked, diverting his attention from these dangerous thoughts.

"No. How about you?"

The wine had warmed him. The wine and her kisses. "I'm fine."

All of a sudden, they were shy with each other.

Probably in an effort to distract herself, Jane started a conversation, mentioning people in town she was beginning to know. Cal eagerly joined in, answering her questions, bringing up other names. At least when they were talking, he wasn't thinking about making love to her.

The hell he wasn't!

"This has got to stop," he said, and at her look of surprise, realized he'd spoken aloud.

"What's got to stop?" Jane asked.

Embarrassed, he couldn't think of a single response. "This," he said, setting his wineglass aside. The next moment she was in his arms again. The kiss started in hunger and progressed to greed. Her response was immediate and she went soft and pliable in his arms.

"Cal?" she whispered, gazing up at him.

"Mmm?" He spread a row of moist kisses on her neck and jaw. She moaned softly and rolled her head to one side. His senses filled with the taste of her, the citrusy scent of her. He couldn't make himself quit, couldn't make himself *want* to quit.

She moaned again when he let his tongue slide along the hollow of her throat.

"You wanted something," he reminded her.

"Yes…"

"What?" He worked his way back to her lips.

He wasn't sure how it happened, but soon her head rested on his lap and he was bent over her.

"You're right—we should stop," she murmured with little conviction.

"I couldn't agree with you more," he said and kissed her again.

She looped her arms around his neck and raised her head from his lap. They strained against each other, trying to get closer, closer. His thoughts—all the reasons kissing Jane wasn't a good idea—didn't mean a thing.

Jane's mouth parted for him and his tongue curled around hers. The next thing he knew, his hand had worked open the front of her blouse and slipped inside to cup a satin-sheathed breast. Her skin was warm to the touch.

This attraction was becoming increasingly dangerous. And harder to resist.

"What should we do?" he asked, needing her to say or do something to stop this.

"I...don't know."

He kissed her again, slowly, thoroughly. "You're a Valley Girl."

"No, I'm not! Anyway, you're a rebel."

"You belong in California."

"You punch cattle for a living."

"There's no future in this."

"None whatsoever."

Cal frowned. "Then why do I feel like this?"

"When you know the answer, tell me."

To his dying day Cal wouldn't know what it was about this stubborn beautiful woman that made him laugh the way he did. He threw back his head and howled.

Jane apparently didn't find it all that amusing. She sat upright, then shocked him by climbing over him and straddling his lap. His eyes grew wide with surprise.

His amusement faded when she threw her arms around his neck and teased him with nibbling kisses that left him hungering for more.

"You taking me to find that ghost town, Rebel?" she whispered.

"Do I have a choice?"

"None whatsoever."

He muttered under his breath. "I'll do it, but I won't like it."

She grinned. "There'll be compensations," she promised.

"I'm counting on that."

And then she really kissed him. By the time she finished, he would gladly have taken her anywhere she asked.

* * *

Frank felt like a schoolboy as he splashed aftershave on his face and studied his reflection in the bathroom mirror. For the first time in eleven years he had a date with someone other than Dovie. He'd rather be with her, but they remained at an impasse and he was tired of fighting a losing battle.

It'd taken him three days to compile a list of candidates and then pare it down to one woman. His decision made, he'd phoned Tammy Lee Kollenborn and invited her to dinner and a movie. It helped soothe his wounded ego when she eagerly accepted.

Of all the eligible women in town, Tammy Lee was the most attractive. She was a fiftyish divorcée who wore a little too much makeup and was friends with Louise Powell; that was the downside. On the other hand, since Louise was the town gossip, word of his seeing Tammy Lee was sure to get back to Dovie.

Tammy Lee had been divorced for twenty years or more, Frank knew, and that was a factor in her favor. She'd dated a number of men in town and revealed no sign of wanting to remarry. Another plus. From what he heard, she received hefty alimony payments. She routinely traveled and had spent one summer in Europe, returning to Promise with some mighty interesting souvenirs. Apparently she'd brought back a giant round mirror festooned with romping nymphs and satyrs. Rumor had it she'd fastened it to the ceiling above her bed. In time, Frank might have the opportunity to investigate that particular piece of gossip for himself.

Frank didn't know Tammy Lee well, but she was exactly the type of date he was looking for. Once Dovie heard about this, she was sure to have a change of heart.

If she didn't, well, that was that. He'd done everything within his power to get her to see reason. Short of marrying her, which he refused to do.

He reached for his jacket and headed out the front door, grateful the rain had ceased. He was starting slow, easing into this relationship. Dinner, followed by a movie. They could chat over the meal, get comfortable with each other. A movie was a good way to end the evening, no pressure to carry on a conversation.

Frank picked up Tammy Lee at her house. She opened the door and beamed him a broad smile. "I can't tell you how pleased I was when you phoned," she said, draping a fringed wrap over her shoulders. "The first person I called was Louise."

Louise Powell. Well, it was no less than he'd expected. Louise might be a blabbermouth, but this time, it was to his advantage.

"You look terrific," he said, thinking a compliment early in the evening would put them on a good footing. She wore a gold lamé jumpsuit with a jeweled belt that emphasized her trim waist and hips. He especially appreciated her high heels, found them sexy. Fewer and fewer women wore them these days.

Tammy Lee stopped and checked her reflection in the hallway mirror, then smiled. "What a nice thing to say."

Frank waited for her to return the compliment, but she didn't. He led her outside and opened the car door, wanting to impress her with his manners. Dovie had always enjoyed the little things he did to show her he cared.

"I'm a modern woman," Tammy Lee said after he'd

climbed into the car and started the engine. "I can get my own door, but it's real sweet of you to do that."

"You don't want me to open your car door?"

"It isn't necessary, Frank."

He smiled and decided he was pleased. This was a woman who spoke her mind, who asked for what she wanted. He respected that.

They chose to eat at the Chili Pepper, and their appearance created something of a stir. Frank felt he should apologize for the attention they received.

"Don't worry about it," she said, graciously dismissing his concern. "I know what it's like when a longtime relationship ends. People are curious, wanting to know the details."

People like Louise Powell, Frank added silently.

Frank ordered a steak and a baked potato with all the fixings. He'd lost a few pounds pining for Dovie, and was ready to make up for lost time.

He was mildly disappointed when Tammy Lee asked for a plain green salad with red-wine vinegar.

"I'm watching my weight," she explained.

Frank guessed that her trim figure demanded sacrifice. He ordered a cold beer to go with his meal, while Tammy Lee requested a highball, her first of three. He wondered about the calories in those, but didn't ask. At four-fifty a drink, she could have ordered the steak. She surprised him further when she asked to see the dessert menu.

"Every once in a while I allow myself a goodie," she said.

Frank never ate restaurant desserts. Dovie, when he could convince her to go out, refused to let him eat a pie baked in an aluminum-foil tin. She insisted she could outbake anything that came from a freezer. He'd never argued with her.

Tammy Lee ordered apple pie à la mode.

"Save room for popcorn," he told her.

She shook her head. "I don't touch the stuff."

"Oh," he said. That was his favorite part of going to the movies. Yes, the theater charged outrageous prices, but it was a rare treat and one of the few indulgences Dovie enjoyed, too. They bought the largest bag, with butter, and shared it.

"I was sorry to hear about your breakup with Dovie," Tammy Lee said, sounding anything but.

"Yes, well, these things happen." Frank wasn't willing to discuss Dovie with another woman.

"I've always liked her," Tammy Lee said.

That statement was patently insincere.

"She's a special lady," Frank said, growing uncomfortable with this conversation.

Tammy Lee frowned slightly. "I did understand you correctly, didn't I? You and Dovie are no longer seeing each other?"

Frank shifted in his seat. "Do you mind if we change the subject?" he asked pointedly.

"Of course not. It's just that, well, I know you and Dovie were…close, if you catch my drift."

Frank wasn't sure he did. "How do you mean?"

"Well…" Tammy Lee lowered her voice significantly. "I understand you spent the night with Dovie at least twice a week."

Frank opened his mouth to tell her it wasn't any of her damn business how close he and Dovie were, but she stopped him.

"The only reason I mention this, Frank, is that…"

She paused and sent him a pained look. "This is rather embarrassing, and I do hope you'll forgive me for being blunt, but I'm in a position to help you through these difficult times."

"Difficult times?" What was she talking about?

"Physically," she whispered, beaming him another one of her smiles. "I'm currently without a man in my life and I'd welcome your attentions, Sheriff Hennessey."

He didn't think a woman had ever shocked him more. Frank shook his head in wonderment. Two years. It'd taken him two full years of courting Dovie before she'd allowed him into her bed. And even after all the time they'd been involved, she was uncomfortable making love without the sanction of marriage. Yet this woman was brazenly letting him know she'd welcome him to her bed on their first date. Sure, he'd admit to a mild fantasy about her supposed sensual bedroom—but checking it out on their first date? What in hell had happened to the world since he'd been out of circulation?

"Well?" Tammy Lee asked.

"Perhaps we should discuss this at a later time," Frank said.

"Have I shocked you, Frank?" she asked, then laughed coyly.

"Shocked me? What makes you ask that?"

"Your ears have gone all red." She snickered as if she found this highly humorous.

Tammy Lee's words irritated him, but he attempted to disguise his reaction. Frank was actually looking forward to the movie for the simple reason that they wouldn't be speaking. She said the most outrageous things, and he was getting tired of it.

The theater in Promise had only one screen. The seats were rather worn, but comfortable. The feature films weren't always first-run, but since it was the only show in town, few complained.

Frank purchased their tickets and was putting his change back into his wallet when Tammy Lee decided to get possessive. She rubbed his back affectionately and cozied up to his side, wrapping her hands around his upper arm. He shouldn't be surprised, he supposed; her actions were certainly in keeping with her conversation.

When he looked up, he saw the reason his date had started to cling to him like a blackberry vine. Standing only a few feet away from him was Dovie Boyd, holding a small bag of popcorn and a paper cup of soda. Her eyes widened with a flash of shock and pain. He feared she was about to drop her drink and admired her for her fast recovery.

Tammy Lee all but draped her arms around his neck, nuzzling his ear like some annoying insect he longed to bat away.

Dovie offered them both a brave if shaky smile. "Hello, Frank. Hello, Tammy Lee," she said. And then, with the grace of the lady she was, she turned and walked into the theater.

Seven

Jane saw Cal every day after their rainy afternoon. The riding lessons continued, but they found other reasons to be together, too. After their first date he no longer made an issue of their not becoming involved and she was glad. She particularly liked meeting him at the ranch, liked seeing him in his own world, which was new and strange and enchanting to her.

It was Sunday, two weeks after the storm. For her riding lesson that afternoon, they rode to the farthest pasture with Digger, Cal's dog, racing along beside them. The day was glorious, a perfect autumn day with temperatures still in the mid-seventies.

Jane had become almost comfortable in the saddle. Either she'd built up calluses on that part of her anatomy, she thought wryly, or she'd gained skill. Probably a combination of both.

Jane frequently mentioned Cal in her letters and phone calls home. She'd taken a great deal of ribbing from her father about this penchant she had for horseback riding. He told her he'd thought she'd outgrown it when she was thirteen. Like many girls, she'd been horse-crazy, reading horse stories and collecting figurines. In a way, what Cal had given her was the opportunity to live a long-ago dream.

"You're quiet this afternoon," Cal remarked when they reached the crest of the hill.

The view of the pasture below was breathtaking. Cattle grazed there, scattered picturesquely about the fields. Cal had explained earlier that most of his herd had been sold off now, and he was wintering a relatively small number of bulls and heifers.

"I'm thinking," she said in response to his observation.

"I hope it isn't taxing you too much."

"The only thing that taxes me is you."

"Me?" He pretended to be insulted.

"You keep putting me off."

The laughter faded from his eyes. He knew exactly what she was talking about. She hated to be a pest, but she wasn't going to let him delay much longer. The ghost town beckoned her; she'd actually started to dream about it. Her mother had mailed her a thick book about Texas ghost towns, but Bitter End wasn't included. It amazed her that an entire town could be tucked away in these hills and so few people knew about it.

"I spoke with Grady and Savannah this afternoon," Cal told her.

"Why didn't you say something sooner?" she asked. It was what she'd been waiting to hear, as Cal knew very well. Savannah had been to the town earlier in the year and apparently found the most incredible old roses blooming in the cemetery. Having visited the town fairly recently, Savannah would be able to give her and Cal directions and save them the trouble of a long search.

When Cal didn't answer, she pressed, "Aren't you going to tell me what they said?"

"In a little while."

Jane was beginning to understand Cal. He didn't like being pressured and would eventually get to the point—but he preferred to do it without coaxing from her. Her patience was usually rewarded, and considering how good he'd been to her, how generous with his time, she could wait.

"This truly is God's country, isn't it?" she said. Cal had helped her develop a love of the land. He didn't preach or lecture about it. Instead, he allowed her to see and feel it for herself. He'd taught her to appreciate what it meant to be a real cowboy, too. Some people thought that cowboys were a dying breed, but for Cal, the work and the life were vital and worthwhile. There wasn't a task on the Lonesome Coyote Ranch he couldn't handle—branding cattle to breaking horses to birthing calves.

"Do you mean that, about this being God's country?" he asked.

"Yes." And she did. The land was astonishingly beautiful. What she'd come to love about it was what Cal referred to as "elbow room." The hill country was gentle rolling hills and pastureland that was fresh, green, limitless.

Cal had told her he could ride as far as the eye could see, to the horizon and beyond, and not meet another soul. This was something she was only beginning to fathom. So much space!

"What about California?" he asked.

"It's beautiful, too, but not like this."

Cal shook his head. "Too populated. That stuff about earthquakes—it seems to me Mother Nature's saying there're just too many people living in one spot and she's just trying to shake them loose."

He glanced her way as if expecting her to argue with him. She merely smiled and shrugged. She had no intention of ruining a perfect afternoon by getting involved in some pointless argument. Not when the wind was gently blowing in her face and the sweet smells of earth and grass rose up to meet her.

The silence out here took time to accept. At first she'd felt the need to fill their rides with chatter, but as she spent more and more time around Cal, she'd begun to appreciate the lack of sound, to stop fearing it. Cal, by his own admission, wasn't much of a talker. He'd shown her that silence had its own sound, but with the frantic pace of her life, she'd been unable to hear it.

They dismounted, and the two horses drank from the creek. Jane walked over to an oak and leaned against the trunk, one leg bent. Cal picked a handful of wildflowers and handed her the small bouquet.

She rewarded him with a kiss on his cheek. From the way his eyes flared she knew he would've liked to kiss her properly. They'd done plenty of that lately, their attraction growing each time they met. Cal backed away from her now, as if that would help remove him from temptation.

"Tell me what it means to be a rancher," she said.

His gaze held hers. "In what way?"

"I want to know about cattle."

He frowned, then squatted down and plucked a blade of grass. "A good cowboy can tell just by looking at a cow if she's healthy. Her coat'll tell him if she's eating right. The eyes let him know if she's in any kind of trouble."

Jane gave him an encouraging nod. "Go on."

"It's gotten to the point where I can look at a heifer and know when she's ready to spill her first calf," Cal continued. "And one glance at a calf'll tell me if it's suckled that day or been separated from its mother."

Jane was fascinated. "Tell me more."

"It's said some folks don't forget a face. A good rancher doesn't forget a cow."

"You're joking, right?"

His smile told her he wasn't. "They have their own personalities, and they're as individual as you and me. I know that the old cow with the missing horn likes to hide in the willow trees, and the one with a patch of white on its backside is a leader. That one with a cut ear—" he pointed "—is likely to charge a horse and rider.

"My job, if that's what you're asking, is to care for the cows. The cows then tend the calves, and trust me, each cow knows her own calf. She can pick out her baby in a herd of hundreds."

Jane was astonished but didn't doubt him for a second.

"Cows are constantly on my mind," he said, then cast her a look and added, "or used to be."

She felt a warm glow and smiled.

"I think about them morning, noon and night," he went on. "I watch them, study them, and work hard to improve the quality of the herd."

"How do you do that?"

"Every year is a gamble. Weather, disease, the price

of beef. With so many things that can go wrong, I cut my losses early and often. If a heifer doesn't breed, she's sold, or if she calves late, she might not get a second chance. I expect a cow to deliver nine calves in nine years, and if she skips a year, I sell her. That might sound harsh, and I often agonize over these decisions. My cattle are more than a commodity to me. The future of Lonesome Coyote is based on the everyday decisions Glen and I make."

Jane had no idea ranching was so complicated. It was a consuming life that required not only hard physical work but research, complex decision-making and business skills.

"Glen and I, along with Grady, have been doing quite a bit of cross-breeding in the past few years, mostly with longhorns. Breeding exceptional cattle isn't as easy as it sounds. Despite the use of artificial insemination and genetics, it's an inexact science that relies on good stock, good weather and good luck." He grinned. "Hey, stop me if I'm lecturing. This is more talking than I normally do in a month."

Jane grinned back. "I hadn't realized there were so many breeds of cattle—although I guess I associate longhorns with Texas."

"At one time there were more than six million longhorns in Texas, but by the late 1920s, they were close to extinction."

"I read that they were making a comeback."

Cal nodded. "They are." He described his cross-breeding program in some detail, and Jane found herself listening avidly to every word. Biology had—naturally—always interested her.

"Cal, I've really enjoyed hearing all this."

His eyes narrowed as if he wasn't sure he should believe her.

"I'm coming to love Texas," she said happily. And Cal Patterson, too, but she kept those feelings buried for now, fearing what would happen if she acknowledged how she felt.

"What about California?"

"It's my home—I love it, too."

"You'll go back," he said, his face tightening.

It seemed as if he was challenging her to deny it. Jane didn't, but every day California seemed farther and farther away. Her life was here in Texas now. After years of planning to go into partnership with her uncle Ken, she found the thought starting to lose its appeal. Promise needed her, and she was only beginning to understand why she needed Promise.

"It's time we headed back," Cal said and went to collect the horses.

"What did Grady and Savannah say about Bitter End?" she blurted, anxious to know.

Cal stopped. "They both tried to talk me out of taking you there."

"Did they succeed?"

He took a long time to answer. "I know you. You're determined to find that town with or without me. You told me as much. And after what they said, I'm inclined to let you try."

"You will take me there, won't you, Cal?" she asked, nervous about his response.

He nodded. "When's your next day off?"

"Wednesday."

"We'll go then."

"Thank you. Oh, thank you!" She raced toward him, threw her arms around his neck and kissed him.

He groaned. "I swear you're going to be the death of me," he muttered.

"But I promise it'll be a great way to die."

The ache inside Dovie refused to go away. When she hadn't seen or heard from Frank in several days, she'd been almost glad. Every time he came to visit her, it was more and more difficult to send him away. She was afraid that her resolve was weakening. She missed him, missed their times together and the companionship they'd shared. She'd never felt more alone, not even after Marvin had died.

Despite his talk, the last thing she expected Frank to do was go out with another woman, especially this soon. It told her everything she needed to know. Seeing him with Tammy Lee had been one of the most disheartening experiences of her life.

Dovie hated to think unkindly about anyone, but Tammy Lee and Louise Powell were enough to try the patience of a saint. From the way Tammy Lee was clinging to Frank, massaging his back, rubbing her leg down his calf, Dovie realized they'd already become lovers. The thought cut with the sharpness of a knife, and she braced herself against the pain.

The fact that business was slow was a blessing in disguise. In her current state of mind, Dovie was practically useless. She wandered around her shop, unable to sit still, unable to think clearly. Her eyes would start to water for no reason, and somehow it always surprised her; she thought she'd cried all the tears left inside her.

Frank was out of her life once and for all.

The bell above the shop door tinkled and Louise Powell casually strolled in wearing a smug look.

Dovie groaned inwardly. "Hello, Louise," she said, determined to reveal none of her feelings.

"Oh, hello, Dovie." The woman bestowed a saccharine-sweet smile on her.

"Is there anything I can help you find?" she asked, silently praying that whatever Louise wanted was out of stock so she'd leave.

"I'm just browsing," Louise said, wandering from one display to another. She picked up a pair of Kirks Folly earrings and held them to her face, examining her reflection in the mirror. "Nice," she said, then glanced at the price, raised a brow and set them back down.

"I don't suppose you have any of those rubber piles of dog do-do? They make the funniest practical jokes."

"I'm afraid not," Dovie said. As if she'd actually sell such an outrageous item!

"Hmm," Louise murmured. "So how are you doing these days, Dovie?"

"Wonderful." Dovie gritted her teeth.

"I understand you're leaving on your cruise soon?"

Dovie was looking forward to it more every day. "Yes."

"It must be coming up next week."

Dovie wondered how Louise knew this. "That's right."

"With Frank out of your life, I imagine you're hoping to meet another man."

Dovie said nothing.

"It's a shame, really," Louise said. "I always thought you and Frank made a handsome couple."

Again Dovie said nothing.

"But your loss appears to be Tammy Lee's gain."

Dovie's nails bit into her palms. "I wish them both well," she said.

Louise shook her head. "You're a marvel, Dovie, a real marvel. I don't know if I could be nearly as magnanimous. Tammy Lee was afraid you were offended about her going out with Frank, but I can see that isn't so. You're the picture of generosity."

Dovie forced a smile and hoped Louise didn't notice how brittle it was.

"Tammy Lee's without a man right now," Louise rambled on, "and she's thrilled to be dating Frank. He's such an attractive man."

"Yes, he is." Dovie eased her way toward the front door. Fortunately Louise followed.

"It was good seeing you again," Louise said.

"You, too," Dovie lied.

Louise left and Dovie sank into a chair. The knot was back in the pit of her stomach, and she wondered if it'd ever go away.

That evening Dovie fixed herself a salad but had no appetite. Her home, after thirty years in the same place, suddenly felt too large. Perhaps this was a sign she was ready for a change, a drastic one. She'd been born and raised in Promise, and she'd seen precious little of the world. The upcoming cruise would give her a sample of what life was like outside the great state of Texas, but the cruise was only a few days long. Afterward she'd be back dealing with people like Louise, who relished rubbing Frank's new relationship in her face.

Dovie didn't know if she could bear it. For the first time in her life she seriously considered moving. With the money from the sale of her home and business, plus what was left of Marvin's life insurance, she could live comfortably. Nothing else held her in Promise. She'd stay in touch with the friends she had and make new ones.

The phone rang. Absently Dovie reached for it, studying her home with fresh eyes, wondering how long it would take to sell.

"Hello, Dovie."

The shock of hearing Frank's voice was nearly her undoing. She grabbed hold of the kitchen chair, feeling as though she might faint.

"Frank."

The telephone line hummed with silence.

"How are you?" Frank asked tentatively as if he didn't know what to say.

She was at a loss about how to respond and decided on a lie, doubting he wanted the truth. "Good, and you?"

"All right. Mostly I was phoning to see if you needed anything."

A new heart to replace the one you stabbed, she answered silently. "I...don't need anything," she said. "Thank you for asking."

Frank said nothing for a moment. "About the other night...I thought I should explain."

"Frank," she said swiftly, "please, there's no need to explain anything to me."

"But I thought—"

"No, please. I prefer not to know."

"But, Dovie—"

"Whom you date is none of my business. I knew when we parted—when we decided we were at an impasse—that you'd be seeking...companionship elsewhere." Only, she'd credited him with more taste.

"You're the one taking the cruise," he reminded her, the coolness in his voice testifying to his displeasure.

Dovie had nothing to say about her vacation plans, especially not to Frank.

"I've heard about those cruises," Frank continued. "I've seen reruns of *Love Boat*. People book those fancy liners looking for romance."

"I'm sure that's true in some cases." Not in hers, however. Now seemed as good a time as any to put his mind to rest regarding the future. "I've been giving some thought to…to making certain changes in my life."

"I'm hoping you're about to tell me you want me back." His eagerness was certainly a balm to her wounded pride.

"No, Frank."

"You're going to be looking for another man, right?" he accused.

"No, Frank," she repeated. "I'm not seeking out a new romantic interest." *Unlike you*—but she refused to say it. "I'm thinking of selling the house and moving."

Her words were met with silence, then, "You don't mean it!"

"Yes, Frank, I do."

"But why?"

"You have to admit it's very awkward for us both. You're dating again now and—"

"One date, Dovie. I swear to you that's all it was."

"It doesn't matter."

"I don't even like Tammy Lee."

But there were bound to be others. Dovie didn't know if she had the strength to stand back and smile while the man she loved became involved with another woman. The only thing worse than seeing Frank with someone like Tammy Lee would be seeing him with someone who could be right for him. A woman who'd love him the way she did.

"What about your antique shop?" he asked. "You care about that store. It took you years to put everything together, and now you've added the Victorian Tea Room."

"I'll have to sell it—either that or close it down."

"But the women in town love your store!"

"Then perhaps one of them will be willing to purchase it."

"You don't mean it," Frank said again, his voice rising. "This is just another ploy to get me to change my mind and marry you."

That he would believe her capable of such a thing hurt. "No, Frank, it's not. I'm contacting the real estate people in the morning. Perhaps I shouldn't have mentioned it, but I felt you should know. Goodbye, Frank."

"I'm not going to marry you or anyone," he shouted as if she was hard of hearing.

"Yes, you've made that quite clear." At this point, if he *had* experienced a sudden change of heart, Dovie wasn't sure she'd agree to marry him, anyway.

Cal wasn't happy with the idea of finding Bitter End and he wouldn't be going there now, but for Jane.

He drove into Promise, hoping that when he arrived she'd have changed her mind, but one look told him he might as well save his breath. Jane opened the front door, and when she saw him, practically launched herself into his arms.

"I'm so excited!" she said, hugging him.

It was beginning to feel damn good to hold her. Beginning, hell, it felt like this was exactly where she belonged. Once again Cal forced himself to remember that Jane would put in her stint here, but when her three years were up, she'd return to California.

"I spent part of the morning with Savannah," he said and withdrew a slip of paper from his shirt pocket. "She drew me a map showing us how to get to Bitter End."

"That's wonderful!"

Cal didn't agree.

"You're sure you'd rather drive?" She sounded disappointed that they wouldn't be going on horseback.

"I'm sure." He spread the map on top of the coffee table for her to examine.

She pored over it and then smiled up at him with such enthusiasm it was difficult not to feel some excitement himself. The problem was, Jane didn't understand what she was asking of him, and he couldn't find the words to explain it.

He'd seen the ghost town once, and that was all it had taken for him to know he never wanted to go back there. As teenagers, he and Glen and Grady had happened to overhear a conversation between his parents and the Westons. They'd been intrigued. Just as Jane was now.

They'd come up with a scheme to locate Bitter End on their own. The adventure had appealed to them; the secrecy, too.

Cal remembered that he'd been the skeptical one of the bunch. He wasn't sure he believed such a place existed. Glen seemed convinced the ghost town was there. Grady was undecided.

In the end it was Glen who turned out to be right. The old town was hidden deep in the hills, just as his parents had said. At first the three of them had been ecstatic, jumping up and down, congratulating each other. Cal remembered thinking that someone would probably include their names in a history book or a magazine article—as the boys who'd found a lost ghost town. Someone might even interview them for television.

None of that had happened—and for a reason. Not one of them ever mentioned finding Bitter End to any of their peers and certainly not to their parents. In fact, they'd never mentioned it again—until recently.

It was almost as though they'd made a secret pact not to discuss what they'd found, but that hadn't been the case. They didn't talk about it because they weren't sure what had happened or how to explain it.

All Cal could recall was how uncomfortable he'd been. How the feelings of fear and oppressiveness had overwhelmed him. The others had reacted the same way. After less than ten minutes all three had hightailed it out of town as if the hounds of hell were in hot pursuit.

"Should I bring a sweater?" Jane asked.

"That's probably a good idea." Cal wished he could talk her out of this, but since that wasn't likely, he was determined to be there with her.

"I brought along a camera, too," Jane said as she swung a backpack over her shoulder. "Mom asked me to get some pictures."

"You mentioned the town to your mother?"

"Wasn't I supposed to?"

Cal wasn't sure how to answer. "No one around here talks about it much."

"I know," she said with a certain exasperation. "I don't understand that."

"Perhaps you will once you've been there."

"I wish I knew why everyone's so secretive about this place."

Cal knew it wouldn't do any good to tell her. She'd soon discover the answer on her own.

The drive out of town went well enough. They discussed Savannah, who'd told Cal about her pregnancy. Cal was happy for her and Laredo. "I imagine Glen and Ellie will be thinking about children soon, too," he said. "I hope so."

"Cal, they're newlyweds."

"Yes, but if my mother'd had anything to say about it, Ellie would've gotten pregnant on their wedding night and delivered their first grandchild nine months and thirty seconds later."

Jane laughed softly. "Your mother is eager for grand-children to spoil. So is mine."

Cal wasn't wading into those shark-infested waters, not for anything.

With the help of Savannah's map, they were able to locate the general vicinity of the town. It would have helped had the tire tracks not been washed away by the recent storm, but every now and then Cal recognized some landmark himself. It amazed him that the memory of these details hadn't been lost. Although it'd been years since his visit, Cal had repeated the journey in his mind many times since.

He parked the truck when they'd driven as far as possible.

"According to Savannah, we'll need to walk in from here."

"I'm ready."

Jane had dressed in khaki shorts, hiking boots and T-shirt; on his advice she'd also worn a hat. Cal held her hand as they climbed over the rocks and limestone ledge.

"There," he said, pointing as the town came into view below. Seeing it again stole his breath. The buildings, the way the streets were laid out, were almost exactly as he remembered, as though the years had stood still. The church, at the far end of town, still stood with its burned-out steeple. The graveyard was beside the church. Some of the buildings along the street were of sun-bleached wood, some of stone, now brown with age. Stores, a saloon, livery stable with a small corral, a mercantile and even a hotel. A corral was situated close to the hotel.

"This is incredible," Jane breathed, slipping the backpack from her shoulders. She pulled out her camera and began shooting. "I can't believe it's here like this…"

Once she'd finished snapping pictures, Jane scrambled forward, bounding energetically over the rocks. Cal followed close behind, watching her, waiting for her reaction once she felt it.

He experienced the first sensation, a feeling of darkness and desolation, when they stepped onto the main street of Bitter End. Jane apparently did, too, because she stopped cold and slowly turned to face Cal. A puzzled frown appeared on her face.

"What *is* that?" she asked, lowering her voice to a whisper.

"What?" he asked, although he knew.

"This…this feeling."

"I don't know."

"You said this place was evil. I didn't know what you meant."

"I wasn't sure how to say it," Cal told her. But he

could find no other word to describe what he and the others had experienced that day.

Jane's grip on his hand tightened as they made their way down the middle of the street. "It's growing stronger," she said in a weak whisper. "Do you feel it, too?"

"I feel it." The sensation grew heavier and more intense with each step they advanced.

"Look!" Jane said, gesturing at a rocking chair outside the saloon.

"What?"

"There's a guitar there."

"A guitar?" It took Cal a moment to see it, propped against the wall.

"That doesn't look like an antique, does it?" Jane said.

Cal went to investigate. He climbed the two short steps onto the boardwalk and reached for the guitar.

"Is it old?" Jane asked.

"This is no antique," Cal said and frowned. Furthermore it was familiar. Where had he seen this guitar before? For the life of him, he couldn't remember.

"Cal, look!"

She was halfway down the street when Cal glanced up. He set the guitar down and raced after her. She was just outside what had once been the mercantile.

"What is it?" he asked.

She held up a half-full can of soda. "Someone's been here recently," she said.

He nodded. "Very recently." He was ready to leave even if she wasn't.

"Let's get out of here," Jane said.

Cal grabbed her hand and they turned to go back the same way they'd come in.

It wasn't until they passed the livery stable that they heard it. A moaning sound, coming from the hotel where Cal had stood only a minute or two ago.

Jane tensed and so did Cal. "What's that?" she whispered. "I didn't think I believed in ghosts, but…"

Cal had a sinking suspicion it wasn't a ghost. All at once he remembered where he'd last seen that guitar.

Bitter End didn't have ghosts, but it appeared to be populated by a single rat.

Eight

Savannah loved visiting Dovie's antique shop with its storehouse of treasures from earlier times. This particular visit was special for another reason—she planned to tell Dovie about the baby. Since Dr. Dickinson had confirmed her pregnancy, the knowledge that her child, Laredo's child, was growing inside her occupied more and more of her thoughts.

Dovie Boyd glanced up from behind the glass counter that displayed some of the shop's pricier antique china and jewelry.

"Savannah, my dear." Dovie's greeting held her usual graciousness and warmth. "It's good to see you."

"It's always a pleasure, Dovie." Savannah noticed that her friend was pale this morning. Come to think of it, she'd seemed tired and listless for a while now. Savannah assumed that had something to do with her separation from Frank Hennessey, although Dovie had never discussed it.

"Can I help you find something?" Dovie asked, stepping around the glass counter.

"I'm looking for something special," Savannah said,

placing her hand on her abdomen, "for our baby's nursery." She waited for Dovie's reaction.

"I don't have much in the way of—" Dovie stopped midsentence and stared at Savannah, her eyes brightening. "So *that's* what's different."

"You noticed already?" Savannah was only about two months along. It didn't seem possible that anyone would be able to detect the pregnancy this soon.

"In your eyes," Dovie explained. "You're fairly glowing with happiness." She smiled. "I know it's a cliché—that pregnant women have a glow about them—but like most clichés it has a basis in truth."

Some days it was all Savannah could do not to burst into tears when she thought about all the wonderful changes that had taken place in her life this past year. The afternoon she'd found the ghost town and dug up the White Lady Banks roses in the church cemetery had forever changed her life. It was on the return drive that she'd seen Laredo Smith walking along the side of the road. To this day she didn't know what had possessed her to stop and offer him a ride. She'd never done anything like that before or since. Within a few months she'd become Laredo's wife and now they were expecting a child.

"I *am* happy," Savannah said.

"You're radiant." They hugged, and as the older woman pulled away, Savannah noticed again how drawn Dovie looked.

"You haven't been ill, have you, Dovie?" she asked, deciding she should ask, just to be sure.

"No. I just haven't been sleeping well." She managed a smile and continued, "I have some news, too."

Savannah had already heard that Mary Patterson had

talked Dovie into a cruise; she was delighted. Dovie could use a vacation, however short, and her absence might clarify a thing or two in Frank's mind. Dovie was a remarkable woman, and if Frank Hennessey didn't realize it, then the sheriff was more of a fool than she'd thought. But she knew Frank almost as well as she did Dovie and suspected that the problem, whatever it was, would soon be resolved.

"I've decided to sell the house." Dovie's announcement was inflated with forced enthusiasm. "I'm going to be moving."

"Moving," Savannah repeated, trying to conceal her shock.

"I talked to a real estate agent this morning and I'll be listing the house this afternoon. I'm...not sure just yet what I'll do about the business."

Speechless, Savannah needed time to recover.

"I know this comes as a surprise," Dovie said.

"Where will you go?" Savannah asked, when in reality her question should have been *why* Dovie would go. Why she'd consider leaving Promise. This was her home. She was an essential part of this community, loved by everyone here. Her shop was the very heart of the town, a mingling of past and present, a constant reminder of the heritage that made Promise special to those who lived there.

"I've decided to do some traveling," Dovie said, again with an eagerness that rang false. "I'm going to explore the world."

"The world..."

"The United States, at any rate. I understand that Charleston's lovely, and I've never seen New York. I've never seen the Rockies..." Her voice tapered off.

This was more than Savannah could take in. She felt the sudden need to sit down. "I realize it's a bit early for tea, but perhaps you wouldn't mind putting on a pot?"

"Of course. And I'll make sure it's decaffeinated."

While Dovie fussed with the tea, Savannah contemplated what she should say. She thought about her own relationship with Laredo, remembering how she'd felt when he returned to Oklahoma and she didn't believe she'd see him again. She'd made changes in her life, too, needing to do *something* to combat the terrible pain of his leaving. The changes hadn't been drastic, although Grady and a few others had behaved as though they no longer knew her. Cutting her hair was a small thing. Dovie planned on packing up her fifty-seven years of life and leaving everything that was familiar.

Savannah noticed that her friend's hand trembled as she poured the tea.

"Why would you leave here?" Savannah asked gently. "I'd like to know the real reason you'd consider moving away from Promise."

Dovie lowered her eyes and folded her hands in her lap. She didn't say anything for several tense moments. "Frank's dating Tammy Lee now and I can't bear—"

"Frank and Tammy Lee?" Savannah interrupted. She could hardly believe her ears. What man in his right mind would prefer that…that trashy Tammy Lee over Dovie?

"If it isn't Tammy Lee, it'll soon be someone else and…I can't abide seeing him fall in love with someone else." Dovie pulled a limp lace-bordered handkerchief from her pocket and dabbed her eyes.

Savannah leaned forward, hugging the woman who'd been both friend and substitute mother to her. She sympathized with the pain Dovie felt and wished there was something she could say or do that would ease her broken heart.

"Obviously I gave Frank more credit for intelligence than he deserves," Savannah snapped. The next time she saw him, she'd give him a tongue-lashing he wouldn't soon forget.

Dovie quickly composed herself, clearly embarrassed by her show of emotion. "It isn't such a bad thing, my leaving Promise," she said on a more cheerful note. "I'm actually looking forward to traveling. Eventually, I'm sure I'll find someplace in Montana or Colorado that reminds me of Promise. I'll settle right in and make a new life for myself." Her enthusiasm appeared more genuine this time. Savannah hated the thought of losing Dovie, especially for a reason as *stupid* as Frank Hennessey's stubborn pride.

She was about to say something else when an antique doll caught her eye. Faded and tattered, it sat on the edge of a dresser. Dovie's gaze followed hers.

"Do you recognize the doll?" Dovie asked. "Jane Dickinson brought it in and asked me about it. Apparently someone brought it into her office and asked her to find the owner. It's quite old and rather fragile. Have you ever seen it before?"

Savannah walked over to look at the antique doll. She picked it up and carefully examined its faded embroidered face. The button eyes seemed to stare back at her. "I've never seen anything like this."

"Me, neither." Dovie shook her head.

"But…it looks like something that might have come from Bitter End."

"Bitter End. That's what I thought," Dovie said excitedly.

"But how would anyone have gotten hold of it?" Savannah asked.

"Your guess is as good as mine." Dovie frowned. "Apparently whoever gave the doll to Jane—she couldn't tell me who—did so because he or she felt guilty about taking it."

"Why would anyone give it to…" Savannah paused.

"I suspect it was a child," Dovie said thoughtfully.

"I was thinking that very thing," Savannah murmured.

"It's highly unlikely that any child's been to Bitter End, though," Dovie pointed out. "Other than a handful of people, who even knows about the town?"

All at once everything fell into place. "*Richard* knows about Bitter End," Savannah said intently. "And he kidnapped Maggie for several hours, remember? What if he took her to Bitter End? He could've either given the doll to Maggie in an attempt to buy her silence or else Maggie took it without him knowing."

"Someone needs to ask Maggie about this," Dovie said.

Her thoughts were a reflection of Savannah's own. Maggie had refused to talk about the time she'd been missing, despite numerous efforts by a number of people, herself included. Even knowing what she did about her brother, Savannah couldn't believe Richard would intentionally take the child. Everyone had been terribly worried—no one more than Savannah, whose fears had been compounded by guilt. The child had been in her care when she disappeared, and Savannah had blamed herself.

Then early the next morning Maggie had come running down the driveway. For the rest of her life, Savannah would remember the way Grady had raced toward the child. At that moment she'd realized how much her brother had come to love Maggie. He might not have fathered her, but he'd always be a real father to the little girl. She'd long had her suspicions about Maggie's biological father, but had kept those to herself.

"Perhaps Grady should be the one to ask Maggie about the doll," Savannah said. The little girl had refused to discuss where she'd been or who'd taken her, but she trusted Grady now and seemed willing to confide in him. Since she hadn't been physically harmed, Frank had felt they should count their blessings and leave it. He doubted Maggie would be able to help them locate Richard, anyway. However, that was before they knew about the doll.

"Someone should bring Frank into this, too," Dovie said. "I understand there's a warrant out for Richard's arrest…" Her voice faltered and she looked away. Whether her reaction was because of Frank or Richard, Savannah couldn't say.

"I'll have Grady call him."

For the next couple of hours Savannah was involved in talking to people. She'd contacted Jane Dickinson's office and learned that it was her day off. Apparently she'd gone somewhere with Cal Patterson.

Caroline agreed Grady would be the right person to discuss the matter of the doll with Maggie. Sheriff Hennessey was brought in, as well, and suggested they talk to her at the ranch house.

Savannah returned to the ranch, baked bread and mulled over what she'd learned from Dovie. She was also worried about Richard. She knew he had a rifle, but didn't like to think that her brother would intentionally hurt anyone. After these past few months, though, she couldn't predict what he might do.

When Caroline and Maggie arrived late in the afternoon, they all gathered in the living room, together with Frank Hennessey. Maggie stayed close to her mother, glancing nervously about the room. Grady held his arms open and Savannah was gratified to see the child willingly sit next to him.

Grady opened the bag Dovie had given Savannah and withdrew the old tattered doll. "Do you recognize this?" he asked Maggie.

The little girl took one look at it and covered her face with both hands. Her shoulders started to shake. "I'm sorry I stole her! I'm sorry!"

"But the doll said she was glad." Grady spoke with such gentle concern that Savannah wanted to kiss him. "She told me how grateful she was that she had someone to love her."

Maggie lowered her hands and gazed at him with searching eyes. "She told you that?"

Grady nodded gravely. "She came from the ghost town, didn't she?"

Maggie's hands flew back to her face. "I'm not supposed to tell!"

"It's all right, Maggie," Grady continued. "You won't be punished."

"But Richard said Mommy would die if I told anyone. He said I'd never see her again and that she'd bleed real bad."

Frank muttered a curse under his breath, and while Savannah wouldn't have used that precise language, she

was in full agreement. That her brother would know-
ingly frighten the child in this manner was inexcusable.
His one redeeming act had been to bring Maggie back.
He'd stolen another truck shortly thereafter, but at least
Maggie had been safely returned.

"Sometimes people say things that aren't true."
Grady placed his arm around the child's shoulders, both
shielding her and comforting her at once.

Maggie kept her head lowered as though she felt undecided about what to do.

"Is Richard at the ghost town?" Caroline asked softly.

"Will you die if I tell?" Maggie asked her mother.

"No, sweetheart, I won't die." Caroline linked her
fingers with Grady's. "I'm going to marry Grady very
soon and we'll all be very happy."

"Will you have other babies so I can be a big sister?"

Savannah watched as Caroline met Grady's eyes,
then nodded. "Yes, sweetheart, you'll have plenty of
opportunities to be a big sister."

"Can I really keep the doll?" Maggie asked next.

Grady raised the rag doll to his ear, his expression
somber. Maggie watched his every move. Slowly, a bit
at a time, Grady's mouth formed a smile. "She says she
needs someone to love her and take care of her and be
kind to her."

"I can do that," Maggie said with a questioning
glance at her mother.

"She needs lots of tender loving care," Caroline
added. "She's fragile and old."

"I'll take good care of her," Maggie promised. "I'll
call her...Isabelle."

Grady handed her the doll, and Maggie pressed Isa-
belle against her shoulder and gently patted her back.

"I'm sorry Richard lied to you," Savannah felt obliged to say.

"I don't like Richard anymore," Maggie said.

"You don't need to worry about seeing him again," Frank Hennessey assured her. "Once I get my hands on him, he won't see the light of day for one hell of a long time."

"In here." Cal's heart pounded as he peered into the hotel. The staircase had collapsed and he was able to make out a figure trapped beneath the boards. Richard Weston, he was sure.

Jane was a few steps behind Cal. They cautiously entered the hotel and began to approach the ruined stairs.

"Stand back," Cal ordered, looking up to make sure nothing else threatened to fall. As soon as he'd assured himself it was safe, he started to remove the boards.

It was indeed Richard, and his groans grew louder, more plaintive. He was in obvious pain and close to unconsciousness.

Jane checked his vital signs. "There's no telling how long he's been here."

"Two days," Richard whispered, his voice weak. "Am I going to die?"

"Not if I have anything to say about it," she said firmly.

Cal understood that to Jane, medicine was a passion the same way ranching was to him, and he respected her for it. *Loved* her for it. He loved her courage and her sense of humor, too, her honesty, her kindness. Why that realization should come to him at a time like this, he didn't know. He'd intended never to make himself vulnerable again after Jennifer had humiliated him in front of the entire town. But he loved Jane. He felt no doubt, not about her or his feelings.

He continued to lift the heavy pieces of wood that trapped the injured man. The way in which Richard's leg was twisted told him it was badly broken.

Richard was moaning for water. Jane carefully lifted his head and dribbled liquid between his parched lips.

"Don't let me die," Richard pleaded between swallows. "Tell my mother I'm not ready."

Jane raised her gaze to Cal's.

"His mother died more than six years ago," he told her.

"He's hallucinating," she explained. "We need to get him out of here. The sooner the better."

"How?" The truck was parked some distance away, and Cal was aware it would be nearly impossible to move him.

"He's lost consciousness," Jane said.

"His right leg's broken."

"I suspect internal injuries, as well."

"How are we going to transport him?" Cal asked, seeking her advice. His biggest fear was that moving Richard, especially in his frail condition, might kill him. Cal didn't need Richard Weston's death on his conscience.

"We have to get help," Jane said, and while her voice was calm, he sensed the urgency in her words. "Leave me here and go back to town. Have Sheriff Hennessey call for a medevac. His injuries are far too extensive for me to handle. He's going to have to be airlifted out of here."

"You'll be all right alone?" he asked, getting to his feet.

She nodded, then looked up at him. "Hurry," she said. "I don't think he'll last much longer."

Cal sprinted out of the hotel, running through the brush and up the hill as fast as he could force his legs to move. He didn't like the idea of leaving Jane in Bitter End, but he didn't have a choice.

By the time he reached the pickup, he was panting and breathless. Sweat poured off his brow as he leaped into the cab and fired the engine to life.

He drove to the highway at a speed far too great for the terrain, and the truck's jolting threw him repeatedly and painfully against the door. Bruises, however, were a small price to pay for saving a man's life.

No sooner had he reached the highway than two patrol cars came into view, their lights flashing. Cal pressed his hand on the horn and slammed on the brakes. He screeched to a stop, swerving partway into the other lane.

Frank Hennessey was out of his patrol car in seconds. "This damn well better be good," he yelled.

"Richard Weston," Cal said, hopping out of the pickup. "At Bitter End. He's injured badly."

To Cal's surprise Savannah and Grady got out of the patrol car, as well.

"So he's holed up in Bitter End?" The question came from Grady.

"Yes. Jane and I were there. We found him. Apparently he was on the stairway in the hotel when it collapsed. He's in bad shape—broken leg, internal injuries."

"Oh, no!" Savannah covered her mouth.

"We shouldn't try to move him. We'll need to arrange for a chopper—he's got to be airlifted out."

Frank was already reaching for his radio, barking out orders.

Cal felt Savannah studying him. All he could say was, "Jane's there. She knows what to do."

He wanted to reassure Savannah that everything would be fine, but he couldn't. He had no way of knowing what had happened since he left the town. From what he'd seen of Richard, and from what Jane had said, it didn't look promising. Cal knew that despite the things her brother had done, Savannah still loved him.

"How is he really?" Grady asked him privately.

"Not good." No point hiding the truth from Grady. They'd been friends since childhood, and Grady counted on him for the truth. "I don't know if he's going to make it, so prepare yourself for the worst."

Grady nodded and moved away. "Maybe it'd be best if we called in Wade McMillen," he said, wiping one hand down his face. "If there's time…"

Grady wanted to give his brother the chance to make his peace with God. Cal had his doubts. Richard had always been unrepentant. Worse, he was unconscious, possibly dying, and nothing short of a miracle would save him now.

Cal suspected that the following hours would repeat themselves in his mind for years to come. Because of the fresh tire tracks left in the soft ground, Cal was able to lead Sheriff Hennessey, Grady and Savannah to Bitter End. The second patrol car returned to Promise for Wade McMillen. If Richard wasn't in need of the pastor's comfort, then Savannah and Grady would be.

Cal's biggest concern wasn't for Richard. Instead, his thoughts were on Jane. He'd hated like hell to leave her, knowing how uneasy she'd felt in the ghost town.

Damn Richard Weston. If he died, leaving Jane alone with a dead man in the middle of that empty town, he'd never forgive the bastard.

As it turned out, Richard was still clinging to life when they reached Bitter End. Grady and Savannah immediately besieged Jane with questions about their brother.

Cal stepped out of the way and watched as Jane skillfully reassured them. She'd been busy while he was away, Cal noticed. Even without medical equipment, Jane had worked to save Richard Weston's life. She'd created a makeshift splint for his leg and managed to shift him onto his side. She'd monitored his pulse and his breathing.

Frank put out a red flare for the helicopter, and it seemed no time at all before he heard the distinctive sound of the blades.

With Jane's help, the medics loaded Richard onto a stretcher and hooked him up to an emergency oxygen supply. Cal and Frank cleared a path, then Richard was carried to the helicopter.

His injuries were determined to be too extensive for the hospital in Brewster, and he was transported to Austin, instead. If he lasted that long, Cal thought grimly. It would be touch and go.

Because of the limited space aboard the helicopter, Jane wouldn't be traveling with them.

They all stood back as the chopper rose, carrying Richard Weston away. Cal placed his arm around Jane's shoulders and felt her trembling.

"Whatever happens is out of my hands now," she whispered.

Cal pressed his chin against the top of her head. "You did everything you could."

"I know." She glanced up and down the streets of Bitter End. "I don't want to come back here," she said with vehemence. "Ever!"

Cal couldn't agree with her more.

It was a day Frank Hennessey would long remember. Richard Weston, if he lived, faced twenty years behind bars without the possibility of parole. Richard deserved that prison sentence, but Frank felt bad for Grady and Savannah.

Wade McMillen had counseled both of them. Frank never had been one to attend church, but he liked and respected Reverend McMillen. As long as Wade didn't preach at him, then Frank wouldn't quote the law at him, either. In a situation like this, he figured, the reverend provided a service nobody else could. Including the sheriff.

Frank was with the brother and sister when the phone rang about eight that night. Grady leaped on it, and after the initial greeting, glanced across the room where Savannah sat with Laredo.

He nodded and murmured a handful of thank-yous before replacing the receiver. "That was the hospital in Austin," Grady announced. His words had everyone's attention.

"He's going to make it," Grady said, and his voice cracked. When Caroline put her arm around him, Grady clung to her tightly.

Savannah burst into tears and hugged her husband.

Frank didn't want to be the one to remind them that once Richard had recovered, he'd be placed in a maximum-security prison. If Frank hadn't disliked the man already, what Richard had said to Maggie to prevent her telling anyone where she'd been would have done it.

Since the deputy who'd driven Wade McMillen out to the Yellow Rose had already left, Frank drove the reverend back to town.

They chatted amicably, sharing insights and theories about the youngest Weston's personality. Frank dropped Wade off, then, on impulse, drove past Dovie's house.

He wasn't sure what he intended to do. Probably nothing. A few weeks ago he would've been spending this night with her. She would probably have waited up for him, brewing a pot of coffee in case he wanted to talk, which he almost always did. He missed those times with Dovie.

Despite everything, he missed her more rather than less with each day that passed. As he'd expected, her lights were out. She might be asleep—or on that cruise she'd mentioned. He'd forgotten the exact date she was supposed to go—although Louise Powell and Tammy Lee could no doubt have told him.

With a heavy heart he turned the corner, and that was when he saw the Realtor's sign. His heart felt as if it'd taken a ten-story tumble. She hadn't been bluffing when she said she'd leave Promise. He stared at the sign, shaken and hurt, trying to imagine Promise without Dovie.

Two days later Frank sat in the café at the bowling alley drinking a mug of coffee. His dour mood had kept his friends at bay. Anyone looking for idle conversation sought out someone else.

He noticed with something of a shock that Wade McMillen had slipped into the seat across from him.

Frank scowled. "I don't remember asking for company."

"You didn't, but I decided to join you, anyway." Wade raised his hand to attract the waitress's attention. Neither spoke again until she'd brought his coffee.

"Look, if you're interested in scintillating conversation, I'd be happy to steer you elsewhere. I'm not in the mood."

"So I noticed, Sheriff. Something on your mind?"

He had to give the preacher credit for guts. "As it happens, there is."

"Want to talk about it?"

"Not particularly."

Wade studied him. "I don't suppose this has something to do with Dovie Boyd."

"Why? Did she come and cry on your shoulder?" Frank muttered angrily.

"Nope. Dovie didn't say a word."

"Then how'd you know?"

Wade smiled, and it was the knowing grin of an observant man. "You might say *you* told me, Frank."

"Me?"

"You've been down in the mouth for weeks. The way I figure it, you can trust me enough to help or you can sit in the café and stare at the wall."

"Is it that obvious?"

"Yup."

Wade certainly didn't pull his punches, Frank thought. "It's not going to do any good to discuss it. My mind's made up. Besides, I already know what you're going to say."

"Do you, now." The knowing smile was back in place.

If Frank hadn't liked the other man so much, he might have been irritated. "You're a preacher."

"Yes, but I'm also a man," Wade told him.

Frank sighed deeply. "Dovie wants me to marry her."

"And you don't love her?"

"Wrong," he snapped. "I love her so damn much I can hardly think straight anymore. We had a good thing, the two of us. I spent the night with her a couple times a week, and we had one of the best damn relationships I've ever had. I always had this sort of vague thought that one day we'd get married—and then I realized I couldn't. I just could not go through with it," he said slowly, shaking his head. "As soon as I told her the truth, it was over. Just like that. Hell, if I'd lied to her, she'd never have known the difference. A lot of good being honest did me." He suspected his words had shocked the minister, and that was exactly what he wanted. To Frank's surprise Wade didn't so much as blink.

"You love her, but you don't want to marry her."

"Yes," Frank said more loudly than he intended.

"Any reason?"

"I've got a long list," Frank muttered.

"I'm not going anywhere," Wade said.

Frank wished he would. Wade McMillen wasn't going to tell him anything he didn't already know. He wasn't going to offer a quick solution to a complex problem. If anything, he'd make Frank feel even guiltier for not marrying Dovie.

"You enjoy your freedom," Wade said. "A man who's been a bachelor all these years is set in his ways."

"Exactly." Frank was impressed at Wade's understanding. "I happen to like the way I live, and much as I love Dovie, I don't want a woman messing with how I do things."

"I'm a bachelor myself," Wade reminded him.

"If I want to belch after dinner, I don't need to worry about offending a woman. I can hang around the house in my underwear if I feel like it. I can pile up all my papers and magazines and read them all at once without hearing about the mess."

"I know what you mean."

"If my dirty clothes litter the floor for a couple days, I won't have someone picking them up for me and then complaining about it."

"That's what I'm like, too," Wade said, "but it does get lonely every now and then."

"Damn lonely," Frank agreed. And nothing helped. The dinner date with Tammy Lee had been a disaster, one that wouldn't be repeated. The only woman he wanted was Dovie.

"I'm going to lose her, Wade," he said, staring into his coffee. "She's put her house up for sale."

"So I understand."

"There's no solution. Either I change who I am or I let her walk out of my life."

"And both of those prospects are making you unhappy. It's eating you up inside."

"I might as well be drinking acid," Frank confessed. The knot in his stomach had become permanent. Even when he went to bed at night, he couldn't make himself relax. He used to fall asleep the instant his head hit the pillow. No longer. His mind constantly churned with the two miserable alternatives—marriage or no Dovie.

"There's no solution," he muttered again.

"I wouldn't say that," Wade countered. "Sometimes people are so caught up in the problem the obvious answer escapes them."

Frank raised his gaze to meet Wade's.

"There's a reason I came to talk to you," Wade continued. "I've got an idea," he said, steepling his fingers in front of him. "One that'll give you both what you're looking for."

Nine

Dusk settled comfortably over the Yellow Rose Ranch. Caroline stood on the porch, savoring the beauty of the sunset and the peace of a Sunday evening. Within minutes the moon would rise to greet her, and a million twinkling stars would nod their welcome.

Grady joined her, standing behind her to slip his arms around her waist. In less than a week they would become husband and wife. As the wedding approached, Caroline tried not to become sidetracked by the events concerning Richard. He'd robbed her and Grady of so much already. All she wanted now was to blend her life with Grady's.

"I thought I'd find you out here," he whispered close to her ear.

She hugged his arms. "I needed a moment of solitude."

"We both do." Grady exhaled slowly. "So much has happened in the past few days it's hard to take it all in."

Savannah and Laredo had moved into their new home. At the same time, Caroline and Maggie had made the transition from their rented house in the city to the ranch house with Grady. They'd spent all day hauling boxes from one place to the other. Later in the afternoon Laredo and Savannah had driven to Austin to visit Richard and had yet to return.

"Maggie's asleep," Grady said, nuzzling her neck.

Caroline closed her eyes, cherishing these moments alone with the man she loved. It was a rare pleasure these last hectic days before the wedding.

"I'm looking forward to just the two of us being together," she told him. Away from the worries about Richard, the wedding, the hard work of merging one household with another. They'd decided to take a four-day honeymoon in Galveston, and just then, getting away seemed to Caroline like a small slice of heaven.

"You're not the only one anticipating our honeymoon!" Grady chuckled softly. "It's beginning to feel like Grand Central Station around here."

"This time next week I'll be your wife."

"And I'll be your husband," Grady said, as if he still had trouble thinking of himself that way. "I swear there's something happening in Promise this year."

"How do you mean?"

"All the weddings." Grady sounded incredulous. "It started with Savannah and Laredo."

"Then Ellie and Glen."

"Now it'll be us."

"I have a sneaking suspicion who's going to be next." Caroline nudged Grady lightly with her elbow. "Cal and Jane." She'd watched them the day Richard was discovered in Bitter End and recognized the signs. She suspected they were only now becoming aware of their feelings for each other. Caroline had noticed something else, too—the rough edges of Cal's personality seemed to be wearing smooth. Perhaps even more telling were the changes Caroline had noticed in Jane. The California native had become one of them. A Texan at heart.

The last time Ellie had stopped by the post office to collect her mail, she'd mentioned that Cal was giving Jane horseback-riding lessons. Caroline would bet that the good doctor was becoming familiar with more than horses. Jane Dickinson had the look. "Yes," she said softly. "Cal and Jane."

"You're suggesting Cal's in love?" Grady shook his head. "No way!"

"We'll see," Caroline said confidently. "I wouldn't be surprised if they announced their engagement before the end of the year."

Grady responded by snickering in her ear. "Boy, are you off base with that one. Cal and I've been best friends for years. If he was thinking of getting married, don't you think he'd mention it to me?"

"Not necessarily."

"You don't know Cal and me—we're like this." He crossed two fingers and waved them under her nose. "Close."

"Uh-huh."

"So," Grady said with conviction, "if Cal was interested in a woman, I'd be the first to know. We don't have secrets from each other."

"Oh, really?" Caroline tried but couldn't keep the sarcasm out of her voice.

"Damn straight."

"Then answer me this," she said smugly. "When did you tell Cal you were in love with me?"

His silence was answer enough.

"Well, I'm waiting." She turned to face him, hooked

her arms around his neck and tilted back her head to get a good look at his face.

Grady's eyes avoided hers. "That's not a fair question."

"Why isn't it?"

"Because...well, because it took me a long time to figure out how I felt about you and even longer to act on it. That being the case, I couldn't very well say anything to Cal."

Caroline rolled her eyes for effect.

"Hey," Grady argued, "the man is always the last to know."

Her cocky grin was wasted on him. "My point exactly. Cal won't mention his feelings for Jane until he's ready to put an engagement ring on her finger. Trust me on this, Weston."

"Is that right," he muttered.

"That's right."

"And how did you get so smart?"

"Practice," she teased and kissed the corner of his mouth. "Lots and lots of practice."

His eyes grew dark and sexy as he focused his gaze on her lips. Slowly he lowered his mouth to hers in a kiss that was open, purposeful and hungry.

The kiss was wonderful. Being right was nice—but not nearly as satisfying as two minutes in the arms of the man she loved.

Jane sat at her desk reviewing her appointment schedule for the following day. She was nearly finished and eager to escape the office for her next riding lesson. In truth it was Cal she really wanted to see, not Atta Girl, fond though she was of the horse. They'd been making steady progress, and when she arrived these days, it wasn't unusual for Atta Girl to gallop to the fence to greet her.

The time Jane spent at the ranch had lengthened to include dinner on her lesson days. Since Cal wouldn't accept payment for teaching her to ride, she'd taken it upon herself to cook his meal afterward. She experimented with traditional Texas recipes, but introduced some "California cuisine," too.

More and more Jane found herself looking forward to being with Cal. This evening she planned to create a special meal, complete with birthday cake and candles. Cal had no way of knowing it was her birthday—but he was the person she wanted to spend it with.

"Do you need anything else?" Jenny Bender, her receptionist, asked a few minutes later.

"Not a thing, Jenny, thanks—and thanks again for the flowers." How Jenny had learned about her birthday, Jane could only guess.

"I'll be heading out, then," Jenny said. "The answering service is on."

As soon as Jane was finished, she locked up the clinic and hurried to her house. The white lab coat was replaced with a freshly laundered snap shirt, and her skirt with comfortable slim-leg jeans. Cal had found an old pair of chaps and she strapped those on over the jeans, then reached for her hat and gloves. She was two minutes from walking out when she heard the doorbell.

Groaning inwardly at the delay, Jane answered the door.

"Surprise!" Her mother and father stood on the other side, their faces revealing guileless pleasure at surprising her.

"Happy birthday, darling," her mother said.

Jane stood there, too shocked to do anything more than stare.

"My goodness," her father said. "Look at you!"

Jane hugged her mother and kissed her father's cheek. "What do you think?" she asked and whirled around to let them have the full effect of her transformation.

"I love it!" her mother cried.

"Cowboy chic," her father added with a grin.

Jane brought them both into the living room. "What are you doing in Texas?"

"Your father's attending a conference in Oklahoma City starting on Wednesday. We decided that since we were going to be this close, it'd only be a hop, skip and a jump to come by and surprise you for your birthday."

Jane had to admit she was surprised, all right.

"We've come to take you to dinner," her father said. He handed her an envelope, which she knew contained a check. "Happy birthday, honey."

"Thanks, Dad, Mom. I can't believe you're really here!" She took a deep breath. "Where are you staying?"

"Your father found a quaint little bed-and-breakfast place here in town."

"Cal's parents own that," Jane said excitedly.

"The same Cal you've been telling us about?" Her mother raised her eyebrows.

"One and the same. Mom, Dad, would you mind if I invited him to join us? I don't know if he can, since it's such short notice, but I do want you to meet him."

"A cowboy?" her father asked.

"One of the best you're likely to meet," she said. "A *real* cowboy."

"You're not falling in love with him, are you?"

"Dad, please! I'm a big girl now and I can make my own decisions."

"Fine, but remember you belong in California, not Texas."

Jane's excitement dimmed as she felt the pressure building inside her. From the time she'd been accepted into medical school, everyone had assumed she'd join her uncle's practice. Everyone including Jane. She wasn't so sure anymore. Cal had said that once her commitment to the government was satisfied, he knew she'd return to California. She'd neither confirmed nor denied it. She couldn't because she didn't know herself. She knew what was expected of her, but her heart had begun to tell her something different. She loved her work at the clinic. It had taken time and effort to become part of this community, and now that she'd established friendships, she didn't want to leave. Nothing needed to be decided right now, she realized that. But the reminder was one she'd rather ignore, especially since she'd never mentioned her uncle Ken to Cal.

"Is this what you've been wearing for your riding lessons?" Her mother wanted to know.

She nodded, proud of her accomplishments.

"Don't get too acclimatized," her father said in a heavyhanded attempt at humor that did nothing to disguise his message.

"Dad, would you stop? I'll be back in just a minute," she said. The phone in the kitchen offered some privacy. She punched out Cal's number and waited through four long rings before he answered.

"You're coming, aren't you?" he asked immediately.

"I can't."

"Why not?"

It thrilled her to hear how disappointed he sounded. "My parents arrived unexpectedly to take me to dinner. They'd like to meet you," she said, stretching the truth, but only a little. "Can you drive into town and join us at the Chili Pepper?"

He hesitated, then said, "I'll need an hour before I can get there."

"We'll wait," she promised, eager for her family to meet the man who'd come to mean so much to her.

When she hung up, Jane discovered that her mother had entered the kitchen. Impulsively Jane hugged her.

"You're happy, aren't you?" Stephanie Dickinson observed.

Jane knew that her parents had worried about her move to Texas, especially in the beginning before she'd made friends. It was the first time she'd lived more than an hour from her family home, the first time she'd been so completely on her own.

"I'm anxious for you to meet Cal," she said, clasping both her mother's hands. She wanted this meeting to go well on both sides, although she wasn't ready to share her feelings for Cal with anyone yet, not even her mother.

"Didn't you say his parents are the owners of the bed-and-breakfast? They certainly seem like nice people. They're packing for a cruise, and apparently they leave in the morning."

"They're wonderful." So was Cal, but she didn't mention that. Jane had met Mary and Phil the night she'd first played bingo and had seen them a number of times since. They were warm gracious folk whose personalities were perfectly suited to operating a bed-and-breakfast.

"You're not really serious about this cowpoke, are you?" her father asked, entering the kitchen.

"Daddy!"

"Don't go losing your heart to a cowboy," her father teased, kissing her soundly on both cheeks. "I can't get over the sight of you in all this cowboy gear. I don't know if I'd have recognized you."

Smiling, Jane went along with his silliness, realizing suddenly how much she missed her parents. She knew her dad could be a little too obvious in his remarks; she also knew he loved her and cared about her welfare.

After changing out of the riding clothes and into a skirt and sweater, she brewed a pot of coffee. The three of them sat in the living room visiting while they waited for Cal. Jane showed them her photographs of Bitter End, and they enjoyed a vigorous discussion of theories about its abandonment.

The instant the doorbell chimed Jane was on her feet. She was unaccountably nervous about Cal's meeting her parents.

"Hi," he said in his soft Texas drawl.

"Hi," Jane returned and held open the screen door for him. Cal looked incredibly attractive, in jeans, polished boots, a white Western shirt and tweed jacket; she'd hardly ever seen him so formally dressed. Since their trip to Bitter End, her feelings for him had solidified. He'd been supportive and helpful, and later, after Richard Weston was airlifted to the hospital in Austin, he'd sat and talked with her. Among other things, he'd told her about Richard Weston's family history. His willingness to do this, to share a part of himself and his community, revealed that he'd come to trust her. It meant more to her than fifty riding lessons and a hundred bingo wins.

"Mom, Dad," she said, taking Cal by the hand and leading him into the room. "This is Cal Patterson."

Her father stood and the two of them exchanged hearty handshakes. Cal held a bouquet of flowers in his left hand, which he gave to her mother.

"You mean to say those aren't for me?" Jane teased, setting her hands on her hips in mock outrage.

Cal flashed her a sexy grin and she blushed. Jane could actually feel the heat enter her cheeks. Only one man was capable of doing this to her, and that was Cal.

"I thought we'd take Mom and Dad to the Chili Pepper," Jane said. "It's the best barbecue in town," she explained to her parents.

"Great. A chance to taste authentic Texas barbecue," her father said jovially.

"Do they have a low-fat menu?" her mother asked.

"No." Jane was adamant. "And don't ask for dressing on the side, either."

"But, Jane—"

"Mother, trust me on this."

"All right, all right," her mother said.

Although the restaurant was only a few blocks away, her father insisted on driving. Since Cal and Jane had been in to eat a couple of times, the hostess greeted them by name and led them to a booth.

"The music's a little loud, isn't it?" her father complained the minute they were seated.

"They like it that way here," Jane said.

"That country music's got a real twang to it." Her mother grimaced as if she could barely stand to hear it.

"I was afraid you were going to develop an accent," her father added, "and you'd end up sounding like that girl who's singing now."

Jane offered Cal an apologetic smile, trying to convey that her parents didn't mean to be condescending. He nodded reassuringly.

A Willie Nelson song came on, and as usual, everyone in the restaurant sang along, Jane included. Her parents lowered their menus and stared, transfixed by the boisterous songfest. The instant the tune ended, patrons and waiters went about their business again.

"This is Willie Nelson country," Jane explained.

"Everyone in California feels the same way about the Beach Boys," her mother said.

"Although I wouldn't call them *boys* anymore," her father put in, and this time Cal and Jane both laughed.

They ordered their drinks—beer for everyone except Stephanie who was having iced tea, "with fresh lemons," she'd specified.

"Can't decide, Mom?" Jane asked.

"It's all…so…"

"Western," Jane supplied.

Her mother nodded.

"Mom, you aren't going to find nouvelle cuisine in Promise."

"Oh, all right," Stephanie Dickinson said with a sigh, closing her menu. "I'll have a salad. I just hope they serve a decent avocado."

It was all Jane could do not to groan out loud. Especially since she was uncomfortably reminded of her own attitude a few months ago.

Her father was the conversationalist in the family and he began telling a story about stopping at a service station in a small town outside San Antonio. "I asked this old geezer how far it was to Promise and he said—" her father paused for effect "—it was down yonder." He laughed until his eyes watered. "Then he corrected himself and said it was *way* down yonder."

Jane noted that Cal didn't laugh nearly as hard. "Dad," she said, "this *is* Texas."

"I know, I know. When in Rome—"

"Yes, Daddy."

Their meals arrived—three orders of barbecue and one green salad—and Jane relaxed as they began to eat.

"Did you know it's Jane's birthday?" her father asked when they were nearly finished.

"Dad!"

"As a matter of fact, I did," Cal said. He reached into his pocket and withdrew a small square box wrapped in white paper with a gold bow.

"Who told you?" Jane asked him.

He hesitated, then confessed, "Jenny."

"My receptionist," Jane told her parents.

"Aren't you going to open it?" her mother asked, eyeing the box.

"It's not an engagement ring, is it?" her father chided. "I don't want a cowpoke to steal my little girl's heart."

"Dad!" Jane hurriedly removed the paper. Inside the jeweler's box was a Black Hills gold pendant and chain. Jane lifted her gaze to Cal's. "Thank you," she whispered. "It's beautiful."

For a second it was only the two of them. His eyes held hers for the sweetest moment. "So are you," he said, for her ears only.

Jane removed the necklace from its cotton bed and Cal helped her put it on. When he'd finished, Jane noticed that her mother and father were watching them closely.

"So…you've adjusted to Texas?" her father asked unnecessarily.

"I like it here."

"Her attitude changed the night she won the Blackout Bingo jackpot," Cal told them.

"You played bingo?" Her mother looked aghast.

"We all do, just about every Friday night." Jane knew they didn't really understand that bingo was one of the few entertainment choices in a town the size of Promise.

"You're joking, I hope." This from her father.

"I bowl, too." Only once, but her family didn't have to know that.

Her mother gasped.

Jane laughed and squeezed Cal's hand. Oh, yes, their attitude was very much what her own had been like when she arrived here. She truly understood now, for the first time, why her reception in town had been cool. "It's another one of those when-in-Rome things."

"Just don't bring these Texas habits with you when you come home," her father said. "I can't imagine what Ken will think."

"Ken is Harry's brother," her mother explained. "Jane will be joining him at his medical clinic when she's finished her assignment here."

"Eventually he's going to make our little girl a full partner," her father said proudly and smiled at her. Jane gave him a feeble smile in return, wishing they'd kept this information to themselves.

"I see," Cal said.

Jane felt him stiffen, and when she squeezed his hand again he didn't respond by squeezing her fingers back.

She should have known this would happen, should have explained to Cal long before now about her uncle Ken. She would have, if she'd known what to say. Now he'd been hit with the information at the worst possible moment. She couldn't explain or reassure, not with her parents there. She'd lost her chance to tell him tactfully and in her own way.

They all rode back in the car to Jane's house, and her parents left shortly afterward, promising to stop by the health clinic the next morning, before they drove on to Oklahoma.

"I need to go, too," Cal said, disappointing Jane. She'd hoped they'd have some time alone together.

"You can't stay a few minutes?" she pressed.

"No."

"You'll phone later?" she asked as she walked him to the door.

"I'll try," he said noncommittally.

"I'd like to explain what my parents said about me joining my uncle Ken's medical practice. I apologize for not mentioning it sooner. Nothing's for sure yet, and—"

"We'll talk about that later."

"All right," she mumbled, her heart sinking. His look told her everything. He was angry now, and felt betrayed, and it would be best to let him sort through his feelings before they talked this out. "Thank you for the necklace," she told him, and despite his being upset with her, kissed him soundly on the lips.

He really knew how to pick 'em, Cal decided, not for the first time. Jennifer, and now Jane. He must have a weakness for deceptive city girls. At least he hadn't made the mistake this time of asking the woman to marry him.

From this point forward he was determined to avoid all women whose names started with the letter *J*.

Cal sat out on the porch in the moonlight and reviewed the evening. He'd been looking forward to meeting Jane's parents, but it hadn't taken him long to discover that the elder Dickinsons viewed him and the entire population of Promise as hicks. However, he could live with that. What he couldn't live with was Jane's plans to join her uncle's medical practice. She might have said something herself, and a hell of a lot sooner. He could only assume she'd kept the information from him on purpose. She intended to go back to California, just the way he'd claimed; it sounded as though her life was already planned for her. Planned years into the future, with no room for someone like him.

His forehead pounded with an increasingly painful headache. Cal walked inside and turned on the kitchen light. Obviously he needed to have his head examined. Not because of the headache, but because he was fool enough to make the same mistake twice. Only this time it hurt more.

This time his heart was fully involved and he'd started to dream again.

Cal expected Jane to show up the following afternoon and she did. A few minutes before five he heard the familiar sound of her car; fortifying himself, he stepped out of the barn, eager to get this confrontation over with.

"Hello," she called, closing her car door. She was dressed in her shirt and jeans and looked as brightly beautiful as a rodeo princess. He wanted to remember her like this.

"Hi," he said, keeping all emotion out of his voice.

"Thanks for being so patient with my parents last night," she said. "I can't believe some of the things they said."

They stood a few feet apart, a little awkwardly.

She sighed and glanced sheepishly at him. "I realized I sounded just like them not so long ago."

"You're right, you did." He wasn't going to disagree with her.

"But I came around, with a little help from my friends."

He nodded.

"Mostly from Dovie and you. Ellie, too."

He didn't respond.

"I'm here for my lesson," she said as if she needed to remind him.

"I'm afraid there won't be one today."

Disappointment flashed from her eyes. "Oh."

"You should have phoned first."

"I…I…" She nodded. "You're right, I should have. Do you have time for a cup of coffee?"

His initial thought was to refuse her and hope she'd be smart enough to figure it out for herself. But he suspected it would take more than the cold shoulder for a woman as stubborn as Jane to get the message.

"All right, I'll make time for coffee," he said, although he wasn't happy about it. He wanted her off his ranch and out of his life *now,* while he had the strength to let her leave.

He walked into the house, reheated the coffee and poured them each a mug. He carried the mugs out to the porch; no need to sit inside on an afternoon as pleasant as this.

"You didn't mention going into partnership with your uncle when you finished your assignment here," he said bluntly.

"No," she said. "It's always been accepted by the family that I would and—"

"It's all right, Jane, you don't need to explain it to me."

Her relief was obvious. "I should have said something much sooner, I know, but I didn't want you to get the wrong idea."

He stared into the distance, training his eyes on the rolling hills nestled against the horizon. It was either that or look at her, and he didn't think he could do that and still say what he had to say.

"You're a very good doctor," he began, and the compliment was sincere. "If I hadn't realized that earlier, you proved it the day we found Richard Weston."

"Thank you."

"You'll be a valuable asset to your uncle's practice."

"I'm not quite sure that's what..." She faltered, and he could see she was having a difficult time.

"Listen, Jane, I've been doing some thinking and I believe it'd be best if we suspended our lessons."

His words were met with stunned silence. "You're serious, aren't you?"

"Very."

"Just because I *might* be joining my uncle's medical practice? I haven't even made up my mind about that! I wish you'd hear me out first."

"No." This was important. "Because you belong in California."

"Hogwash."

"You might adapt to life here in Texas for a while, but it isn't going to last. The writing's on the wall."

"And just when did you become a handwriting expert?"

"Last night."

She snorted. "Oh, come on, Ca—"

Cal interrupted her. "I was wrong. You aren't Dr. Texas, you're Dr. Big City. Big plans. Big bucks, platinum charge cards, high-powered friends."

Jane vaulted to her feet, spilling her coffee on the porch. "Don't give me that, Phillip Calvin Patterson."

He was surprised she knew his full name, but this wasn't the time to ask how come she did.

"You know what the real problem is, don't you?" She dragged in a deep breath, preparing to answer her own question. "You're a coward."

"I'm not going to trade insults with you, if that's what you're looking for," he said.

"I'm not stupid."

"I didn't say you were."

Hands on her hips, she threw her head back and glared at the sky. "You might as well have said it," she returned, calmer now. "I love you and I'm fairly certain you feel the same way about me."

"You're taking a lot for granted."

"Perhaps, I am," she agreed, "but if you're idiotic enough to send me away because you're afraid…"

His eyes flared at the word.

"Afraid," she repeated, "then you're a fool, as well."

"It might be best if you left," he said. His head was beginning to pound again. He wasn't up to dealing with a tirade.

"If that's what you want, I will. And I won't be back—"

"That's what I was hoping," he said and hated himself for being so cruel.

"—unless you ask," she finished as though he hadn't spoken.

With her head held high, she walked in the direction of her parked car, then stopped halfway across the yard. For a moment he figured she was planning to argue with him some more, but he was wrong. Instead, she turned toward the corral where Atta Girl stood, her sleek neck stretched over the top rail.

Jane stroked the mare's nose and whatever she said apparently met with Atta Girl's approval, because the animal nodded and snorted. Climbing onto the bottom fence rail, Jane put her arms around Atta Girl's neck and hugged her. Then she leaped down, stroked Atta Girl's nose again and walked over to her car and climbed inside.

A minute later she was gone. She'd retained her dignity—and his heart.

Ten

Jane had called Cal Patterson a coward and a fool, and she'd meant it. Add to that stubborn, unreasonable, infuriating…and worse.

Dr. Big City. Big plans. Big bucks. Each time his words came to mind she grew more furious. After all the time she'd spent with him how could he know so little about her? That really hurt.

By Thursday she was exhausted. Sleep eluded her and she'd rarely been so frustrated or out of sorts.

Ellie stopped by the clinic late Thursday afternoon when the office was technically closed. Jenny led her back to the office, where Jane sat making a desultory attempt to organize the top of her desk.

"I take it this is a personal visit," Jane said after Jenny had left.

"Have you got a few minutes?" Ellie asked.

Jane nodded. "For you I do, but not if you're here to talk about Cal."

"Fair enough," Ellie said, entering the room. She sat in the chair across from Jane's desk.

"You know what infuriates me most?" Jane blurted,

her anger spilling over. "It's that Cal didn't have the common decency to talk this over with me. Oh, no, he just *assumes* I'm returning to California without so much as waiting to hear my side."

"Jane, I thought you didn't want to talk about him."

"Forget I said that." Jane shook her head. "And you know? That's not the worst of it," she went on. "Not only doesn't he hear me out, he sends me away like I'm a child he can order around."

"I'll admit—"

Jane interrupted her. "He was completely out of line in what he said. If he didn't want to see me again, fine, but to insult me—that was going too far."

"He insulted you?" Ellie sounded appropriately outraged.

"Tell me, do I look like a big-city doctor to you?" Jane demanded without expecting a response. "I don't even wear makeup anymore. Well, maybe a little mascara and lipstick, but that's all. I haven't washed my car in months. I wear jeans practically all the time." She took a deep breath. "And when's the last time you saw a big-city doctor asking some disgruntled rancher to teach her how to ride? A rancher who implies that this supposed big-city doctor is only interested in money, by the way."

"He said that?" Ellie was clearly shocked.

"Sort of. And more—like it was time I left."

"Cal suggested you leave Promise?"

"No, the ranch, which I did, but not before I put in my two cents' worth."

"Good for you!"

"I told him he was a coward."

Ellie's eyes widened. "You told Cal *what?*"

"That he's a coward, and I said it to his face."

"What did *he* say?"

Jane paused and tried to remember. "Nothing."

"Nothing?"

"Nothing memorable, anyway."

Ellie clapped her hands, apparently enjoying the details of Jane's final skirmish with Cal. Her outrage, however, only helped so much. "I hope you're here to tell me how utterly miserable he is." It would boost Jane's deflated ego to learn he was pining away for her.

"Actually," Ellie said, her gaze warm with sympathy, "I haven't seen him, so I can't. But Glen has."

"Oh?" Jane's spirits lifted hopefully.

"Apparently Cal's been pretty closemouthed about you."

Those same spirits sank again, even lower than before.

"But Glen did say Cal's been in a bitch of a mood."

Jane couldn't have held back a smile to save her soul. So…the man was suffering. Good.

"I don't mean to be nosy—" Ellie's gaze shifted uncomfortably to her hands "—but what happened? Everything seemed to be going so nicely."

"You tell me!" Jane cried. "My parents arrived as a birthday surprise, and we went to dinner and Cal joined us."

"So he's met your parents."

"Yes, but I rue the day. No," she said, changing her mind, "I'm glad it happened before…" She hesitated. "Actually, it's too late for that."

"You're falling in love with Cal?" Ellie asked bluntly.

"I've already fallen." Might as well admit it. "I felt close to him—closer than I have to anyone. For the first time since my college days there was someone in my life who…" She let the rest fade.

Ellie was silent for a minute. "You weren't far off, you know."

"About what?"

"Cal being a coward. He *is* afraid."

"Of what? Me moving back to California? Give me a break, Ellie. I've been here less than a year and my contract's for three. Do I need to decide right this minute if I'm going to live in Promise for the rest of my life?"

"No."

Jane ignored the response, too keyed up to stop now. "He's being more than a little unreasonable, if you ask me."

"I agree with you."

"I'm not another Jennifer Healy."

"I know that. Glen knows that. You know that," Ellie said.

"But not Cal."

"Not Cal."

Jane brushed a stray hair from her face. "I told him I loved him," she said, revealing the most intimate and embarrassing part of their argument. She'd exposed her heart to him, and he'd not only dismissed *her* feelings, he'd denied his own.

"Oh, Jane, just be patient. He'll figure it out. Eventually."

"He might have offered me a reason to stay," she said, her voice little more than a whisper.

Ellie sighed expressively. "I don't know what it is about men in Texas. They're stubborn as the day is long."

"Proud, too," Jane added. "Way too proud."

"Impatient."

"Uncommunicative."

Ellie nodded, then sighed again. "Wonderful. Loving. Protective and gentle and passionate."

Jane closed her eyes, not wanting to confuse the issue with anything positive.

"Are you going to Caroline and Grady's wedding on Saturday?" Ellie asked her, abruptly changing the subject.

"Caroline asked me to cut the cake."

"Cal will be there," Ellie warned.

"Cal is Grady's best man." For half a heartbeat Jane toyed with the idea of finding an excuse to skip the wedding, but she refused to let Cal Patterson influence where she went or what she did. "I'd better get used to seeing him around town," Jane said, more for her own sake than Ellie's. "We won't be able to avoid running into each other now and then."

A saucy grin appeared on Ellie's face. "That's exactly what I was thinking. Cal's going to see you at the wedding. He'll see you at the grocery store and the Chili Pepper and bingo. And every time he goes to the post office he'll drive by the clinic."

"Heaven help him if he gets sick," Jane said.

"That would be horrible, wouldn't it?" Ellie said, sounding almost gleeful at the prospect.

"Absolutely horrible," Jane agreed.

Ellie shivered delightedly. "I can hardly wait."

Jane laughed for the first time in days. "I can't wait to give this stubborn Texas rancher a booster shot in places men don't like to talk about."

The last night of the three-day midweek cruise, Dovie decided to join Mary and Phil Patterson in the lounge for drinks and dancing. Mary had been after her the entire trip to make herself more accessible to the single men on board, but Dovie couldn't see the point.

The music was from the forties and fifties, and judging by the crowd on the dance floor, the audience appreciated it.

"I'm so glad you decided to join us," Mary said, greeting Dovie at the door and leading her to a small table at the back of the room.

"I couldn't see spending our last night aboard doing something silly like sleeping," Dovie teased.

Mary patted her hand. "I wish you'd enjoyed the cruise more."

"But I did," Dovie assured her friend. It had been the perfect escape. Being away from Frank had given her some perspective on the relationship and on the difficulties she and Frank had encountered.

A waiter came for her drink order, and Dovie asked for a glass of white wine. Maybe what she needed was a little something to loosen her inhibitions. Actually she felt better than she had in weeks—although she still missed Frank.

"I couldn't believe the way you took to the water! I wouldn't have guessed you were that much of a swimmer."

It'd been years since she'd gone swimming, but Dovie'd had no intention of wasting an opportunity like this. For her, the highlight of the cruise had been snorkeling off the Yucatán Peninsula. Viewing the different species of colorful and exotic sea life was an experience she would long remember. She said as much to Mary.

"But your thoughts were on Frank," Mary replied.

Dovie couldn't deny it. Three days away, and she was

dreadfully homesick, feeling more than a little lost and confused. Mostly she was angry with herself for having done something as foolish as putting her home up for sale. Promise was where she belonged, and she wasn't about to let Frank Hennessey chase her away. Dovie didn't blame Frank, but herself; she'd simply overreacted to his dating Tammy Lee.

The music started again and Phil stood, ready to escort his wife onto the dance floor.

Mary hesitated.

"Go on, you two," Dovie urged, her own foot tapping to the music.

To her surprise, no more than thirty seconds had passed before a distinguished-looking man approached her table. "Would you care to dance?"

Dovie stared at him as if this was the most complex question she'd ever been asked. "Yes," she said, deciding suddenly. She stood up and placed her hand in his.

"I'm Gordon Pawling," he said as he slid his arm around her waist and guided her onto the dance floor.

"Dovie Boyd," she said.

"I know."

She looked at him in surprise. "How?"

"I asked your friends the first night of the cruise."

Dovie remembered Mary mentioning a tall handsome man who'd questioned her about Dovie. While it had salved her ego to know that someone had asked to meet her, Dovie wasn't interested in a holiday romance. The only man she'd ever loved other than her husband was Frank Hennessey. She still did love Frank. She wasn't a woman who loved lightly or gave her heart easily.

The crowded floor forced Dovie and her partner to

dance more closely than she would have liked. Gordon, too, seemed uncomfortable with the way they were shoved together, but as the dance went on, they both relaxed.

She liked him. He didn't talk her ear off with tales of how successful or well-known he was. He simply held her close. It surprised her how good it felt to be in a man's arms again, even if the man was little more than a stranger.

When the number was finished, Gordon escorted her back to the table. "Thank you, Dovie."

"Thank *you.*"

Mary and Phil approached.

"He's a lucky man, whoever he is," Gordon said.

Dovie frowned, wondering how he knew she was in love with someone else. Mary must have said something.

"I see you've met your admirer," Mary said, dabbing her handkerchief on her damp brow. "Won't you join us—Gordon, isn't it?"

Gordon looked to Dovie to second the invitation.

She could see no harm in it. "Please," she said and gestured toward the empty chair next to her own.

"Thank you."

Gordon bought a round of drinks.

"Phil Patterson," Phil said, stretching his hand across the table for Gordon to shake.

"Gordon Pawling."

"Where are you from, Gordon?" Mary asked.

"Toronto, Canada."

Phil nodded. "I understand that's a beautiful city."

"It is," Gordon agreed.

"We're from Texas," Mary said, and Dovie nearly

laughed out loud. No one listening to their accent would have guessed anywhere else.

"A little town in the hill country called Promise," Phil put in.

"Promise," Gordon repeated.

"Dovie owns an antique store there." Mary's voice held a note of pride.

"And we have the bed-and-breakfast," Phil added.

"I'm a retired judge," Gordon said.

"A judge." Mary's eyebrows rose slightly as she glanced at Dovie. She seemed to be saying that Gordon was a catch she shouldn't let slip through her fingers.

"Retired," Gordon was quick to remind them. "I haven't served on the bench for three years now."

"Do you travel much?" Mary asked. "Is that how you're spending your retirement?"

"Let's dance, Mary," her husband said pointedly. He got up and didn't give his wife much of an option.

Mary's reluctance showed as she rose to her feet.

As soon as they were out of earshot, Dovie felt she should apologize for Mary's questions. "You'll have to forgive my friend," Dovie said. "It's just that Mary's encouraging me to see other men." Once the words left her lips, she realized more explanation was required. "I've been seeing someone…in Promise…for quite a few years. We had a difference of opinion and now he's dating another woman." It hurt to say the words even to someone she wasn't likely to see after tonight.

Gordon reached across the table and squeezed her hand. "I need to revise my opinion of your male friend. He didn't know a treasure when he found it."

Dovie smiled. "Have you been talking to Mary?"

Gordon's smile was gentle. "No."

Dovie looked toward the dance floor and smiled, too. "Shall we?" she asked, preferring that they dance rather than discuss her relationship with Frank.

"It'd be my pleasure." Gordon stood and offered Dovie his hand.

They danced every dance for the rest of the night. At midnight they attended the buffet. Dovie's appetite had been lacking; even the lavish display of pastries and other goodies hadn't tempted her. Not once during the three days had she stayed awake long enough to partake of the midnight buffet.

Tonight, however, she was famished. Gordon Pawling filled his plate, and Dovie wasn't shy about helping herself, either. Mary and Phil were right behind them in the buffet line.

"I'm going to have to diet for a month after this," Mary complained.

"Make that two," Phil teased, and Mary elbowed him in the ribs.

Too full to think about sleeping, Dovie gladly accepted Gordon's invitation for a stroll on the deck when they'd finished eating.

The night was beautiful. Out in the middle of the Gulf of Mexico, miles from land and the lights of the city, the stars blazed, filling the sky.

"I don't think I've ever seen so many stars," Dovie said, leaning against the ship's railing.

"In Northern Ontario," Gordon said, "in the dead of winter when it seems like spring is only a distant promise, the stars look like this. When a fresh snowfall reflects the moonlight and starlight, it's almost as bright as day."

"It sounds lovely," Dovie said wistfully. "I've never

been to Canada," she confessed. "I'm afraid I'm not much of a traveler. This is my first cruise."

"Mine, too."

"I wouldn't have come if it wasn't for Mary and Phil. Mary thought it was what I needed—to get away for a time."

"Was it?"

"Yes," she admitted after a moment. "I think it was exactly the right thing to do."

"I came because of my son."

Dovie heard the smile in his voice.

"Bill seemed to think that two years was enough time for me to grieve the loss of his mother. He insisted I take a cruise, and when I balked, he purchased the ticket himself and presented it to me on my birthday."

"He sounds like a determined young man."

"Very much so," Gordon said. "He's a younger version of me, I fear. He followed in my footsteps and seems headed for the bench."

"Your wife's been gone two years, then?"

"Yes," he said, and sadness weighted his words. "I loved her for forty years and I don't know if it's possible for me to love anyone else."

"It is possible," Dovie told him. Her own experience had taught her that.

"I'm beginning to think you're right," he said.

They turned away from the railing and Gordon tucked her hand in the crook of his arm. They walked together in silence, their pace leisurely, and they spoke of their lives and marriages and dreams.

An hour later she still wasn't tired, but they'd be disembarking the next morning and things would be hectic. She knew she should get some sleep.

Gordon escorted Dovie to her cabin. "Thank you," she murmured. The night had been perfect in every way.

"All the appreciation is mine," Gordon said, then very slowly leaned forward and kissed her on the lips.

Dovie blinked back sudden tears.

Gordon reached into his suit jacket and pulled out a business card. "My home phone number is listed here," he said. "In case things don't work out with your friend…"

Dovie accepted the card.

"Will you call?" he asked.

"I…I don't know." She didn't want to lead him into believing something might come of this one night.

"I'm very grateful to you, Dovie Boyd," he said. "For this evening. And for showing me that my son might possibly be right."

But Dovie was the one who needed to thank him. She'd learned something, too.

Her life could go on without Frank. And in time, she might fall in love again…

Cal was aware of Jane's presence the minute he escorted Savannah Smith down the church aisle. Grady's sister was serving as matron of honor to Caroline Daniels, and he was best man.

Every pew in Promise Christian Church was filled. It seemed as if half the town—and half the county—had come to Caroline and Grady's wedding. Being the postmistress, Caroline knew just about everyone, and they knew and liked her. Grady, too. The integrity with which he'd handled Richard's debts was no small thing, and the merchants of Promise felt both gratitude and respect. This was a chance for the townspeople and ranchers to show how much Grady and Caroline meant to their community.

Cal didn't see Jane, but he knew she was in the church. He *felt* her there, and as hard as he tried to ignore her, he found it impossible. After walking with Savannah down the aisle, Cal joined Grady, who stood next to the altar. The organ music swelled through the sanctuary as Caroline appeared at the back of the church.

Cal heard Grady's soft intake of breath as he gazed at his bride. Caroline looked lovely in her dress, complete with veil and a long train. Cal smiled as he glanced at Maggie, wearing a green velvet dress for her role as flower girl.

Then his eyes sought out Jane. She sat on the bride's side, wearing a pearl-white suit with big gold buttons. Accustomed to seeing her in jeans and a Western shirt, he didn't recognize her for a moment. Damn, but she was beautiful.

Cal forced his attention away from her and looked at Caroline, whom Frank Hennessey was walking down the aisle. He soon found his gaze wandering back to Jane. Her eyes refused to meet his, which was just as well.

He regretted the way they'd parted. Both of them had been angry, saying hurtful things, things they didn't mean. He'd told himself that sometimes it was necessary to be cruel to be kind—only in this case he was the one who'd suffered. He'd been miserable and lonely since that day. He knew their confrontation hadn't been easy for her, either, but she certainly seemed to be faring better than he was.

She might still be angry, but after a while she'd see

that this was for the best. When the time came, she'd return to the life she'd always known in California. Her career plans were already in place—and they didn't include practicing medicine in rural America. They didn't include falling in love with a rancher.

The organ music faded, and Caroline joined Grady at the front of the church. Wade McMillen stepped forward to preside over the ceremony, smiling at the happy couple.

Before Caroline and Grady exchanged their vows, Wade had a few words to say about love and marriage.

Since he intended never to fall in love again, Cal only listened with half an ear. It wasn't until Wade said, "Love doesn't come with any guarantees," that Cal paid attention.

That was what he'd wanted. A guarantee. He wanted Jane to promise she'd never leave him. He'd been waiting for her to assure him that her future would always include him.

Without that guarantee, he hadn't been willing to take the risk.

The remainder of the ceremony was a blur in Cal's mind. He handed Grady the wedding band at the appropriate moment and escorted Savannah back down the center aisle following the ceremony.

Later, at the reception, he stood in the receiving line and exchanged chitchat with the guests as they paused to greet the newlyweds and other members of the wedding party.

Grady and Caroline were ecstatic. Maggie was with them and proudly referred to Grady as her daddy. As Cal watched he felt a sharp emptiness in the pit of his stomach. Overnight Grady had a wife and a daughter, and he'd pledged his life to them with nothing to safeguard the future. He'd stood before his family, friends and God and promised to love Caroline for the rest of his life. Without knowing what the next day held, or the next year. Whatever the future might bring, he was willing to love Caroline and Maggie.

The emptiness inside Cal increased. He loved Jane, but unless he was offered a money-back guarantee, he hadn't been willing to risk his heart by telling her how he felt.

When he lost Jennifer, he'd simply stepped aside and let her walk out of his life without saying one word to stop her. He'd done the same thing with Jane, only this time he'd loved much more deeply. Because of that, he hadn't just let her go; he'd pushed her out the door with both hands.

He'd refused to commit himself to the love he felt. Not without reassurances first.

As the wedding guests progressed down the receiving line, Cal saw Jane moving toward him. His heart reacted immediately, leaping with a rush of excitement at the mere sight of her. His mind buzzed with ideas of what he should say. Something pithy, something profound; he couldn't decide what.

Before he had the opportunity to display his wit and charm, she was there, standing in front of him, her hand in his.

"Hello, Cal," she said. Her eyes seemed to sear right through him. Then without warning she proceeded to the next person in line.

Cal yearned to call her back, to say he deserved more than a casual greeting, but he couldn't. The next guests stood directly in front of him and he was obliged to greet them.

Cal continued to greet the wedding guests. Whenever he could, he sought out Jane with his eyes. He saw her serve wedding cake and chat with each person, joking and laughing. If she was miserable without him, he'd be hard pressed to prove it.

He recalled the first few months after Jane had moved to Promise and how the people in town had avoided her. The fault had been on both sides. Jane had arrived with her newfangled ideas and big-city attitude, and folks in town hadn't been too tolerant. There'd been some unwarranted assumptions made by Jane, but also by the people of Promise.

All that had changed in the past two months. Jane had mellowed, made new friends, gained the confidence of people here. He remembered the night Jeremy Bishop had broken his arm and the gentleness she'd displayed to both the boy and his terrified mother.

Little Maggie Daniels had brought her the rag doll because she knew Dr. Jane could be trusted.

Cal had seen for himself her passion for medicine and the way she'd squared off against death, fighting every way she knew how to save Richard Weston's life.

Damn it all, he was in love with her, and his feelings weren't likely to change. If he wanted a guarantee for the future, he wasn't going to find one. Not with Jane. Not with any woman.

He hadn't liked it when Jane called him a coward. Even now it wasn't easy to admit she'd been right.

The cake was almost gone before Cal found the courage to approach the table.

"Is there a piece for me?" he asked.

Jane glanced up and he could tell by the look on her face that she was surprised to see him.

"I believe there are a few pieces left," she said cordially enough, but she gave herself away when she refused to meet his eyes. She reached for a plate and handed it to him.

He cleared his throat and said, "You look very pretty."

"Thank you. I bought this suit in downtown Los Angeles."

Cal let the comment slide. "Something's wrong with Atta Girl." He said the first thing that came to mind.

That got her attention. "What?"

"It's nothing to worry about," he told her, then grabbed a glass of punch and walked away. That was a dirty trick, but he was willing to use whatever he had to.

Cal found a vacant table at the other end of the hall and sat down. He hadn't been there a minute when Jane pulled out a chair and joined him.

"What's wrong with Atta Girl?" she demanded.

"She misses you," Cal said between bites of cake.

Jane stared at him as if she hadn't understood a word.

"I miss you, too," he said, swallowing his pride along with the wedding cake.

"Oh, Cal."

"Do they have cattle ranches in California?" he asked.

Her brow puckered in a frown. "I don't know—I'm sure they must."

"Good. I was thinking of moving there."

"To California?" Her voice rose a full octave. "In the name of heaven, *why?*"

This was where it became difficult, but having made

his decision, he wasn't going to renege now. "Looks like I'm going to have to if I want to be near you."

Jane was on her feet so fast the chair nearly toppled backward. "You're taking a lot for granted, Cal Patterson."

"Perhaps," he agreed, recognizing his own response the day they'd argued and she told him she loved him. "But the way I figure it, if we're going to get married and you've already agreed to join your uncle's medical practice, this is the only solution."

Jane glared at him as though it was all she could do not to slap him.

"You *are* going to marry me, aren't you?" he asked.

Eleven

Back less than twenty-four hours from her cruise, Dovie worked endlessly in the church kitchen, helping the women's group with Caroline and Grady's wedding. She had artfully arranged hors d'oeuvres on silver platters and set them on the counter to be picked up.

Actually Dovie was grateful to be in here, away from the reception, although it was considered the least enviable of the jobs the women's group performed for weddings and other social events. At least while she was here, she needn't fear seeing Frank dance with Tammy Lee or flirt with any other women.

She hadn't seen him since her return, but then, it was still early. She steeled herself for their next confrontation, dreading it already.

Humming softly to herself, Edwina Moorhouse entered the kitchen. "Pastor McMillen is looking for you."

"Me?" Dovie couldn't imagine what he wanted.

"He asked me to send you to his office."

"Really?" Dovie washed her hands and reached for a towel. "Did he happen to mention what this was about?"

"Not a word," the older woman said.

But Dovie noticed that Edwina's eyes were twinkling. If she didn't know better, she'd think Wade and the Moorhouse sisters had something up their sleeves.

Tucking a stray curl behind her ear, Dovie left the kitchen. Pastor McMillen's office was just down the hallway and around the corner. His door was closed and she tapped on it politely.

"Come in," he called.

Dovie opened the door, and the first person she saw was Frank Hennessey, rising to his feet from a chair opposite Wade's desk. The sheriff also stood when she entered the room, his eyes focused intently on her. Dovie's pulse accelerated to an alarming rate, and she was grateful when Wade motioned for her to take a seat.

"Hello, Dovie," Frank said.

"Frank." She nodded once, but avoided looking in his direction. He sat down when she did.

"Actually I need to get back to the wedding," Wade announced. "My purpose here is to bring the two of you together to talk this out." With that, he left the room.

Dovie was too shocked to speak.

"I asked Wade to bring you here," Frank explained.

"Why?"

"Well, because I didn't think you'd come if I asked."

"I mean, why did you want to talk to me? As far as I can see, everything's already been said. You're dating other women now."

"One date, Dovie, and that was a disaster." He got to his feet and walked across the room to stare out the window. "There's only one woman I love and that's you."

"That's all well and good, but it hasn't gotten us very far to this point, has it?"

"No," he agreed with a certain reluctance.

Dovie's mind whirled. She couldn't imagine that Wade McMillen, a man of God, would condone Frank and her resuming their previous relationship, especially considering its physical aspects.

"You talked to Wade about us?" she asked.

"Actually he came to me."

"Wade?" Dovie had never heard of such a thing.

"I've been feeling pretty down lately," Frank admitted. "I assumed that once you saw me with Tammy Lee, you'd realize how much you missed me and want me back."

Dovie's mouth thinned with irritation.

"I don't think any idea of mine has backfired worse. I accept the blame for that—it was a sign of how desperate I was without you."

It didn't hurt Dovie's feelings any to learn he'd had a miserable time with Tammy Lee.

"Then you left on the cruise and...and I worried the entire time that you'd meet someone else." He hesitated, then asked, "Did you...meet someone?"

"Yes, a retired judge. He lives in Toronto."

"Oh." Frank turned to face her, eyes narrowed. "Will you be seeing him again?"

"I...I..."

"Don't answer that," Frank said, holding up his hand. "It's none of my business. Like I started to say, while you were away, I was pretty miserable. But then, nothing's been right since we split. Wade and I had a long talk, and I told him about you and me."

Dovie could feel the color fill her face even before she asked the question. "You didn't mention anything about...spending the night at my house, did you?"

"Yes."

"Oh, Frank, how could you?" She covered her face with both hands.

"He isn't going to judge us, Dovie," Frank hastened to assure her. "It's not his job. He told me that himself."

It was one thing for Frank to refuse to marry her, but to embarrass her in front of the pastor was something else entirely.

"I explained to Wade why I've had such a struggle with this marriage idea."

She hoped he'd done a better job of it with Wade than he had with her. As far as she was concerned, telling her he wasn't "the marrying kind" was a mighty poor excuse!

"I've lived alone all these years, and a man grows accustomed to having things his own way—to certain freedoms." He paused and his eyes pleaded with hers for understanding. "These freedoms I'm talking about don't have anything to do with other women, either."

"We've been through all this before," Dovie said, tired of the same old argument. She didn't want to hear his excuses again, especially when she could practically recite them herself.

"I couldn't find any solution to it, either," Frank said, his voice gaining speed and volume. "But, Dovie, don't you see, that's been the whole problem."

"What do you mean?"

"Wade said we'd overlooked the obvious solution, and by God, he's right. We can get married and I can still have my freedom."

"How?" she asked incredulously.

Frank's smile lit up his entire face. "It's so obvious I can't believe we didn't see it earlier. I'll keep my house and you keep yours. Some nights I'll spend with you—and if you want, you can sleep over at my house, too."

Dovie's head came up.

"I won't feel the walls closing in on me, but at the same time you'd have what you want. You'd be my wife, Dovie."

If she was tongue-tied earlier, it didn't compare to what she was now.

Frank's eyes were bright with hope as he reached for her hands. "Dovie Boyd, would you do me the honor of becoming my bride?"

She blinked back tears and smiled so hard it hurt. "Oh, Frank, I love you so much. Yes, I'll marry you." It was all she'd ever wanted. It didn't matter what other people thought or said. This was a plan that worked for *them*.

She didn't know who moved first, but they were in each other's arms and kissing.

God bless Wade McMillen, Dovie mused as Frank's lips found hers.

If Cal Patterson made her cry now, with half the town looking on, Jane swore she'd never forgive him.

He held her gaze, his feelings for her glowing in his eyes. "I'm asking you to be my wife."

She brought her hand to her forehead. "I heard you the first time." Which, she had to admit in retrospect, wasn't a very gracious thing to say.

"Do you want me to get down on one knee in front of all these people, Jane?" he asked. Cal was standing now, too.

"No." She shook her head and retreated a step.

"I've got an engagement ring. It's a good one, big diamond and only slightly used, but I'm afraid the damn thing's cursed. If you don't mind, I'd prefer to buy you a new one. I'm hoping Harley will take the other as a trade-in."

"You'd sell your share of the ranch?" she asked, afraid she'd been hearing things.

"If I had to."

"Why?" she demanded.

"Because I love you."

Damn, he'd done it to her. Jane could feel the tears welling in her eyes, threatening to spill down her cheeks.

"After what Wade said earlier, I've given up demanding guarantees. Like the preacher said, love just doesn't come with one. I don't know what the future holds for either of us. All I know about my future is that I want you in it."

Jane pressed her index fingers under her eyes in a desperate effort to keep the tears at bay. "You make me weep in public, Cal Patterson, and I swear you'll live to regret it."

"You'd cry for me?"

"Yes, you fool!"

His lazy grin spread from ear to ear. "That's the most beautiful thing you've ever said to me."

"Oh, puh-leeze!" She whirled around while she could still see straight and stormed across the room. She wasn't surprised to find that Cal had followed her.

The music started, and after Caroline and Grady had danced the first number, other couples stepped onto the floor.

"I'm not light on my feet, but I'd be willing to give it a try, if you are," Cal said, offering her his hand.

Jane didn't think she could refuse him anything at that moment. She placed her hand in his and nearly sighed aloud when he touched her. The sense of rightness she felt in his arms was…miraculous. Incredible. And so exciting.

Cal's chin rubbed the side of her face. "You love me, don't you?" he whispered.

"You know I do."

"I love you, too, Dr. Texas."

"You're serious about moving to California?"

"If that's what it takes to be close to you."

It astonished her that he'd agree to leave Promise. It shocked her, moved her deeply, inspired her. "As it happens, I love living here," she whispered, resting her head on his shoulder. She closed her eyes and savored the feel of his arms around her.

"You'd be willing to live here?" he asked.

"Promise needs a doctor, doesn't it? Everyone here feels like family. I enjoy the challenge of my job. It didn't take me long to realize that joining Uncle Ken wasn't really what I wanted." She shook her head. "Before I came to Promise, I just didn't have enough experience to know that."

"What about your uncle?"

"He'll be disappointed, but he'll get over it."

"Your parents?"

"Give them time and they'll learn to love Willie Nelson as much as they do the Beach Boys."

"And me?"

"That may take some doing," she teased. "However, if you promise to make them grandparents…"

His arms tightened about her waist. "I'm feeling this

very strong urge to kiss you, and either I embarrass us both right here and now or we sneak outside."

Jane smiled softly, so much in love that the emotion burned inside her. "I don't know about you, but I could do with a bit of fresh air."

In the middle of the song Cal stopped dancing, clasped her hand and led her off the dance floor.

Ellie Patterson lifted her head from Glen's shoulder, looking worried. Jane smiled broadly and gave her a thumbs-up. Ellie signaled back with a wink and laid her head back on her husband's shoulder again.

Once they were outside in the shadows of the church, Cal pulled Jane into his arms. She went there without resistance. His mouth found hers and his tongue licked the edges of her lips. With a small sigh of welcome, she opened her heart and her life to him. They kissed with a need that was so deep she forgot to breathe.

"You'll marry me?" he asked, his voice a whisper.

"Yes." The decision had already been made for her the instant he asked. She'd known then that this was what she wanted, that Promise was where she belonged. This was her home now, with Cal.

"When?"

"You in a hurry?" she asked, grinning delightedly. She couldn't see any reason to wait, either, not when they both knew what they wanted. Even waiting another minute seemed too long.

"You're damn straight I'm in a hurry," Cal said. "Let's talk to Wade right now."

Jane laughed and hugged him close. "Just remember, the future has no guarantees, Rebel."

"Well, it does come with at least one," he said, lifting her several inches off the ground. "My love for you."

"And mine for you," she whispered before her lips met his.

* * * * *

#1 *New York Times* bestselling author

DEBBIE MACOMBER

**welcomes you to Promise, a small town
in the heart of Texas.**

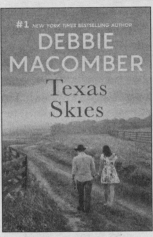

Lonesome Cowboy
Everyone in Promise thinks
Savannah Weston is content
to stay on the quiet family
ranch with her brother.
Life is busy but lonely, yet
Savannah has her passions—
particularly for the vintage
roses she grows. Then she
meets a disenchanted cowboy.
He doesn't plan on staying
long, but he may just change
Savannah's life...for the better.

Texas Two-Step
Ellie Frasier takes over running the feed store in town
after her father's death. Still in mourning, she relies on
her friends for comfort. She was always close with her
childhood buddy Glen Patterson, but they never shared
"those" feelings for each other. But now her long-standing
friendship feels like it's turning into something else...

Available now, wherever books are sold.

Be sure to connect with us at:
Harlequin.com/Newsletters
Facebook.com/HarlequinBooks
Twitter.com/HarlequinBooks

#1 *New York Times* bestselling author

DEBBIE MACOMBER

returns with the eleventh novel
in the beloved Cedar Cove series

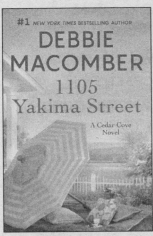

Dear Reader,

You've probably heard that my wife has left me. Rachel is pregnant, and she says she can't handle the stress in our household anymore. My thirteen-year-old daughter, Jolene, is jealous of her. Maybe it's my fault. As a widower I spoiled her—

Jolene was reading over my shoulder just now and says that's not true. She claims Rachel ruined everything. But *that's* not true. The real question is: How can I get my wife back? I don't even know where she is. She's not with Teri Polgar or any of her other friends from the salon. The other question is...when will Jolene grow up and stop acting like such a brat?

Available now, wherever books are sold!

DEBBIE MACOMBER

36869	CHOIR OF ANGELS	___	$7.99 U.S.	___	$9.99 CAN.
33125	NAVY FAMILIES	___	$7.99 U.S.	___	$9.99 CAN.
33121	NAVY BRIDES	___	$7.99 U.S.	___	$9.99 CAN.
33032	HANNAH'S LIST	___	$7.99 U.S.	___	$9.99 CAN.
33019	ALASKA HOME	___	$7.99 U.S.	___	$9.99 CAN.
33018	ALASKA NIGHTS	___	$7.99 U.S.	___	$9.99 CAN.
33017	ALASKA SKIES	___	$7.99 U.S.	___	$9.99 CAN.
32918	AN ENGAGEMENT IN SEATTLE	___	$7.99 U.S.	___	$9.99 CAN.
31926	THE SOONER THE BETTER	___	$7.99 U.S.	___	$9.99 CAN
31917	BECAUSE IT'S CHRISTMAS	___	$7.99 U.S.	___	$9.99 CAN.
31913	CHRISTMAS IN ALASKA	___	$7.99 U.S.	___	$9.99 CAN.
31903	WEDDING DREAMS	___	$7.99 U.S.	___	$9.99 CAN.
31894	ALWAYS DAKOTA	___	$7.99 U.S.	___	$9.99 CAN.
31888	DAKOTA HOME	___	$7.99 U.S.	___	$9.99 CAN.
31883	DAKOTA BORN	___	$7.99 U.S.	___	$9.99 CAN.
31860	THE MANNING BRIDES	___	$7.99 U.S.	___	$9.99 CAN.
31624	ON A CLEAR DAY	___	$7.99 U.S.	___	$8.99 CAN.
31580	MARRIAGE BETWEEN FRIENDS	___	$7.99 U.S.	___	$8.99 CAN.
31551	A REAL PRINCE	___	$7.99 U.S.	___	$8.99 CAN.
31535	PROMISE TEXAS	___	$7.99 U.S.	___	$8.99 CAN.
31441	HEART OF TEXAS VOLUME 2	___	$7.99 U.S.	___	$8.99 CAN.
31413	LOVE IN PLAIN SIGHT	___	$7.99 U.S.	___	$9.99 CAN.

(limited quantities available)

TOTAL AMOUNT	$ _____
POSTAGE & HANDLING	$ _____
($1.00 for 1 book, 50¢ for each additional)	
APPLICABLE TAXES*	$ _____
TOTAL PAYABLE	$ _____

(check or money order—please do not send cash)

To order, complete this form and send it, along with a check or money order for the total above, payable to MIRA Books, to: **In the U.S.:** 3010 Walden Avenue, P.O. Box 9077, Buffalo, NY 14269-9077; **In Canada:** P.O. Box 636, Fort Erie, Ontario, L2A 5X3.

Name: _____

Address: _____ City: _____

State/Prov.: _____ Zip/Postal Code: _____

Account Number (if applicable): _____
075 CSAS

Harlequin.com

*New York residents remit applicable sales taxes.
*Canadian residents remit applicable GST and provincial taxes.

MDM0519BL